FIGHT FIRE
WITH FIRE

FIGHT FIRE
WITH FIRE

AMY J. FETZER

WITHDRAWN

BRAVA

KENSINGTON PUBLISHING CORP.
www.kensingtonbooks.com

BRAVA BOOKS are published by

Kensington Publishing Corp.
119 West 40th Street
New York, NY 10018

All Kensington titles, imprints and distributed lines are available at special quantity discounts for bulk purchases for sales promotion, premiums, fund-raising, educational or institutional use.

Special book excerpts or customized printings can also be created to fit specific needs. For details, write or phone the office of the Kensington Special Sales Manager: Kensington Publishing Corp., 119 West 40th Street, New York, NY 10018. Attn. Special Sales Department. Phone: 1-800-221-2647.

Brava and the B logo are Reg. U.S. Pat. & TM Off.

ISBN-13: 978-0-7582-3137-6
ISBN-10: 0-7582-3137-7

First Kensington Trade Paperback Printing: May 2009

10 9 8 7 6 5 4 3 2 1

Printed in the United States of America

To Rhonda Pollero

For 16 years of friendship in a life that often
doesn't allow the luxury.

For your wit and humor, even with 59 staples holding you
together
For private laughs in overpriced hotel rooms,
warding off bad prom dates,
and ditching just about anything for a smoke.

For letting me pick that incredible mind,
and always seeing the calm, logical approach that
makes me think deeper on just about everything.

Love you, girl.

One

10 years earlier, somewhere in the Southern Hemisphere

He wanted to break her. To let her skim the edge of madness.

He'd almost succeeded.

On the stone floor, Safia folded her body tightly, her legs beneath her. A turtle backing into its shell. She kept her head down, her grimy hands shielding her skull. Her Mao pajamas lay like a damp layer of filth over her skin and did nothing to protect her from the cold, wet stones. Or him.

Between his boots crunching lightly on the stone floor, she listened to his indrawn breath, the almost imperceptible brush of his clothing as his arm rose. She tightened down her muscles. The cane snapped, the lash licking across her back and wrapping under her ribs. Her teeth sank into her lip as ungodly pain burned in stripes over her spine.

Warm blood pooled in her mouth. *swallowswalloswallow*

The moan slid back down her throat, denying him victory.

He enjoyed her screams, but she offered no sound except her struggle for air.

Water dripped somewhere.

"I will have to think of something else then," he said.

His accent scraped with a guttural sound. She could never

put her finger on the region. It didn't matter. She wanted to kill him. He probably knew it. His visits were less frequent and theirs was a twisted relationship. He talked. She never spoke. Never. Well, except to scream her freaking head off the first time he'd struck her. She wondered if his nose still hurt.

Her stomach coiled noisily, acid stewing on nothing. Food was a memory and she closed that mental door and kept in position. Waiting for another strike. Waiting till he dropped the lash made from strips of sugar cane. Layered, the cane could hold a man's weight, yet woven in a tubular braid, its flexing tongue didn't cut right away, the welts swelling till they burst the skin. He enjoyed letting it slither in front of her vision. It wasn't his only threat. He favored waterboarding in the beginning, bringing her so close to her death she'd felt the last of her air trade with water. How many times had he visited?

Her captivity was meaningless stretches between sessions. Without a shred of light, she no longer counted the days, her brain occupied with trying to understand why she'd been captured. She was in the field, but spent most of her days in a flat, monitoring movement of the local police and relaying information to experienced officers. Then she'd received an assignment, just a carrier pigeon. It wasn't unusual nor the first time. She'd been delivering a piece of art, a Chinese urn to an antique shop in Hong Kong. An exchange for information. As far as she knew, that's all it was, a jar. She remembered standing at the shop door, reaching for the latch and feeling someone move up behind her, then nothing. Not even collapsing.

She'd been tied up until recently; her wrists were still swollen with torn and blistered flesh. Her skin there was warm; infection was setting in. She peeked between her fingers and spied his boots, the toes polished, yet this time, the laces were wet. Dirt and a tiny bit of green clung to the rim of his heel. He'd been fastidious before, the boots unusually tidy when everything around here was filthy and medieval.

She didn't know where *here* was exactly. She'd woken up in this cell. As far as she knew, she was the only prisoner. She never heard or saw anyone except him and one guard. Their faces were a mystery, always hooded, and when she'd tried to look, he struck her down. Yet she'd glimpsed mud-brown material with small slits in the hood for eyes and mouth. He smelled vaguely of garlic. People who hid behind masks drew strength from anonymity. Her body was feeling every bit of his freedom.

He dropped the braided canes. She turned her head a fraction more to watch his retreat, but again, saw only his boots. He wouldn't leave the whip. She could use it to hang herself and he wanted her alive, this man with no name. If he'd said it, she didn't give a damn. Chung, was how she thought of him. Bluish light from the single lantern on the floor outside the door reflected in, and she imagined him taking the measured steps. Like small warnings. He would do as he'd done before. Step. Look back, then turn on his heels and two steps back into the cell to bend for the whip. He wasn't aware of the tell, but he was aware of the threat. Daring her to react. If she did, he'd strike.

At the cell door, he stopped. Before he turned to face her, she inched her arm to see him more clearly. All that encompassed was a view of his legs, his gloved hand loose at his side. He was never without the tight-fitting black gloves. Big hands. If he was armed, she couldn't see it. A single guard stood outside with the keys.

The tell came. He spun on his toes this time, then stepped. One, two. . . .

She sprang from her crouch and grabbed the cane handle first, snapping it hard. The braided rope circled his neck, and she gripped both ends and yanked, dragging him till her back hit the wall. He struggled, but she held on, remembering each violation to her body. Chung grunted, clawing at her hands. The officer with the keys was stunned from his boredom and drew his club. He rushed her and she shoved her captive into his chest. Their heads hit with a solid *thunk*, but she held the whip ends, dragging Chung back and cutting off his air. But he was taller and bigger, and when he started to get his footing, she twisted, jammed her hip into his back and knocked him off balance. His polished boots slipped, his weight grinding her shoulder into the stone wall.

He squawked like a seal with a sore throat, and she felt warm liquid on the floor at her feet. He stopped struggling. His hands fell away from her and flopped loosely at his sides. She held still to catch her breath and had to concentrate on her hands, unfurling her stiff fingers. A knuckle popped. He slid to the floor. Three fingers pressed below his ear got her nothing, and she jerked back, her head swimming. Her breath rushed, and she licked her lips, tried to swallow. The burn rising in the back of her throat made her slow her breathing. Her hands trembled as she covered her face. *I killed him.* Her memory bloomed with the last days; his threats to remove her knee caps with a power drill, water boarding, and then humiliation, leaving her naked for days, making her beg for the one bowl of maggot infested rice . . . and his touching her. He'd treated her as if he owned her soul. She hoped his was frying somewhere in hell.

She lowered her hands, then sank to her knees. She reached for the hood, afraid of what she'd find. She worked it up enough to see under it, and wasn't surprised by the dark skin, yet his face was obviously swollen. She pulled it further up. Skin was distended around her eyes, nose, and lips, all of it surrounded with deep purple bruises. There was no telling what he really looked like. She touched his cheek and felt a hardness unlike bone. It shifted. *Oh no they didn't.* Implants.

She turned her back on the body and crossed to the rookie. When they'd slammed, it knocked him out, but it also cracked the lantern. The phosphorous light was quickly dying and she searched him, taking the keys and night stick. He carried no other weapons. Not even a knife.

What kind of prison is this?

She found chewing gum in the rookie's shirt pocket and shoved a stick in her mouth. Pineapple and it tasted like heaven. She stripped off his shoes, but they were too big and she settled for the pants, rolling the cuffs. She cinched the belt but was forced to knot it. Some fried foods were in her near future, and she was going to enjoy gaining weight.

She took the rookie's shirt, and ripped off anything that would reflect, then knelt at Chung's body, freeing the belt. In her torturer's trouser back pocket she found exactly five hundred dollars, American. It was the newness of the bills that puzzled her, too pristine to have been in circulation yet. The bills were bound with a money clip, silver plated metal with the outline of a griffin or dragon. She pocketed the cash and clip.

The lack of a weapon bothered her. He wasn't the type to go around unarmed and she ground her hands down his hips and thighs, searching, then stopped, shoving up the pant leg to take the knife strapped to his upper calf. She felt a little better to be armed, but someone was going miss these two soon.

She stood, then instantly slapped her hand on the stone wall as her world tilted rudely. Her stomach joined in for the ride. She pushed gingerly back, knife in one hand, and wrapped the belt around her other palm, the buckle on the outside where it could do the most damage. She moved to the entrance.

No one came to investigate. Cautiously, she flattened to the stone wall. The only natural light was reflected farther down the corridor. She stepped out.

Sound had always come from the left. Never the right. Left led out. She hurried down the corridor. The floor was flooded a couple inches and she heard water rushing somewhere above her. Her bare feet barely made a sound on the uneven stone floor, and she kept moving, her hand on the wall for support. Everything swayed. Her muscles shook. If they caught her, they'd kill her. She had to get out of here and headed up, toward the sound of water. Then she slowed in front of empty cells.

The prison might be old, but the cells were retrofitted with steel doors, but that's where it ended. Inside were a few scraps of cloth wrapped around iron cuffs, slave shackles really. She hadn't been the only guest, and passing the next cell, she realized the light came from gaps in the roof. Vines and ferns shielded the sun, water misting like crystal rain. She tried the door, thinking she could climb to the surface, but it was locked. She tried the guard's keys and it surprised her that none of them worked. The guard had always opened her cell.

Don't analyze, she thought, turning away. She hurried down the corridor, stopping at each junction to check her bearings. The light diminished, and she felt as if she was heading downhill. Confused, she stopped, her back to the wall, holding the knife with a white knuckled grip. She took a slow breath, listening. The sound of water had changed and she frowned. It's splashing, she realized, but hesitated, dissecting echoes from hollow reverberation bouncing in a passageway. She'd be in total darkness in a few steps. A scraping sound came from behind her, the scuffle of footsteps.

Without a choice, she walked into the darkness, blinking to let her eyes adjust, and then advanced, her shadow glinting off the wet floor. She smelled something different—like raw mushrooms—and kept moving forward. It was several yards before her hands touched wood. Her fingers nimbly shaped a door, felt for the hinge and found a padlock. Shoving the knife in the belt, Safia tried the keys. Were they just for looks, she wondered when none of them worked. Dropping the keys, she held the nightstick like a bat and beat the metal. The sound vibrated like a clap, and the footsteps grew closer, faster. She slammed again, and the lock popped suddenly. A crazy surprised laugh escaped her and she worked it off and pulled, but the door was stuck, the wood damp and swollen. Footsteps crowded, closing the distance, voices calling now. She didn't understand a word, but knew she'd less than a minute before they found her.

She unwound the belt from her fist, sliding it through one of the rings that held the lock. Gripping the leather, she pulled, her foot against the wall. They were coming closer, and she prayed they got lost as she stretched herself out, pulling, the belt bearing most of her weight. The door gave, the wood against stone fracturing with rot. Light blossomed beyond and she flinched, turning her face away for a second, then pulled harder, her freedom inches away. It gave a little more and she wedged herself between the opening, then fell back against the door.

Free.

Twisted trees and overgrown vegetation surrounded her. The sunlight splintered, shadowing the landscape. She stood on a hillside, behind her, steep with rocks and thick vines, a worn path led away from the door. Frowning, she skimmed to her right, close to the wall of stones covered in moss. It looked like ruins, an old fortress or something. The crumbling formation jutted out, casting shadows, yet she could see the reflection of sunlight spilling somewhere beyond. She hoped it led down and edged along till the forest thinned. Gripping the wall, she peered around the jagged rocks.

Two men stood on an outcropping of rocks drenched in sunlight. A few yards behind them, a narrow waterfall poured from a small brook higher in the hill. Their backs faced her. She studied them, determined they were armed, but concealing it. They looked completely out of place, both in light shirts and dark trousers as if they'd stepped away from their office cubicles only moments before.

One man twisted a look over his shoulder, then turned fully. "Well done, Safia."

It was her boss. The shock of it sent her back a couple steps and she hit something, then jerked around. A hooded man stood near, still concealed. Then he reached under the hood's hem and pulled a long strap of flesh colored leather from around his throat. She'd missed that, but not that he could anticipate what she would do.

"You almost killed me."

"Almost wasn't what I was aiming for." She raised the knife a little higher and looked at her boss. "Somebody needs to start talking, or I'll finish this." She backed away, gripping the knife, point down. Her warden held up his hands as if it would stop her. After what he did to her? She looked at her boss. "Why?"

"We had to be certain your integrity couldn't be breeched," he said calmly, moving nearer.

A test. Staged. *What arrogant bastards.* Her eyes narrowed to slits. "And beating me like a rug was necessary?"

"No." He walked closer. "He went too far." There was a tightness in his words, the only sign of his displeasure.

Safia stepped back from them both. "He did more than that," she said in a low voice, her gaze pinning her shrouded tormentor.

Where did they find him? Was five hundred U.S. the going rate for torture-for-hire? Five hundred to enjoy inflicting pure misery on another human being? Because this one liked it. *He's an outside asset,* she realized, and didn't want to be near him. What she really wanted was his death to be real. She owed him, but she also understood she'd probably never learn his identity. It didn't mean she wouldn't try.

She kept her attention on the hooded man, committing everything to memory. "You said I lacked enough field experience," she aimed at her boss.

"You have it now." Her boss gestured to the black van several yards below on level ground, the single windowless door open and showing its luxurious interior. "Let's get some food in you first."

His tone was dismissive, as if this was just a rude interruption at a party. She wasn't going to forget the past days anytime soon and looked at the reason. He didn't move, brown eyes barely visible inside the dingy hood. His fingers flexed and she remembered them around her throat, holding her off the ground like a rag. In two steps, she was in his face, the knife sinking into his side as she drove her knee deep into his groin. He buckled with an *oof* and she gripped the hood hard enough to hear it tear and whispered, "Someday, I'll repay that game. On my terms."

"No. You won't," he gasped, and he was right. He'd have a different face. But she wouldn't forget the voice, or the pain.

"That's not wise!" her boss said somewhere behind her.

She twisted the knife as she pulled it out and shoved him off, stepping back. "But it felt good." She turned away as the man tried to straighten and failed. "Is that face courtesy of U.S. dollars?"

Her boss froze, nodding to the driver who moved to the van. "You saw his face?" He waved to her tormentor, and she didn't have to look to know he was slipping back into the stone prison. He gave off the stench of his own urine.

"You know I did. That beast didn't do a damn thing without your approval. Who is he?"

"That's classified."

"Not if you want me to work for you again."

He snorted disdainfully. "It's above your pay grade."

"Then give me a raise." She walked past him. She'd have time to address that subject later. This was far from over. "How long was I in there?"

"Twelve days." He picked his way downhill. "A record, I believe."

How could he look unruffled and dignified when she smelled like rat droppings and could feel blood warming down her back? "You're a parasite and I want to beat the living hell out of you . . . *sir*."

"Good, keep that close." He flicked a hand at the prison behind them. "Remember it often, nothing is as it seems."

She stopped, but he kept going. "That includes you. I don't trust you anymore. Your ethics are wretched and I'm debating continuing to work for you."

The bastard stopped and looked back at her. Then he had the gall to smile. "Welcome to the inner ring."

That caught her breath for a second.

"You were outstanding."

"You couldn't just trust me? Have a little faith?" Instead, they hurt her before the enemy could. Sounded like Munchausen's syndrome and she wanted him to have a taste of it, but then he had the decency to help her in the van. He was also better trained and signed her paychecks. Halfway in, she froze, her gaze landing on the woman sitting in the rear, looking pristine and regal.

Now she knew who'd really orchestrated this. "I'll remember who did this to me," she said with undisguised rancor.

The woman only tipped her head, her lips curving with approval.

Safia gripped the knife, her expression warning them not to push her further. Message sent, she thought, and was damned amused when both of her superiors kept their attention on the knife till she laid it across her lap. When someone let out a noisy breath, she settled in the plush bucket seat with a little satisfaction. But not nearly enough.

Her boss produced a bottle of water, sweating condensation. She broke it open and drank deeply, and as the van pulled away, she shifted to look out the rear window at her prison growing smaller by the moment.

The rush of water she'd heard was the narrow waterfall that fell into a small pool shaped by stones. On the whole, it was supposed to look natural. She didn't get that feeling.

Aside from the citadel behind it, it was too beautiful, artfully overgrown and perfectly concealed. She wondered what else had happened in a place like that.

"So . . . I'm guessing the Philippines, maybe? Not Okinawa, too many American eyes." Her gaze sailed over the grounds, picking out plants and trees. It reminded her of a canyon in the monkey forest. "Indonesia?" Only her gaze shifted to her boss, waiting for confirmation.

"Very good."

She doubted he'd give her the truth anyway. How many places like this were located around the world? Who was using them? Was her phantom just waiting for his next victim? It made her sick. She'd no intention of letting her superior forget this perverse test of honor, and decided she'd watch her own back from now on.

When the van rolled onto even ground, she settled gingerly into the seat, feeling the scrape of wet fabric against the welts swelling on her spine. The woman was already on satellite communications, her world quickly changing. She took a long drink of water, a salute to herself.

Well, I guess it's official then.

I'm a spy.

2 years later, Serbia,
4 miles from the Kosovo border

Riley recognized the shrill whine of an incoming missile and rushed toward the crumbling building. Each step was a struggle, Captain Sam Wyatt's weight bearing down on him. The missile hit, throwing them forward and obliterating half the street. Riley's knees hit the ground, driving pain up his thighs. Debris struck him in the back, his burden threatening collapse. The enemy wasn't done with them and a trail of bullets chased toward his heels as he pushed to his feet, dragging the wounded pilot along. Thirty feet, twenty . . . Riley fell behind the remains of a wall, the rest of the building destroyed by Russian missiles to keep the border uncrossable. It was working—but it was where he needed to go.

He lifted Wyatt's arm from around his neck, then leaned him against the wall before easing him to the ground. The morphine deadened the pain, but Riley worried the splint he'd made wouldn't hold. The leg was already at an odd angle. Sam needed better medical care and soon. He was bleeding again.

Snaps of gunfire struck the ground, the wall, and Riley considered how to get his ass out of this one. The air moved slowly, thick with smoke and dust and covering the sun. No place was safe. Smart people fled to the countryside. The city was deserted except for scatters of rebel resistance trying to protect themselves from Serb soldiers bent on genocide. Oh yeah, that wee bit of U.N. cease-fire negotiations worked splendidly. He took his bearings, then surveyed his immediate surroundings for better cover.

He had maybe a half hour before the patrol caught up with them, and they had trucks. Time to eat crow and call in the cavalry, he decided, and reached for his radio. He found a smoldering jumble of wires and melted plastic. "Bugger me. So. Fighting it is then." He checked his supplies, but he knew exactly how much ammunition he had left. Not enough to keep renegade Serb soldiers off his back for long.

Jagged cinder block shattered above his head in a spray of chalky rocks. A chunk hit Wyatt's cheek as Riley pushed him further to the ground. He howled, and Riley let him, but held him down to keep him from thrashing. Bullets chunked away at their position, intermittent, taunting. Northeast, he thought, and hovering over Wyatt, he aimed. He didn't get off a shot.

A line of bullets sliced across his position and he felt each hit vibrate the wall, chip near his boot. *Jesus Mary. Two directions.* It wouldn't be long before the barrier was gone. He looked at Sam, thinking he'd made it worse for him, dragging him all this way. Now the fractured bone threatened to come through the torn skin. He couldn't pull the tourniquet any tighter or risk Wyatt losing his leg. Riley glanced behind them. The border was less than four miles away. The closer he got to it, the better his chances of friendlies.

Three successive shots hit the ground twenty yards to his right and made a chunk of rock dance. Immediately, a second shot knocked it over. Excellent shooting, he had to admit, and followed the trajectory, his gaze climbing. A three-story building lay about forty yards south. The lower outer walls were scarred by fire, marked with soot and shattered windows. The upper-floor windows were blown out, the interior a blackened skeleton.

That's the target.

He searched each floor, moving right to see the south side. Gunshots peppered around him, keeping him pinned, but he peered just enough to focus his binoculars. From the top floor of the building just beyond it, he spotted a rifle barrel before it slid out of sight. A second later, a hand appeared, held up two fingers, then a fist, then pointed. Riley felt a chill at the familiar military signals.

The disembodied hand repeated the gesture. Wait two minutes, then go.

If this wasn't a fine one, he thought, aware he risked a trap. Yet the sniper had several chances to kill them already, and didn't. But there were other shooters out there.

A mortar round hit fifty yards away, the impact throwing cars, street benches and toppling a statue. "Shoulda worn the smart shirt, Donovan," he muttered as he quickly knelt beside Wyatt, checking his wounds before he worked off his Kevlar vest and strapped it on the pilot. He hoisted him on his back and prayed his legs were strong enough to make the distance. Testing the field, he raised his hand and nearly got it shot off.

Instantly, the sniper returned automatic fire to the north, covering him as he rushed out into the open, crossing the street like a hunchback, then moving alongside walls shattered by bombs. Sidestepping rubble challenged each step. The building loomed. The sniper laid down constant cover fire, and he glimpsed a shooter drop from a window, another from a balcony. Riley pushed on, the burden of Sam's weight pounding his hips. Safety loomed in the shell of steel and concrete.

Bullets chewed the ground at his heels, and he felt a muscle pull in his thigh as he rounded the charred edge. He stumbled into the safety of darkness, Wyatt's weight slamming him to his knees. He rolled Wyatt off his back, then crawled to his head, gripped his flight suit at the shoulders and dragged him from the opening. He returned to aim out the doorway blown wider by missiles. Smoke twisted on the air. The tat-tat of gun fire spun closer.

Where was the sniper?

His gaze ripped over the streets once more before he turned to Wyatt, taking him deeper into the remnants of a restaurant, a yawning hole in the ceiling exposing three floors above. At least it was defensible. He dragged the six-foot-tall man onto a fallen piece of drywall, then inspected his wounds. Blood saturated his pant leg, and although the wood splint held, the fractured bones threatened to cut an artery.

Wyatt's head lolled on his neck and his eyes opened. "Donovan."

"Sir?"

"You're a brave man to do this." Sam reached to offer his hand and flinched. Riley had tied his arm to his waist. His ribs were broken.

"I bet the C.O. has a different opinion."

Wyatt tried to laugh, but only coughed. "I'll put in a good word." He breathed in short gasps.

"After you just crashed one of his jets? Begging your pardon, sir, but you're on his shit list too." It didn't matter. A court-martial was in his future, he knew.

"Call me Sam, will you?"

"Certainly." Riley grinned. "But command's going to call us both dead if we don't get out of here."

Riley offered him water, then made him comfortable in the rear of the building. From his position, he could see anything coming, and had solid wall at his back, but he knew time was ticking by before the patrol found them. Armed, he scoured for anything useful, stuffing it in the bag he'd stolen from the medic's supply. He used the painkillers sparingly. Whatever was left in the kit had to do. He hoped it was enough.

Then he focused on Sam's wounds. Resetting the fracture was going to hurt like hell. He broke open the morphine capsule and injected Sam's thigh, then inspected the break. He felt the jagged crack of bone under Sam's skin and formed a plan to reset it. They couldn't travel another four miles with it tearing inside his body.

"You don't have time for that."

Instantly Riley scooped up the pistol and spun on his knees, aiming.

A figure stood near the blown out entrance. Shit. He hadn't heard a thing.

Still as glass, the man's head and shoulders were wrapped in dark scarves over a green military jacket, now a dull gray like the weather. The only skin exposed was his eyes. Around his waist, a utility belt sagged, and the sniper rifle was slung on his shoulder, the weapon held across his body, ready to sight and fire. Yet he stood casually, without threat.

"If I wanted you dead, I wouldn't have wasted bullets to see you two safe and alive."

The sniper, Riley realized with a wee shock, was a woman.

She advanced with easy grace, stepping over piles of rubble to hop down at his level. Her rifle looked all too familiar.

"Yes, it's American," she said, noticing his attention. He lowered his weapon. She stood a couple feet away, staring down at Sam. "He doesn't look good." She unwound her head scarf and a braided rope of shiny dark hair spilled down one shoulder. She met his gaze. Beneath arched brows, whiskey colored eyes stared back at him.

"Sweet mother a' *Jaasus*." She was younger than him.

"I get that a lot." She gestured at Sam. "What do you need to do?"

"Set his leg again and get a tighter splint on it."

She nodded as her gaze bounced around the interior. "Let's get busy. I don't know how much time we have."

Though the pop of gunfire was lazier now, Riley wasn't ignoring the help, or the danger of staying put too long. He instructed, glad Sam was unconscious or he'd be screaming to the heavens. After unbuckling her utility belt, she got behind Sam, her legs and arms wrapping his torso and hips as Riley grasped his calf and ankle. On a count, he pulled. Even drugged, Sam arched with silent agony. Riley ripped the flight suit more and pushed the bone down, forcing it to align closely. Blood oozed from the gash. He met her gaze and nodded.

"It's set. Well . . . better than it was."

She eased from Sam and unclipped her canteen, offering it.

He cleaned his hands and the wound, then Riley worked against the cold. With the needle poised over Sam's flesh, he shook too much to stitch. "For the love of Mike." He dropped the needle, sanding his hands, blowing on them. She quickly grasped them both, wrapping her scarf around them, then brought his fists to her lips. She breathed hotly against the fabric, and Riley felt the warmth sting his icy skin. She rubbed and breathed, her gaze flashing up. He felt struck, her soulful eyes hiding so much.

"Better?"

He nodded, unwound the scarf. "The rest of me is a bit chilly still."

It took a second for that to sink in and she made a face. He chuckled, then said, "Get yourself on the other side, woman, and let's make some quick work here."

She snickered to herself, yet obeyed, holding Sam's skin closed as he stitched. She still wore gloves and though she was dressed warmly, he noticed everything was cinched down, nothing to catch, and her rifle would collapse. It was a weapon he'd seen in spec, a prototype of the MP5. Not in production, yet she had one. And if the bodies outside indicated, she knew how to use it. It was at her right, by her knee with a bullet chambered.

"You're Company." CIA. Probably attached to NATO.

He had to give her credit, she didn't look up or make even a single nuance. If she was any good, she wouldn't give anything away.

"Tell me how an Irishman got to be in the Marines."

Okay, he could go that direction. "I was a runner for the IRA and my older sister caught me. Dragged me home by my ear, she did." His lips curved with the memory as he took another stitch. "My parents, fearing for my immortal soul, sent me to America to live with relatives." He shrugged.

"So dodging bullets comes easy, huh?"

"Yeah, I guess."

Then he went and chose a career in it. He glanced at Sam, knowing this would cost him what he held dear. His Marine enlistment. But he couldn't let the one man who treated him like a friend instead of his superior die in the frigid Serbian forests.

"I saw the jet go down."

His gaze briefly slid to hers.

"He was doing some amazing flying before the missile hit. I've been behind you for a day."

"So you're the reason the patrol didn't catch up to us?"

Bless her, that blank expression didn't change a fraction.

"Thank you for our lives." He clipped the thread. "I'm Riley." He held out his hand. She bit off her glove and shook it. Her skin was warm, her palm smooth and dry.

"Safia," was all she offered with her disarming smile.

He wondered why someone so young was in the field alone.

She helped him work the inflatable air cast over Sam's upper thigh, then wrapped him in rags and curtains Riley'd found to keep him warm. Sam's fever would spike and he had to get him some antibiotics. He'd used his last just now.

The woman unwound from the floor, strapped her belt back on, then dug in her pack like a purse and blindly reloaded her magazines. He recognized C4 packs and some gadgets he didn't. She was a little fire team all by herself, he thought, smiling. Armed, she went to each opening. He reached for his gun when she disappeared out a gap in the wall. He waited, chambering a bullet and aiming.

Tell me I can't be that much of a sucker. Icy wind spun through the building. Seconds ticked by. She reappeared and stopped short, then cocked her head. She smiled almost appreciatively, and he lowered his weapon. She moved to him with an elegance that defied her crude surroundings and the two pistols in her belt. Her exotic features and tanned skin puzzled him. Without head scarves, she looked completely out of place.

Then the radio hooked on her belt buzzed and she brought it to her ear, listening. The language sounded Albanian. She didn't make contact, only listened, then said, "We need to go. I'll help you to the border."

Riley opened his mouth to say he didn't need her to risk her life again.

"Don't argue. The Serbian patrol after you have already murdered seventy women and children along their way. Brutally." Her accented voice snapped with anger as she wrapped her scarves. "Those soldiers don't care about life or freedom. They wanted him." Her voice softened a notch. "To display for the press . . . preferably dead and bloodied."

He agreed. The reports out of this region were an abomination to humanity, and while nobody was happy about not going after one of their own because of some negotiations going on, Riley just couldn't live with it. But a one-man rescue wasn't the smartest move he'd ever made.

Sam stirred, moaning, and Riley grabbed the preloaded syringe.

"No. No more drugs. We need him mobile. It's now or never." Waving him to hurry, she crossed to the opening, weapon at her shoulder. She aimed up the street and sighted, then suddenly said, "Get him up, now!" then vaulted over debris to get to him. "They found us!"

Riley tried. "Come on, cowboy, time to run."

She helped him get two hundred pounds of man off the ground, and he shouldered Sam, then drew his weapon. Out the rear of their haven, she led them to the alley behind.

Sam focused on her, then gave him a sluggish smile. "Trust you to find the only woman within miles, Donovan."

"It's the accent." Riley grinned and winked at Safia. "Gives them all sorts of wily thoughts."

She rolled her eyes, a smile coasting her lips. "Everyone has an accent. We go that way." She nodded left and advanced. "And stay in the alleys—"

A blast struck the building across the street, fiery debris rocketing into their hideout and knocking out remaining windows. The supports gone, the building listed as they hurried away. Another rocket finished it off and before the wave of smoke and fire reached them, Riley dragged Sam out of the path. Shielded by a building, dust and debris shot past them and he turned his face away.

"That's mortar fire," he said. "They're trying to get a lock on this location."

Her gaze jerked to his, suspicious.

"I'm clean, and the beacon is in the ejected seat fifty miles north."

She eyed him a second, then turned away. "Then it's thermal and someone's close enough to give them coordinates."

"Well shit," Sam said.

"That's what we'll be if we stay." She agilely stepped over rubbish, and they kept up, but it was costing Sam. His breathing was fast and hard through gritted teeth. Safia slowed in the alley littered with debris and ahead, she stopped briefly, her shoulders sagging before she continued. When he passed, he saw the pair of legs, thin and small, the rest covered in trash and broken windows. Aw hell. It wasn't the first time he'd seen children discarded as collateral damage, but as he left the alley, the image haunted. Three blocks and two turns from the last hit, Riley stopped her.

"This isn't working. We need a ride." He moved up behind her, and Sam fell against the wall, exhausted and shaky. He looked a little gray.

"I don't think a cab will come to this neighborhood."

Riley passed her, pistol drawn, then edged the building. "There's a truck about two blocks up."

She shifted to see, then shook her head. "It'll never run or it'd be gone."

"So negative," he chided, studying the terrain. "We don't have another option. He can't walk to the border, and we need to get the hell out of here."

Riley took off, keeping low and reached the truck. Mortar rounds hit, each impact coming closer. They were hunting for them by destroying anything in their path. He didn't get it. All for one pilot?

At the truck, Riley threw open the door, ducked under the steering column and pulled wires, striking them. The engine caught and sputtered, smoke billowing from the exhaust. He climbed behind the wheel and drove to them.

He jumped out to help Sam. "You drive."

"I planned to," she said climbing in and putting it in gear.

Sam in, she accelerated before he closed the door. Their speed increased and he leaned out the window, watching their back. "Faster woman."

"It won't go any faster!" Smoke was filling the cab.

He drew inside to add, "It better, because ugly has brothers."

"Don't they always," she muttered, shifting gears.

He saw the truck cornering the street, the gun mount swinging into position. Oh, crap. Law rockets. "Turn! Turn left! Now!" he shouted and she did, the truck fish tailing, throwing Sam against the cab. The mortar hit the crossroad they'd just left.

"What do you have, a sixth sense?" she said checking the mirrors, never letting her guard down.

"I saw the ignition flash before it launched."

"Good." She pointed in front of his face. "Now shoot them please."

His eyes flared when a stripped down Land Rover barreled toward his side. The gunner behind a fifty caliber machine gun fired, a line of rounds chewing the ground and taking out the tire.

"Riley, shoot!"

He leaned out the window and fired, unloading seven rounds in the tires, engine, and driver. The driver fell back, hitting the gun barrel and tumbling out of the seat. The out of control Rover clipped their ass, tearing off wood slats and knocking them sideways. The impact dumped the gunner and Riley experienced a sick feeling as they rolled over a bump.

Safia struggled with the wheel, turning hard and the truck tipped for a few feet, then slammed down. The tireless wheel screamed with sparks, riding on the rims.

"That was fun."

Armored vehicles swarmed in behind the last, knocking the downed rover and barreling hard toward them. Christ. They'd get blown out of their seats any second.

"Come on, baby," she coaxed the smoking truck. "Just a little further."

"To where?"

"There," she said, nodding to the hills.

On a high slope, he saw flickering movement, the endless black sky growing lighter as a helicopter lifted over the mountains. It swept near and illuminated a line of trucks and tanks cresting the hill ahead of it. NATO forces. Ooh-rah.

Behind them, the renegade patrol raced, the convoy grown

in size, and he heard the scrape of a tank turret. They were trapped between.

"Time to bail!" She hit the breaks, and he jumped out, helping Sam.

She grabbed the radio and shouted into it. He didn't understand a syllable. A moment later, the gun ships launched duel rockets. The noise deafened as they whizzed past and impacted in the tank's turret. Orange-red fire erupted, the explosion peeled open the metal, sending chunks fifty feet into the sky. It was close enough that he felt the heat of the flames.

Shouldering Sam, Riley hurried to the small clearing, the chopper rotors beating the air and smashing trees and grass as the pilot set it down swiftly. Two helmeted men ran toward them. Then above and behind the chopper, two more gunships rose over the hillside and swept forward. *The cavalry's here.* The aircrafts laid down cover fire, and the Marines took Sam, helping him in the chopper.

He turned to her. "Come with us!"

She shook her head, the wind tearing her scarves free. "Still have to fight the good fight." She didn't smile, then grabbed him close. In his ear, she said clearly, "Ask yourself, why no rescue launch when he went down so close to the border."

His muscles tightened and he scowled at her, their faces close.

"Your radio was enough to track you." Then she brushed her mouth across his as she forced paper into his palm. "Watch your back, Irish." She turned away.

"Safia!" But she was running into the fight.

A Marine grabbed his shoulder. "Sir, we got to go!" Riley threw himself in as rocket-propelled grenades launched, fifty calibers ripped across the Serb fighters, cutting anything in half. The chopper lifted off. Below, the ground was alive with battle. Flames and smoke stirred.

He searched for Safia and prayed she was fast on her feet, yet even after someone handed him headphones, he still couldn't turn away. The chopper climbed higher, and he pulled his legs inside. A medic hovered over Sam on a stretcher as the aircraft banked.

Riley fell back against the bulkhead and opened his hand. It was a dollar bill, American. He spread it.

In black ink, one word defaced it. *Fundraiser.*

Two

The barrier islands scattered like strings of torn white lace mixed with plots of lush green. This one looked like a Chia Pet growing in the middle of the ocean, Riley thought. Storms had eroded the shore till there was little more than a small stretch of beach maybe seventy-five yards wide, but it dropped off into deep water. The rubber motorboat floated on the outer rim of the reef, and with his hand on the rudder, he idled as he watched the men emerge on shore. At high tide, they could swim over the jagged reef and while Jim Clatt wanted to go alone, Riley was on board the research ship to make sure the boatload of geeks didn't do anything stupid.

It was a surprisingly easy job.

Walking alongside Jim was his twenty-year-old research assistant, Derek. The kid was having a blast sailing on the high seas before his senior year and facing the real world. When the pair turned to wave, Riley tapped his dive watch as a reminder. One hour and the tides would rapidly change. The rip current wasn't too bad, but getting across the barrier reef would be nearly impossible until high tide. He didn't think the bone diggers wanted to be stuck there all night. He heeled the rubber boat around on a swell of white water and headed back to the research ship.

Two hundred miles east of the Philippines and about a hundred south of Palau, the islands were small, mostly uninhabited, a couple acres at best, and during the rainy season, they were a few feet underwater. Riley didn't know what the pair thought they'd find, but he doubted much of anything could have survived the last round of typhoons.

Cabin fever, he figured. They needed to be on land. Riley knew if he set foot on solid ground, it would take him another day to regain his sea legs again. He'd rather skip shoving his face in the commode any day. At Derek's age, it was the reason he'd joined the Marines and not the Navy. Years ago and too old to look back, he thought as he steered the boat alongside the 180-foot white research vessel.

From the deck of *The Traveler*, a technician waved acknowledgment, then swung the rail gate aside. After he secured the rubber boat, Riley slung a small duffle across his body, then climbed the steel ladder forged into the hull of the ship. He stepped through the opened gate in time to see his older sister give orders, her Irish accent a wee heavier. It seemed to charm the lads. He wasn't fooled. Of his four sisters, she was the tyrant of the lot.

Yet he smiled just the same. Bridget was in her glory. A marine biologist with her doctorate in marine archaeology, she was the head of an expedition to gather data on the effects of the 2006 tsunami on the Pacific marine life. Her fully funded gig came with equipment, technicians, a botanist, an archaeologist, a climatologist, and a ship's staff. Partnered with her was his brother-in-law, Travis McFadden, an oceanographer. The man smiled an awful lot for someone who stared at weather patterns most of the time, but Trav and his sister had raised three boys, all in college, and from the looks of them lately, they were reviving their twenty-three-year-old marriage like honeymooners. Best not go there, he thought and looked back toward the shore.

Because of the depth, the ship was anchored a quarter mile from the reef. Standing at the prow out of the way of activity, he unzipped his waterproof duffle and drew out binoculars, sighting in on the two men. The pair was still inspecting the shore of sea-battered coral less than ten yards deep. A storm had raged across this area only two days ago, what did they think was left?

He followed them as they strolled toward a towering rock formation half shrouded in palms and betel nut trees and he didn't lower the glasses until they walked into the forest. Their steps were awkwardly high over the untouched vegetation as Jim swung a machete.

Then they were gone, swallowed into the darkness.

Jim Clatt liked that he was probably the first person to be here in centuries. He felt like the only person in the world. Derek was fortunately a quiet young man, his music tastes not withstanding. Jim brushed at the rocks, sweeping powdery white sand and dirt, smiling when the fossil emerged.

Then just as quickly, Jim felt a ripple of unease move down his spine that wasn't there a moment ago. Slowly, he lifted his gaze from the fossilized snail. The air was suddenly very still. He glanced back toward the ship, yet through the dense foliage, he could see only splashes of white shore and blues skies.

"Derek?"

When he didn't respond, Jim looked to his right. A few yards away, the young man was frozen, staring into the forest.

He didn't look at Jim as he said, "There's something in there."

"Impossible. Monsoons would drown anything out."

But he knew Derek was right. He could almost smell it.

Sweat pearled on Jim's temples and the base of his throat, rivering with gravity into his tank shirt. He let go of the brush he'd been using and slowly reached for the spade. He felt a measure of relief when his hand closed around the handle. It was short and folding, but heavy. His gaze darted to the undergrowth, then the tops of the wildly twisting trees. No animals in sight. Not even a bird.

Then what was out there?

Paranoid, he touched the waterproof walkie-talkie Riley insisted he take along. He hooked it on his waistband, then shifted back on his haunches, his gaze flicking over the darkness. This was the only clearing on the island they'd found. The rest was dense and too thick to even move through without chopping away half the jungle.

He heard something dart to his left, barely a whisper of sound and he flinched. Yet nothing moved. Not a single leaf. But he'd heard it. Creeped out, he felt like he was in a slasher movie and blindly he shoved his belongings into his waterproof bag, taking the fossil rock. He glimpsed at Derek. His student was moving forward on his hands and knees.

"Derek no," Jim whispered hotly.

"There's an animal in there, Dr. Clatt. I saw something."

Jim frowned and eased toward him, the shovel primed. He watched the forest, then whispered Derek's name and shoved the machete across the rocks and sand. Derek tilted to reach it, then held it like a baseball bat. He inched forward, and with the curiosity of youth and lacking all caution, he stood. He took a step.

Jim rose slowly. "What did you see?"

"Just movement, might be a lizard." He swiped the machete, clearing away nearly five feet of brush.

Jim stepped slightly away from Derek and advanced, pushing fronds aside. He drew the flashlight and flicked it on, focusing the beam into the darkest area. Derek's steps crunched on the dry, dead fronds and they stilled.

"I think we need to leave."

"Why?" Derek asked.

"If there is anything alive in here, it's never been in contact with humans."

"But what could be here? Dr. Bridget said the islands didn't even have monkeys or iguanas."

"Regardless, we're here and the good doctor is not."

Movement shot to the far left, this time stirring leaves. For an instant, Jim thought someone fired an arrow, the beam of movement was so fast and straight. He met Derek's gaze, but damn if the kid wasn't beaming.

"New species?"

"I doubt it and get that look off your face, we're not investigating." Jim reached for the walkie-talkie. "Back away."

Derek obeyed, thank God. Jim grabbed the waterproof sack and slung the strap over his head, the small shovel still primed to strike.

Derek inhaled. "It's close."

"I know." Jim felt the presence, indistinguishable but definitely there. "Keep moving, but go slow." He couldn't take his gaze off the jungle.

Then between the fronds and branches, nearly blending into the foliage, he saw it.

One golden-brown eye stared back at him.

Riley watched his sister approach, smiling. In her forties, she had the beam of a good life radiating from her, and he wished he knew her secret. Her passion about her work eluded Riley. He was a little jaded now, he got that, but while one mission nearly killed him, another nasty mess had the CIA kissing ass any way they could. It left Dragon One not only debt free, but at their disposal. Riley wasn't keen on that. He trusted very few and the Company wasn't even in the running. From his experience, they lacked a decent moral center.

As she neared, Bridget pulled her frayed slouch hat low. It was one of his old desert booney covers from his tour in the Marines. She was never without it considering she had the hair and skin of a true Irish lass. Fair and freckled. Even a tube of sunscreen hung from a belt loop on her shorts.

"Thanks for humoring them," she said, inclining her head toward the island.

"It gives me a break from that heavy metal noise Derek is so fond of."

She rolled her eyes. "Try living with that every day."

She was referring to his nephews who enjoyed head banging music. It just gave Riley a headache. "You really don't need me here, Bri." After two weeks, he was little more than an extra pair of hands.

She glanced, blue eyes soft with concern. "Getting antsy?"

"Not really, but security on a research ship?"

"I wanted you near me, Riley. I missed you." She leaned her head on his shoulder and he swept his arm around her waist. With four sisters, she'd practically raised him, letting him tag along as a kid. He'd probably be dead on the streets of Belfast if it wasn't for her, but he knew this went deeper. It had taken him two years to recover from a mission that put him in a coma along with several broken bones and a gunshot to the chest that barely missed his heart and lungs. According to his buddies, he'd drowned, but he barely remembered any of it.

"Your job attracts the wrong sort of people. Why do you insist on chasing such danger—" She stopped herself, let out a breath, then said, "I worry . . . we all do. I thought this might be a nice break."

And show him a different life, he thought. He was wise to his sister. "You're hoping I won't go back to Dragon One? It's my job. I can't freeload off you forever."

She cocked her head, a hand on her hip. "Do you know what an electrician makes in the states?"

"Yes I do, but installing lights isn't as rewarding. Besides, I've been on a couple missions since then."

"I know," she snapped, then softened. "I know. But I keep seeing you in the hospital in traction, machines helping you breathe, tubes running everywhere. You're lucky to be alive and I thank Logan for that. A doctor on sight saved you."

He knew he owed Sam and Logan more than he could re-pay. "But I've got better equipment now." He bent his knee, the surgical scars still plump against his tanned skin, but be-neath the stitches were hydrogel kneecaps and titanium rods that replaced shattered bones. "Want to arm wrestle?" He flexed one bicep like Arnold.

She elbowed him. "Don't tease. It was hard on us all."

He squeezed her, pressing his lips to her temple. It was the first time she'd really spoken about it. "I'm sorry." His fam-ily was close knit, and yet he was only just learning the effect his injuries had taken on the Donovan clan. His teammates were just as coddling. He put up with it because he wasn't in any hurry to return to work and focused his attention on more leisurely activities these days.

"I'll say this once—"

"Once? Since when?"

She crossed her eyes and made a face, then sobered, facing him. "Don't take so many risks with your life . . . and I never thought I'd say this, but shoot first."

He chuckled to himself. "Now there's me Belfast girl."

She laughed, then her assistant called to her, and she moved away.

Riley checked his watch, waiting for signs of Jim and Derek. Then he heard his name and turned.

"You have a call." Bridget clutched his satellite phone.

Riley tensed. No one but the team knew he was here.

"I was hoping there were no SATs in range for that to be of any use." It wasn't like this part of the world was a threat to humanity. There wasn't anyone else around for nearly a thousand miles.

"Kate said it's rung four times in the last hour."

That can't be good. Frowning, he took the phone, holding it to his chest. "Is it a female?"

"No, me handsome boy." She patted his face. "It's not."

"Then you should have hung up."

"Who left it turned on?" she said, already turning away and waving over her head.

He put the phone to his ear. "Riley Donovan isn't available for at least another three weeks."

"Really? Is she blond or brunette?"

Riley smiled.

"Neither," he said to Sam. "A redhead, and we're related. Don't go there."

Sam chuckled, then said, "Had enough sun and sea? Ready for work?"

"Not especially." But he admitted he was bored silly.

"We have a hand me down job."

Instantly Riley's radar went up. "Whose?"

"The State Department, more specifically, the Bureau of Diplomatic Security."

The law enforcement agency charged with the security of diplomats and just about anyone traveling abroad on State Department business, DS agents were assigned to a hundred-fifty-some foreign offices around the world. They used their diplomatic connections and with in-country police and Interpol, tracked and apprehended international fugitives who posed a threat to U.S. national security and dignitaries.

A heavy hitter, whoever they wanted to retrieve. After Venezuela, did the team really want to do anything remotely connected to government intelligence work again? One thing he knew for certain . . . "You're two stepping, Sam, and I'm wondering what's so bad that you can't spit it out."

He heard him sigh through the phone. "It's Vaghn."

For a moment, his muscles locked. The name burst with memories he wanted to forget. He turned away from the crew working around the mini sub he'd repaired only yesterday. "He fled the country, didn't he?"

"Quite easily, from what we can tell."

Well, he couldn't say he didn't warn them. "So why don't the DS just go get him?"

"It's a little trickier than that. You need to hear it all first, but it's your call, partner."

At least it wasn't CIA clean up. But the DS weren't slackers. They knew about his ties to Vaghn before they contacted D1. That meant someone was doing him a favor and he needed to know who.

"I'm about six hundred miles out in the middle of the South Pacific. It'll take a day to get to land with an airport."

"Got it covered. Tessa is coming by seaplane. She should be in your sights in a couple hours."

He looked at the horizon, cloudless and blue. He didn't ask for details, wanting to take this contract through a filter. He ended the call and tapped the satellite phone against his thigh, remembering the trial; Vaghn smiling when he was sentenced to five years minimum security. He'd planted his fist in the man's face about a minute later. But beating him wouldn't make Vaghn care. Vaghn was soulless, bloody arrogant and unfortunately—a brilliant weapons designer. The combination created a lethal genius with the attitude of a psychopath.

Vaghn testified that he'd released the pair of newly designed rifles for field-testing after they were given the required controlled tests. Evidence said he had, but only twice before the weapon was in the hands of Riley's team. Two of his troops had paid with their lives when the misfired laser weapon struck across their faces, severing their heads at an angle. It was the worst accident he'd ever witnessed. That his friends, his Marines, had died because of Vaghn's arrogant carelessness and sloppy miscalculations, put him on Riley's needs-to-die list for a long time. He was off radar till now.

He felt suddenly anxious to get on dry land.

Travis came out of the pilothouse and hurried down the steep metal staircase to the first deck. He held a hand radio. "Riley, something's wrong."

Immediately Riley grabbed his binoculars and focused on

the shore. There was no sign of Jim and Derek. As Travis neared, he heard the transmission.

Hard breathing came with, *"Can you hear me? ... the shore ... hurry!"*

Riley grabbed his duffle and ran to the rail. Travis followed.

"No, Trav, let Riley handle it," Bridget shouted, rushing to the rail. But her husband simply blew her a kiss as he went over the side.

A scream came through the radio, cut short, but he was already priming the motor, frustration mounting as he yanked the pull cord once, twice. The engine roared, water swelled around the propellers and as soon as Travis was seated, he gunned it.

"We'll never make it over the reef," Travis shouted. He kept the radio to his ear, transmitting they were coming. There was no response.

"We don't have time to go around." Leaving the boat and hoofing it wouldn't help them now.

Riley pushed the throttle down, the rubber craft bouncing over the water toward the reef. He glanced back to the ship, judging the push of his wake, and when white water swelled beneath the lightweight boat, he gunned the engine. The boat sailed over the razor sharp reef to the tidal basin. Riley kept going, rushed the boat onto shore and cut the engine. He climbed out. Travis started to follow.

"Take it back out into the lagoon, keep it running. No telling what spooked them."

"I'm betting it's lizards, the weenies." Though his expression said otherwise as Travis immediately moved into Riley's position, then tossed him the radio.

Riley grabbed his Glock from the duffle and followed the footprints from the water's edge. A few yards in, he was at the edge of the jungle.

Nothing moved. The walkie-talkie remained silent.

Riley went left to the jagged rock extending over the shore where they'd first entered the forest. Footprints confirmed it, and he followed them into the darkness, pausing to let his eyes adjust before advancing. The ground was soft beneath his dive boots, a mossy wet odor stirring with each step. And something else he couldn't put a finger on, but it was rank. About thirty yards in, he came to a small shadowy clearing. They'd been digging here, he realized, but no tools, no struggle. No men.

A rustle made him duck near a tree. Then he saw a figure plowing through the foliage, but couldn't tell who it was. Riley called out seconds before Jim burst through the darkness, tripped, then regained his footing.

"Riley! Go back, don't stay!" he said, pushing him, then glanced behind himself. Derek came running full force and Jim caught him, both winded and not wasting a moment to get to shore. "Come on!"

But Riley wasn't easily spooked and watched the forest, backing away slowly till daylight touched his back. He turned, maneuvering around the rocks to shore.

Whatever scared the two men sent them splashing into the water. Travis motored near, but Riley could tell Jim was having trouble. Riley dove into the water, swimming furiously. He grabbed Jim, pushed him to the boat, then reached for Derek. He shoved his ass up and in, then treading water, he watched the shore. The jungle beyond came alive. From the trees to the ground, it rustled.

Three heartbeats later, it stopped, only the breeze pushing leaves. Something survived the last major storm, he thought, then waved to Travis. He skidded closer and Riley grabbed the ropes and rolled smoothly into the craft. He pointed down the long stretch of lagoon. "We have to go around it."

Travis headed out of the basin. Jim and Derek lay face down in the bottom of the boat, breathing hard, neither talking. Riley exchanged a look with Travis, then leaned forward to roll Jim on his back.

"Oh, Christ on a cross," Travis said, releasing the throttle.

There were two bloody slashes across the left side of Jim's neck.

48 hours earlier, Singapore

With the package tucked under his arm, he watched the deliveryman return down the hall to the staircase, then closed and locked the door. Walking back to the table, he picked up the phone.

"What the hell are you doing?" the voice on the line snapped. "We'll miss the window!"

"Hardly." He checked his watch. "Do it now."

A few seconds passed, then, "It's done, Jesus, if anyone finds—"

"They won't. I'm smarter than you, remember."

"Christ, you're a bastard."

"My parents would agree, I'm sure."

He ended the call and tore open the wrapping, smiling at the paperback novel. At the table, he sat and opened his Yahoo account. There were five spam messages, subject line, Viagra. Figures. The world was one big dick, he thought as he checked the date and time of each. He clicked on one, opening it. The single row of letters and numbers marked it as spam. On a pad, he jotted down the sequence, deleted them all, then opened the book and found the page he needed.

He'd been warned to expect a way out. He thought he'd had that in a non-extradition country. Or any other one with the least friendly diplomatic ties to the U.S. of A. But the perfect opportunity would never arrive.

Waiting longer put his life in greater danger. They were watching him. He knew that a week ago. He didn't know how many, but felt them. Whether they were friend or foe, it didn't matter. His new employer would keep his word. He'd wanted his skills enough to offer ten million American. Half that was already in his Swiss account as a show of good faith.

Yeah, he could risk it.

His own calm surprised him, and he wondered if he really thought that five million in the bank would protect him. Because that's about all the backup he had. Moving to the table, he shut down the laptop, popped out the flash drive, then pocketed it safely in the seam of his jacket. Insurance was always near. He carefully replaced his equipment in the cases, then methodically arranged them in the satchel. More was required of him. Rich beyond his imagination meant now he had to earn it.

By betraying his country a little more than he did the last time.

Three

Jason Vaghn III was the Jeffrey Dahmer of weapon designers.

A silver spoon in the mouth, "daddy pay his way out of trouble" genius that had military contractors begging for his talent—until they witnessed his macabre skill at work. His weapons didn't kill, they maimed. Now, all banned by the U.S. military.

Vaghn's very existence bit a raw nerve that hadn't deadened with age.

Riley didn't take a life easily, but for *Tripp* Vaghn, he'd make an exception.

He should be satisfied, but a five-year prison sentence for two deaths wasn't enough. Riley knew Vaghn; the attitude bred into the spoiled boy had created a man who thought his genius put him above the law. While he'd been clean since his release, he had virtually no assets (the guy didn't even own a car), and he'd lived on a trust fund from his great-grandfather that barely kept his electricity on.

To the FBI, he wasn't a flight risk. Oh yeah, that was good Intel.

Taking surveillance off him was their first mistake. The second was believing that his sentence to not design or recreate any weapons or fuels of any kind, permanently, would matter. Not only was he too egotistical to think rules applied to him, he wouldn't even try.

He's already put something out there.

Vaghn wasn't in Singapore in the hopes of disappearing. He had help getting this far, Riley thought, rubbing the back of his neck and watching the surveillance screens. Vaghn was privileged to reams of classified material. The judge warned that if he disclosed even one word, she'd charge him with treason, a death sentence. Why she didn't sentence him adequately years ago was more political than handing down justice. Vaghn had been an employee of Noble Richards, a government contractor, and the projects were top secret. The company had influence in Washington. Riley would bet half of congress didn't know how much classified R&D work the National Intelligence Council farmed out to "outside resources." The secrets of the super power in shaky hands, as far as he was concerned.

Vaghn was proof of genius run amuck.

The door opened suddenly behind him and he scraped up the gun and turned.

Max put his hands up as best he could with a sack of groceries in his arms. "Jeez! No wonder your sister cut you a liberty pass off her ship."

"She had enough people to boss around." Riley laid the pistol aside.

Max chuckled as he set the bag down and pulled out bundles. Riley turned back to the camera feeds.

A breeze barely moved the torn bamboo shades. The paddle fan spun in a crooked thump overhead, and they were lucky to have some electricity. The unending humidity kept the air heavy and odors from the street fermented, occasionally masked by a whiff of frying bean curd or *hokkien* noodles. Somewhere tinny music played. They were positioned on the third floor of a row house, and high enough to have a wide vantage point. Like tired souls leaning on each other, the narrow homes were destined for demolition, most already uninhabitable, he thought with a glance left at the six-foot gap of missing floorboards. But people stayed, refusing progress until it was forced on them.

On the off chance that Vaghn might recognize him from their past, Riley stayed out of sight. After a month of Intel, cornering the guy was the plan. He didn't doubt Vaghn would run. He was hunted and the squalor he was living in said as much. From inside the small flat, he watched the feed from mini cameras positioned around Vaghn's last location. A DS agent gathering information on another case had spotted him after the FBI flooded U.S. agencies with his photo. Pinpointing it had taken a week. They'd been here twenty-four seven since then and still no sign of him.

Riley expected Vaghn to have changed his looks, a little dye, some facial hair so he could blend in.

"Any clue what that guy saw in the jungle?" Max asked.

"Bridget thinks it was an iguana. Jim says bigger." He'd believe the archaeologist's version. The man was too much of a detail nut not to be accurate. "He said he was spooked, fell, then claws swiped at him. He got up and ran." Screaming into the walkie-talkie. He'd lost that and his bag. Dumbshit, he had a weapon, the spade. But his sister reminded him in that superior tone of hers that most people didn't respond well under duress. Maybe he'd call Jim in a couple days to see if he remembered anything new.

"The assistant?"

"He didn't encounter it. But said it was like something big behind a curtain." He shook his head and remembered the jungle shivering. "Bri won't bother with it. It's not on her expedition budget program, and that he was injured will make her more stubborn." *That* he was glad to avoid. "Besides, she was too damn eager to dive the Yonaguni ruins off the coast of Okinawa."

"Man, I'd kill for the chance to get wet there."

He glanced up. "I think I can arrange that after this is secure." He waved at the screens on the desk.

"You're on." Max handed a paper wrapped lump.

He found a fried bean curd wrap filled with steaming meat. It was probably wise not to ask after the species, but it smelled great. He chowed down, his attention on the three laptops. Each had four views in a grid on the screen. They covered a four-block radius from where Vaghn was last spotted. Sebastian was on the streets. His dark hair and perpetually tanned skin coupled with the right clothes let him blend in easier than any of the team. He was getting to know the locals by now, turning down dinner invitations.

Riley wanted out there to search for the little prick, but the whole idea of surveillance was not to be seen. "What do you think he's doing?"

On the screen, he watched Sebastian stop a teenager with a package, slip him money and head this way. "*He has a delivery,*" came through the speaker.

Sebastian gave the address and Riley glanced at the street map, then keyed in the correct camera. So, there's your hideout.

"*He's going by Wang Chung, by the way. I thought he was smart?*"

He was. So what's with the giveaway? Riley took a bite of the sandwich, his gaze flicking to each picture. "Something's not right."

Just as Sebastian entered the building, movement at the far edge of the roof caught Riley's attention. Thinking it was birds, Riley went to the window, pushing back the bamboo shade. "Heads up! He's using the fire escape. West side!" He dropped the food, then scooped up the gun and radios. "Max, direct me."

"You got it."

He didn't take the door, exiting out the window and using the fire escape. He hit the ground in a crouch and straightened to hear Max say, "*He's on the roof heading to the north end, but he's not running.*"

Excellent. He was still blind to us. "Tell me when he's on the ground. Sebastian?"

"Headed west, I'll try to cut him off before he gets to the markets."

If Vaghn reached the crowded food kiosks, their chances would quickly thin.

Riley hurried to the end of the building, knocking aside trash in the alley. At the edge, his gaze slid over the crowds of patrons and vendors, then jerked back to a man with shaggy hair. The light shade stood out against the throngs of dark haired people. Just as the awning shadowed him, the man looked over his shoulder.

"It's him." Riley was already advancing. "Sebastian, watch my flank. I've got him."

"He made you?"

"No, not yet. Come east. He's cutting through *Kopi tiam*s." The two-acre mall of food vendors was impressive, the entire complex covered against the blistering sun. Even in the late afternoon, the crowds were heavy. He moved left, careful not to get too close. Steam shot up from cookers behind the counters, orders called out in Malay and Mandarin. Riley saw Sebastian hanging back when Vaghn stopped at a vendor and handed over money for *Ngo Hiang*; spiced pork and prawn rolled inside a bean curd skin and deep-fried. Everything around here was fried, he thought, stooping a little when Vaghn looked around before taking a bite.

He was between them, along with five aisles of tables, chairs, and forty vendors serving over a thousand people. Riley paralleled Vaghn, a few yards behind. The guy was afraid, stopping to look behind himself and using the reflection in windows to do it. He had the fugitive life down well. Vaghn walked to the entrance on Woodlands Road, around the pillars supporting the roof of the two-acre food court squashed between high-rise housing complexes.

Riley noticed he had a satchel and a backpack. He wasn't

coming back. He nodded to Sebastian. Riley was within earshot of him, then within reach. Sebastian came around from the east to the front, cutting Vaghn off.

Riley moved up behind him.

E ring
Pentagon

Colonel Hank Jansen kept a brisk pace down the corridor. To those who were aware, his presence on this floor spoke of trouble. Today was no exception. He glanced at his watch. He'd have to cancel dinner plans, but disappointing his wife came with the job.

A Marine guard snapped to attention and he paused long enough for security, then turned the next corner and opened the large oak door. Few looked up or stopped their discussion as he entered, yet he noticed that at least three were already answering their phones. The word was out.

He went directly to the screen controls and typed, linking the feed from his operation, then stepped back and picked up the remote. "Gentlemen."

The room quieted.

"Delta class intelligence. Direct your attention to the screen." Chairs swiveled around, but Jansen didn't wait. He keyed in the satellite feed. "This is an air strip in Britain. Eighteen minutes ago." It showed a glimpse of the runway, but focus was on a gray building, small and heavily fortified with two-stage security. He drew the image back a few feet, exposing the surrounding grounds and the bodies tumbled like pillars.

"Good God. The count?" someone asked above some colorful curses.

"A detachment of fifteen. Ours."

"I'm not familiar with the target," an admiral said.

"The shipment of RZ10 stored and bound for R&D Ordnance."

The joint chiefs murmured among themselves.

Once the shipment was turned over for storage, Americans guarded it, but it was the British military's responsibility to see it to ordnance specialists from both countries—and Jansen's job to keep track of it. All was well until about a half hour ago.

"This is thirty minutes prior." Jansen watched the attack that was so carefully executed he'd have thought it was one of his own teams. The men standing guard dropped like rags, no force, no gunshots. They simply collapsed. Gas? he wondered. A moment later, two men in full black ops gear approached, set charges and broke through to the container, a building created to protect the RDX fuel to the degree that a tornado or even an earthquake wouldn't harm it.

The thieves quickly passed through without explosives, using a composition that smoldered yet didn't blast. From what he could see, it cut through the titanium door and one man simply pulled off the lock and tossed it. His fury pushed up his blood pressure. America had billions in Research and Development and analysts to anticipate different types of attacks, and some slipper faction gets in without trouble? And what the hell did they use?

He waited till the escape was apparent, then turned it to live-mode so the joint chiefs could see that British Royal Marines had arrived and the MI5 investigation was underway. "I will contact MI5 in thirty for a report. Diplomatic Security is in the area to assist."

He moved to the head of the table near the screens linking them to major movement across the globe.

"We have ascertained this. The British knew when we did. The alarms tripped after the first blast." He played the long-range video, drawing back to before the guards fell. "We've learned in this frame," he froze it briefly, "the shots were fired out of range of surveillance cameras. All but one camera, intentionally concealed, were taken out simultaneously. Prior to that, sensors picked up no more movement than a squirrel.

Not a single pressure sensor went off. That means the weapons were not only silent, but had a tremendous range. The building was fifty yards from the nearest solid marker, a military motor transport section of vehicles recently repaired and awaiting transport to Iraq."

"So what did they do? Drop out of the sky?" a three star general asked.

"I haven't had time to speculate, sir."

"How much did they take?" the Secretary of the Navy asked.

"One canister."

"Only one?"

"Yes, sir." It confused him too. They'd passed the opportunity to steal mass quantities of the most highly explosive liquid component created. One question loomed over all others. How did anyone know it existed? Getting it to Britain was a logistics nightmare, and Hank thought the fuel should be destroyed. It was too unstable, and the reason it was kept in two binary agents. They were still volatile, but manageable. A canister was one half liter, unmixed.

"We've never seen anything this tightly executed," an officer said, watching the replay.

"Looks like one of ours."

"I agree," Jansen said. "They could be ours turned mercenary." Blackwater had already coaxed their highly trained military away, paying them more than the government could even consider.

Discussion tripped around the long polished oak table as Jansen's phone vibrated softly. He glanced at the text message and immediately crossed the room. His aide waited on the other side. The lieutenant handed him a printout from MI5. Hank scanned it, then looked up.

"Puzzling, isn't it, sir?"

"It certainly is."

He turned back into the room, striding to the front and attention came with him. "Gentlemen, we have a surprising development. MI5 tells us that all the sentries are alive."

A stir of shock rippled around him. In an age when hundreds of people were being blown up at once, this was unexpected. He grabbed the remote and with his eye on the counter, he drew the image back and rewound the stream. "MI5 reports the men were struck with darts." He froze the image, the needle-like barbs only light streaks on the screen. "The area is locked down and British Intelligence has the ball." He turned to the joint chiefs, his attention on Major General Al Gerardo. "I'd like to hear your opinion, sir." Gerardo was the JCS expert on the latest weaponry.

"I don't have one yet. But the man that steals one container of RZ10 is a thousand times more dangerous than a few IED's and some militants."

No one asked for more explanation, waiting.

Gerardo leaned forward, hands clasped over a small stack of files. "RZ10 is a highly explosive composite fuel. Thermobaric. Ignited, its oxidizing flash point is so high that it results in a vacuum. Everything collapses. Special Forces used it in the Afghan caves, but it didn't leave enough debris to sift."

Good lord. Who thinks up this stuff? "What can one container do?" Jansen asked.

Casually, Gerardo dipped his coffee spoon into his mug and lifted out no more than a taste. "With the right detonation, this alone would destroy this building."

Jansen experienced a familiar tremor shoot down his arms to his fingertips. He clenched his fist, waiting for the general to continue.

"That makes it highly cost effective and powerful enough to need only small quantities. It's used in enclosed spaces, but one half-liter container detonated, say inside an aircraft over land, would create a massive pressure wave of sonic magnitude, and depending how low it was when it ignited, would crush everything for . . . well . . . about the size of Texas."

The general glanced at his colleagues. "Over water, it could cause a tsunami that'd make the one in 2006 look like a surfer's day out."

Gerardo leaned back in his chair. "In the vacuum, nothing survives. Nothing."

48 hours earlier
Satellite surveillance post
Mariana Islands, U.S.
Western Pacific

"I graduated summa cum laude for this?" Owen said, leaning back in his office chair, his headset cockeyed.

"So did I," the voice on the other side of the divider answered. "Get over it."

The frosted glass partition was more for toning down glare than privacy. "Didn't you think when you were recruited, you'd end up doing something remotely James Bond?"

"No," his partner Greg said, leaning back and pulling the headset aside.

Owen was listening with half an ear too. The satellite wasn't in range for another three minutes. "That's because you like eavesdropping too much, perv."

"You don't think the Farsi and three dialects are doing it for me?"

"Not till you find the Farsi word for lap dance." Owen snickered to himself as he turned back to his screen, adjusted his headset, then checked the countdown.

Time to go to work.

He watched the timer trip and adjusted his frequency wave. He'd been instructed to focus on five sets of coordinates—at the same time. The range decreased, and he worked to isolate each one, assigning them names. He sifted through each, holding for a few seconds, then onto the next. He'd record and store if the chatter was too fast, but the system would pop open a window when it heard a key word. It didn't happen as often as people would think, but these five points were of vital interest or he wouldn't be tracking them. It wasn't in his pay grade to know why.

He glanced at the counter and watched the animated replica of the satellite moving into position to do its job. He hit record one minute prior to zero. It was down to ten seconds when the words came.

"Ee . . . ine," he caught and scrambled to replay. The satellite was in full range rolling through the first promenade, but the stream dropped off.

"Greg, did you get that stream?"

Greg leaned back. "The burst just before range? It was too short to get a lock, why?"

Teasing faded, the pair were all business. "I've got a flag on it." In his section, Owen's responsibility.

"No shit. What level?"

"Just a three."

Greg frowned. "What did you hear?"

"I'm not sure." Owen tuned the sound up and hit replay while keeping an eye on the tracking that was sweeping across the Pacific back to the points of origin.

Greg listened, then played it twice more. He looked at Owen. "We can't track that for another twenty-four hours." And that's if it comes again.

"God, it was just barely on the edge before the satellite came in range," Owen muttered as he typed. "I'm alerting Australia, see if they have anything on it. It should be a full stream on their part of the world."

Dotted like bugs across the globe were American and ally listening posts along with their dangerous counterparts of China, Russia and a few others with the budgets to do it. We all listen, but few act, he thought, sending the message down under, then relaying it back to the U.S. where analysts better than him would be the first to see it and understand his suspicions.

Ee . . . ine. . . . He tumbled it over in his brain, trying to match it to full words. "Geez, can I buy a consonant?"

Spinning to another computer, he accessed the data bank and the search brought up twelve languages and about three thousand possibilities. It might be just radio backwash or another satellite out of kilter, but he had to be sure. He set search parameters, narrowing by category, then filtering casual conversation from eerily listed words like timer, device, slaughter, conspiracy. The computer did most of the work to match up common words that usually preceded suspicious conversations. But for the life of him, he couldn't pinpoint the grouping.

Vigilant, he glanced at the relay, waiting for Australia to reply.

Marina Bay
Singapore

The entire purpose of standing on her feet all day waiting tables was to get close to table number eight. It was on a dais, shielded from the sun by a conical roof and perched out over a man-made lagoon. But the private dining gazebo wasn't her station and the waitress who had it was protective.

Beyond, the sea view was spectacular, but Safia didn't have time to enjoy it as she served a woman from the right, then delivered meals around table six. The patrons barely spared her a glance, deep in conversation. The hired help were nonexistent to the few elitists. Finished, she held her tray and kept her head bowed, asking if she could bring them anything else. Even her question was subservient. The more submissive, the better the tip, and considering the men wouldn't give the hired help a glance, it kept her in the background. Just where she wanted to be.

She was filling in for Miya, a waitress and an asset with a shrewd eye for oddities in people. Singapore was full of them so picking out something non-indigenous was a skill Safia needed and Miya offered. The woman worked too hard for too little pay, and Safia was more than willing to fund her and her four-year-old daughter. Tax dollars well spent, she thought, because putting her in danger was out of the question. When the "golden skinned man," showed again, Miya called in sick and sent a replacement. The boss barely gave her a glance when she showed at the height of the lunch hour.

She stopped at each of her assigned tables to be certain all were happy little diners. She had a half hour left on the shift and needed to get closer to the dais. Two of her tables were vacated recently and the busboy was clearing the dishes. She grabbed the freshly pressed linens and crossed the restaurant, waiting till he'd removed the dirty dishes and swept up the soiled linens. She snapped out a fresh cloth and let it sail down over the table, her position offering a clear view of her objective. Table eight.

Cale Barasa enjoyed a meal with the casual grace of a king. His light brown skin glowed like polished copper in the glare of the sun, the carefully manicured goatee added a dash of piracy. She'd give him props for looking suave. But if he didn't want notice, he shouldn't have worn a thousand dollar suit to a seaside Polynesian restaurant. She couldn't see his eyes, hidden behind sunglasses and he didn't take them off when a bodyguard hopped up from a nearby table and lowered the sunscreen. She caught a whiff of his Cuban cigar as the busboy returned with fresh dishes and set the table. She folded napkins precisely as Miya taught her and set them in the wine glass to resemble a coral flower. Hers looked a little limp.

In her line of vision, Barasa answered his phone, then sat up a bit straighter.

His lunch date was a slim black haired woman perched on the edge of the chair in a practiced pose designed to get attention. Gorgeous woman. Did she know the company she kept? Safia doubted it. The woman questioned him, and he waved her off rudely, then shifted away. Conveniently toward

Safia. A quick glance to the next table told her his bodyguards were more interested in their meals than watching his back. The piglets had requested a male waiter, and she was happy to oblige. They were ugly when they ate, a fact that put them apart from their boss.

She moved to the next table, a step closer, and tried to read his lips, but she hadn't heard him speak to know his accent. Her sources couldn't pinpoint it beyond maybe Congolese or African. He had a Euro look going on, yet even before intelligence made the connection of arms to Barasa, she knew he was a scuzbag in designer duds. He'd crossed her path one too many times, often followed by people dying.

It was the company he kept that brought more attention. A deal maker, he put elements together. Like Hezbollah and necessary weapons. He didn't have a conscience or a cause. While he was very careful to never be seen in a country the U.S. or Britain could extradite him from quickly, he'd slip up. She wanted to be there when it happened.

Safia felt an odd tremor to be so close to this man.

She could liquidate him right now, but that wouldn't get who was pulling his strings. Barasa might be careful about his conduct, but he had deadly friends who could turn on him at any moment—a threat that ruled his actions with ruthless paranoia. She'd tracked him a month ago and he'd hopped countries so fast it was like trying to follow a fly. Plus, his past didn't exist. Point number forty-four in the suspicious behavior manual, she thought making it harder to understand him and catch him in the act. He was rarely close to his own hardware, and knew which rock to slip under and be protected. On the surface, he was sophisticated, but he didn't flaunt his wealth with the ease of someone who'd grown up with it.

People didn't die around Barasa, they disappeared. Proven a moment later when his bodyguard hopped from his table, a phone to his ear as he went to the dais. It wasn't the same man as three days ago, nor was he as refined as the last. This guy's like a farmer in a suit, she realized. His walk was too stooped for his age, yet with a broad back and shoulders. It was the hands that cinched it. Leathery with thick white calluses. Not a guy accustomed to the high life and firing a weapon. She could tell when his holster jabbed him as he sat and he had to adjust it. Anyone familiar with carrying a weapon would have made allowances. He did it again when Barasa waved him back.

So who was on the phone that changed his mood?

Forced to turn her back on him for the job, she backed up, hoping to catch some conversation. She'd have saved herself the trouble and bugged the reserved table if Miya hadn't warned her his people check it for just that before he entered the restaurant. She finished refilling glasses, then moved to the ice machine outside the dining area and a bit down the hall. She had a clear view.

Barasa checked his watch, then suddenly stood and tossed a wad of bills on the table. He said something to the woman, then turned his back on her. The woman pouted, grabbed some of the bills and left. The bodyguards jumped up and followed. Barasa came toward her, head down, still on the phone. The guards went out the front. When he passed her, Safia followed him through the restaurant.

He was mad and in a hurry. It delighted her no end. His long legs overtook the distance. She hurried after him, keeping back just enough that he wouldn't make her till she remembered she was supposed to be here, not him. He went in the kitchen.

She stopped short. *Who are you running from? Or to?*

The door swung closed. Through the frosted glass, she saw him move away from the door and she pushed through. He shouldered workers out of his way and she glimpsed him stop near the dishwasher station, then continue through to the back door. Stopping about thirty feet behind him, she pinched the hem of her tropical print apron, flicking on the microphone.

"He's coming your way."

"Got him. Just exiting now."

Agents were her eyes on the perimeter. "His ride is marked?"

"Tagged and running."

"Tail him just the same." She'd blow her cover if she followed him in her uniform and quickly turned back into the kitchen, moving around the chaos of cooks, dishwashers, and busboys to where Barasa had stopped briefly. She glanced around. To the left was the dishwasher station, steam coiling up as a young boy sprayed the racks. Across from it were four lined trash cans, no lids, brooms, mops, and a large slop bucket sold to local farmers.

She looked down into the pail of vile brown muck.

"Oh no he *didn't*," she said softly.

The cell phone sank beneath a day's worth of restaurant leftovers. Gross.

A busboy stared with wide eyes as she rolled back her sleeve and plunged her hand into the slop. *I deserve extra pay for this.* She swished her hand and found the phone, shaking off glop, then grabbing a rag. Wiping it down, she prayed the moisture hadn't ruined the memory. She turned it on, and scrolled to the last number.

The prefix said it was the other side of the island.

She hurried to the locker room, stripped, washed off the foul smell of spoiled food and Chinese five spice, then dressed in her street clothes. Removing the mic, she tossed the uniform in a laundry bin, and before she left, she slipped an envelope into Miya's locker vent. The day's wages and tips were a payback for Miya's keen eye.

She zippered her tight fitting jacket and left. Outside, she hurried to the far corner of the lot and threw her leg over her silver motorcycle. She twisted her hair up to put on her helmet, then started the bike and left the lot at a moderate speed till she cleared the next street. She urged the machine faster. Two blocks away, she turned on the small GPS screen on the dash. Her mic relay went through her helmet.

"I've got him. Damn, he's passing Changi and heading to

Seletar airport." And not in the direction of his last phone call. She followed and Barasa's car took the Central expressway, gaining speed. "Get me some SAT info, now, Base."

"Yes ma'am. We have imagery of the field. A plane is landing."

"Check for clearance of *his* jet. He can't leave till I tag it." Tracking Barasa was a lesson in international hopscotch. He paid bribes to get in and out of countries without notice, but most often, he was welcomed by the latest regime.

She spotted the dark blue town car that was larger than most of the vehicles on the road and slowed, keeping at least a hundred yards back. She leaned, taking a turn that put her on the other side of the runway. It was a private air strip, reserved for those who could pay the fees to land. Three hangars located at the far end were open, a helicopter shadowed inside one. She stopped the bike near a park bench off the highway, her position secluded enough by trees and shrubs someone took the time to trim. The runway was off Seletar's 747 traffic, yet further up the road the highway split, dividing smaller towns and villages on the edge of the water. A stone's throw would land on the poorest of Singapore.

She left the bike, bringing her backpack and digging out her binoculars.

She sat on the metal table with four chairs permanently attached and flipped up her visor. She focused on the field. The town car was just making it around the long drive to the airstrip. Tires are a little low, she thought, waiting for the show to begin. Too often, he was legit, magically producing the right papers for his cargo. Interpol hadn't given up on catching him, but Safia knew that letting him have some rope would get them more. He'd been in very bad company lately and following the money trail didn't get her enough. While his accounts were modest enough not to draw the attention of the international banking community, recent increases in the millions said otherwise. Whatever he was up to, was big.

The roar of engines whining down for a landing made her

swing the glasses left. Too fast to be safe, the Gulfstream jet touched down. Barasa left the car and stood next to it, his bodyguards at the rear looking like Secret Service in bad suits. She noticed several feet to the right of him was a shade cabana, a table and—oh you've got to be kidding—linens and set for a tea?

She swung her attention to the jet as it powered down and the door opened, lowering the steps. A figure moved in the dark interior and Safia was surprised when a woman stepped out. That explains the tea set.

The woman wore a pale gray suit, cut close, the skirt longer than fashion but her shoes were the bomb. Bright red. She sighed, wishing for playtime to be a girl. The woman descended the jet's stairs and walked straight to Barasa before he could meet her. She didn't offer her hand nor did he. Red shoes went to the shade and sat. Barasa was slower to follow, his attention on the woman's rear. Clearly, he'd other plans for her, but Safia was interested in Red Shoes.

Women didn't fit in the world of arms dealers. Aside from the fact that half the buyers seeking weapons were Muslims and therefore still in the dark ages, she thought snidely, most men had ego problems with strong women. They felt threatened. Barasa didn't. He seemed amused.

She needed to get closer and hopped on her bike, riding it to the fork, then doubling back to the airfield. She stopped the bike behind a tall *chengal pasir* tree. They were sitting at the table, a servant who must have come from the jet, pouring for them. A sharp breeze battered the cabana, taking away a piece of linen. The woman didn't notice nor acknowledge the servant chasing after it. Was she the money?

Safia raised the cell phone and snapped a picture of the two, then hailed Base. She worked the slideout keyboard. "Base, I'm sending you a photo. Run everything."

"Confirmed jpeg and running."

"Ya know, you can drop the military speak, Ell."

"Yes ma'am."

Safia shook her head, and sighted through the monocular, using its digital camera to get a full face shot as she watched the pair converse. The woman was beautiful, her black hair twisted up to show off her slender neck and reminding Safia a little of Audrey Hepburn. Way out of place. The suit was designer, the shoes . . . fifteen hundred easy. Though this was Singapore; knock-offs were sold on every street corner.

She studied the unlikely pair.

Who are you Red Shoes, and what are you doing with that nasty arms dealing trash?

Four

Max was finishing off Riley's wrap when he saw movement behind the salty glass of a storefront. He grabbed his binoculars, sighted, shifting his position on the windowsill. His side of the neighborhood was empty except for a couple of dogs that would end up as dinner if they weren't careful. A few entrances up from Vaghn's suspected address, a bell plinked as a shop door opened.

A man appeared, then turned west. That he didn't look left kept Max watching. Who didn't check for oncoming anything? Max slipped back inside and went to the laptops, keying up the next street in their four-block radius. He focused the tiny pen-sized cameras, then saw the man turn the corner. A few seconds passed before he could get a face shot.

The man appeared, his image clarifying with each step closer.

Max grabbed the radio. "Riley. It's not him!"

"*Repeat last?*" came back. "*I'm three feet away.*"

Max grabbed his weapon, holstering it behind his back. "I'm telling you, he's *here*. Your guy's a freakin' decoy!"

Over the wire, he heard a scuffle, then cursing. When Riley's voice came back on, he could tell he was hoofing it fast. "*Some*

Australian. Vaghn paid him a hundred. Where the hell is Vaghn now?"

"On Pi Nang Road, west. I'm going after him." Max went out the fire escape, and when he hit the ground, the ladder shot off its track. He darted out of the way as it crashed to the pavement and crumbled in a pile of rusted iron. "One step closer to demolition."

He took off in a hard run and glimpsed the guy's brown tee shirt that hung to his thighs, his jeans rippling with fabric. "Behind the village, toward the river," he said over the personal roll radio. "Same clothes, same pack."

Where was he going? There wasn't a damn thing on the water except shanty homes slapped together with tin and wood discards from recent construction. The river was so shallow along tributaries the next monsoon would wash away any evidence of their existence. He hauled ass past new construction toward the old and almost untouched. Lush with palms and towering banana trees, the paved land blended into dirt roads, rutted and sloping toward the water.

Far ahead, Vaghn walked a steady pace, unaware. Then two men in a flat bottom boat appeared around the curve of a jetty. Vaghn quickened his steps.

"Put some fire under it, buddy," Max said into the mic. "He's got a ride."

Seletar Airstrip

He knew her by no other name than Odette.

"What I don't understand is why you aren't handling it yourself," she said, then sipped warm tea.

He couldn't place her accent and wondered if, like him, she strove to cover it. The less people knew of him the better. It was something they had in common. "Like your employer, I can delegate."

"We have warned you." She set her cup down with a click.

"He's immature and a genius. Those are qualities not easily handled, neh?"

"I'm due a measure of trust."

She scoffed, her smile tinged with patience delivered to the mentally incapable. Barasa felt his shoulders tighten. The pretty little bitch would learn not to dare more than that with him.

"Trust is not a commodity in business. Any business."

At least they agreed on that and planned for it. "When will he show himself?"

"When we have completed the next phase."

"He promised the perfect delivery system."

Something skated across her flawless face just then, and he didn't try to decipher it. The woman was not the force in this dangerous bargain, but merely the messenger.

"You will have it." She made a show of checking the time. "We will expect to hear from you within the deadlines you set."

"You came all this way to say that?"

"No. I'm here to demonstrate that, should you betray us, we will find you."

"If he wishes to fold"—he shrugged—"I won't oppose."

Her smile was slow and thin, her blue eyes taking on a victorious gleam he'd seen only in the pump of sex.

"And you're prepared to return the money he has already fronted? Won't that be difficult when you've already spent most of your share?"

His features stretched tight. How did they know anything? No one knew . . . his gaze immediately scanned his surroundings. Their position was in the open, yes, but also far enough to see anyone approach. He saw nothing unusual.

"No one has betrayed you, Barasa."

He looked at her and she tilted her head, the move coy yet somehow ill-fitting on this woman. He offered the truth. "Had they, they would be dead."

She nodded once, regally. "Sometimes loyalty accompanies

strict rules of self-preservation. Your clever discretion and influence has earned his admiration."

His brows knit as he considered what would bend her loyalty.

He stood with her.

"It's in your best interest to keep the genius alive and out of Western hands." She tossed the napkin on the table. "Bring him to us." She turned away, starting toward the plane.

He called to her, but she didn't stop, and he rushed to grasp her arm. He heard the click of bullets chambered and looked at the plane. From under the open staircase, two men advanced from either side and aimed rifles with infrared scopes. The gaping entrance in the fuselage remained empty, yet a gun barrel slid from hiding.

She didn't have to tell him to let go. He put his hands up, stepping back.

"Again you have underestimated, Cale."

His gaze narrowed. He didn't like anyone calling him that.

"Anticipating your enemy is necessary for success," she said.

"I'm not your enemy. We are equal partners."

"Equal?"

"I am risking everything while your boss hides in the shadows giving orders," he snarled at her, taking a step closer and ignoring the men with weapons.

"Are you not capable of the task?"

"Do not insult me, woman. Of course I—"

"Then enough."

The words weren't sharply spoken, but he felt their bite. Something shifted between them and not in his favor.

"Do you want more money, is that it? Or simply to see a face when it's shown to you several times already?" She flicked her hand at the jet and men. "We have step one. Now stop this . . . *whining* and fulfill your obligations." She spun away and mounted the steps. "Succeed, and the rewards will be many, Barasa." She paused to look back at him, smile, and add, "And I don't mean in virgins."

Barasa chuckled under his breath, admiring her ass shifting inside the gray cloth as she took the stairs. She never once looked back as she was swallowed inside the jet. The guards filed in, the door raising on a hydraulic hush and the locks clamped it seamlessly. Barasa hurried away as the engine powered up for takeoff.

"Hey," someone said and he looked at the guard standing near his car.

"Address me as sir and nothing else. What do I pay you for?"

"Answering your phones." The beefy man held out a clean one.

He suddenly realized that the woman couldn't have arrived so quickly if she hadn't known where he was first. He stared at the phone. She must have tracked it and while removing the GPS would end her watchful eye, the phone wouldn't work without it. Disposable cells were easier. He put the phone to his ear.

"We have the package," the gravely voice said.

Barasa snickered. Of that, he did not doubt. "Bring him to me, and take away his phone."

"Yes sir."

He waited till the jet banked off the runway and into the sky, then slid into the back of the town car. He wasn't without influence and scrolled through his phone numbers for just the right advantage. He didn't doubt Odette and her mysterious master were doing the same to him. He hadn't survived in this business by being careless.

Max's words pushed Riley, his arms pumping as he ran. He darted into the street, around people and cyclists, then jumped a cart, spilling baskets to the ground. A hunched man shouted at him in Mandarin, and his new kneecaps held up as he sprinted out of the dreary projects onto a newly paved street. Cars raced dangerously close together. He stopped, catching his breath. A traffic circle was packed with little cars like bugs marching to a nest. It led off in three directions but not anywhere he wanted to go. He watched the cars, then stepped into traffic. Horns honked, drivers shouted. A cab came so close he felt it brush and he figured it was now or get killed standing here. He darted between cars, then hopped on the back of a pint sized Carmen Gia, holding on as it took him around the curve. The driver shouted at him and Riley felt the bumper give under his weight. He had to jump, his target coming fast.

This is gonna hurt. He pushed off, but the driver sped up a fraction, and he tumbled to the road. His elbow burned as he rolled away from the street, then hopped to his feet.

"Finn, come back."

Riley frowned. Why was he using call signs? "I hear you."

"He's on the docks." Max's voice popped in his ear. *"Two men in a boat heading toward him. Christ, the package waves like a pansy."*

Riley paused on the balls of his feet, spying between the trees. The river looked almost black from the road. It was deceiving, the tributaries only hip deep. It confused him when he heard the soft putt of a motor and he rushed into the trees toward the water. Two men in a flat bottom boat floated toward the dock, the trolling motor small enough to accommodate the low water level. The pair in the boat looked like any local; big shirts over a muscle tank, but that's where it ended. Riley was thinking fast as Vaghn waved with big gestures. It annoyed his chauffeur as he expertly slid the boat sideways to the dock.

"Back off, Drac."

"We'll lose him."

"They've been here before and the locals know it. Look at them." On their approach, people vanished, retreating into huts, dropping what they were doing and melting into the forest along the banks. "That's too familiar."

He recognized fear in their faces. If just showing up provoked that, then it was probably a smuggling trail. Within moments, there was only Vaghn, the docks, and his cabbies. The boat rocked as Vaghn stepped in and apparently not fast enough. The cabbie yanked him into the center seat, his partner in the rear. They used the long handled paddles to push away and under their loose shirts, Riley saw weapons.

"Christ, they've got an Israeli Galeils, and I've got two magazines. Sebastian where are you, man?"

"Stuck behind a rickshaw," Sebastian said. *"I could walk there."*

He looked back at the road and saw the hood of the truck behind a cycle cart. "When you can, go north, cut them off."

"What are you thinking?"

He told them.

Sebastian snorted. *"You don't actually think that will work, do you?"*

"We don't have much choice now that he has help. And I'm not into automatic gunfire with so many locals nearby."

He wasn't leaving without Vaghn. No bloody question about it. He hauled ass to get further ahead of them. The craft was moving slow, idling in the short canal as one man used a cell phone, the call no more than seconds. The main body of water was just a few yards ahead. The only path was around hundreds of soggy juts of land. Riley moved out on one of them, stopping to yank on thick green vines and cut a portion. He turned in a small circle to wrap it around his chest, then moved further out on the peninsula.

Max appeared in the forest several yards to his right. He crouched low, winded, then swiped his hand over his face. "That's some definite skill there."

"The norm lately, huh?" Riley approached a tree and quickly climbed.

Max moved into position. "This better work."

The armed twins kept an eye on their surroundings and only the dense undergrowth concealed Riley. Broad branches curled without direction, the porous limbs seeking water and light. Soft moss coated the north side, and he slipped, hitting his chin, nearly biting off his tongue. He shimmied quickly toward a thick branch hanging over the river. Stringy green-gray moss draped inside the trees so dense it felt like a cave. Riley slid a length of vine free, rolling it, then feeding it down and up. This would be tricky, but automatic gunfire could spray the huts hiding villagers.

"Eagle's in the nest."

The craft was about fifteen feet long. He'd seen the like all over Asia. Farmers used them to bring goods to market. They could accommodate a lot of weight. *Lucky for me, they tip easy.* The boat slipped forward on the current, its motor silent, the pair of guards using the paddles to guide. He could tell it was shallow, too flat and clear nearly to the center. Drowning their asses wasn't an option. Vaghn wore a satchel and pack like the last guy, yet it was his death grip hug on it that clued Riley in. No telling what that guy could invent when he wasn't restrained.

Fifteen feet away, Max laid on the branch hanging over the water, his legs hooked around the wood. The boat passed. Max waited till it was nearly beyond his reach to grab the rear man and drag him off the back. It rocked the craft, and Riley dropped the vine around Vaghn's head and shoulders. He swatted at it, lifting one arm to take it off and Riley pulled. He jerked up, his legs scraping the boat and the man in front turned, drew his gun. Vaghn kicked, dangling over the water, and Riley almost laughed when crocs slid into the river from the opposite bank.

Vaghn saw them and screamed. "Help me! You have to help me! Shoot them! Shoot *them*!"

The twins didn't. The boat driver was on the bank, out cold and face down already. *Way to whip on it, Max.*

Riley's muscles strained and he swung Vaghn, the branch bending under their weight. He heard a crack. Maybe this wasn't such a great idea. Vaghn was sliding out of the loop.

The second guard had recovered, aiming his weapon, but he didn't shoot, searching the foliage for a target. Crocs moved in. Riley heaved, giving the guy a chance and let go. Vaghn barely landed on the bank, wet to his thighs and digging at the mud to get out.

"Drac," Riley warned.

"*I'm on him,*" Max said.

Riley moved briskly down, tough to do going backwards, then he jumped. Max held the vines, having a little too much fun sweeping the jungle floor with Vaghn. The geek clawed the ground and screamed like a slasher movie victim, false arrest or something. Riley was on him, a knee in his back, and pushing his face into the ground so he'd shut up. He pulled off his backpack. Max tossed him cuffs and he twisted Vaghn's arms behind his back and locked them down.

"Help me, you have to!" he shouted at the boat trolling just out of range.

One man was looking for his buddy. Oh yeah, feel the love. Riley stood, pulling Vaghn to his feet. Recognition was instant and Riley smiled. "You knew this would happen."

"Give it up, Donovan. You have no jurisdiction here!"

"Ahh, but today, I do."

Max flipped the Diplomatic Security ID in front of his face. It paid to have friends in the intelligence community.

"That's bullshit. You're Dragon One." Vaghn struggled.

Riley tightened his grip, pulling him back toward the dirt road, Max covering his back. It didn't surprise him that Vaghn knew his business.

Mud and dirt spewed as Sebastian braked nearby. "My God. It worked?" He jumped out and sighted over the open door at the river.

"Not for long." The boat moved swiftly upriver toward the bridge.

Quickly, Riley threw open the door, and with a hand on his head, pushed Vaghn into the back of the truck cab. Like a panicked toddler, Vaghn tried to go out the other side, but

Max was already there, moving in and closing the door. Sebastian hit the gas.

"You won't get away with this. Are you stupid? Wait, I forgot, you all are."

"It'd be wise to shut your mouth about now," Sebastian said.

"You shouldn't have messed with me again."

Riley unclipped the satchel, and Vaghn kicked out to keep it. With his arm across his throat, Riley pinned him. "Don't make me wish I'd killed you the first time."

"You don't scare me, Donovan."

He met his gaze. "I should." He punched, once.

Vaghn didn't make another sound, blood trickling out his nose.

"Did that feel as good as the last time?" Max said.

"Neither was enough. Head to the jet," Riley said. "We leave this country now." Damn cops. There were too many unknown factors going on. Who was helping Vaghn? The guys in the boat were muscle and using a familiar route. But it wasn't their assignment to investigate further, just bring him in. Besides, Vaghn wouldn't admit to anything. He never had, even under oath.

"You know we're kissing off about ten grand in equipment?" Max said, poking through Vaghn's gear. In the satchel was a laptop. The backpack contained a couple disposable phones, an MP3 player, a PSP, a couple games, clothes, booze, and a bottle of pills. The small handgun made Max snicker as he turned on the laptop.

"I'll take the loss." Vaghn slumped and Riley pushed him off. "That was too easy."

"Tell that to my aching back," Max said. He inserted a flash drive and with a few swift key strokes, downloaded the hard drive.

"They could have shot us and taken him, and the lack of cops says something." He waved to the area. Still not a Singapore police vehicle in sight. From behind the driver's seat,

Riley scanned the streets, the cars. The men in the boats were more than prepared.

Max replaced the laptop in the case, then searched Vaghn, emptying his pockets.

Riley picked up a cell phone, then found another just like it. He turned one on and was scrolling the numbers when Sebastian said, "We have road warriors."

He leaned to see. An all terrain vehicle popped out from under the trees.

"Strap in," Sebastian said. "They're out for blood."

Seletar Airstrip

Safia backed her bike out of view in between some bushes as the car zipped past her position. She didn't need to track him. The marker on his car was working just fine. But he didn't seem happy and she needed to know why.

"Did you get that call?" she asked Ellie.

"Sorry, too short to triangulate. The plane, however, is heading toward Thailand. I'll track."

Well, it was clear that Red Shoes was more than just a pretty face in this. Safia'd recognized Barasa's fury, and for an instant there, thought he'd smack Red Shoes. Till she saw the backup in black hidden under the jet's stairs. Smart woman. Safia half expected the commandos to put two in Barasa if things didn't go their way.

Red Shoes was the money, a shocker, decent firepower notwithstanding. She didn't trust Barasa, wise move. Not being seen with him only slightly wiser. But then, that's the game, bad versus bad, and the good guys have to fight harder. Safia swung her leg over the bike and started the engine, then flipped down her visor. The tracking beacon showed Barasa was headed toward his hotel. The call from the restaurant phone was from the other side of the island, but there had been too many crowded signals on cell towers to pinpoint the call's exact location.

Out in the open now, she could put a laser sight on him.

Not that it was a consideration. Probably annoy the big cheese though. She didn't want this guy in U.S. custody—yet. His usefulness was limited from behind bars. She'd learned the hard way that when criminals had a benefit, the Company exploited them. She agreed, let them dig their own graves, but her boss wasn't in the field with a twenty-three-year old female Marine intelligence expert as her only link. Though Ellie wasn't just her relay, but more like a little sister who completely ignored her good advice on men and pushed the fashion envelope. Yet they were both alone. Once they'd been tanked on Singapore Slings, and almost got arrested for hot-dogging a couple of borrowed jet skis down the channel. Her lips curved. That's where her invisible friendships with the local police came in handy. The Company would have hated to bail them out of that one.

"Base to Raven."

Okay, Raven was a new one. Ellie came up with the names and changed them often. Safia could always tell when she was upset. The names got a little raunchy. She could care less, though she thought "maggot breath" for their last subject was inventive.

"Gotcha."

"He's on the phone again and changing directions."

She glanced at the GPS tracker on the dash screen and slowed to take a residential street. "Can you intercept the call, let me hear?"

"That wouldn't be authorized."

"Screw waiting for Langley. They're not here right now."

A sigh came through the microphone. Safia even heard the rustle of papers while Ellie wrestled with her conscience. Langley would approve or she'd threaten something. It'd worked before and Safia wasn't above sticking some pins in people to get what she needed. If they wanted her to fight the good fights, she had to have access to intelligence and quickly.

"*I'm on him.*" A pause and then, "*Damn, he's got a scrambler.*"

"Ohh, he's a nasty boy." Scramblers weren't easy to come by, no matter who you bribed. But one the CIA couldn't extract?

"*Let's hope it's a phone sex line.*"

Safia smiled to herself.

"*The longer he chats, the more time to track,*" Ellie said. "*Why aren't you moving?*"

"I want to wait to see what direction he takes and alter my route." She couldn't risk exposing her cover by tailing too close.

"*I'd reconsider that. He's either going to have a suit made or he's headed to the heliport.*"

Safia keyed in a search for the nearest helipad from her position. Just about every high rise had one, four were on the same street. But Ellie was right, he was in the garment district. She started to ask for satellite imaging when Ellie said, "*He's speeding. Okay he's turning. You need to move.*"

"I'll get there. You keep tabs because if he takes off for the far reaches, I'm sunk."

She couldn't outrun a chopper. Leaning over the handlebars, she turned back onto the Central Expressway and toward the garment district. She rode a wide berth. No telling which direction he'd fly, but she stayed in the open for the best opportunities to get close, fast. Impatient for him to move and give her something to chase, she hailed Ellie.

"*SAT has him on the roof. Must have taken the express lift.*"

That always punched her stomach to her knees. Safia slowed, pulling off the road to a petrol station. She refilled the tank, then stretched, her gaze on the small screen showing the chopper lift off a mile away.

"The north channel," Ellie said, then sounded confused. *"Where's he going? There's no place to land beyond Seletar airport."*

"What have I told you about bad guys?"

"They ignore all the laws, all the time."

She said it like a kid reciting dry poetry. "Think twisted and depraved."

"That's easy for you."

Safia laughed as she merged onto the highway. This wouldn't be so hard. The chopper was air traffic and well, less up there to trace. She angled around cars, squeezed the motorcycle places she shouldn't, then saw the black chopper. It was still gaining altitude. *Who's got you jumping through hoops again, nasty boy?*

"They're doing a pattern sweep. Looking for something," Base said. *"Their central area is Sungei Kadut."*

"Inland?"

"Negative, the water side."

It would be, she thought, and shot off the Seletar Expressway to Sungei Kadut, beneath several confusing overpasses, then past the new high rises. The chopper hovered over land, then paralleled the river. Drug trafficking, she wondered, aware the local police had problems with small time players using the river, yet when the chopper banked hard toward the *Johor Bahru* bridge, she shot north to get ahead of it. Six blocks and she lost it as the land dipped. It forced her to higher ground on the east side. Singapore, she thought, was sinking under its own weight. She was never going to identify Barasa's target if she didn't locate the man.

Safia stopped the bike near the bridge walking path. Pedestrians ignored her, marching across. She unlatched the bike's pack and grabbed her monocular. She sighted on the cars and trucks filing toward Malaysia, then saw a Land Rover ATV, stripped down and crowding a truck. Light bounced off weapons. Damn.

"Be my eyes, Base, get that dark green truck."

Her gaze darted from the chopper to the truck to the Land Rover. The chopper hovered over the west bridge traffic, scaring drivers. Most drove faster to get away from the chaos, and when the Rover shot ahead, Safia understood the tactic. Use the bridge to box them in and shoot. She parked the bike and ran to the ladder of bars maintenance workers used for repairs and climbed. She reached the top as the Rover spun sideways and stopped traffic. Cars skidded, veering to the sides, several impacted, but Barasa's desperation was clear. He wanted what was in that truck.

And Safia couldn't let him have it.

Sungei Kadut
Singapore

Riley and Max leaned over the backseat, gathering ammo. Vaghn slumped sideways, still out. The ATV chased parallel, joining them on the expressway to the bridge.

"Get off this road!"

"I can't. Traffic's too heavy!" Sebastian pointed and like a swarm, little cars darted around them, blocking exits.

The bridge was wide, a walkway on either side, lanes feeding traffic to Johbar, Malaysia and Singapore, but it was nearly rush hour. The cars weren't the worst. Rickshaws and overloaded cyclists clogged the highway, some stacked with so many goods it's a wonder they didn't topple over. Hoping for a turn signal was useless. The ATV sped up alongside and Riley aimed out the window as Max flattened over Vaghn to join him. The ATV pulled away, speeding ahead, then clipping a car. The sloped, white two-door spun, smashing into another lane and the pile-up began.

Sebastian swerved left, finding a hole.

A helicopter rose from sea level, hovering over the water on the left.

"Jaasus. Look at the size of that thing!" It was rigged for rescue.

Max shook the prisoner awake. "Who's after you?"

Vaghn blinked, looked around at the smoking cars and smiled. "I told you not to fuck with me."

Riley shoved Vaghn's head down and removed the hand-cuffs, securing his hands in front. Vaghn frowned and Riley said, "I want you alive." *To stand trial for treason.*

Vaghn smirked. "You don't have orders to shoot me, do yah?"

"That's never stopped me before." Riley cinched the cuffs tight. "And laddie, I'm volunteering for your firing squad."

Vaghn paled and Riley pushed him to the floor. The chopper rose and backed away, then its side door slid back. Men in Singapore rescue uniforms confused him. A chopper wasn't necessary and where the hell were the police?

"Sebastian, get us off this bridge. And where the hell is the ATV?"

"In front. He wants to play chicken."

The ATV was crowding again and Riley searched for a way off the bridge, then spotted a dark figure crouched on the walkway, hidden behind the slatted rails. He recognized the long slim barrel a second too late and saw a muzzle flash an instant before the right front tire exploded.

At this speed, it was all over. Riley braced himself seconds before the truck flipped.

Safia hunched down as the truck fell on its side and kept skidding. Cars collided, smashing into the barriers and the truck slid a good forty feet before it stopped.

"Tell me that's not what you intended!" Ellie shouted and Safia winced at the high pitch.

Not really, but . . . "Barasa wants them badly and that's good enough reason to screw with his plans." It wouldn't stop him, but it might give her time to learn more. The chopper was being tracked by Singapore Air Force right now.

"But in the middle of rush hour?"

"Hey, I didn't pick the place for this!" Enough people had seen the Rover and truck dogfight to get out of the way.

Barasa was in the helicopter, his suit jacket flapping in the wind as he shouted orders into a hand radio. But what scared her was the two men in Singapore emergency rescue uniforms hovering on the edge, ready to deploy on cables. Fakes, she thought. But who was in the truck that he'd risk this destruction and notice?

Safia aimed at a fake and fired. He flailed, and the body rolled out of the craft and fell, caught short on the cable. Two men leapt from the Rover and ran toward the truck. They didn't bother to hide their weapons. She'd seen that murderous look before and put in a call to the Singapore Police Force to protect the locals.

The impact drove them into the ground, everything inside the truck slapped to the left, including Vaghn. The windows shattered with a pop, the sparks of metal to asphalt spraying like fireworks till it stopped sliding.

"Everyone okay?" Sebastian asked. "Sorry about that."

"Yeah," Max said. "What the hell did that?" He rubbed his shoulder, trying to get his footing.

"There's a shooter on the bridge, right side!" Sebastian kicked out the front glass and climbed out, weapon first. Max was behind him. Vaghn crawled frantically through the back like an inchworm. Riley caught his leg, but he kicked violently, leaving his shoe behind and rolling onto the pavement. Drivers spilled out of cars to rubberneck, a few abandoning them and running.

"Later sucker, that's my ride!"

"My dyin' ass."

Riley was right behind him as Vaghn ran toward the chopper, waving handcuffed arms. He reached for Vaghn's shirt and grabbed hold as the chopper swept in low. But the ATV guys were shooting and machine-gun fire chewed the road toward him. He ducked for cover, losing his grip. Vaghn fell, slamming to the ground.

A young family was trapped in a compact car and he motioned them to stay down, then darted behind an empty car and bolted toward Vaghn. Intermittent gunfire pushed him back as Vaghn reached the side of the bridge. The chopper rose high, then dipped nose-down and swept in. A uniformed man hung out the door, reaching for their package. Shots hit around Riley as he aimed for Vaghn and fired. A bullet gouged his leg and Vaghn folded to the ground. Riley hauled ass, but a commando instantly dropped from the cable and grabbed the geek. Bloody hell, he couldn't loose him! But bullets chunked the asphalt at his ankles, and he dove behind an abandoned car, then shouted to Max.

"The markers! Max! Get the markers!"

From the north end of the bridge, the ATV guys advanced, covering for the chopper. One man fired a stream and an elderly man with stacks of goods on a bike fell back as bullets went through the boxes and into him. Jesus. Riley checked his pulse, cursing Vaghn as Max crawled into their wrecked truck and came back with the biomarker pistol. On his back, he loaded the cartridges, came to his knees and hurled it. Riley caught the stubby gun before it hit the ground, then ran as the guy pulled Vaghn into the chopper.

You're not getting away that easy, he thought and with smoke coiling around him, he aimed for precision and fired. It hit Vaghn in the rear, throwing him inside. Four successive shots flew past him and punctured the aircraft, liquid spewing before smoke snaked from the fuselage. *Who's the enemy here?*

The chopper struggled in the air, then rose a thousand feet and flew out to sea.

Riley spun and saw a helmet disappear over the edge of the barrier. The ATV twins were only thirty yards away. Riley hurried to his buddies. Max was on the ground, his upper body in the truck wreckage. For a second he thought Mat was hit till he came back with two machine pistols and tossed one to Sebastian. Max was wearing Vaghn's backpack.

Now the playing field was even. "Hey!" he shouted, his hands out. "Where's mine?"

"Smashed, and you're armed," Max said, using the truck for cover and shouting for people to get off the bridge.

Sebastian fired a single shot at a time at the ATV guy's feet. It didn't stop them and they fired back. "We need to question them!" Riley rushed to cover them, but Sebastian waved him off. "Get that shooter!"

Riley didn't hesitate and ran, then vaulted onto the walkway. He leaned out to see the land below. No sign of the shooter. Damn. He swung over the edge and rappelled down the cables and joints. He dropped to the ground, then pushed his hydrogel kneecaps to perform.

Jason Vaghn grappled to get inside the chopper and hands pulled at him, thank God. Gray-black wind swirled through the interior, the odor of burning oil pungent as someone shoved him against the bulkhead. Pain shot up his leg, blossomed to his ass, and he inhaled through clenched teeth. Goddamn Donovan, he thought, and finally opened his eyes. A man in a jumpsuit uniform knelt, tore his pant leg to his thigh and probed his wound. He said something Jason thought was Malaysian as he wrapped his leg in a field bandage. Jason pushed him away and finished it himself.

Three men were in rescue uniforms, one of them dead and lying near the door, the trail of blood spread wide. There was a rack of rifles anchored to the back with gear he recognized for thermal tracking. A dark skinned man handed him a set of headphones and he worked them on, his wrists still cuffed.

Jason looked up at the guy in a suit, for crissakes, and said, "Just who the hell are you people?" They weren't what he'd been warned to expect.

The man didn't say anything, as he leaned to pull a latch.

It released the cable on the dead man, and as smoke sucked inside the tottering craft, he shoved the body. It rolled over the edge and dropped to the sea. The other men did no more than salute the air and close the door. And Jason realized he'd gone from one fire, right into another.

five

Riley didn't get the chance to run.

A motorcycle shot out from under the bridge supports and headed right for him. He tried to knock the rider off, but he swerved and shot past. Riley ran after it, uphill to the main road. Traffic was snarled, people milling around their cars. Riley moved swiftly between, but ahead, the biker puttered slowly around the bottleneck of humans. They didn't take kindly to a bike on the sidewalk, but it gave him time to catch up. Then the rider found open space and blasted through. Damn. He ran up the back of a cab and stood on the trunk, ignoring angry shouts in three languages as he searched the crowds. He spotted his target and jumped to the sidewalk, pushing his way between the throngs and when forced, showing his badge and making a hole. It wasn't happening fast enough, but in the stillness of traffic, he heard the sharp whine of the motorcycle. The water. The coils of smoke from the chopper was a marker to follow. That biker had some answers and he needed them. It didn't make sense to shoot out the truck tire, then plant a handful of bullets in the helicopter. Was the biker a rival to the men who nabbed Vaghn? His suspicions brewed as he turned off the street and ran down an alley toward the water. He didn't know what he'd do, but at least the view was better and he could see further up the coastline. He hustled between buildings and surveyed. The shoreline was ragged from floods and typhoons. The giant cement X's piled to halt erosion were worn down like broken bones.

Gray vapor lingered in the early twilight and he spotted the spinning tail prop of the chopper, the rest blocked by a building that extended to the banks. Still in the air, it wobbled as the pilot tried to set the wounded bird down when his controls were smoking. They'll end up in the brink, he thought and quickly worked his way to the pier, running out on the floating dock, then hopping to another. The weathered wood listed and rocked. Riley paused till it settled, then headed for the Jet Ski tied up at the end of the pier. He slid onto the seat, and drew his penknife to start it, then saw the key on the floorboard. Irish luck is shining, he thought.

The engine purred as he pushed the throttle and swirled away from the dock, taking it slow and staying as close to the shore as depth would allow. He was less than a half mile away riding around a jetty when he saw the chopper fly inland. Riley gunned the ski onto the sand, abandoned it, then climbed the slope to the crumbling service road.

Red painted buildings crowded the shore and reeked of rotting shellfish. A cannery, he thought and walked closer to the structure. He heard the beat of blades, saw the smoke trail. Stopping at the edge of the building, he saw their target further upriver; a parking lot for small craft launching. The tide sloshed on the ramp, deserted for the evening. He hurried alongside the building back to the street, noticing exits and wondered just what he could do right now, outnumbered and outgunned.

Leaning against a shop wall to catch his breath, he pressed the mic on voice activate and hailed Sebastian, but couldn't get a signal. He tried it again before he moved away from the wall, nearly in the street, yet when he looked farther up the avenue, he glimpsed the rear of the motorcycle before it disappeared between buildings.

He forgot about the signal and followed the rider.

* * *

Sebastian hurried around the dented cars and fractured glass. The smell of gasoline boiled in the heat, the sun punishing and low in the sky. People scattered. He prayed the bad guys didn't spray the place with random fire again, and signaled Max. They bolted, drawing attention to themselves and not the locals, but as they reached the side of the bridge, he realized the ATV pair were turning back. So did Max.

"Now what do they think they're doing?"

"Not a clue, they're boxed in," Max said, straightening from a crouch.

From the Malaysia side, the blue lights of the Singapore border police raced closer and he could hear sirens from somewhere in the city behind him.

"So are we." Max left his hiding place and walked into the open, ignoring Sebastian's calls, then looked back at him. "They're ditching over the side."

Sebastian frowned. "Not unless they have ropes there." It was a hundred foot drop into a depth that was debatable given the weather. He hurried to stop them when the men split apart and climbed the railing. "Oh crap." He ran to reach the closest, but the guy simply met his gaze, then smirked sadly. He turned and jumped.

"No!" Sebastian lurched, grabbing a fistful of shirt, and held on. The fabric ripped. The weight nearly took him over the side and he jammed his knees between the steel rail slats and felt the painful pressure on his thighs. The man dangled, made no effort to reach him. Then he yanked at his shirt buttons.

"Don't do this, man, it's not worth it!" Sebastian shouted, his arm feeling ripped from the socket. "We can help you!"

The man looked up, his expression almost relieved. "I am already dead."

With both hands, he ripped the shirt open and slid out of the sleeves. As he fell to the water, he twisted his body so he'd hit headfirst. The splash was abrupt and Sebastian turned his face away, but caught the burst of red in the murky green water.

"Dammit. Who's got these guys so scared?"

He hurried toward Max on the other side of the bridge. He had a hold of the other guy, keeping him back from the edge. Then the man leveled his weapon at his face and Max let go, backing away. Instantly, the guy ran to the side and jumped. Max hurdled the rail onto the walkway to look over the side.

"It's deeper. He's alive." He hopped back to the road. He headed to the the only thing running, the ATV. "You get that asshole, and I'll get us some wheels and block escape."

"How do you expect me to get down there?"

Max hitched the backpack and shrugged. "Jump. He made it."

Sebastian groaned, looked down. The river was a sewer. "It's going to take me forever to clean this gun." He swung over the side.

Safia heard sirens. At least the injured would get help.

"Raven, give me status, please."

She heard the fear in Ellie's voice. "I blew it. One of them spotted me and he's on my tail." And that wasn't all, Safia thought, tumbling her suspicions over in her mind.

"Can you lose him?"

"I'm trying," she said as she found a space and rode between it. "He doesn't matter right now."

Barasa was going to leave the country, she could feel it. He wanted the blond man enough to risk this spectacle and that need alone put the target on the side of darkness. He'd go underground and locating him would be nearly impossible. He had all those low friends in skuzzy places and she didn't expect the GPS to be on his car long. He was paranoid enough to sweep the restaurant, he'd certainly do double duty on the car. Then he'd know how closely he was watched. No, this mess won't be good.

She angled the bike up the street, weaving around pedestrians and cars, and generally pissing off the locals. Buildings were emptying for the day, people hailing cabs and boarding buses. But the accidents on the bridge brought the artery to a standstill.

"Base, did you get the license on that green truck?"

"*It's a rental. Signed by Maxwell Renfield. I bet he's lost the deposit now. U.S. passport, by the way.*"

"An *American*? Great." She just crashed a fellow countryman's truck. The handcuffs should have been enough of a clue. Though she never knew terrorists to use cuffs, there was always a first time. The possibilities weren't looking good, but she'd trusted her instincts till he shot his own captive in the butt.

"*It doesn't get better.*"

Figures. "Spill it."

"*The bill went to the U.S. Consulate.*"

"Well . . . this day is going downhill nicely, isn't it?"

She didn't want to get into a political exchange. Firing her weapon would do it though. Diplomat Security along with all the others were stinkers for behaving by the international rules when other countries ignored half of them. Singapore was nothing if not corrupt.

She bent over the handlebars, shooting between two trucks and jetting ahead. The chopper rode the skies like a Frisbee, rocking violently. The doors were shut, the windows tinted dark, but the curls of smoke were obvious.

"Do you have SAT to track Barasa?"

"*No, we're out of range. I'm silent.*"

Damn. "Hop onto Singapore Air Force frequency, and don't give me lip about authorized."

"*Yes ma'am.*"

She couldn't risk losing him and slowed the motorcycle, then shut off the engine and coasted it between a coffee shop and a printer service. She stretched, then left the bike behind a couple of overflowing trash cans and wildly growing palms. She moved toward the water side behind the buildings hemmed in dense grasses and sandwiched herself between a small dozer and a pit. The air was rank, but after a minute of working off her helmet, she was used to the odor. Cement formed a box where fishermen deposited their catch. The cannery didn't export outside the country. The fisheries around here were nearly spent and the unkempt grounds said the industry wasn't doing well.

She looked to the sky as the chopper struggled in the air. Smoke rolled from under the pilot's position, then a sharp loss of power sent it crashing the last ten feet to the ground. The pilot bailed first, rushing around with an extinguisher, spraying the hull.

Safia smiled, appreciating that at least that round went where she aimed. She glanced over her shoulder, fixing the radio mic in her ear. Onlookers noticed the smoke, yet none came close; a couple girls ran in the other direction. She wondered if they'd recognized Barasa as he stepped out. His eyes shielded by sunglasses, he adjusted his jacket and sleeves as a uniformed man pulled another man from inside. Barasa's body blocked a clear view, but his prisoner was hooded and bound. *The guy from the truck everyone wants.* His lower thigh was bloody and crudely wrapped. He was a shaggy blond, a head shorter than the other two and sandwiched between. Barasa's thug of the day wore the right uniform, but lacked the correct insignia. Knock-offs made anywhere, she thought, but admitted it was clever. It also warned her that he was well prepared for his latest weapons deal. Enough to have help standing by.

While the pilot had the smoke under control, they weren't going anywhere without a ride. Barasa led the package toward the opposite side of the lot. She moved to see and thought, *now it's in my court.* His familiar navy blue Town Car pulled in, then circled as if to go back out. She drew her single scope monocular to check the plates before the position blocked it. She'd only delayed the inevitable. Barasa had what he wanted.

She backed into hiding. "Base, you still have the GPS tag on the limo?"

"Roger that."

"Tell me it's on the east side of the bridge."

"Confirmed."

She let out a breath, then returned to her position. At least he hadn't found it yet. "I've got visual on his sedan and the chopper."

"Your plan?"

"Don't have one. You?"

"I don't do field work."

Safia chuckled to herself, then pulled the silencer from inside her jacket and screwed it into position. Rather the conceal till necessary type, she returned it to the holster, but felt it hit something. She unzipped. The jacket was designed to give her the straight shape of a man, and the padding housed pockets for her favorite tools. It was custom made by Miya's sister. She found the cell phone from the slop bucket and turned it on. She considered how to use it as a distraction, then arched a brow when the hourglass rolled on the little screen, surprised it worked after swimming with the fish-special.

She worked to find the last number and nearly jumped out of her skin when it rang in her hand.

Riley watched her. That he'd been chasing a woman wasn't so much of a shock. Once he got a good look, he knew the rider was either female or a skinny man. She was a bloody master over that race bike though, but he didn't have time for games. When he saw the phone in her hand, he took a chance. He could hear the soft ring from here, and hit the speaker on Vaghn's phone.

When she looked up, he waved.

That didn't go over well, considering he was aiming his .45 at her. He had a good angle, just not a clear shot. She was tight against the shed, but only thirty feet away. She started to draw her weapon, and he shook his head, motioning her to stand and walk left, into the shade and out of plain view. He waited.

She stood, but didn't move.

Instead, she answered the phone. He spoke first.

"I believe this is what I call a Mexican standoff."

"It's what I call pissing in my yard. Who are you? Maxwell Renfield?"

Riley frowned. "Clearly your resources are better than mine."

From his position, he could see his target several yards upriver. The chopper was empty, but there was movement around it. A uniformed man raced to the docks and dropped into a skiff. Still wearing the crash helmet, the man yanked the pull rope and backed the skiff out, then hauled ass downriver. Where was he going in such a hurry?

Pocketing the phone, he darted to the next bit of cover, a rusty boat trailer, its cargo a chunk of driftwood that vaguely resembled a sailboat. He ducked low and looked back to see her scramble to his left.

"Go, shoo. Don't get involved in this." She made a face and Riley laid flat on the ground, then shimmied under the boat trailer for a look at the lot.

Safia moved in closer, kneeling. She couldn't put her finger on it, but something felt suddenly familiar, making her senses keen. "What are you trying to do?"

Now there's an interrogator's question, he thought, hiding his smile. "Find a way to get my prisoner back."

"Prisoner?" *Oh no he wasn't.*

He glanced at her. "Yes, you shot the wrong tire."

She'd been aiming for the ATV, but at the last moment, they'd moved ahead. She hadn't meant to crash it, just slow it down. Still, it had the desired effect. Trouble for Barasa, and this guy apparently.

Riley watched the men milling near the rear of the car. The gag and blindfold first made him think they were holding Vaghn hostage. Vaghn's family was wealthy, but disowning him after his conviction was a sure bet no one would pay a ransom. If the captors knew anything about Vaghn, it would be his finances, so what's with the blind and gag treatment? Surrounded, Vaghn would feel isolated, without control. Interesting. The guy normally didn't know when to shut up.

"This is a new box of frogs, isn't it?"

Safia's gaze shot to him and she ducked in, her gaze soaking in his face. She experienced a strange sense of dejà vu. "I know you," she said, frowning.

He scoffed. "I doubt it."

What *was* it about him? Then she saw him again, younger, bloodied, that teasing smile, and she knew. "Fundraiser. The pilot."

His features tightened, and he backed up from under the trailer and sat up. His gaze ripped over her face and she felt devoured by that look.

"Safia? From Serbia?"

She smiled, nodded. His shock was adorable. "Nice to have made an impression, Riley."

"A lifetime wouldn't change that day." Then he grabbed her close, hugged her tight, then laid a deep, quick kiss on her that rocked her to her knees. "That's a proper thank you."

She sputtered, unaccustomed to anyone treating her like that. She didn't want to dissect the wonderful little spin of heat, but she didn't back away either.

Then he said, "So who's the suit?"

Moving out of his arms, she crawled to the rear of the trailer and spied around the rotting tire. "Someone to watch carefully. The kid?"

It amused him that she wasn't giving up any information. "A parole fugitive."

She scowled and glanced. "You're a chaser?"

"For this guy, I am." He drew out his billfold and flipped it open. Diplomatic Security.

"I thought you'd still be a Marine."

"So did I," he murmured, pocketing it and watching.

She settled beside him, looking through a monocular. When Barasa ducked into the backseat, she stood and retraced her steps to the bike, but she had company. "It's great to see you again, Riley, but we part here, and I think you should forget about that kid."

"I won't."

And she knew it. He'd gone after his friend in Serbia against direct orders. She wasn't getting rid of him that easily. She went to her bike, backing it out of hiding, then swung her leg over.

"You owe me."

Gripping her helmet, she tipped her head. "I thought it was you who owed *me*."

"That too. But I won't go away."

Safia knew when she'd hit a brick wall and was about to concede when he scowled suddenly and tipped his head, pre-occupied. She realized he was miked up as he strode nearer to the water and looked toward the bridge.

"I need a ride."

She shook her head. "I'm tracking a target and he's leaving." The town car was moving.

"I can find him again, trust me." Riley climbed on behind her. "But Sebastian's in trouble, west of the bridge, and he's unarmed."

Oh jeez, she thought, the clean-up was in the skiff. She kicked over the engine, then worked on her helmet.

Riley wrapped his arms around her waist and turned his ball cap around. "Just be gentle with me, lass."

"Been that long, has it?"

She gunned the engine and maneuvered the bike through a narrow alley, then shot west. The limousine turned in the opposite direction and he felt her tense. He should probably tell her he shot a bio-marker in Vaghn's ass, but he needed to know exactly how she was involved. Because Vaghn wasn't just a parole jumper anymore. He was caught up in a deadly business that brought in the CIA. She was the best lead he had, he admitted, yet riding behind her was a test of his pucker factor as she raced at spine numbing speed toward the bridge.

Safia was glad she had communication inside her helmet. "Base, get me what you can on Riley Donovan and Maxwell Renfield."

"How do you have two names?"

"Donovan is a passenger."

A bark of laughter came through and then, *"How's that feel?"*

Warm and protected, she thought for a second, his body pressed tight to her back. She couldn't recall the last time she had a man wrapped around her. December, Spain, she decided, Antonio. She could call on him any time, but the Spanish matador had a narcissistic ego she barely tolerated and that made it easy to use him just for sex. Shallow, she knew, but there you go, the life of a spy. Relationships brought questions. She didn't like lying to someone she cared about so she solved it by not getting too involved.

Why she was thinking like that with Riley on the back of her bike, she didn't have a clue, but she'd take the rare attraction for what it was, a man who knew and accepted what she did for a living. Sorta.

"You're in good company," Ellie said. *"That much I'll say."*

Safia could hear the laughter barely concealed. "Spill it, you little witch. You like tormenting me."

"Well it's just so hard to do, Raven. Or should I change that to Riley's Girl? Oh my, he's hot."

This wasn't the oddest conversation she'd ever had with Ellie, but it was close.

Yes, Riley was good looking, but it wasn't his looks that made him so likeable. He definitely had that Irish charm going for him still. "He's too old for you."

"They all are. Dragon One, freelance retrieval experts, former USMC. Ooh-rah. Sebastian Fontenot, Maxwell Renfield, Killian Moore, Sam Wyatt and Doctor Logan Chambliss, he was a Navy Seal. Cool."

"Keep going," she said, wondering what constituted retrieval.

"Private hire, well-equipped, and from the look of their record, very dangerous. You should get along fine."

"Last job?" She needed something current.

There was a stretch of silence so long that she thought she'd lost the signal.

"Raven," Ellie said softly, *"I just got an access denied to files on them."*

"Interesting."

"No, it locks me out. I can't bring up any details. It has a notation for referencing Major General McGill for authorization."

"Our last director, that McGill?"

"Roger that."

That changed everything, she thought. McGill's command had been temporary, only for a few months but she felt the shake up all the way in Asia. He was the reason she had direct relay with Ellie twenty-four/seven. Intel in her hands. She adored the man for that.

"Okay back off. Don't send up any signals. They're after Barasa's package. He's a fugitive and no, I don't know his name yet, but Riley has Diplomatic Security credentials and they're legit."

"So . . ." Ellie said and Safia could imagine her leaning on her elbow, her chin in her palm. *"What I'm thinking is they were heading out of Singapore with their prisoner already secured, and you screwed it up."*

"Yes. I did." She was never going to live this down and supposed she had to take her hits. She deserved them. Thankfully, she wasn't normally wrong or she'd be out of a job. "It was difficult to tell the good guys from the bad at the moment." Lame, Safia, really lame.

"Dragon One are the white hats, confirmed."

It wasn't so much of a relief. She worked alone and didn't like bringing anyone inside her operations. Too many chances for leaks and breaks in cover. Yet Dragon One had a McGill stamp of approval and ignoring another set of expert eyes was asinine, this Op was quickly blossoming out of control.

2 hours earlier
6°21´N, 134°28´E
Sonsoral Islands, Philippine Sea

Bridget braced her footing and sighted on the island. Like a string of pearls unraveling, the islands were scattered south of Palau. This one was nearly two hundred miles away from the main island.

She lowered the glasses and unclipped her radio, then looked to the pilothouse as she spoke. "Circle it once. There's a better spot to come ashore in the southwest."

Travis responded with a cheeky, "Are you questioning my topography or getting a wee lazy?"

She brought the radio up. "Funny, love, that's not what you said last night."

She heard the hoots from the sailors and captain, and smiled. The only two sharing a bed on board, they were the brunt of jokes often. But they'd been married too long to take offense and joined in the fun.

"I'd rather dive in, but after the ruins, I've got another twenty-four hours before I can go deep again."

She was eager to return, yet she'd spent too long diving off Okinawa with minimal surface time between. It forced her to stop longer to let her blood refresh with oxygen. She clipped her radio to her belt and sighted in again. Returning to this island was her decision. Despite Jim's reluctance, she'd pitched the side expedition to the project board. Jim was wounded by something, and the lack of trails or any reported inhabitants convinced her and the money. The prospect of animal survival worked into her Tsunami expedition. She kept her expectations low, but Jim deserved an answer. And well, she was just plain curious as to what had attacked him.

She lowered the field glasses and saw Jim bend over a duffle of equipment, the claw marks on his throat no longer inflamed, but deep. An invisible spray bandage protected it. Occasionally, she caught him touching it and knew the trauma lingered in his mind. The man spent most of his career inside a testing lab, just being in the field was new to him.

She walked toward him, her hand on the rail as the ship cut through the sea. "Jim, you can reconsider going ashore." He looked up, a little offended maybe.

"I'm going. Even if it's just a monkey surviving the storms around here,"—he zipped the duffle and straightened—"I need to know."

She nodded and didn't press. She had a habit of mothering her staff, but honestly, some of these men needed guidance. When the vessel came around the most southern point, she recognized the shoreline formation she'd brought up earlier on satellite. She radioed the captain to stop. They would go ashore on the rubber skiff.

A little tingle of excitement danced on her skin as she went to properly suit up. She walked the passageway, cornering toward their room when her radio hit the bulkhead. It fell, spinning across the deck, and she dove to catch it before it slid under the rail and into the sea. She barely nabbed it and crawled her fingers over it to get a better grip. Then it crackled and clicked. No one spoke. She stood, checking the setting. The frequency was off by a couple degrees. The channel was open.

She looked at the island, and for a second, wished her brother was here.

Because she swore she heard *breathing*.

Six

Deep Six
Satellite Intelligence
Virginia

David Lorimer checked his email first, frowning when he didn't find a priority message. He imagined his analysis report sitting upstairs somewhere on a large stack to be read by someone with authority. It wasn't as if he was paid per trace, but he didn't have authorization to go further than he had. He wanted the chance.

While the report gathered dust, he was in a satellite communications room deep underground. The black hole of computers had three separate and different locks to get through the door several yards behind him. Lucky for him he wasn't claustrophobic because inside the crypt, he lost all sense of time. More than once, he'd had the crap scared out of him because he forgot about the intelligence officer on a dais behind and to his left.

At a slick console desk with his feet on top was Major Mitch Beckham, an officer who was pretty much the voice of the strategic defense command, better known as the Joint Chiefs of Staff. He was cool though, a laid-back kind of guy, which was good. It got tense around here sometimes. With only one-half of the earphone in his ear, he listened to intelligence traffic, and despite that his eyes were closed, David knew the Major's hand was on a control, sliding over the globe.

The dais had the perfect view of the six-foot screens on the wall in front of David's station. He rarely looked at them, and focused on his string of five monitors. The last time he was in a pit of electronics was with Major General Joe McGill. He'd learned a lot about the man, and how intelligence really worked. He admired the people in the field. In the cheap seats, as McGill would say, it was easy to be objective. He'd heard McGill was retiring soon, and David was a little disappointed. He reminded him of his dad. *A no bullshit officer if I ever met one.* The three-star's recommendation had put him here, at the beck and call of the JCS, but he lived for it. Every assignment they gave him tested his skills. And so far, so good. He twisted in his chair.

Though David didn't have to, he addressed the major as "Sir?"

Beckham cracked open one eye.

"There's something behind that burst."

He made a rolling motion.

"It wasn't garbage, but a live send. Australia post got the same burst Mariana Island did, but they didn't start a trace till it was out of range."

"What do you expect to do?"

"We have a section of transmission. Granted it was a mega ton of information, but sent right on the cusp of the satellite range of two birds so neither destination would have a complete piece."

"That could be mere chance. There are hundreds of companies with their own satellites. Didn't you conclude that a stream crossed?"

He nodded. "At this level, it would explain the red flag."

Communications needed line of sight, direct range in a straight line. Waves didn't bend, they bounced. Like an octagon circling the earth, signals jumped from one satellite to another till it reached its destination. They weren't in a straight

line, more like a jagged moving equator. This last one didn't
reach anywhere that he could tell. He had a piece between two
points of reference, the satellites. Problem was, that was just
on our birds. The rest could have bounced off of any number
of birds up there. Getting clearance to examine deep classified satellite imagery wasn't a hill he could take alone.

"You want to pursue?"

"Yes, I believe it warrants it. If anything, to confirm or
deny."

Immediately, Beckham dropped his legs off the counter
and sat up, then reached for the phone. He dialed, sipped his
coffee, then got comfortable again. David listened as Beckham pitched his case.

There was a stretch of silence, Beckham's gaze flicked to
him, then he ended the call. "You have thirty minutes to get a
brief together."

"For who?"

"Major General Al Gerardo. He's sending his car."

David let out a deep breath and sat back for a second,
then thought, here we go again.

Sebastian treaded water, swiped his face, then searched for
the twin, spotting him several yards up river. The guy wasn't
struggling and went under. *Christ.* He thought only his hill-
billy relatives were that stupid and swam, his long arms pulling
through the water. The guy bobbed. Sebastian grabbed a
handful of hair and yanked him above the surface.

"No! Let me go—"

"Sure pal, I jumped thirty feet to do that."

Sebastian dunked him long enough to lock his arm around
his throat, then pulled him up for air and started toward the
shore. The package clawed at Sebastian's arm, and when that
didn't work, he reached for his weapon.

"Give me a break," Sebastian said, then felt the ground
beneath his feet. He swung the machine pistol around and
pulled the trigger. It clicked. The guy inhaled and coughed

again. "Now that I know the caliber of dumb ass I've got, tell me why you want to die so quickly?"

He didn't respond, choking out water, and Sebastian dragged him into the shadows under the bridge. He ordered his hands on his head and searched him, finding a knife. The machine gun he used to kill the old man was at the bottom of the river. The careless slaughter told him the young scientist was up to no good in a big way. Sebastian had read Vaghn's dossier. The kid belonged in the psych ward as far as he was concerned.

He forced his captive to his knees. Water drained off them both, a muddy river pooling and spilling down the cement incline. Sebastian removed the strap from his machine pistol and used it to secure his prisoner. He searched him again, but the guy was clean right down to the labels cut from his shirt. Professional, he thought, pulling him to his feet. Then why go for suicide? Not the way of Mercs. Anyone could hide if they knew how.

"Want to talk now and save me hours of crapola?"

"You won't get anything. Ever." He spat, the mucus landing on his chin.

Sebastian tisked softly, then pulled his bandana from his neck, wiped the spittle, then used the bandana to gag him. The man glared and his eyes said there'd be payback. Not a problem. Sebastian wanted some of his own. He shook water out of the machine pistol he knew was toast, then heard a motor and turned. A skiff burled a huge wake as it sped under the bridge, and a reflector glinted off the white crash helmet just as the driver raised his arm and leveled a long barreled pistol.

Oh crap. Sebastian dropped to the ground as the shooter fired. He rolled into the darkness beneath the bridge. Cement chipped over his head. The boater spun the craft around, stirring the dark river. Sebastian stayed flat, trying to hail his teammates for the third time and figured the water ruined his ear mic, but where the hell was Max with the wheels? The boater wasn't leaving, and Sebastian realized the man was gunning for him.

A real clue came when he saw his prisoner and the perfect hole in his pasty forehead.

Jason thought, *I might be young but I'm not stupid.* He'd expected a simple transfer. Take the boat escort to the Land Rover and drive away. What a fuckup.

Donovan, he thought, laying the blame in the Irishman's lap. The shock of seeing him didn't hold against being snatched out of the boat. Christ. He was surrounded by idiots, and Jason wondered who fucked him over to send that particular man. Donovan wasn't an element he factored into this deal. He had hoped he wasn't worth the trouble to send a chaser since he'd paid his debt. So he broke parole, big deal. As far as he was concerned, his slate was clean. Hell, leaving the country had been effortless, his prison mates proving their advantage on the outside. What little cash he had went a long way with illiterate cons. The stupid were so easy to use, he thought and though he didn't lack for cash now, accessing his five million was impossible.

He flinched when someone jabbed his elbow into his side for no apparent reason. He didn't know who it was, nor did he care. No one had spoken since shoving him in the car, at least not in a language he could understand, and he was fluent in three. Once they were moving, a man traded the cloth gag and blindfold for a hood, doing it so quickly, he didn't have the chance to focus on a face. The Suit was near though. He could smell his cologne, but above that, the air conditioning didn't help the ripeness of sweat and BO. Did no one bathe around here?

"Who were they?" a voice said close to his ear.

Jason shrugged. Let them figure it out. He wasn't ready to give up Dragon One just yet and put Donovan's patriotic ass in his back pocket for now.

"How did they find you?"

He wasn't talking. Ever. This bunch was the hired help and didn't warrant a damn thing, but he'd been warned. His silent partner stated it obviously by delivering the stray cat he'd been feeding, dead and in a basket. It wasn't the dead cat that got him, he could give a damn, or that he'd found him easily. But that the animal was severed into neat little pieces. Even the gray fur was combed. He got the message. He understood from the start that he might never meet the source of all his new money. But his partner's intelligence was a worthy match, and he was intrigued enough to wait it out. He didn't do five years in prison by losing his patience or wasting his time.

The car rocked to the left as the driver took a corner too fast. Someone barked a command and it sounded like Afrikaans. It wasn't important, just mental amusement as they carted him around. He shifted and his leg throbbed harder, pain reaching his hip. It stirred his loathing and he vowed to pay Donovan back in spades. With less effort than firing a damn gun, he thought, reaching with cuffed hands to touch the wound. The bandage was soaked. He needed medical attention, then realized he wouldn't get a damn thing if he didn't let these yokels know in no uncertain terms that they couldn't make a move without him.

He'd made sure of it.

Riley's muscles clamped as Safia maneuvered the bike, speeding between oncoming traffic, then through alleys. He wondered where she was going as she rode down a street, onto the sidewalk, then cut through yards and alleys. They popped out between buildings and around the traffic circle to the bridge. He tapped her, pointing. He could barely hear Sebastian on the radio, and when they skirted the building nearest the bridge, she braked.

Riley hopped off the bike and ran toward the water, but he glimpsed the boater and flattened to the cement bridge support. The man aimed somewhere to his left, under the bridge. Riley fired three shots, forcing the shooter to duck and punching holes in the boat hull. Then a *thip thip* sound came from behind him, and the boater knocked backwards, bullets impacting his chest. It didn't stop him. Kevlar, he realized as the man struggled to grab the rudder and fire. Riley popped in his last magazine, and Safia was beside him, the tip of her pistol barrel curling with smoke. When he stepped out to aim, she put her hand on his arm, pushing it down. He glared.

"Don't waste your ammo. He's out of range." The boater sped downriver.

Riley rushed under the bridge. "Sebastian!"

Within the shadows, he saw a lump on the ground and his heart skipped, thinking Sebastian was hit till he sat up. His face and throat were splattered with blood.

"These people are too damn ready to die for the cause." He rolled the body over.

Safia stepped near and studied the face. "No clue," she said.

Riley eyed her. "But you're not surprised."

"No. The boater was clean up." She pulled out her cell phone and dialed, looking at the tall dark haired man as he stood. "You were lucky."

Sebastian swiped at the blood on his jaw and throat, and his gaze shifted to Riley. He inclined his head at the woman. "The cause of the crash?"

Riley nodded. "The Company."

"Holy hell," Sebastian muttered and eyeballed her with more detail.

"What are you doing?" Riley asked her.

She covered the phone. "Cleaning this up." She paced for a few steps, and when he heard her speak rapid Malay, his brows shot up.

She stopped short, her voice rising a couple octaves and her expression said she wasn't getting the results she wanted. When she finished the call, she closed the phone and walked near. "Singapore police are notified of his location." She flicked her hand toward the corpse.

Riley scowled. "Was that wise?"

"Got to give info to get it," she said almost absently. "But we have a short window and we need to disappear. Now. All of us."

Riley's cell vibrated, and he flipped it open. "Max has wheels. He's on Wilson Road."

She looked at Sebastian as she swung onto her motorcycle. "Go to the next street, then left and keep walking," she said. "He'll be coming toward you. It's the only paved road." The sirens grew in number, the shrill screams coming closer. She gave Sebastian an address as she pulled on the helmet. "Riley. Come on, chop chop," she said, tightening the chinstrap.

But he didn't. "Who has my package, Safia?"

"Cale Barasa, an arms dealer."

"Shit," Riley and Sebastian said at once.

"An extremely slippery one, and I'll get you what you need, I swear, but you do *not* want to spend a night in a Singapore jail." Her friendship with the police would only take her so far. She turned over the engine.

"We're going to have a long talk tonight," he said, climbing on behind her.

"Sure, but let's not have it in a cell."

Sebastian was already heading to the street, a wet trail behind him. Safia drove slowly up the incline. Tall buildings crowded the corner, traffic lights flashed and the congestion was more pedestrian than vehicles, but at least it was finally moving again. But so were the police; nearly a dozen uniformed officers directed traffic. Then a pair talking into radios headed toward them. She nodded imperceptibly to Sebastian, then rode in the other direction. Once they were clear of the congestion, she defied physics and took her crotch rocket to its limits.

Riley peered over her shoulder at the dash of the motorcycle. Normally the dash was sparse, speedometers and gauges, but beneath the handlebars was a touch-sensitive flat screen lit up like jet controls and shielded by the windscreen. He suspected it was connected to the helmet, and he'd bet she had a night vision visor. She was certainly outfitted properly for spying, he thought as she angled in front of a three-story house and touched a combination on the dash. A slim door opened and she rode the bike inside a courtyard. Real estate like this was hard to come by this close to Singapore City and he could smell the water from here. She parked the bike and Riley stood, stretched and looked at the house.

Three floors and weather beaten, it had the pagoda style of Asia, but that's where the similarity ended. The house was on cinder block stilts, and the courtyard garden wall shielded the place from the street. Infrared and motion sensors were tucked around stone urns filled with tall wispy bamboo. Her helmet under her arm, Safia stood near a rain duct, her hand raised to hit some switch concealed behind it. The first gate closed, and another on the street side opened.

He frowned.

"Your buddies," she said, and he heard the car roll to a stop. "Direct them in, will you?"

Riley went to the entrance as Max drove into the enclosure. The motorized gate sealed them in. When the two climbed out of the boxy blue car, she faced them, looking them over.

"Lo, but you're a sad bunch. Come on. I think I can make this day end a little better."

They followed her around to the front door, yet when he expected another key lock, she just opened it. Inside, it looked like a normal home, wood floors in the foyer, staircase to the right, rooms flanking the entrance, furnished and clean.

"This your place?" Riley said, glancing around.

"I don't stink that badly at design, thank you very much." She walked down the hall and waited till they were beside her, then hit a switch. A door sealed them off so tightly Riley felt his ears pop. She let out a hard sigh, then turned down the hall, and walked further inside. She stopped to push her helmet onto an overhead shelf, then hung her jacket and sling bag on a line of silver hooks. She replaced her ear mic, curling the mic wire around her ear.

"Do you ever disconnect?" Riley said.

"Not when I'm expecting information. Besides, base is like my alter ego, just smarter." She looked at the others, then held out her hand. "Hi. I'm Safia Troy."

"Troy?" Riley said. "I never knew and couldn't find out."

"Those were my NOC days."

Non-official covert, he thought and wondered what she considered herself now. NOC's worked alone, without any help, delivering information from undercover. It was a strange life, and passion and self-confidence were necessary, plus a certain thrill-junkie attitude. Teammate Killian Moore's wife Alexa Gavlin had been a deep cover NOC. They were the die-hard operatives. Alexa had been left to die and still finished her mission. Riley introduced his buddies.

"Where's the rest of Dragon One?"

"Whoa, really good Intel."

She flashed a smile. "You'd be surprised."

"So we're sharing? We've dealt with the Company before," he said in a low tone. "I don't trust them one bit."

She scoffed. "Neither do I."

His brows shot up.

"That Fundraiser in Serbia wasn't the first time the political agenda stepped on my toes."

"Don't they always," he said cryptically, then plucked a tiny pod from his ear, a less than half-inch mic protruding. It was flesh colored and visible only at an angle.

She peered. "Gawd. You guys have better gadgets."

"One of them is in Jason Vaghn, 28, child prodigy and genius. *Doctor* Vaghn actually." He wiggled his ear and pocketed the comm-link.

"In? I saw you shoot his leg and butt."

"One was a bio-marker." He showed her the small short gun that looked like a .357 magnum before pushing his pant leg back over it again. "It dissolves in seventy-two hours. Where he goes, we go."

"Excellent! If we can get one on Barasa . . ."

Riley shook his head. "Only reason Vaghn doesn't know it's in there is that I shot him in the butt and it's soft tissue."

"Bet that stung." She grinned. "I'm trusting you to locate Barasa. I have a tag on the car, but he's paranoid. It won't be there long." She looked at Sebastian, wrinkling her nose. "There's a bedroom that way. Second on the right." She pointed over her shoulder to the hall lined with doors. "You'll find everything you need to change out of those wet clothes."

Before Sebastian headed that way, he paused to grip her arms and kiss her forehead. "Thank you, *cheri*. I'm itching all over and was trying to be polite and not scratch."

She blinked, stepping back from him and looked uncomfortable just then. "Just helping a fellow troublemaker," she said uneasily.

Max hadn't spoken, watching her carefully. He handed Riley the flash drive, then shouldered off Vaghn's backpack. "He's got a handgun in there with some toys. I'll take it apart when I get back. I'm going back for our gear," he said gruffly. "If it's still there."

Safia showed him how to get past the gates and Riley understood how much trust she was putting in Dragon One right now. Technically, she was breaking a lot of rules just by bringing them into a covert CIA station. He searched the pack, removing the gun, yet finding nothing unusual for a young man on the run.

"He okay?" she said when Max had left.

He unloaded the weapon. "He's as ticked off as I am that we don't have Vaghn on a plane to the U.S. right now."

"I'm sorry, really." She met his gaze. "I take full blame for that. I'll pay for the truck too."

Laying the weapon aside, he hooked the backpack along-side her jacket. "Then I'll refrain from rehashing it again." He had to admire her candor.

"I'm trying to make up for it." She threw her hands wide to encase the house.

"But you *are* going to do everything in your power to get him back, aren't you?"

"You can get him back right now."

"I'm ready."

"Really?" She folded her arms and cocked her hip. "Then what's it worth to you?"

Hagia Irene
Istanbul, Turkey

He passed through the pale blue door and into the monument of Byzantine architecture, his steps echoing enough to make him slow down as he walked beneath the arches. With his partner, he meandered with the tourists, gradually making their way past the scaffolding around a center statue. Restoration was constant, and people circled the workers to watch. Hagia Irene had been a church, a mosque, and now a museum at closing time.

Hooking the leather pack on his shoulder, they followed instructions and went to the west wall mosaic under restoration. A young woman knelt with a tool, and scraped away centuries of Muslim plaster, revealing the intricate mosaic of Jesus beneath.

He ignored the cobalt blue eyes staring at him with accusation and waited.

All communication was through computer or cell phone text. If the financier wanted to remain an entity, he was all for it. As long as he was paid the balance, the guy could dance in the streets in his skivvies for all he cared.

"Don't turn around," he heard and glanced at his partner in surprise. The voice was female, accented.

"You have something to say?" When she didn't respond he started to turn, then heard what he needed.

"Daedalus."

He slid the pack off his shoulder, and held it at his side by the strap, then felt a small hand close over his and pull the backpack away. He was glad to be rid of it. A moment later, she pushed a broader strap into his hand. He gripped it, the contents much heavier than the first. He glanced at his partner and nodded.

"Join the tour and leave slowly. Don't turn around. Get in your vehicle. Wait five minutes more, then leave."

He obeyed, bringing the black leather pack up and unzipping it. American bills bound with paper bands filled it. He tipped it enough to show his partner. Smiling, he closed it and slung the pack, keeping an even pace with tourists circling the mosque to the blue door. He didn't dare glance behind. The operation had gone exactly as planned, a first for him. Once outside, they crossed the parking lot and got into the rental car. He let out a breath, handing over the pack.

"So . . . this is what two million feels like? Do I count it?"

He lit a smoke. "If it makes you happy," he said, glancing in the rearview mirror, then the sides before he checked his watch. He marked the five minutes till they could get the hell gone. He wouldn't screw with perfection, even this late. It'd sour, he thought and kept his attention on the exits.

The setting sun blistered the three-story dome as tourists filed out and he kept his eye out for the pack. No less than four people had similar bags, not one of them was female.

This entire operation went off flawlessly, and their employer had fulfilled their end of the bargain. An old part of him was repulsed by their methods, but money always soothed that niggle of conscience. Tourists strolled past to their cars, and he caught a whiff of a fragrance, something flowery. He studied the people, a family of five, a small child with braided hair skipping on ahead. Two women, sisters, he decided, checked their guidebooks, stopped to read from one to speak to the attendant, then clomped by in their Birkenstocks and fanny packs. *Bet they have a few cats, too.*

He glanced at his partner, frowning. He had his head back and mouth open, sleeping. They'd been traveling fast for days till now. Then he realized his chest wasn't moving. He grabbed his face, turning his head and saw the dart in his throat.

A breath later, he felt the prick.

The bastards was his last thought.

Seven

Riley didn't like the sound of that. "Just what do you mean?"

"What are you willing to do to get this guy?"

He scowled. "Anything."

She gave a short laugh. "God, those are loaded words. Don't agree so fast. I'm talking about leaving Vaghn where he is and giving Barasa some rope to learn what they're selling and to whom." She dropped in a club chair and worked off her boots, then neatly set them aside, and stood. "Your package is the hot property of the day and we need to know exactly why."

"He's a weapons designer and not limited to his own imagination," he said, conceding that he couldn't go in there with guns blazing and take Vaghn back. Certainly not without a plan. Returning him to US custody and on a plane stateside was still the assignment, but Safia didn't know he'd never give up. He wasn't ready to trust her, and had to see how far she'd let him press her with information, because she clearly had an agenda for Barasa. His gaze followed her as she went to the wall and pulled a metal frame out a few inches. On the box frame was a padded half circle, centered and thick, but before he realized what it was, she bent, head down and kicked up into a handstand.

"How very Zen," he said.

"It helps when I've been on that motorcycle too long. My hips and butt are numb."

He tipped his head to look at her and said, "Need a volunteer to put the feeling back?"

She laughed and almost toppled out of her stand. "What I really need is your Intel on Vaghn," she said. "I want to know how Barasa found him."

"And I need access to your satellite communications—to start."

She lowered one leg at a time, then came up right slowly and stayed on her knees for a second. "I'm okay with that. You have the clearance, but it might take a bit to convince Base. She's gotta territorial thing." She stretched on the floor, then stood. Her skin was flushed, brightening her whiskey-colored eyes.

He pointed to her ear mic. "Can you turn that off?"

That confused Safia. "Of course, why?" She pulled out the mic and thumbnailed the tiny switch.

"I didn't want Base to hear you moan."

She blinked. "Excuse me?"

Then she didn't need an explanation. He was there, trapping her against him and laying his mouth over hers. Oh my God, he was *good* at this. She braced her hands on his shoulders and soaked in the moment for what it was; a man kissing her for no other reason than he needed to, right then. Antonio had nothing on him. Every inch of her simmered with sensations she hadn't felt in a long time. The reasons why made her push out of his arms.

"Stop doing that. It's unprofessional," she said, giving him a shove yet admitted she'd walked right into that.

"Really? You taste better than I recall."

She just sputtered, yet her body, which was spinning toward another planet, screamed for more. She really didn't need this kind of disruption, she thought when his smile widened.

"Well, I have at least one weapon in my arsenal."

She replaced the ear mic, glad Ellie didn't hear that. She didn't just moan, she purred. "I'm bullet proof." *Liar.*

"Don't be challengin' an Irishman, lass. You won't win."

That got her back up. "I have enough people to fight, Riley, I don't need you complicating things. Keep it in its place." The truth was she liked him, and while kissing him was a feast for her senses, and God, her mouth, relationships were an emotional distraction.

"Consider it kept," he said, but that cheesy smile didn't alter a fraction. Damn. "And sticking with the real subject . . ." He winked. "What do you have on Barasa?"

She couldn't move fast enough. "Very little." She crossed the room and pressed a wood cabinet. A drawer slid out, and she removed a thick file. Tangible files in her hands always gave her a perspective she never saw on a computer. "Some light reading. Cale Barasa, no known origin, no background beyond the last five years or so. Whoever he really is, we'll never learn the truth." She handed over the dossier. "He has no fingerprints. Burned or cut them off, I suppose." Riley started to speak, but she said, "We had a clean one off a glass and sent it through the databases. It was too mutilated. We think he's African, but not a Muslim. He has no cause, no loyalty. He's been seen recently with the Russian mafia, and he's on friendly terms with Hezbollah, Colombian FARCs, Bolivian radicals . . ."

"A real well-rounded guy, huh?" he said, thumbing through the file.

"Oh yes, and he's used every loophole and soaked up the corruption to keep out of prison. The recent buzz is that he's suddenly distanced himself from his other clients, but he's got a few million in the bank. Fine, he's selling or buying." She shrugged. "No deliveries recently that we've detected. Then earlier today, he met with this woman." She opened her cell phone and showed him the snapshot of Red Shoes.

Riley shook his head. "Pretty, but no clue."

"We're running it. She's the money."

His brows shot up.

"Yeah, I know. In this part of the world, not so common."

"I've met a few women vicious enough," he said.

"Bad love life?"

"Great as a matter of fact." He looked her over with slow detail. "Better now."

She felt a blush steal up her body from her knees and her traitorous skin did a little happy dance. The betrayal annoyed her and she turned away, but when she glanced back, he was smiling like he had from the first moment she'd met him. Sort of amused and hungry. How surreal was that?

She needed some perspective and said, "You want to look at that?" She pointed to the black flash drive he twirled on his finger. He nodded, still with that goofy smile.

She went to the polished dark wood counter that ran the length of the north wall. The moment she stepped in front of it, the area illuminated from overhead. With both hands, she pressed the wood and a rectangle sprang up. She flipped the wireless console over, entered a numbered password, and the wall directly in front of her lowered, revealing a large screen. She always thought that was so cool and loved her gadgets.

She stepped back. "Scan it first." She gestured to a block housing USB ports on a separate unit. "I'll give you a hand if you need it, but I need a half hour to clean up first. The kitchen is that way." She pointed back over her shoulder. "And if you find anything good, share." She grabbed her boots and walked down the corridor.

Riley watched her go, a pleasant view in those worn jeans. She unbraided her hair and when she turned into a room, he went back to the console and pulled up a chair, scanning the flash drive. When the light blinked, indicating no viruses, he opened the hard drive, running through the files. Vaghn was definitely intelligent. It was encrypted.

Damned smart ass. Riley ran an encryption program, then left the desk and headed to the kitchen. He found the beer first, then prowled in the cupboards. Lucky for him, a few minutes later, Sebastian entered the room, clean-shaven and dressed in dark trousers and a gray tee shirt. Riley handed him a beer.

"She's got a disguise room." Sebastian tossed a thumb toward the hall. "Fully stocked. Even a priest's cassock." He took a long pull on the beer, then made a face and looked at the Tiger label. "The CIA can't get American beer delivered?"

Riley didn't think she was still exclusively CIA, but kept that to himself.

He glanced around the room clearly designed to hide its purpose. The long polished counter appeared suspended on pale green walls. Light flooded down on every surface, but it wasn't natural. There were no windows on this side, and he suspected the place went further back than these dimensions showed. An L shaped sofa separated the place and gave it a lived-in feeling, but it was the high gloss surface of a couple tables that looked deceiving, and the Company was all about deception.

He glanced at Sebastian. He could tell the man was itching to get busy. "She said to help yourself to the kitchen."

Sebastian motioned him to the other side of the island, then snooped in the fridge and cabinets, making noise over the improperly stocked spices. "What do you know about her?" He pulled out pans and a cutting board.

"Nothing. I wasn't going to try back then. I was in enough hot water at the time." But he'd play some catch up, and find out what she knew about the Fundraiser. She'd dropped that 800-pound gorilla on him, and he'd never been able to prove it.

It had cost him far too much to let it fade away.

Safia slipped into the room and closed the door, signaling Ellie. "Get me a secure connection to the DDO." Deputy Director of Operations.

"Making the connection," Ellie said. *"So give, do they match their pictures?"*

Yes, she thought, and if anything, Riley got better looking with age. "Come down and have a look."

"*No, no, I like my perch.*"

Two-hundred-eighty meters in the sky on top of the Overseas Union Bank Center was definitely a crow's nest. "You don't know what you're missing."

"*Ew, like a bunch of uncles,*" Ellie said.

Safia smothered a laugh, grasped the headset, briefly wondering where her mobile phone went missing this time. She focused, and listened for the familiar pauses and clicks through secure scrambles. The call went through and when he answered, she started in with, "There were Federal agents in the area and you didn't tell me?"

"*I can't know everything.*"

"It's your job to know, dammit. It's one small country. How hard was that? I ruined their op!"

"*So what are you, embarrassed?*"

He sounded distant. "They're Diplomatic Security, Dragon One."

He hesitated for a few seconds. "*Confirmed?*"

"You know them." These guys get around, she thought. "Explain."

"*Our operations crossed once. Your former Colombian counterpart is married to one of the team, I understand.*"

Safia's brows rose and she sat back. Jade Everett? Aka Alexa Gavlin. They'd been trained together by the same woman, Lania Price. The only difference was Alexa wasn't so willing. Safia had wanted to hunt the worst of the world since she was sixteen. Price was the first person they'd learned not to trust. She dismissed the connection.

"Not a concern. I want the locations and assignments of any Feds in this country. Today. And I want a dossier on Jason Vaghn, and anyone he worked with in the last ten years."

"*Sounds fair.*"

God, she hated him sometimes. It wasn't like they weren't on the same team, but he was a skinflint on information. Another reason not to trust Adam Kincade to give her the whole story. But she knew Riley could.

After the call, and reviewing the dossier Safia strode into the great room, letting her anger take her the last few steps. She stopped short when she smelled frying onions. Sebastian was at the stove, stirring. She'd never seen a man cook and certainly not in here. It threw her for a second.

Riley sat on a stool at the island and looked up.

Her gaze pinned him. "You didn't tell me you knew Vaghn."

"I haven't told you a lot of things."

"I thought you'd studied your target," she said. "But you have *history* with this guy?"

His gaze dropped to the papers she held and he scowled. "Yes. A big one."

"Then we're done. I don't do vendettas."

He left the counter stool, facing her head on. "Someone did me a favor with this dandy assignment, and I'll find out who, but that doesn't change a damn thing. He's a fugitive and we have every indication he's committing treason right now. I'll get authority to go after him for stronger charges, but I'll wipe his ass off the map if I have to, so no Safia, we are not done."

"Riley, you get emotional and it rules you. I know. I've let it."

His look turned dark. "Too bad. That's how the CIA works, but Dragon One doesn't goose step." She scowled at him, yet he went on. "We accept assignments *on* emotion, for reasons that matter to us as a team. And we give a damn about the people hurt in the process. Vaghn massacred my Marines, then smiled about it. He told me he'd do five years and not a day more and he was right. He orchestrated it all, knew how to bring his flight-risk status down. The minute the FBI took surveillance off him, he split without a trace. Dragon One spent a week in that pesthole looking twenty-four seven. We had him, Safia, and he'd be in U.S. territory by now but because of *you*, he's right where he planned to be, out of our reach."

"You won't make me feel the least bit guilty over blowing the tire. I didn't know your team was in the area, a tidbit that took Base less than a minute to learn. This could have been avoided." She'd hold the Diplomat Security accountable, but it wouldn't help the situation now. "That said, I cannot risk emotional decisions made at the wrong time, even if it's for the right reasons."

"Understandable." He nodded, his temper fading. "But our judgment has been spot on so far." He took a step nearer, his gaze locked with hers. "When it's not, I expect you to say so."

She frowned. "You'd defer?"

"I didn't say that, but I don't claim to have the answers all the time." His brows knit for a second, his eyes softening. "You'll be the one having a tough time of it, I'm thinking."

She folded her arms. "How's that exactly?"

"Ahh, don't get your knickers in a twist. You've been alone except for that," he gestured to the comm-link she wore. "And considering another opinion when you've had the run of it," he shrugged, "could be a problem."

She smiled, and knew where this was leading. "I'm all for more mutual exchanges and debate since the lack of it got us here."

"Well then, I guess you'll be keeping a watch on my emotions." A smile tilted his lips. "Wouldn't want them to get the best of me, eh?"

She stared at him for a few seconds, then said, "You've already been scolded once."

"I'll deny myself for the sake of national security."

She shook her head, wondering when the fight went out of her and who was really doing the denying here. She needed a shower and some sleep, but didn't think that would keep her on her toes enough for Donovan.

"Safia," he said, catching her arm before she turned away. "In the future, ask me what you want to know."

"I will, but paper isn't emotional." She shook the print-outs.

"Apparently, neither are you."

She inhaled, a little insulted.

"You keep a terrific objective, but its got to vanish sometime."

Something tightened in her chest. "This is too deep for a first day." She pulled free and his expression said, *See what I mean?* But if she dropped her guard, she'd lose the fight. Experience taught her that. She wasn't protecting her heart. She was protecting her *life*. She needed a clear head at all times. She flinched when Ellie's voice popped in her ear.

"Our target has stopped," Safia said, and crossed the room to a modern black lacquer table. She took a seat, flicked the switch under the top, and a screen rose out of the table as a touch keyboard whispered over her lap.

"Mary mother, you have all the bells and whistles, don't you?"

He hasn't seen the really good stuff, she thought. "Why do you think I went with the Company. America has more money."

"There was a choice?"

She glanced. "My mother was Egyptian. I was born in Cairo. Raised half there, half in the U.S. My father was a U.S. diplomat." She shrugged. "I have duel citizenship."

So did he, but . . . "That explains the accent in Serbia." It was barely detectable now. Something, he gathered, she struggled to cover.

She typed, then sat back, pointing to the screen. "He's with bigger fish. The car's at the home of a member of the Hong Kong Triads." It was a pricey gated neighborhood, small. Most millionaires in Singapore were on the top floor penthouses.

"Bloody hell."

"His deal could involve the Triads, but I doubt it."

"Why?"

"They don't want attention. They're low key even in their own backyard. Plus, they don't need him. They have a network of their own suppliers and don't like outsiders. We put a ripple in his plan. Barasa's calling in favors to hide." A neon stripe showed the beacon's path on a street map.

Riley leaned close and she felt hemmed in. "And surrounding himself with a wee bit of firepower, I'm thinking."

Then the car's tracking signal died.

"Oh no he didn't," she muttered, and typed soundlessly, trying to get it back. She tilted to look at Riley. "Now it's up to Dragon One."

"Scoot that sweet behind over, love." He waved at her. "And let me introduce you to our resident geek." He worked the keyboard and only seconds passed before the screen blinked with images. Logan was fitting a head set on when it focused.

Logan frowned and inclined his head. "You're not alone."

"No," Riley said. "Don't pry. It's not polite."

Safia started to lean in, but he pushed her back, his funny smile making her frown. She sat back, going with it.

"Bio-marker tracking, Logan."

"That's it? Wait, Sebastian said you had him already."

"Long story, different Op now."

Logan leaned in and filled the screen as he typed. Riley tapped a key and Logan's image disappeared, and the screen generated on its own. The satellite map reappeared, and Riley watched the imagery split and divide as Logan narrowed it down to Singapore.

The biomarker was doing its job, blinking.

"How did you get past the security?" she whispered.

He slid her a glance. "We have our secret weapons too, ya know." She nudged him.

Logan peered, grinning, then shaking his head. "Figured it would be female," he said and Safia eyed Riley, lifting a brow. The Irishman only shrugged.

Behind Logan, Safia could see a comfortable living room

in pale tropical colors. Nice. She wondered if he was Alexa's husband.

"We have our resources," Riley said. "And yes, we are very expensive." Though the last mission put the team in the black, he didn't want to go that route again.

"Satisfied?" he said, pointing at the biomarker signal. "Same place, hasn't moved." He tapped a few more keys. "Now when it goes thirty feet past his present surroundings, it will tell us. You can get some rest."

She wished she could. "Thank you." She left the bench and was heading to the shower when Sebastian stopped her.

"Sit and eat." From a sizzling pan, he spilled glazed chicken and vegetables onto a large white plate, then set it in front of her. Standing on the other side of the counter, he set the service perfectly, then said, "If Max beats you to it, there won't be anything left."

Safia looked at the food and her stomach growled with anticipation. She slid onto the stool, tasting a bite. It would be rude otherwise, she thought, before the explosion of flavors made her moan.

"Why are you with Dragon One? You should have your own business."

"I do, the Craw Daddy in N'Orleans, but it runs itself. Or Jasmine does."

"Wife?"

He shook his head. "Half sister."

They talked and Safia tried to eat slowly, hungry yet eager to leave. Definitely a problem tonight, she thought, absently glancing at her watch. She was partnering with them for this operation, but that's where she drew the line. Dragon One might have the clearance and all the pals in the right places today, but in her book, that bought them only so close—and no further.

Max wasn't keen on being in bed with the CIA again.

Yeah, he knew Riley had a past with Safia, and he was

glad his buddies were alive, no doubt about that, but he didn't trust many, and never Central Intel. They left a bad taste in his mouth the last time and he'd reserve his judgment until he got to know the woman.

He slid the last case into the back of the car and closed the hatch, ready to call it a night.

On the bridge, his credentials saved him some fast-talking to get near the wreck and clear it of their gear. The Kevlar would have been hard to explain. He'd sat through some questioning and gave them anything he could without blowing Safia's cover, but it took a call to the U.S. Embassy to keep him out of jail when they'd discovered the old man riddled with bullets. Poor guy never had a chance, and he'd intentionally left the murder weapon with the suicide guy. It would have to do but he didn't think they would get any information off the dead regardless. Not when they were so eager to die.

He rounded the front of the car to get in and heard the tinkling bell again. He spun, scowling, then saw a child race out of a narrow building, and head off between the next alley.

Grabbing a flashlight, he locked the car and walked to the shop front. The odor of mold hit him as he stepped inside. A staircase led to the second floor, the hand rail missing. He investigated the lower floor and found little more than trash and weathered discards. It had been stripped of anything useful and easy to carry.

Vaghn's decoy had come from the roof on the north side, he recalled and took the staircase that was missing a few treads. Old footprints left a path in the sandy floor, and he carefully inspected each apartment. Wasn't much to them, more efficiencies than homes and all vacant. One door was half-open, and he nudged it, drawing his weapon. The wood swung wide and a not-so-pleasant breeze pushed through the open windows on the street side.

He shined light around the rooms and saw rats burrow into crannies. Bet this is a real let down after the Hamptons, he thought as he went to the window. The only fire escape still intact was outside this apartment. He turned back inside and flowed the light slowly over the pitch black room, then crossed to the kitchenette, searching each cabinet, finding the makings for coffee and little else. In a corner, a trash can was piled high and spilling. He crossed to it, overturning the can.

He used a pen to poke through the remains of several packaged meals dripping in sauces, toiletry wrappings, a paperback novel, and a couple porn magazines. A lot of booze, he thought when he saw the row of empty liquor bottles lining the table like trophies.

"Courage in a can," he muttered, rooting though the flat.

For a second Max sat at the table, trying to think like a fugitive. *Travel light, pay cash, leave nothing to trace.*

He caught a whiff of ash and ran his hand over the table; his sooty fingers confirmed Vaghn had burned anything they could link to him. He shined the light on his immediate surroundings and spotted paper under the table. He ducked and grabbed a thin scratch pad, thumbing through the cheap newsprint. All blank and half gone. Then he tipped it toward his light and smiled. Smart guy made a mistake.

E Ring
Pentagon

Hank Jansen knocked softly, then entered the office. Gerardo sat behind his desk, the phone to his ear, yet he waved him in closer. The general cracked a joke about meeting on the golf course to do battle, then hung up and gestured to the coffee service nearby. Hank poured himself a cup.

"That was Joe McGill. Are you familiar with David Lorimer?"

He added cream and turned. "He's General McGill's favored tech and he's worked with him a couple times, but I don't know anything about the operations."

"Neither do I."

Hank stopped mid-sip, and his brows shot up. "Excuse me, sir, but you don't?" It was hard to believe that an operation of any kind was beyond Gerardo's clearance. He had the ear of the president, for pity's sake.

"No, and I'm not digging either. There are some doors that should stay sealed. Joe insists it's a closed case and David can be trusted. He said Lorimer could pull a needle out of a haystack."

"Why do you need him? He's Sat Com."

"Yes, but he's assigned to Deep Six right now."

Good God. Deep Six was just that. Clandestine field intelligence, a relay to stations around the world. His clearance had to be just as stellar. "How come we've never used him?"

"He's a well-kept secret. Young, twenty-eight maybe. He should be here any moment."

Hank waited while Al did his organizing moment. He'd worked with him long enough to recognize that tidying his desk was a mind-prep before he'd explain his purpose.

"We'd received a flag on a random burst off one of our satellites in the South Pacific. Analysts there tracked it, but only picked up a portion of a stream and they thought, some vocals."

Hank frowned. "But it wasn't?"

"That's the problem, the noise." Gerardo reached for his mug, cupping it. "The report was sent to Langley for deeper analysis and given to this David Lorimer to pick apart. This morning I got a call from Major Beckham with Lorimer's concerns. Someone in the Company was backlogged or wasn't on it fast enough." He shrugged and pushed the young man's file across the desk. "McGill was just confirming what I knew."

Hank opened it, scanning the most recent pages and felt his smile broaden to almost painful. David Lorimer exposed Deputy Director Lania Price, who'd not only released classified satellite patterns to see who'd take the bait, but enlisted an outside asset to assassinate a field operative when the agent learned the truth.

He whistled softly. "That took guts, especially knowing Price." Her wealthy suburbanite appearance was a façade. There was a vicious pit bull underneath all that Lily Pulitzer. Now she wore Leavenworth gray. Lorimer had been her executive assistant, but she hadn't included him in her plans.

He closed the file. "What's your decision?"

"I'm bringing him in. If it's a crossed stream, fine. If not, then someone knows when they're in orbit to jump it. We need to know if it's viable."

It sounded like a lot of man-hours for something as trivial as a commercial satellite straying out of alignment for a few minutes. It didn't happen that frequently, but Lorimer's career was exemplary and with McGill, it was wise to shut up and listen.

The intercom buzzed, a gentle voice announcing Lorimer. A moment later, he entered the office, and Hank wondered if there was a pocket protector under that tailored navy suit. His short dark hair was neatly combed but he could tell it hid a funky haircut, like his sons. He was tall, but not a big man, yet beyond anything, the intelligence in his eyes was unmistakable, and he was all business.

"Thank you for seeing me, sir."

Gerardo put up a hand. "I understand why you want to investigate this further, but you're Deep Six. Why didn't you just keep going with your suspicions?"

Hank's gaze moved between the two men, and he wondered what Gerardo sought.

David frowned. "I was assigned to analyze the stream to learn if the hit posed a threat, not its origin."

"But you did."

"No sir, that was a hit between the birds. Two portions of one stream. We have half, I believe. It isn't impossible to hop from one country's satellite to another's. Likely why we have this chunk and nothing else."

"What do you believe it is?"

"Other than it hit on one of ours, I have no idea."

He frowned.

"And I can't know until I have authority to go postal on it."

Gerardo smiled, then glanced at Hank. It's what he needed to hear. "You have it."

"I can tell you the data is encrypted."

Gerardo arched a bushy black brow at that bit of news.

"That's what clued me in. Encryption in the data sometimes makes noise that sounds like stretching vowels."

"I've never heard of that," Hank said.

David met his gaze. "No one has, sir, just something I recognized a while back. It's sort of like listening to whales. Certain transmissions make no sound, some crackle, but very few have steady enough tones to track and learn what's in it. I haven't decided if it's coincidence or confirmed, but I'm keeping a record. Classified, of course."

Their expression must have startled him because David straightened and shuffled. "General McGill authorized it."

Hank shook himself out of awed stupor and stood. If his *sound* theory was authenticated, the young man would revolutionize the intelligence world with a way to catch encrypted, often treason worthy, data from leaving the country.

"Not a problem," Al said. "What do you need to crack this burst?"

"Nothing I don't already have right now sir. But if it gives me fits, permission to contact Nolan Deets, NSA? He's a wizard."

Hank blinked at both, then smiled. Apparently, the young man was aware of more than they were.

"I'll warn him," Gerardo said, and jotted a note.

"Then I have your full permission to continue?" The young man looked ready to come out of his skin for the chance to get at it.

"Yes."

"Excellent! Sorry," he added, blushing.

Chuckling, Gerardo leaned to open a drawer and slipped out a small file box, and flipped through the contents and pulled out a blue plastic card, handing it to David. "Authority to use Deep Six to go *postal*." It was the access codes to sensitive transmissions, Hank knew.

David grinned, placing it carefully away.

"What are your suspicions?" Gerardo asked.

David's expression turned serious again. "That burst transmission wasn't all of a single send, and this portion was big. You'd need a system strong enough to launch that much data. And somewhere for it to land." He sanded his fingers together. "It's pricey and that narrows the field. Besides, you can send anything in increment pulses so it doesn't have to be in one big chunk. That it was on the cusp is just a little too accurate for my comfort zone. I'm betting it hopped a sister satellite or two before jumping off."

"Can you learn who and where?"

"I believe so, yes."

Gerardo nodded, then handed him a business card. "My cell number, report to me whatever you find."

David immediately slipped it into his wallet behind his CIA credentials and the code card. "Any further instructions?"

Hank glanced at the general and got a nod before he said, "How are you at deciphering satellite imagery?"

David frowned. "What do you have?"

Eight

Singapore

The moment Safia was out of the room, Riley went to her jacket hanging on the hook, found the phone he'd called her on, and with Vaghn's, he went to the computer. He opened Vaghn's phone, removed the SIM memory card, and inserted it into the reader. The list of calls was short. He repeated the process with her phone, then did a comparison.

"Ohh-rahh," he said under his breath, then replaced the cards and quickly returned her phone to the jacket still on the hook.

Sebastian shook his head, looking disappointed. "You don't trust her."

Riley shrugged it off. Sebastian knew as well as he did that the checks and balances of the intelligence community weren't fair. Sebastian was the only member of the team who left the military when he wanted—before he lost something vital, he used to say. But his superiors abandoning Sam in hostile Serbia was Riley's first lesson, and he was a quick study. "Brilliant lass, but she's been CIA for a *long* time."

Dragon One had done a lot of clean up recently for the Company and too many renegades used their influence outside the SOP, Standard Operating Procedure. It was breaking those same checks and balances that got them there and he didn't expect any less from Safia. He hoped, but he didn't expect.

"I have a common number. If we can track it, maybe we can learn who is orchestrating this weapon's deal."

"You're convinced it's bigger now?"

He laid Vaghn's phone aside, turned off. "Never doubted it. Just the degree of Company involvement. Which is still out to lunch," he said, working the computer for a trace then went the simple route and just dialed the common number. After two rings, someone picked up.

"Who is this?"

Female and annoyed. "Wrong number," he croaked in Gaelic and cut the call. "It has a GPS, and I think it's Red Shoes. She's the only woman."

"So far," Sebastian said, cleaning up dishes. "And why is the money talking to Vaghn if Barasa already has him?"

"Good question. I'm thinking this Barasa is being played like a gopher. He's an arms dealer, so he's bargained a prize out of this, probably, but the woman and Vaghn know each other." Riley loaded the numbers and GPS into his hand held *Recon* computer, then wedged it into his back pocket.

"How well?"

"Three calls to her phone."

"New target?"

He shook his head. "A phone won't get us much until she uses it again."

Sebastian tossed a towel on the counter and came around the edge, then flung himself over the back of the sofa and stretched out his long frame. Riley stood, wishing he had Sebastian's ability to relax in a tense situation. Probably a good thing for the guy since Sebastian was a close quarter's explosives expert.

"Listen for the biomarker's tone," Riley said, scowling and moving to the door.

"I've got the comm, Obi Wan. Where you going?" Sebastian said, wiggling his shoulders into the plump cushions.

But Riley was already moving through the CIA station house, his fury building when he heard the roar of a motorcycle.

Triad house
Singapore

The knock was loud and short. Barasa paused in wiping his face.

"Come in," he said and swiped the last bit of shave cream, then tossed the towel aside. He reached for his cologne as Rahjan entered the suite. Barasa patted his smooth face, then picked up a fresh shirt and slid it on.

Rahjan stopped in the middle of the grand rooms, and his presence was almost offensive to the lavish décor. No longer wearing the rescue jumpsuit, he was clothed in his favored dirt gray trousers and shirt. Too loose for a man his size. Rahjan was powerful, though not a tall fellow. Barasa suspected even now he was armed with his long curved dagger, a Ghurka soldier's weapon of choice. It was his Nepal training that Barasa had hired years ago, and for that Rahjan, above all, was his most trusted. They were not equals, but comrades, he thought. Good ones.

"Relax," he said and gestured to the bar on the far side of the master bedroom, already open. His half-finished drink waited on the granite counter.

Rahjan glanced, yet didn't move. "You do not want a report?"

"Is everything secure?"

Rahjan frowned slightly. "Yes."

Cale crossed the room to the bar. "Splendid. Then reveal the details at your leisure." He picked up his drink and drained the remains, then grabbed a second glass and filled both with ice. Rahjan joined him, pointing to a twenty-year-old bourbon.

"You will leave the scientist in there all night?"

He referred to the isolation room where the beetle of man sat, secured and unaware of his location. "Yes. He'll talk soon enough."

Barasa passed him the drink, and Rahjan crooked a finger for the bottle. Cale slid it to him, then walked past the living room furniture positioned in front of a bank of tall windows, a pair of doors between. He threw the doors open and stepped out onto the stone balcony. Four floors above the street, he could see the lights of Singapore City in a soft glow against the twilight sky. He surveyed the shadows, the buildings across the street, yet knew he was well protected.

The house belonged to him, yet anyone searching for ownership would find a Chinese owner on paper. He'd become quite skilled at burying his trail, and paying bribes to keep his actions quiet. He was always aware of law enforcement, legal and not. Today's incident was a thorn in his otherwise unnoticed life.

His skin tightened when he thought of the risks he was taking for a weapon he did not possess. His client would only wait so long.

Rahjan startled him when he appeared at his side, staring straight ahead and taking a drink.

"You should be accustomed to me by now," Rahjan said.

"All but your stealth, my friend, and I am glad of it," he said. "As I've said before, you are worth your price."

"Perhaps you should wait until you have my bill," he said into the glass, then sipped.

Cale chuckled shortly. Rahjan cared little about money and more about enjoying the challenges he was offered. He hadn't hesitated to hunt the last driver and had tied up the loose ends. The men had failed and they knew the consequences. They were paid handsomely for the risk. Though the death of Rahjan's teammate wasn't expected. Cale still wondered over the shooters on the bridge and their purpose. He'd yet to learn who'd snatched the scientist from his drivers, but he would, soon. Dr. Vaghn's countrymen, he supposed, then shook his head.

Even now, he found it difficult to believe the young man was as brilliant as Odette had claimed. Thus far, he'd been a moaning adolescent.

"The helicopter was repaired enough to fly it back to the hangar," Rahjan said. "It will be ready for flight by morning. Your calls to your associates helped me expedite the disguise."

All traces back to them had been sanitized. "The drivers?"

"The bodies are left to the authorities. The weapons, if they can recover them, are in the river."

Neither the men nor the weapons could be traced to him. "Release their families," Cale said.

Rahjan nodded and pulled out his cell phone, hit a button, then a moment later, spoke to his man. "Drop them near their homes, but keep them blindfolded," he said, then ended the call. He took a sip of his drink.

"You saw the people who took Vaghn from the drivers?"

He nodded. "I counted two men, perhaps three." He rubbed his chest.

"You should have dealt with them as well."

Rahjan looked at him, his curry brown skin creased in a scowl. "Unnecessary, and no price."

That statement reminded him that Rahjan's work ethic was unique. He assessed threats quickly, made decisive decisions, but he didn't do anything for free. "The authorities hunting Dr. Vaghn were his own, and they will show themselves again. Increase security. Start with my neighbors," he said, waved at the town spread out around them. He set his glass on the balcony stone rail, then tucked in his shirt. "I think I'll join you for the first session."

"You do not want to be a witness."

"But I do. I have several questions for our bit of cargo."

Rahjan sighed and finished off his drink in one swallow.

Despite the trouble on the bridge, Cale possessed the most important piece; the creator and his computer. However, no one could access the information on it and extracting the password would offer an insight into the man's character. He always enjoyed observing how far people would go to save their own lives.

The heat was cloying and her dark tee shirt clung at the small of her back. The humidity was relentless and lying on the flat rooftop felt like a bed of hot rocks beneath her. Her body wept with perspiration, her bra already soggy. So much for the refreshing shower, she thought as she watched through a night vision scope.

The Triad house was still, yet the windows brightly lit. The mansion stretched for a block and had several levels. A bank of windows faced the south, toward Singapore City. Barasa was in there. She'd seen him on the terrace, but it was the man beside him she didn't recognize. A clear picture would help to run through the databases.

While she'd never heard of a biomarker before, it was doing its job. Ellie had a duplicate trace on it off the station computers. She should have invited Riley to join her, but his type had the "protect the womenfolk" attitude and she didn't need it. Not to observe and follow. From here, she could see the infrared sensors surrounding the house or she'd be a lot closer than a block. She'd buzz him when she had something concrete, she told herself.

Her position on top of a neighboring building was just a street's width outside the stone wall that separated the wealthy elite from the people scrounging daily for work.

Suddenly the sensors blinked off, and she saw two figures cross the courtyard to the garage designed like a carriage house. Barasa, she thought, recognizing him instantly. The other, she'd let Ellie figure out and held her cell, waiting for a clearer face shot. Hired muscle, she decided, but didn't disregard him. Barasa trusted few to keep them around for long. Their path had them flickering in and out of the darkness until they stopped outside the side door to the guest house. A light came on above them and she photographed them. The second man paused behind Barasa, scanning the grounds and the rooftops.

She slid lower. They went inside. The windows were blackened, her first clue Vaghn might be there and not in the big house. She couldn't do more than wait and backed up a bit, then flinched when her backside hit something.

Instantly she rolled onto her back, weapon drawn. "Damn."

Riley knelt, and looked really ticked off right now. Not that she didn't blame him.

"I wanted to trust you," he said.

"And taking the phone from my jacket was an example of that?"

His brows shot up and she grabbed his shirt and pulled him down to the roof. "Don't spy much do you, Donovan?" She rolled back on her stomach and looked through the scope again.

"We can't work together if you don't trust me." He settled beside her.

She scoffed. "I don't trust anyone, least of all a government hired civilian."

"And here I thought we were making such progress."

She ignored the sting of that. Guilt wasn't something she'd felt in a long time and she shook it off. "What did you find in the phones?"

"Vaghn and Red Shoes have knowledge of each other. The extent . . . ?" He shrugged. "It gives me the notion your arms dealer is being well used."

Her brows shot up. "Good work, Donovan. I agree, Barasa's working his own deal."

"What are you planning to do from here?"

She spied. "Have to know the players before you can anticipate their moves."

"Hand someone else that weak crap, but not me."

She tipped a look at him, night vision scope still poised.

"I want Vaghn back. I cannot let him slip away."

"You've got him tagged. Be satisfied with that for now. You said you would do anything. This is it. We'll never get in there. Sensors, guards, alarms. He's surrounded and protected. No, you can't take him back. He's the perfect bait."

When he didn't respond, she turned her head to look at him and judged his expression best she could. "Yes, I will fight you on this."

"Then you best not be giving me the slip again. Because I can put an end to your operation right now."

"I don't think so."

"Lass. I know people." He smiled. "And they owe Dragon One."

She arched a tapered black brow, her gaze searching his face. She felt her skin tighten when it sunk in. She didn't doubt him. McGill was first on his list, and Safia didn't want to butt heads with the one man who'd helped her do her job in the field. She shifted enough to hold out her hand. "You have my word on it. Partners. No secrets."

His gaze dropped to her palm, and she wasn't surprised when he leaned in and said, "This has a bit more truth to it," then kissed her so hard she almost lost the scope over the edge of the roof.

Oh Lord, she'd keep him with her just for this, she thought, sinking into him. He snaked an arm around her, pulling her against him with a soft crush. It was a moment before he drew back, gently kissed her forehead, then pried the monocular from her hand.

"I adore it when you let me in." He sighted on the carriage house, smiling.

She nudged him. "You're just growing on me."

"Good, I'm not leaving your side till Vaghn is back in custody."

She sighed. That could take a while.

Barasa walked into the room and stared at the young man in the chair. He was bound, but his blind had been removed. His chin rested on his chest, his light hair matted. He barely breathed, lifeless. Barasa glanced at Rahjan who stepped close and shoved the prisoner.

Vaghn tipped his head back, his eyes bloodshot. "You have no idea what you're messing with, do you?"

"The men who captured you, who were they?"

"I don't know. Federal agents, I guess."

Barasa assumed so, and could not ignore that they were still out there hunting for their target. Absently he wondered how to eliminate them completely. Perhaps this will do it, he thought as he slid Vaghn's laptop onto a small table. He opened it. "What do they have?"

"Nothing."

He glanced up.

"And neither do you," Vaghn said.

Barasa scowled.

"You can't do a damn thing without me and at the moment"—Vaghn looked at his surroundings—"I'm not happy. You should make me happy. There are people hunting us right now. Some really good ones, so if you don't get me where I need to be, now, you might as well give up."

"You Americans are so cocky."

"I'm not an American anymore." He snickered to himself, his head lolling and Barasa realized he was feverish. His gaze dropped to Vaghn's leg wound that was minimally but properly tended. The man was in pain, certainly, but so childishly vocal that Rahjan had drugged him after that. He was, as Odette had warned, juvenile.

"The password." The computer screen stalled, a window popping up as it had the last five times. He waited for the sequence. "Dr. Vaghn, please. It won't be pleasant."

The young man gave him a rebellious glance. He nodded to Rahjan, and he withdrew his blade.

Vaghn's eyes flared, fear coloring his face. "You can't be serious? He'll kill you. The Professor, he will kill you if you hurt me. I have a job to do."

"Really? I want the weapon, Dr. Vaghn. I suggest you relinquish it."

Vaghn smiled for the first time, tilting his head back and meeting Barasa's gaze. "You don't even know what it is?"

"You will tell me."

"Try to find it." Vaghn laughed to himself a bit drunkenly and Barasa wondered if the wound was affecting him or the drugs. "It's an undetectable weapon that can be detonated anywhere, anytime. But only by *me*."

And Odette had promised the perfect delivery system, Barasa thought, hating that he didn't have all the answers. "Show me, now."

He shook his head. "You didn't pay for it."

He'll change his mind, Barasa thought. Vaghn wasn't the first to refuse him what he desired. Rahjan was more than skilled at extracting information. At his nod, Rahjan nicked Vaghn's arm and he winced, then glanced at the wound and rolled his eyes.

"We going right to the hard stuff, huh?" Vaghn said.

It was minor, a scratch, but then, that was just the first one.

Jason gasped for breath, his exposed skin burning with little cuts the bastard had salted. He threw his head back as the man Rahjan grabbed his leg wound and squeezed. Blinding pain raced up his thigh, crashed into his hip. He tried not to scream. That only made it worse. To say this was part of any deal was a goddamm understatement. They wanted into his computer and thought a password would get them there. He couldn't give it to them. He had to prove his worth to the Professor, not to this guy.

When the man held a claw hammer, aiming for his kneecap, Jason flinched to the side, pain racking him in sharp blades. Jesus Christ. "Alright alright! Stop. The Professor can kill you himself! Because I'll be sure to tell him about this!"

He inhaled hard, wondering how it came to knuckling under to a stupid thug.

"Cale," the guard said. "Perhaps—"

Barasa signaled him into silence.

"Barasa," Jason muttered. "I've heard of you. I'm not impressed. You're a fuckup."

Cale made to strike him, then dropped his arm, letting Rahjan do his bidding. Jason caught the imperceptible nod before his partner sliced open his cheek. Pain burst with heat and he spat to keep from biting off his tongue.

"Well," the man pressed.

Vaghn lifted his head, the warm trickle of blood spilling down his jaw.

"I'll not ask again."

Rahjan raised the knife already dripping with his own blood.

"Okay! Okay! Geez!" He gasped, his skin dancing with pain. "I need my phone."

Barasa frowned. "What phone?"

Somewhere over the South Pacific

Aboard the aircraft, Odette glanced at the steward, making certain he was out of earshot before she reached for the buzzing phone in the seat's console. She sat back and crossed her legs as she brought it to her ear.

"The meeting went rather well," she said. Barasa needed to know he was never out of their reach.

"And your assessment, my dear?"

"He'll do the necessary work." She'd never considered the South African a wise choice. He had too many enemies. "But the scientist . . . I still don't think it's wise to bring him too close."

"I thought we ended this last week. I've heard your opinion, Odette. The facilities are ready."

She stiffened. "I'm only thinking of your privacy."

"Good, then I know he will be secure. Any difficulty retrieving our cargo?"

She glanced at the long bench sofa. It was hidden in its
base. "No, of course not." She didn't want to be near it and
certainly didn't like transporting the canister, but she'd do as
he wished. As she'd always done.

"You've taken care of the remaining ties as well?"

"Again, of course." Some trails must be obliterated for the
good of the project.

"What would I do without you, my sweet Odette?"

She felt her face warm with his praise. "Go on as you have."

"Not as well, of that I know."

They'd spoken this same conversation countless times,
and his constant gentle tone always assured her of a place in
his life.

"Let's not allow Mr. Barasa to get comfortable, neh?"

Wasn't that what she accomplished earlier? "He needs us
as well and while he might think of me as your secretary," the
bark of laughter that came through made her smile, "he's paranoid and won't ignore anything peculiar."

"He's also watched."

"Not that we've seen. I can handle him. Haven't I always
taken every precaution?" She didn't like reminding him that
she'd never failed him, but understood his concern. Even she
wasn't privy to some details, but he enjoyed his secrecy. She
didn't concern herself with it. He was far too brilliant to question.

"Very good, my dear. Call if you should need me."

"Thank you." She slid the phone into the charging slot,
and turned to find the steward with a tray filled with a de-
lightful little repast. For a moment, she suspected he'd eaves-
dropped, then dismissed it. He'd been preparing the meal.
She nodded and sat back as he adjusted the coffee table, then
laid out the plates and cups. She'd missed tea.

He poured, then she waved him away. Alone in the front
of the aircraft, she slipped off her shoes and curled her toes.

Her guards were in the rear of the cabin. Dining, she thought, catching the scent of spiced chicken. A partition separated them.

No one part of this delicate dance would meet another until he chose. His plan was flawless and yet, she risked more. Her face was in the public, she thought, plucking a peeled, seeded and quartered apricot from the carefully arranged pile. And for that, she wielded his power.

Exhaustion battered her and her eyelids felt heavy. She glanced at the tray, suspicious, then checked her watch. She'd been on a plane far too long today and was about to call for a hot towel when she heard a door open behind her, the soft suction in the pressurized cabin.

She leaned out to see her captain cross the threshold. "William? What is the reason for this interruption?"

He held up one finger as he went to the console of controls and tapped keys. A panel slid down, exposing the flat screen. He turned it on and flipped to a channel. "I thought you'd be interested in this." He turned away and left her alone.

Odette frowned, then increased the volume. It was a news report on an accident on the Singapore side of the Johar Bridge. What did he want her to see? The video played, blurred and jumpy. Taken from a cell phone or the like, she thought. A rescue helicopter hovered in the background, the men descending on cables. Then she recognized the figure standing inside the helicopter. Fool, she thought and reached for the phone. If she could recognize Barasa, others would as well. If one whisper came near them, her mentor's plans would be destroyed.

This was intolerable.

Triad house
Singapore

Barasa answered the buzzing cell phone.

Her voice was crisp and tight. "What are you doing with my scientist, Barasa?"

Vaghn screamed like a child and Barasa waved at Rahjan, scowling. He was enjoying himself too much.

"I'm gaining information you refuse to hand over. Neither of you have offered proof of such a weapon. And my services do come for a price."

"You will receive nothing if you destroy his plans. No one takes possession till the Professor has had his glory. That was the bargain. I will not be swayed. Neither will he."

"I hardly think—"

"Don't think, Barasa. Clearly you were the incorrect choice and you are very close to becoming a deterrent instead of an asset," she hissed. "Agents already took him from you once."

His features tightened. How did she know so much so quickly? "They have no evidence to follow, nor do the police."

"A victim has your photo. It was on the news."

He'd expected someone to get it on film. They'd halted the bridge traffic for a few hours. "It's local and easily remedied."

"I hope so, for your sake."

"I grow weary of your threats, woman."

"I do not threaten. Veer from the plan and you will feel it by morning." Her tone sent a chill over his skin and he remembered the armed men traveling with her. "We have taken great pains to assure no positive trails lead to him till he wishes it."

"They've been eradicated."

"I doubt that. Agents will continue to hunt him and you. They are shadows that must be erased. *Now*."

"You might reconsider. They possess his prototype."

He heard her sharp intake of air. "Let me speak to Vaghn."

Barasa muted the cell phone's microphone, crossed to Vaghn and tipped his head back. "Be careful what you say," he reminded with a meaningful glance at Rahjan. He switched it to speaker.

"You really need to get me the hell out of here," Vaghn said, breathing hard.

"Doctor Vaghn." Her voice was gentle, almost motherly. "I will and believe me," she said. "You will not regret it."

"I already do, God dammit. I'm wounded, tortured, tired and starving. This was not part of the bargain!"

"Try to remain calm, Jason. I will personally see you have the best of care. But first, is it true? American agents have the prototype?"

"Yeah, but they don't know it. He must have taken—"

"Inconsequential," she cut in ruthlessly. "It must be destroyed, no traces back to the final outcome, understood?"

"No," Vaghn said. "We can't. I can't. It's the Professor's."

She hesitated, then said, "Would you like confirmation directly from him?"

Vaghn glanced at Barasa, his smile thin. "Yes, I would."

Barasa heard two clicks and it was a moment before a male voice came on the line. "Doctor Vaghn."

"How do I know it's you? We've never spoken."

Barasa frowned. Had they created all this by computer messaging?

"Daedelus," the Professor said.

Vaghn's features pulled tight, then he smiled. "Very good, sir." He glanced at Barasa. "Do you really want that attention?"

"They'll be too busy sorting it out because you have designed a *brilliant* weapon, Dr. Vaghn." The young man sat up a bit straighter. "Now is an excellent time to test it. Then you're that much closer to spending your millions at your leisure."

"Fine, agreed, but sitting here in my own piss is not doing either of us any good."

Grow up, Barasa wanted to say, then heard the authority in the Professor's tone.

"Then it is time to make that step, Jason. If you choose not to fulfill your end of the bargain—"

"No. Not a chance. I'm in. God, after all this, how can you doubt me?" he practically cried.

"Good. Odette is my authority. This changes plans a bit. We will meet, Jason. I look forward to it."

A couple clicks and a short moment, Odette came back on the line. "Satisfied?"

"Yes, quite," Vaghn said and seemed to preen in the chair.

"Then ignite it. Destroy all trails, gentlemen. And Cale? Did you really think we couldn't tell you were listening."

His features tightened. Vaghn smirked and Barasa wanted to slap him. Though he had to admit the young man hadn't given him anything beyond his own cryptic explanation.

"Be useful or be gone," Odette said. "Bring him to Seletar airport and wait. Quietly." Her voice was tinny through the speaker. "I will retrieve him myself. Treat him with the utmost care till then. He is the heart of this."

Vaghn smiled smugly, and red heat slipped over Barasa's face. "I will deliver him at the appointed time and no sooner," Barasa said and noted the quick spark of fear in Vaghn's sweaty face. He enjoyed it; the little prick was too damn full of his own importance.

"Absolutely not. You've done enough damage."

"I am invisible, Odette, and if you want your little pet," he said patting Vaghn on the head as he strolled around him, "you will accommodate me." He gave her instructions and before she could respond, he ended the call.

"Now, Dr. Vaghn. It's time to see your work."

The scientist tilted his head, and said, "I need a phone with satellite and text message capabilities, and my laptop."

Barasa waved at the table, the laptop running. Rahjan cut his bonds.

Jason slumped forward and slowly worked the feeling back into his arms and shoulders. Christ, these guys needed to die and he wanted to be around to watch it. He'd make an asshole bomb just for it. He swiped his bloody face across his shoulder, then rolled his wrists. Rahjan nudged him with a bulky phone. Vaghn snatched it and stood. His knees went mushy.

Rahjan reached for him, but he slapped him away. "Don't. You've done enough already." The bastard had the balls to smile.

He opened the satellite phone, bringing up the text screen, then hobbled to the laptop. Agony punched each step, and he stopped, gripping the table ledge and catching his breath for a second. Then he pressed a button on the side of the computer and a latched cavity opened. He pulled out a universal cord, then attached it to the phone.

He punched in a sequence, then stopped. "There's no turning back now. You better hope they aren't nearby or we die with them."

Rahjan looked at Barasa. "We don't know. You cannot risk this."

Jason felt a prickle of conscience. Donovan likely had it. An old part of him recognized the determination in the former Marine, and his deep sense of honor. However useless, he'd been seeking justice for the deaths. Any sympathy vanished as pain softened his muscles and he flattened his palms on the surface to steady himself.

Blood dripped off his chin and onto the keyboard.

He grabbed the phone. "Bye-bye, Donovan."

He hit *Send*.

Nine

Deep Six
Satellite Intelligence

David's special assignment was giving him fits. He still didn't know what the transmission contained, but he was close to narrowing the field of the send. With Gerardo's play-for-free card, access to several other pieces of hardware in the sky was easy and kind of scary. The government was everywhere, he thought. He'd spent hours going through data and looking for something similar to the encryption. He just had to find the primer, the sequence embedded in the binary code. He was afraid the General would call it quits before he learned the truth. Although there were about two dozen analysts working inside Deep Six, divided only by sound muffling partitions, someone else was taking his daily workload while he hunted.

"Whoa, what was that?" Beckham said from behind him, sliding his feet off the desktop.

David frowned at the neon red signal that wasn't there a moment ago. Saving his work, he turned away from his station and rode his chair across to another area. Immediately he switched frequencies and turned all his attention to it. The computer started spewing data down the screen.

"It has a high heat signature."

"God damn suicide bombers."

"No sir, bigger, South Pacific." He glanced back at the Major. "Like Chernobyl."

"Holy Hanna." Major Beckham sent the message to the proper authorities. No one wanted to get caught with their pants down.

The eye in the sky slid east from Indonesia. David felt adrenaline pump through him as he manipulated the signals, shifting billion dollar pieces of engineering to be able to see the topography ten thousand miles across the globe.

"Singapore, Johor Straits."

"Magnify," Major Beckham said, leaving his console and moving off the dais. He stopped beside him and watched on the smaller screens.

The Hawkeye satellite system had the capability to return deeper imagery than any of its kind, then proved it as the graphics on the wall of screens in front of them refined and divided, narrowing their view. He could look inside a kitchen window if he tried hard enough. He slowed the process and focused on the thermal signature.

"It's hot, minor explosions near the epicenter."

"Pull back five hundred meters."

David did as ordered. They could see the results.

"I need an address, Davey boy. A-sap."

David typed, filling in with a street map, then waiting for the overlay. "Oh man," he said. "It's ours. A station house."

Beckham's features pulled tight. "I thought so. Give me all records for that location. Recent transmissions, agents in the area, Sat use times, everything."

David pushed off, his chair skating across the floor to another computer station. He pulled up the records. He'd spoken to Ellie Mullins only this morning. Deep Six was mostly covert Intel; he relayed and assisted the base operations with her and numerous other stations. He was glad she wasn't near that place.

E Ring
Pentagon

Hank Jansen didn't stop writing when his clerk buzzed him.

"Sir, Agent Choufani, Interpol, is on the line for you."

There was a little question in the clerk's voice and Hank suspected it was the agent's Middle Eastern accent that put him on alert.

Hank picked up the phone. "Agent Choufani, how can I help you?"

"It is I who am returning a favor to you, sir."

Antone Choufani had been tracking a Hezbollah bomb maker who'd detonated at a Yemen wedding, Choufani's own sister's. It was Antone's police work in tracing a slip of specialty paper found on a deceased bomber that helped uncover an arms network in the Peruvian jungle. Taking out the terrorist who'd killed his sister and forty-eight other people had been the agent's sole pleasure.

"Can you please scramble this line, sir?"

Hank hit a button and the tone hummed. "Done. Go ahead."

"I am in Istanbul, Hagia Irene. Can you bring up your email?"

Frowning Hank wondered at the cryptic tone of the call. He did as he asked, then opened the picture sent from a cell phone. He saw a small European car, the doors open. The bodies of two men in street clothes were inside, slumped over each other like lovers. Deceased, he assumed.

"I believe I've uncovered a link," Choufani began. "You should know that I have followed the two men from Syria. From a cell training camp. They have criss-crossed their own paths several times without resistance, assisted as if the followers dared not have them in their camps for long. I do not feel it's because American agents could be searching for one of them already."

"Why are you contacting me with this?"

"He's one of yours. A U.S. Army Ranger. He has the emblem tattooed over his heart."

Damn, Hank thought.

"I have run prints, he is—was Daniel Porter."

Hank worked the military database. "He was declared Killed in Action four years ago in Iraq." Apparently, he crossed the border and worked for the other side. The press did not need to know this. Not now.

"I found dirty black ops clothing in duffels, and two million in cash in the car."

It just gets better, he thought. "Cause of death?"

"I haven't had time to confirm, but I believe they were killed by some sort of dart."

Hank stilled, the connection outrageous, but he suddenly needed to be there with Choufani. "You're right, Antone. You have a link. I need that evidence. All of it. It can't be tested. If I'm guessing correctly, what they'd find would be classified."

"I understand."

"It's imperative that word not leak of a U.S. soldier dead in Turkey with two million in cash." Not with so many bases in Turkey, and the latest Blackwater scandal, he thought. "Can you send the evidence to me, A-sap?"

"I have already done so, sir. It should arrive by morning, diplomatic courier."

Hank's brows shot up, and he sat back in his leather chair.

"Your silence is meaningful," Choufani said with a light chuckle. "The less the local constables know, the less of a trail they'll follow that could get them killed. These two men were a cog, and unfortunately, whatever they sold for two million is gone."

Hank had the feeling it was a half liter of RZ10 and now there was no chance of locating the deadly chemicals until it was used.

Fifteen minutes later, a call from Major Beckham confirmed his worst nightmare.

Sungei Kadut
Singapore

Max was damned pleased with himself and hoped he had enough of an imprint on the pad to get Vaghn's notes. He down-shifted around a curve, heading north back to the CIA station, zipping along till something shook the ground. He braked slowly. Earthquake, he thought as the small hatchback car shivered like a nervous terrier. He stopped, but it was a struggle to get out and he stared over the car roof toward the water. It was too dark to see much, but he heard a rumbling, like rocks falling down a mountain.

He felt it before he saw it, the collapse of buildings, cars and my God, people in a wave that wouldn't crest. It neared and he realized he was facing the wrong direction to escape it. He jumped back in the car, shoved it into reverse, and stomped on the gas. He threw his arm over the seat, steering backwards through the streets. Pitch dark, the tail lights didn't illuminate enough and he rode over anything in his path. A glance ahead said he wasn't going to make it. The spew of glass, concrete, dirt, and steel chased him in a thick cloud, and he maneuvered wildly, clipping cars and buildings.

"*Ohgodohgodohgod.*" He cut sharply to the right, the rear end fishtailing and he braked, spinning the car around. He threw the gear, slammed his foot to the floor, and rode over curbs, then clipped a sandwich board sign, kicking it into the air. He passed it as it crashed to the ground behind him, the shattered wood ricocheting like spears.

But the blast caught up with him and a chunk of debris hit the rear window. He braked hard and ducked as glass pummeled him. Fractures embedded in the dash.

He felt blood trickle warmly near his ear a breath before his world went quiet.

* * *

"Base? Confirm the tag," Safia said from the rooftop.

"Roger that. I have thermal as well. Three figures, one seated."

"Interrogation," Safia muttered.

"There are incoming and outgoing calls," Base said. *"Tracking. Something's going on. Too many appliances to isolate."*

Riley sighted in and saw the long town car pull from the garage, the indoor lights brightening the area for a moment before the door lowered. It was Barasa's car.

"They're leaving," she said.

On the rooftop, Riley sat back on his haunches, then scooted further from the edge. "Do you feel that?"

Safia twisted to look at him, then caught the sensation. "The shaking? Yeah." Earthquake, she thought, a minor one. She backed up to avoid a shadow, then stood.

Scowling, he rose and looked around, then moved to the edge of the building's roof to view Queen City. The traffic signals and neon signs sparkled like on any other night. The snail of headlights blinked in and out as traffic moved.

"Raven, I lost the station," Base said.

Safia touched the volume on her comm-link. "Repeat last."

Riley scowled at her.

"I lost connect to the station."

"Which one?"

"All of them!" Ellie said and Safia could hear her typing furiously. *"There's nothing there. No computer tracking, no land lines, cable, nothing."*

"Oh sweet mother Jaasus," Riley said.

Safia rushed to him. "Base has no communications."

He didn't answer, staring, and Safia moved around him.

In the distance along the water, an intense burst of light radiated in a pinwheel, suspended, and she flipped off the night vision on the scope and sighted. It was there for a moment, then it was gone and in that instant, she felt as if there wasn't enough air to breathe in. She reached for him, and he gripped back, scowling darkly at the sight.

Then a wave of heat came like a slap, the temperature rising in seconds and she felt it on her skin, her hair. Like she was cooking in the noonday sun.

"Are you mad, woman?" Riley pulled her down below the roof's rim, and covered her with his body. A second later, a flash of heat passed over them like a molten river and he wedged them closer to the only barrier. Sweat flushed down her body, the air baking in her lungs.

It lasted only a moment longer. The temperature quickly returned to the cloying humidity. Riley unwound from her and she met his gaze.

"That wasn't anything good," she said.

"You're telling me." He rubbed the top of his head and she smelled singed hair.

Cautiously, she rose to peer over the edge, sighting through the scope. "Oh my lord." It wasn't over.

As if a giant fist slammed into the land, buildings collapsed, flattened effortlessly. The percussion took the same path as the first blast of heat, a crushing force she'd only seen in movies. Scream after scream punctured the night air, the scrapping compression of metal and concrete fast and destructive. It was over a mile away.

"I've never seen anything like it," she said.

Then it simply stopped. Alarms went off in all directions. The dust hadn't begun settling before people rushed in panic.

Safia's stomach sank hard. "Base, what do you have on satellite, where is it?" Ellie told her. "Riley?"

He met her gaze. "It's the station, isn't it?"

She nodded, her chest tightening.

"I told you we should have taken him back," he said without malice. "The only thing we brought into the station was Vaghn's backpack. And I left Sebastian sleeping right beside it."

His voice broke, a slight fracture that told her just how close those guys were. She looked at the destruction. Sebastian couldn't have survived that.

Riley headed for the rooftop door, vaulting over abandoned planters then threw open the door. He raced down the interior staircase, Safia close but his heart was pounding too fast to care if she caught up. Outside he scanned for a ride, and saw her motorcycle tucked between the buildings, leaning. He maneuvered it into the open.

"Hurry up," he said as she burst through the tenement doors.

She swung her leg over, and started it with one touch. She pulled on her helmet as he slid on. "Base, track on all traffic in that area." She rode.

"Raven, there isn't anything coming from there. Electricity and phone circuits are down all the way to Sungei Kadut."

Safia didn't have to ask Riley. That's where Max had gone.

They rode closer, streetlights sputtering out as the damage spread. The debris forced Safia to move slowly and she passed a car crushed to two feet thick, the driver still inside. A body lay in the road, the victim on his back. His skin clung tight to his bones, as if mummified. Her heart lurched when she recognized the red apron of the old man who sold vegetables in the common market. She slowed, the rubble heavier, some of it flaming, and she was forced to stop.

Riley slid off and ran the rest of the way to the station. She didn't follow immediately, the terrain no longer familiar. Homes and shops she'd frequented were crushed as if the bones were missing, all the support stolen. She slid off the bike and turned in a circle, stunned by the landscape. It looked like a nuclear blast.

Five blocks of Singapore coastline was simply *gone*.

She stepped carefully, forcing herself not to look too closely, then spotted the leg of a child under tons of concrete, steel, and glass. "Oh geez," she moaned. She'd seen worse in her career, but it was the children that always tore at her soul. Singapore was densely populated. The death toll would be high.

Yards ahead, Riley stood on a pile of bricks and stones, and she climbed the rubble to his side. She stared down into a smoldering hole in the ground a hundred feet wide. The house was gone. They stood on what was left of the building that had been across the street.

She slipped on jagged cement, then just sat. A few feet from her, Riley stared at the cavern, then sank to his knees. "Oh Sebastian," he said softly.

"I'm so sorry." Her throat ached and she reached for him, then hesitated.

Safia felt his grief as if she wore it, his body trembling a little, his breathing fast. She touched his shoulder, slid her hand down to grip his. He squeezed, then suddenly grabbed her close, almost painfully, and Safia simply held on. He breathed hard into the curve of her neck, his fingers digging into her skin as he fought the scream she felt boiling up in him. Then as if he broke inside, the tension snapped. He sagged against her and after a moment, he let her go and turned away. Riley stared at the spot where he'd left his friend.

She blinked, feeling helpless, and angrily brushed at her own tears. "Base? Alert all emergency services. Start with outside the blast perimeter."

"Why past it?"

"There is noting left inside it."

She ignored Ellie's moans of sympathy and added, "Send a directive to NMCC, the JCS. Don't wait for DDO approval, go right to the top."

Riley turned, his emotions in a hot glare that softened instantly.

She was going to piss some people off, but the Joint Chiefs needed to know this, now. "This is going to ring across the world," she said. "Maybe someone knows what that explosive is." Then to Base she said, "I need Intel. Now, all channels. Flash priority."

"Yes ma'am."

"Riley, come on." She grabbed his elbow, pulling, and he seemed to snap himself back from his grief.

"We need to find Max." Riley turned his attention to the Johor straits, the slums along the river. He prayed Max wasn't caught in that. His throat tightened, the thrust of guilt coating his skin. God. Sebastian. Max. Riley pulled his comm-link from his back pocket and hit speed dial. There was no signal. Please, he thought. Not both of them.

"Let's get out of here," he said, grasping her hand. "Now. Police get to you and it's all over. This is going diplomatic, a terror attack. If anyone learns that was a CIA owned house, then the U.S. will be blamed."

"We've never had a concern, it's covert."

"But I'm betting thirty thousand people didn't die around it before either." Riley tried his phone again, shaking his head.

"We still have satellite contact," she said to him and held his gaze as she addressed Ellie. "Base, total access for Riley."

"Excuse me?"

"You heard me, give him total access. Link to his comm. Talk to Riley as if it's me, got that? Whatever he needs, do it." He met her gaze, features pulling taut. She understood the look. She was breaking all the rules for him.

"Yes ma'am."

Riley gripped her hand. "Thank you."

She squeezed back. "We'll find the truth, I swear it."

"All I want now is to locate Max."

"Base?" Safia said. "Keep calling Max till you have a link."

"But he won't know what it's about."

Safia looked back at the destruction, the splashes of blood against window and door frames. People were under all that. People she knew and who had nothing to do with Barasa, Red Shoes and this damn weapon.

"Yes, he will."

Triad house

Barasa grabbed Vaghn and ushered him belowstairs. He carried the laptop and phone, not about to let the young man near either.

He looked over the roof of the car at Vaghn, the fluorescent bulbs turned a harsh light down on them.

"I must commend you."

Vaghn frowned, looking confused.

"How does it feel to have just murdered about thirty thousand people to pad your bank account?"

Vaghn paled, the blood draining from his face. Suddenly he turned away and vomited, stumbling, his shoulder hitting a support post. He wretched violently, his hands braced on the nearest wall. Then he fell against it, his cheek on the cool concrete.

"I thought as much. Rahjan."

Rahjan pulled him upright, then shoved a handkerchief in his fist before pushing him into the car. Vaghn curled into a ball in the corner, clutching his skull. Barasa got into the rear as Rahjan slid behind the wheel and started the engine. He eased the car onto the street. Emergency vehicle lights flashed as they passed them. Rahjan drove past the highway, taking side streets to their next location.

He would not accommodate Odette. To do so would give her and this Professor the upper hand. Something he rarely relinquished. He'd take care of his little package, but he would use his own jet to deliver him. Being a hostage to the kindness of Odette was never his plan.

Barasa glanced out the rear window when the car suddenly rocked on the road. Another smaller explosion, he thought. Gray smoke boiled toward the sky, bright against the moonless night. They were nearly ten miles from the explosion now.

"Well done, Dr. Vaghn."

His gaze slid to the blond man where he huddled on the other side of the seat, clutching the door handle as if ready to leap to his death. Barasa doubted it. Vaghn was a bit less than a coward, yet without conscience. Until now apparently. Vaghn scrunched tighter to the door, staring into the sky, the flicker of neon signs and traffic lights making his skin sallow and gray. He hadn't moved since emptying his stomach.

Barasa dipped his hand inside his jacket, the feel of Italian silk reminding him that he had two more suits ready as he withdrew a cigar. He bit the tip, spitting it into his palm, then dumping it in the ashtray. Striking a match, he puffed.

"Do you mind?" Vaghn whined.

"Ah, feeling better?"

"Not with that thing." He opened the window a bit, turned his face into the breeze.

Barasa handed him a bottle of water. He drank deeply, but kept his face in the wind. He really was young, Barasa thought.

"Your ass is grass, ya know," Vaghn said. "She's pissed."

Barasa didn't care. "I didn't lose it, and they have paid the price."

Vaghn turned his head slowly, his skin paler.

"Did you not think your success would have a cost you couldn't put in your pocket? If this is a test, Dr. Vaghn, imagine what your creations will do in the hands of the Professor."

"You don't know him either?"

He shook his head. "My preference, actually."

He didn't need to know, and though he'd spent considerable time searching for his identity, he'd been unsuccessful. It warned him that he'd underestimated the Professor. The man had come to him through Barasa's own connections. It was the first time he'd taken his associates at their word, and would be the last.

Vaghn coughed, then slumped in the seat. "Where are we going now?"

"Do you really care?"

"No," he said sullenly, and closed his eyes. "Not anymore."

"Then get some rest, Vaghn. You'll need it. We have just begun this ride."

Vaghn lifted his head, met his gaze. "What do you mean?"

"Millions for one device that's already destroyed? You will create more, Dr. Vaghn."

His expression went flat. "Not for *you*."

Barasa laughed, then relaxed into the seat, dragging on his cigar. "I believe the Professor will have a different opinion. Or he doesn't get to have you."

Vaghn would be put to work. Barasa didn't know how exactly since that blast would bring considerable news interest. But the Professor had a plan for the weapons and whatever it was, he'd leave his mark on the world. Experience had taught Barasa that anyone wanting a weapon—already had a target.

Sungei Kadut
Singapore

Riley kept his balance with hers as she rode them around the perimeter of the damage. He scanned the area for the square hatchback. All he saw was rubble. The blast had reached to the tenements where Dragon One had set up a command post. The structure looked as if the mortar between the bricks had dissolved, and the building simply fell over.

He pointed over her shoulder and she veered right, turning between buildings. He spotted the car just as she did and she sped toward it, sliding sideways as she braked. He was off the bike in a heartbeat, pushing debris from the crushed roof. The door was crumbled and Riley swung over the hood, coming in from the windshield. Max was head down and Riley saw blood.

Safia left the motorcycle's headlight turned on them.

"Max? Buddy? Can you hear me?"

Safia was on the other side, bending in and reaching for the seat latch. She pulled and the seat rolled back a few inches. Max moved, moaning.

"Thank God," Riley said, then louder, "Tell me where you're injured."

"Well, it isn't my hearing, for crissake."

Riley smiled and worked himself in. "Lean back if you can."

Max tried and Riley gripped the already cracked steering wheel and forced his weight on it. It broke, giving him room. The dented car ceiling was just a couple inches above his head and Max wasn't small. It forced Max to work his shoulder around the crumpled roof, and he managed to get onto the seat, but with little leverage. Riley pulled Max out.

He lay on the hood of the car for a moment, chips of glass sparkling around him. "So tell me . . ." He breathed deep for a second. "What the hell was that?"

When Riley didn't respond Max lifted his head, then winced. He sat up slowly.

"Let me look at that," Safia said and held a square of cloth that looked like old draperies. "Best I could do." She probed his wound, blotting it.

Max ducked and took it from her, whispering, "Thanks, I'm okay."

"You need a couple stitches."

"Later, thanks." Holding the cloth to his head, he looked at Riley, "You're too quiet."

Riley didn't think it was any harder to accept than it was to see the explosion up close. His emotions crowded him, and he understood what his family and friends had felt when he was in a coma with about twenty broken bones. His sister's words came back to him, *it was hard for us all.* At least they'd had hope. This time, there was none. One of their own was dead.

Max's expression fell. He and Sebastian were close, had served together in the Marines. Max pinched the bridge of his nose with thumb and forefinger, quiet. Riley felt the freshness of his own grief again and as if she knew it, Safia moved beside him. He curled his arm around her waist, kissed the top of her head.

Max collected himself quickly. "The equipment *had* survived till this," he said after a moment, flicking a hand at the car as he slid off. "Looks like we'll need it." He leaned on the fender for a few seconds. "We need something to pry back the metal."

Safia went to the rear of the car, inspecting. "I can get at it," she said and tossed back bricks and shattered wood. Riley was behind her as she crawled inside. She was small enough to get between the crushed hood and tailgate, lying over jagged metal to reach the cases. He accepted whatever she handed out.

"One of them is toast." She pushed the thick silver case out the broken tailgate window. The dent was deep. "There's only a bag of trash left." She started to back out.

"It's from Vaghn's apartment, get it," Max said. "I'll find some transport." He started walking, but Riley stopped him, forcing him to just sit while he went in search of wheels. Max nodded but didn't stay still, walking away from the car and staring in the distance. The sky glowed with fire and smoke.

Safia let him have his peace and when he looked at her, she said, "Let's find the little psycho. But Riley has first dibs on his method of madness."

Max smiled weakly. "Ya know, there's a really ugly irony in an explosives expert being killed by a bomb while he slept." He frowned. "There wasn't anything else we brought inside?"

"Barasa's cell phone, Vaghn's and his backpack. Do you remember what was inside it?"

"Travel stuff. Music, games, cell phone, some clothes, and pills." He shook his head, as confused as she was.

"The sensors in the house are designed to pick up explosives. I don't understand how it missed it."

"Maybe it's new, whatever he used. The components didn't register in the data."

She considered that. The system was updated regularly, but that didn't mean there was something they hadn't seen yet. She hated being unprepared. Now they had to start from scratch, she thought, turning with Max as car headlights bounced toward them.

"Follow me," she said when Riley braked beside them.

"Where to?"

"My place."

Ten

The elevator doors opened with a soft hush.

Riley glanced at Max as they hauled gear out of the lift. "My stomach is twenty floors below." To prove it, his steps faltered.

"She did mention it was the express elevator," Max said, looking a little spacey too.

Unaffected by the sixty-mile-an-hour ride up the skyscraper, Safia strode ahead to the only door in the corridor, whipped out a card and swiped it. She pushed inside and held the door for them, then shut it behind them before she went to an oblong control panel on the wall and reset alarms.

She let out a short breath, then turned inside. "Welcome."

Riley looked around. "You live here?"

"Home sweet home as it were."

"The government pays you a grand sight more than I thought."

It was huge, more like a house than a penthouse. Well, it wasn't exactly the penthouse, but close. About forty floors up, there were only two more levels above. He set the cases down and Max went off to find a bathroom and wash up. Riley walked in, taking the two wide steps into the living room. Nothing blocked the panoramic view outside the long line of floor to ceiling windows. He could see most of Singapore and the bay. He crossed for a closer look, weaving around sofas and chairs wide enough for two people.

"I got it for a song," she said, striding toward the kitchen that faced the view. "It once belonged to a Chinese diplomat or something." He glanced as she tapped a row of buttons on the wall, switching on the lights. "Some people are superstitious about living anywhere a murder was committed."

He turned from staring out the window, arching a brow.

"Three actually. It was a brothel type place, for trysts with pricey escort services to visiting dignitaries."

A common practice around here, he thought and now he knew how she'd snagged it. Insider Intel. At least it was tastefully decorated in warm hues and not all tarted up. His gaze followed her as she moved quickly around the condominium, even pulling out her earphone before signing off. "We still have your tag on Vaghn, and we really can't do anything till we get some information on the explosion," she said.

"There wasn't anything left." Riley felt his loss all over again and clenched his fists.

"I know," she said in a softer tone, walking closer. "Maybe Ellie can find something in a few hours."

"Are you telling me to go to bed?"

"Yeah, I guess."

At about two in the morning, a bed sounded like a bit of peace in a bloody awful day. "Sharing it with me?" He couldn't help tease.

She tilted her head. "If it will make you feel better."

"Oh love, I don't want you coming to me with sympathy."

She frowned, then he swore she blushed. The woman was completely unaware of what those brown eyes did to him. She was an expert in guarding her emotions and granted, her job wasn't easy, but he liked pecking at that CIA shell.

"See if the news has anything." She went to the coffee

table and opened a box, then held out the remote control. "I'm going to take that shower."

Riley's lips tugged at the corners, a rather provocative image exploding in his mind.

As if she read it, she said, "There are four bedrooms, all master suites and furnished. With the exception of the carpet and some drywall, it came that way. Make yourself at home." She started to turn away, then met his gaze, something cracking in her expression. She crossed to him. "I'm sorry he's gone." She laid her warm hand on his chest and he covered it, then laced his fingers with hers. "I'm sorry. He seemed like a great guy, and I swear, I won't give up until we get him some justice. I've got sources and we can go beat the ugly out of them whenever you're ready."

"To learn what?"

"Barasa, he's the key to this."

"I disagree."

She shook her head before he went on. "Vaghn is his prisoner now, and don't forget the woman. He was jumping to her tune. A complete contradiction to the arms dealer I've been tailing. Barasa throws his weight around, and he was on his phone just before that explosion. Ellie is trying to narrow it and maybe trace."

"We can track it from the cell tower that logs GPS and even turned off, it would show a charge."

"Base couldn't lock on them all at that Triad house, but since she's usually working so fast at the moment, she records everything via satellite."

Then she can pick it apart later, he thought. "That helps, but if it goes outside the Singapore tower area, we get only the last location. I need Base to access the GPS logs now and when it's on, start a triangulation on the towers to get a lock."

She made a call, instructing exactly that, then hung up. "Now let's hope Red Shoes makes it easier and uses it." She stepped back from him. "Going for that shower," she said, pointing over her shoulder and walking backwards. "American beer is in the fridge." She turned away and disappeared down a corridor that ran behind the kitchen.

Alone, Riley glanced around, trying to make sense of this day. He went to the sofa and dropped onto it, then worked off his boots. He was tempted to makes some calls, but it could wait. Nothing would change till morning, and Riley admitted he was still trying to grasp that Sebastian was gone.

He tried to focus on details, the equipment, and manpower they'd need if Vaghn left this country. Barasa owned a small jet, so it was a given he'd use it. But they couldn't fly out after him. Neither Max nor Riley could fly the team's Dragon Six, a C-30 dinosaur. The transport aircraft was large enough to house a helicopter they could use right now. Sebastian could have landed that on the roof.

His friend's image floated in his mind. His throat burned, and he braced his elbows on his knees, then gripped his skull. He'd brought the pack inside without examining it closer, and he shouldered the blame for that, but knew he couldn't have anticipated any of this. His mind focused on two schools of thought. Where was the explosive that they *and* the sensors missed it, and what chemical caused that much damage? A genius with a bratty ego, Vaghn's creations were over the top, but aside from the hand gun, nothing in the pack appeared any different than if it came right out of the box. Was it hidden in there? In the MP3 player? The game, the pen light?

He fell back on the sofa. Killing Sebastian changed everything. There was no eternity behind bars for Vaghn. Eliminating the treasonous bastard was their only choice.

He was good with that.

Safia spent longer than usual in the shower and rubbed a towel over her hair, fluffing it as she walked into the living room. In bike shorts and a loose tee-shirt, she crossed to the sofa and found Riley stretched out, asleep. She turned down the lights, then tossed a coverlet over him. She started to turn away, then sat on the edge of the coffee table near him. Her heart ached for him. She'd lost friends before, but not *friends*. She didn't have many. It was tough to do what she did with pals calling to shop or have a drink together. Then there were the targets. She hunted the worst, criminals with no conscience, no moral center. Allowing monsters anywhere near people like Miya was the reason she kept herself guarded. Being around Riley, there wasn't so much of a barrier. At least not between the two of them. Even with the death of his team-mate, he hadn't lost those easy smiles. There was a strength in him she hadn't seen in a while. *Since Serbia*, she thought and without realizing it, she reached, pushing his hair off his forehead. The dim light caught the sparkle of russet in the soft brown curls. His eyes opened slowly, and he held her gaze for a long moment. Then suddenly he reached for her.

"I changed my mind," he said sleepily, pulling her onto the sofa with him.

Safia didn't bother fighting it and went willingly, needing his arms around her. He shifted her back against him, his body curling around hers and she settled with a slow breath. She'd never been so comfortable in her life. "I could get used to this so easily."

"That's the idea, love." He kissed her temple and snuggled warmly, yet as Safia drifted into an exhausted sleep, she realized for the first time in years she experienced a bit of role reversal, feeling truly safe and protected. So rare, she thought, and she wanted to keep it close; it smothered the loneliness she could never escape.

Singapore City

Barasa crossed the avenue, dodging late night traffic. Neon lights and music colored the darkness, creating a hazy shield over the ugliness. The streets were thick with squalor and the sordid that came out at night, he thought, spotting hookers pulling young men in as the last customer passed them in the doorway. The aroma of frying food mixed with heat and sweat. It was the reason he'd discarded his suit for a Philippine *barong*, the whispery thin fabric showing his sleeveless tee-shirt beneath. Yet it clung, his cotton trousers feeling heavy. Tall buildings hemmed in the heat, and most vendors had huge fans blowing the hot air and streamers. He thought of Vaghn in the air-conditioned hotel room, under tight guard and the care of a doctor. Keeping the man sedated with a little morphine gave Cale the quiet he coveted. Moving him quickly was easier with him in a wheelchair, the sympathy alone getting them into hiding quickly.

He spotted the sandwich shop, the fruit vendor before it just closing up. Halfway to his target, he stopped to buy a newspaper from a stand, and look back down the street. His contact would certainly have protection with him, he thought, then continued walking. Cale wanted no one to witness the meeting.

He strolled another block, buying a drink, and making his way nearer to the shop. He ordered from the street window, then stepped back, sitting on the short cement wall and opening the newspaper. A few moments later, a man in a green tee-shirt and black shorts ordered the same meal. When he turned from the window, he met Barama's gaze, then sat beside him. He crossed one leg at the ankle, and held it there. The man had followed his instructions to the letter.

"We want it now," the buyer said.

Barasa turned the page, and said, "Learn some patience."

"Arrangements have been made for transport."

"Then change them. I'm not overnight express."

The man glared, his clean-shaven face showing jagged scars on his jaw and the lack of sun on his smooth skin was obvious. "You go back on this and we'll kill you."

Barasa scoffed. Everyone threatened him with death. "Then neither of us will have what we want."

The vendor called his order number and Barasa closed the newspaper and folded it, then went to the window and took his order. He looked back at the man and said, "Have you seen this evening's show?" His buyer frowned, then looked toward the coast. The spinning lights and fires were barely visible even at this distance. "That is proof of its power."

The man cursed in surprise, still staring.

Barasa grasped the white paper bag, then tucked the newspaper under his arm. "Don't summon me again," he warned. "I have several buyers who'd be interested in taking your place."

"Then we expect to be repaid."

Barasa looked at the man probably five years senior, and said, "Then perhaps you should consider it a deposit for the demonstration?"

The man's face flamed with anger, but Barasa turned away, strolling casually, yet noticed the two men flanking him, one across the street, the other ahead a few yards. He smiled to himself and continued, intentionally coming close to his watchers. When one brushed against him, Cale ignored it, walking past the threshold of a dingy hotel.

Rahjan stepped out, meeting his gaze briefly. "I told you," he said, then headed in the opposite direction, toward the buyer.

"Discourage them only." He didn't want his buyers dead, simply warned back. The stalling was for his own benefit. He had yet to see this weapon, hold it, and until then, it didn't exist. For him, the only exchange in the bargain was in his bank account and the lives of three men.

Marina Bay
Singapore

The sun was hinting on the horizon when Safia woke. She lay still, absorbing the incredible comfort of Riley wrapped around her. She'd never wanted to just sleep near Antonio, she thought, mentally comparing. In fact, she was usually out the door before he woke. But she didn't want to greet this day if it meant losing the closeness she hadn't had . . . well, since taking this job, she thought back. Frowning, she felt the prickle of her isolation and inched closer to Riley.

She heard the coffee maker click on, and tried to disengage herself from him, but he squeezed back.

"A wee bit longer," he said sleepily and she smiled, closing her eyes and settling in again.

Sleep nearly overtook her again until he whispered, "Why did you do this?"

She stirred, and turned a bit to look at him. "The CIA?"

He nodded and simply waited. His blue eyes were so intense right now, and she thought, he doesn't have the right to know, but then, the words just spilled.

"My mother was a teacher at the embassy, Dad was the U.S. Ambassador to Egypt."

His brows rose high. She tried to focus on his face and not the memories suddenly crowding her brain. "He was controversial, always talking about bringing Christian, Arab, and Muslim together for cultural discussions. Some didn't want that and thought a bomb in his staff car would shut him up."

"Mary mother," he said softly.

The familiar ache started tightening in her chest. "They were on their way to pick me up. I was at a boarding school, a senior. My little sister was with them." She inhaled a shuddering breath. "The killers were house staff. They knew every move we made. I witnessed it." He didn't comment, his thumb rubbing slowly over the back of her hand, mimicking the little circles she was drawing on his chest.

"I wondered why not me too. My sister was waving out the window. The car was coming toward me outside the school. When the explosion detonated, it was a block away. Nanya was still waving when her arm was ripped off." She shifted on the sofa, fighting the urge to leave, to duck and hide from the images she couldn't smother. "All at once I was alone with just a lot of stuff that used to be my family. I caught some debris and was hospitalized. A neighbor took me in until I went to college at the University of Maryland. Then I applied to the Company."

"And you went after the killers?"

She tipped her head back and met his gaze. "Not at first. I had a lot of psych evaluations because of that though. I found them living rather well in Syria. They'd progressed to killing a few hundred at a time by then."

"That's a long time to be so alone."

She cocked a look at him. "Who says I was?"

He arched a brow. "Is there some bloke I should be challenging?"

She busted with laughter, touching the side of his face. "You're one of a kind," she said, searching his gaze.

He grinned. "That's what me Mum says."

She shifted on her back and her breath caught when he slid his hand across her stomach. It made her more aware of him, and that he touched her with an almost natural ease. "My director said one of your team is married to Alexa Gavlin."

"Yes, Killian. You know her?"

"We were both trained by Lania Price."

Riley muttered a curse.

"Ahh, so you're acquainted."

"She blackmailed Killian into going after Alexa. When that didn't work, she sent a contractor after Alexa to cover her tracks."

Safia hadn't heard all the details, but enough to know that Lania Price's method of intelligence gathering had finally caught up with her. "Well, she was a flaming bitch with no soul," she said and he chuckled lowly. "She had me tossed in a cell for two weeks in the jungle, and I wasn't left alone."

"You've got to be kidding."

"I wish." She told him of her imprisonment and what she

thought was her first elimination. "There's not a moment of those days I don't recall. I can smell the cell, the mud, *him*. I can see his shoes, his bruised face." She shook her head. "That's one bastard I'd have no trouble double tapping." She recited the details, unleashing it softly, and it wasn't until he brushed a folded handkerchief along her cheek that she realized she was crying. She curled into him and he simply held her, rubbing her spine. She thumped his shoulder, angry all over again. "Guess I haven't dealt with it well."

"I'd disagree."

"You're always disagreeing with me."

He rubbed her spine for a few moments, then said close to her ear. "Who else do you work for?"

She leaned back, met his gaze. "You know this is classified, right?"

"My lips are sealed."

She hesitated for a second. "Any intelligence agency that needs my skills." He only nodded and she reared back a bit when a thought occurred. "How'd you know?"

"Access to more Intel than I've ever seen started me wondering. Then there was the motorcycle."

"Cool ride, huh? The latest from R&D."

"I'd love to get a look at it." She frowned. "I'm an electrician."

She patted his shoulder, smiling. "Good to know you have something to fall back on if this Dragon One thing doesn't work out." He chuckled softly. "Coffee's ready," she said, her eyes flicking toward the kitchen that seemed miles away.

"I'm certain we can find something else that tastes far better," he said before his mouth covered hers.

Oh yeah, Safia thought, throwing her leg over his hip. Delicious.

He palmed her behind, the thin black cloth a weak barrier, his warm hands slow and subtle. Safia experienced a shudder of pleasure as his hand swept up her spine and under her teeshirt. She wanted to rip off her bra and give him better access, and she pushed her hips into his, his hardness flush against her center. Her control slipped a little more, and her hand sculpted his chest, seeking, and when her hand covered the bulge, he moaned and his kiss grew stronger.

"You're madness," he whispered feasting on her throat, her mouth, as his hands mapped a rough ride over her body, hunger barely tempered.

"Then go a little crazy with me." Even as she said the words, she knew she wanted more from Riley than a little foreplay on the sofa. But for now, this would do.

Somewhere in the South Pacific

In the rear of the open safari cart, Odette leaned her head back against the seat cushion. It was a short ride from the airstrip and the driver kept an even speed on the narrow road. The shade tarp above her snapped with the wind, her silk blouse fluttering around her throat. She was tempted to remove her jacket, but she wanted to look her best. The early morning sunlight popped in soft flashes between tall coconut trees, the fallen fruit already collected this morning. When her driver slowed, she sat up, checking her appearance. She waited till the cart stopped and he was coming toward her before she slid her legs out and stood, then reached for her handbag.

He wore a broad smile.

"You saw it?" she said.

"It was spectacular, my dear, well done."

Odette walked into his arms and felt the instant comfort of his strength. He patted her back gently, then leaned back to look her in the eye. He smiled, kissed her forehead, then steered her up the stone walkway toward the tea service waiting on the veranda. She took her seat on the far side of the table, smoothing her skirt before she sat, then snapped out her napkin and dragged it over her lap.

On a small pedestal table behind her, a bouquet of fresh

cut flowers filled the covered porch with fragrance. She un-buttoned her tailored jacket and slipped it off. A servant moved to take it and she sat back, her hands limp on the armrest. She closed her eyes briefly, allowing her familiar world to en-velop her and calm her anger to nothing. She'd been home-sick, she realized, and didn't want to leave again for a long while.

Servants neared, pouring tea, offering her favorite little chilled crab sandwiches. She glanced at him, smiling her thanks as she selected one. They didn't need to speak just yet, and she hoped that like her, he'd missed the peace and routine they shared. He folded his hands over the head of his wooden cane. He rarely needed it, but the panther head molded in silver brought him the same comfort, she supposed, that he did to her.

"You mustn't be angry with Barasa."

Her mood instantly changed, fresh anger pricking her spine and she straightened in the chair. "He failed and brought no-tice."

"On himself," he stressed. "We can keep it that way eas-ily. It was essential that you and the American never be to-gether any place that wasn't completely secure."

It was for her benefit, she understood that, but somehow it felt as if he lacked faith in her abilities to do it herself. She added cream and a dip of sugar to her cup and she stirred, watching her moves.

"He was a decoy" he reminded, "but I believe he can main-tain his level of security." His shoulders shifted beneath the batiste lawn shirt she'd bought him in Belgium. "If not, he does not land. Simple."

"He has already sold his weapon."

His thick silver brows rose. "Then he sells air." He laughed under his breath, settling in the high-backed chair. With his straw hat tipped down a bit, he reminded her of an ancient emperor and not for the first time. Perhaps it was the almond shape of his eyes, or the carefully manicured beard reflecting the Manchu dynasty.

"Selling the weapon is his choice, and his concern, not ours. As long as he refrains from delivering it till our day, it's of no consequence." He waved a hand as if to sweep the subject aside, yet he waited for her agreement.

She nodded, aware that it was her own ego that had taken a slap and little more. Her solace was in the final outcome of his plan.

"But . . . I will give you what you desire."

Her gaze flashed to his as she bit into the crustless sandwich. She chewed, and swallowed before she spoke. "As if any man, forgive me but I must include you as well, would know what I truly desire."

Even she didn't, because she had everything she needed to be happy right here.

He tilted his head, his eyes shaded by his straw hat, yet his mouth curved. "You want to punish Barasa for his failure. And his disrespect of your authority."

Barasa's refusal to obey her instructions didn't anger her as much as his disbelief in her skills. "He failed and it forced us to ignite the prototype." It was part of the agreement. Fail and you get nothing, including your life. The incentive was in the millions the professor offered and delivered. Yet on that, they'd disagreed. She thought it no better than throwing his money into the sea, but he'd insisted that the financial temptation would be irresistible to both the scientist and Barasa. With the threat of elimination if they failed, Barasa didn't hesitate. Yet the arms dealer had a trail, and the explosion was not enough proof the American agents were dead. She wanted assurances that nothing Barasa had done would lead here.

"You haven't answered me," he said.

She glanced, popped the remains of the sandwich into her mouth, then used the napkin. His chuckle was barely audible, but she caught the shake of his shoulders.

"Yes, you do know me well," she said, then lifted her cup and saucer.

Odette sipped her tea, and stared out over the magnificent landscape that always soothed her. The aroma of Chinese Oolong tea filled her senses. She thought of Barasa and his arrival. And she smiled.

"If you two are done necking like teenagers," Riley heard Max say, then grinned when she ripped out of his arms. When he expected her to end on the floor, she swiped her hand under the cushion as she knelt, then aimed a Glock.

"Whoa!" Max pointed to himself. "Friendly, a friendly!"

She lowered the weapon. "Sorry." Flicking the safety on, she pushed it back under the cushions.

Riley laughed more to himself. "Wound up a wee tight this morning, are you?"

"Yes, quite nicely, thank you," she said for his ear alone, letting her hand slide provocatively over his chest as she stood.

Riley swung his legs over the side, but didn't stand. He'd crack in half if he did. She knew it too, her smile like a cat with a mouthful of cream as she walked to the kitchen. He watched the tight behind he'd had in his palms a moment ago.

Max winked at her as she went to the cabinets and grabbed mugs. "You could have cleared your throat or something," she said, pouring coffee for all three.

"A man needs Kevlar around you. Have you considered decaf?" Max leaned over and added cream to one of the pair she held. "He's Irish."

She walked to Riley, handing him a mug. He took it and tossed a pillow over his lap. "Not a word," he warned.

"The advantage of being a woman. No evidence. Though . . . I've a mind to take you yonder, suh," she said, affecting a perfect southern accent. "And have my delights with you."

He reared back, smiling.

"Or would you rather be hearing something a wee familiar?" she said with an Irish burl.

"My sister has to hear that. She swears there are no good imitators."

"I inherited it from my father, I guess. He spoke seven languages."

"I can't keep one straight," Max said, sliding onto an upholstered stool at the kitchen counter and nursing his coffee.

"He's lying," Riley muttered and stood slowly. When she looked him over like he was a buttered scone, he motioned her toward the kitchen. Close proximity to her wasn't helpful right now.

"I've got the gear booting up," Max said. "And someone named Ellie called, it rang in the bedroom with the mirror on the ceiling."

Mirror? Riley mouthed and Max's expression said he should go look for himself.

"Oh man." She rushed to where she'd left her link and switched it on. There was nothing there and she grabbed the phone, hitting the speed dial.

"Ellie?"

"Vaghn's marker has moved."

She hit the speaker. "Repeat last."

"That biomarker, Commander Chambliss notified me. Vaghn is in the Singapore Four Seasons on Orchard Boulevard now."

"Did you tell him about the blast?" Riley's gaze flicked to Max.

"No sir. Not authorized."

"Thank you," Riley said. "They're going to hear about it soon." He and Max walked toward the bedrooms and privacy.

Safia switched to the handset and ended the call. Ellie didn't need orders. She was an overachiever and would notify Safia if the situation changed. She went to the windows, the sun lighting the gray rooftops and washing the world clean. Well, for a few minutes anyway, she thought, sipping, then thought of Riley and Max in the bedroom telling their friends about Sebastian. She hadn't been touched by a death since her family's murder. She wouldn't let it. But when Riley knew he had to tell them, his stricken expression made her throat hurt. They were more than mates, they were lifelong friends. She wondered what that felt like, and had a lovely "woe is me" moment before she shook it off and went back to the kitchen. She needed to be productive.

Riley smelled bacon before he left the room.

"Marry her," Max said, inhaling the aroma. "She can cook and spy."

Riley laughed to himself. "I can't see it. Sorry." He wanted to, and the thought startled him.

Max glanced. "Sometimes you don't have a choice. Killian sure didn't."

Riley wasn't listening and stopped at the edge of the kitchen counter. Any old-fashioned image he might have had was shattered. She was loading a weapon with a croissant in her mouth. The bacon jiggled as she popped in the magazine.

"Guess I was wrong," Max said under a laugh.

She bit into the pastry, and laid the gun on the counter near a box of breakfast croissants. She waved at them, telling them to help themselves before she sat in front of the computers.

"Base is downloading that file you had on the flash drive."

"Fantastic," Max said and took her place at the long dining table set up with computers.

On the floor was a stack of old newspapers and Vaghn's bag of trash. "You think there's evidence in there?" she said to Max.

"I wanted to be sure." He handed her a pad of paper. "I have this, but so far, it's meaningless. The pad has his last impression on it. It's a sequence of symbols, numbers, letters, and crap that may just be doodling."

Riley examined it. Max had used graphite to bring up the impressions. "Not doodling," he said. "It's repeated a couple times." With his little finger, he pointed out two more. "Memorizing."

When the download finished, Max typed at the computer, then said, "Doesn't work, at least not in that sequence." He left the chair, spread newspapers on the tile floor, and dumped the trash in the middle. There were several pieces of balled up scrap paper in the heap along with some moldy garbage. Safia grabbed a wooden spoon from a ceramic crock of tools, then knelt at the pile. She flipped the food containers and tipped her head to read the names.

"He likes sweet and sour pork." She turned another. "He lived in the projects, the buildings due for destruction." She glanced up and Riley nodded, impressed. "These containers are from restaurants all on the same street, each with window service you can walk right up to and order and don't have to be seated inside." Someone on the run didn't want to be closed off from escape, he thought.

She moved aside a damp novel and newspapers with sauce staining the pages, then nudged what looked like a gum wrapper, trying to flip it over. Max leaned to one of their cases, unzipped the side and pulled out gloves, handing them to her. She snapped them on and picked it up. "It's a peel off, like a label backing." She tipped it to the ceiling light. "There's an impression."

Max took it, slid it into a mini scanner. From the floor, he leaned to tap keys, and the image appeared. He increased the size a thousand-fold.

"That looks like a computer chip," she said.

"Possible." Max reversed it.

"It's a wireless booster," Riley said, then popped the breakfast sandwich in the microwave. "That just protects it for transport, but the chip enables a computer to pick up a wider wireless range and hop off private networks." He hit the buttons.

"He's hopping networks? Geez," Max said. "Probably cloaked too."

Safia sat on the floor, and wrapped her arms around her knees. She stared at the trash for a second, then said, "Profilers say each bomb maker has a signature."

"Except Vaghn didn't create bombs." Riley tossed the hot sandwich from hand to hand. "He developed hand-held and transport mounted weapons. This isn't his usual forte. I'm not sure it was in the pack."

"What else could it be?" she asked.

"It was a CIA station, take your pick," Riley said. "Covert or not, there is such a thing as leaks. We have to consider other reasons until we know for certain."

"Know what for certain?" Max snapped. "That a bomb exploded? That Sebastian is dead!" Riley frowned, and Max took a slow breath, then apologized. "The timing of the calls and them on the line is not coincidence." He looked at Safia. "You said so yourself."

She agreed.

"We're assuming there was something in the pack. It can't be the phone," Riley said. "Because I *know* I shut it off."

Safia stood and went to refill her coffee. "The station's back up data is with Langley, but even if I ask them to send it, we don't have the equipment to handle it here. Not all of it. There are only two other stations and they aren't outfitted nearly as well. Singapore isn't a national security threat, just the people passing though it."

Riley pulled his TDS Recon from his back pocket and wiggled it. "We have a common number." Her brow knit. "Both phones had one caller that matched and I called it."

She leaned to look at the screen and under her breath, she added, "And you're giving *me* lip service about trust?"

His glance slid to hers. "It's the lip service that did it," he said giving her a really goober look.

She rolled her eyes, shaking her head. "So Barasa and Vaghn called this woman."

"No. She did. Incoming only."

She looked thoughtful. "The money doesn't usually get

that close. Often, it's just a pick up and a drop off. International electronic accounting isn't a venue either. Money has to be washed a few times first." She frowned, held up her hand for a moment. "Wait a second. I assumed she's the money with the production she made about meeting Barasa and showing her firepower. But it's possible she's after just Vaghn. Since Barasa has him, he might be using Vaghn as a chip in his favor."

"Barasa has Vaghn, his fat brain and his laptop with whatever that bleeding thing is—" Riley gestured to the computer screen that was encrypted into a colorful mess. "And we have zip."

"Let Base work on getting the GPS log for the number, but I say it's time to use and abuse some resources." The phone rang. She glanced at the caller ID before she hit the speaker.

"Will you put your comm-link back on?" a young voice said and Riley smiled. *"This phoning you is annoying."*

"Wow, must be like the stone ages for you, actually dialing," Safia said. "Report."

"I hope you're dressed," Base said. *"The target is moving. Fast."*

Eleven

Woodbridge, Virginia

The ringing phone disturbed the first rest Hank could grab since the chemical theft. His wife nudged him, handing the cordless over his shoulder and he wondered why she insisted the phone be in her side of the bed when it was always for him.

He glanced at the clock. At this hour, it wouldn't be good, he thought, glancing at the number. He propped on his elbow, then put the phone to his ear. "Jansen." He yawned and blinked, then rubbed his face.

"Sir, Major Beckham. At twenty-two hundred forty-six hours, a blast with a two-megaton range occurred in Singapore."

"Drop the Intel speak, Beckham, and give me the shit," Hank said and his wife smacked his rear.

"Analysts believe the RZ10 was used."

"Good God."

"Just enough to flatten about eighteen acres and kill an estimated thirty thousand," the major added.

Hank sat up and swung his legs over the side of the bed. "Jesus, how'd it get that far?" he said, switching on the lamp. It had only been days since the theft, he thought as he moved to the closet and pulled out his uniform.

"That's the problem. According to Agent Choufani it was passed off in the last twenty-four hours."

He went still for a second. "Then it's something else. Notify General Gerardo. I'm on my way in."

"Yes, sir, but you should know the center of the blast was a CIA station."

He closed his eyes for a second. "Find out what you can about the agents assigned there." He ended the call, then shaved and dressed quickly, pausing long enough to kiss his sleeping wife before heading to the Pentagon.

He'd missed his exit and was on his second turn around DuPont circle when he wanted to pull off for some coffee, but the city was still sleeping. Gerardo was likely waking the Joint Chiefs.

Marina Bay
Singapore

Safia went to the doorway between the dining room and kitchen, then hip-checked the wall. It sprang, a bank of shelves hidden behind. Riley's eyes widened. "God, I love a woman with her own arsenal," he said, his gaze flicking over the stash of hand weapons.

She laughed lightly. "Your tax dollars, so help yourself." He reached for a rack of glass tubes and Safia snatched his wrist. He met her gaze. "Poison, and mishandling them will kill you before you realize it."

"I remember something like that from Thailand," Max said.

"That's where I got it." She turned down the hall toward a bedroom. "Riley, you might find some clothes in the mirrored room," she called over her shoulder.

"You should see it," Max said, taking ammunition for his own nine millimeter sidearm. "Really kinky stuff. With costumes."

Pocketing ammo, Riley swung a look at him. "Bugger me."

She did say she bought it as is, and he went to investigate the room, finding clothing with tags, dusty but serviceable. The costumes ranged from Arabian nights sheik robes to an innocent schoolgirl's with a kilt that gave him the creeps. He changed into a clean black tee-shirt still in tissue wrapping, and cargo pants that looked like his old marine uniform in solid gray. He met Safia in the hall, frowning at the difference in her appearance.

Her long dark hair was pulled tight into a ponytail high on her head and braided, but it was the bit of makeup around her eyes that gave an Asian appearance to her Middle Eastern looks. Her sexy body-shaping tank top and rolled shorts had his attention as she wrapped a hoodie around her waist, then knelt to lace ankle boots. Man, she had great legs, he thought, and asked for her comm-link. He reset them with Base control so they could hear Ellie, but not each other. He didn't plan on being separated from her, but Safia's voice would echo.

Heading to the garage, Riley feared this was their last chance to take Vaghn back. Within minutes, they were in the underground garage, and Riley knew he'd never get used to that speed-demon lift ride.

"What do you want," she said, pointing at the two vehicles in the furthermost corner of the garage. "Fast or inconspicuous?" One was a green Land Rover covered in dirt, the other, a dark British Racing blue BMW hardtop.

"Fast," he said. "I don't think covert is an option anymore." It was a given that Vaghn wouldn't keep his mouth shut about Dragon One.

"Agreed." She tossed him the keys.

He sailed them right back. "Your town and I hope you can get us around morning rush hour."

Safia smiled and climbed in. They had tracking on a GPS on the dash, and he'd already loaded the biomarker trace on his Recon. He concealed his weapons as she drove from ground level to the street. "You should probably buckle up," she said, then rocketed into morning traffic.

Riley slapped a hand on the dash, giving her a side glance and her girly giggle made him smile. Singapore was awake, and he navigated her toward the biomarker, then frowned when the beacon turned toward the water. "Pasir Panjang Terminal."

"The docks?" she said, glancing, then down shifting. "Shipping him out to where? It would be easier to fly him, and Barasa's jet is in a hangar."

"Marked?" he asked.

She shook her head. "Too well guarded to get that close. His men won't let anyone without custom's credentials within a hundred yards." Riley's look questioned. "He's got official connections and uses them."

She downshifted, putting the car into a corridor between two trucks, then like a bullet, popped through and skirted a traffic jam on side streets. An old woman tossed water on her walkway as they zipped past. Then the area opened, the shadow of tall buildings no longer crowding as she drove to the docks. Warehouses lined the road in, then split off in wide streets to different companies and cargos. A granary was at the farthest end, but Riley didn't think they'd stash him on a barge. They moved too slow.

"Can you narrow the location?" she said, coming to a fork. "It's a big place."

"Pier twenty-two," he said, watching the neon dot blink.

"That's Chang Ju Shipping." She frowned. "Triad owned." She cornered the sports car, cutting between dockyards and loading ramps, then slid into the parking lot. They both left the vehicle, moving quickly down the pier.

The morning dew sheened the metal surfaces. Trucks and forklifts were still, the smell of oil and fuel blended in the air with the scent of coffee. Workers didn't pay them any attention as they hurried past. Riley glanced at his comm-link to judge location, then stopped and backed up in the shadows of a warehouse. Workers hosed down the concrete and buckets on chains that swung from the dock to dump the fish into iced storage. Women walked in groups toward the fishery.

Some milled, waiting for the first catch to arrive to prepare it for sale. Yards beyond, stretching into the water, the pier was nearly deserted except for a handful of people.

They moved alongside the warehouse, a shabby metal building with three wide doors. Only one was open and Riley glanced inside. Water dripped and trickled off equipment. A young man with a large hose propped on his shoulder sprayed the concrete, washing fish guts into the sea. Probably why the waters were shark infested, he thought, then glanced at his comm-link.

"The marker stopped." He nodded ahead. "He's near the water."

A tugboat and a fishing trawler were side by side. The crewmen cast lines from the pier, the stack burping smoke as the hundred-foot fishing trawler started to float away from the dock.

Riley's gaze flicked between the two boats. "Which one?"

"The trawler," she said beside him. "That will take him up river, even as far as Indonesia and Thailand without much notice." It was backing away from the pier and swinging toward open seas. "We're going to lose him." She started for the dock, but he stopped her.

"Something doesn't feel right," Riley said and they backed into the shadows of the fishery again.

"The bad guys never do the norm."

"But why would they put him on a boat? Barasa has a jet." His gaze moved to the high spots. Two men sat on the steel girder of an unfinished warehouse like magpies on a branch. About twenty feet above the ground, the pair drank from Styrofoam cups and stared out at the water. Several yards across the loading dock, a small work crew checked in at a toll booth–sized shack. One dark skinned man lingered back, dressed a bit heavy for the tropics. Riley couldn't tell if they were tearing the structure down or building it; the area below the warf road was packed with construction equipment sitting idle.

He studied the faces again, the position of the marker. A few yards ahead, men pushed open the tall steel doors, metal to metal shrieking like a Banshee howl broken short. At the tip of the piers, trawlers were already heading out to sea, the slow process marked with seagulls flocking the nets. He moved forward and glanced inside the warehouse. Against the back wall, a line of industrial ice machines groaned with their own weight, ready to melt in the Singapore heat. Why here? he wondered.

His gaze swung to the girders. The men were gone. His gaze lowered over the skeleton of the building. He saw the muzzle flash and threw himself back into Safia. The round hit the warehouse, ringing the metal wall.

"Silencer," she said, huddled behind a forklift, her weapon drawn.

Aiming his gun, Riley glanced up at the bullet hole in the metal where he'd been standing. "Well. Clearly these weren't the clever trousers in the closet."

Safia snickered a laugh. "Guess you were right. They're using Vaghn."

"*The marker is heading east now,*" Base said over the radio. "*About fifteen miles an hour. It's fifty yards west of your position. You should be able to see something.*"

Safia darted for a quick look at the road bordering the wharf. "It's got to be the truck. It's the only thing moving."

"The shooter wants me," he said, searching for the magpie guys. "I'll be returning the favor."

She met his gaze. "Then I'm going after Vaghn. I want to meet this idiot."

He kissed her, deep and quick. "Watch your six, love," he murmured, and she squeezed his arm.

"You too. Don't be a hero." She shifted past him and walked inside the warehouse. She crossed the damp concrete and out the right side door. Riley turned his attention to the shooter, and thought it was almost flattering to be such a threat.

* * *

CIA communications expert Ellie Mullins sounded like she was twelve and far too young to be in this business, Max thought, but she was no slouch. Safia had downloaded the flash drive from the station back-up, and Ellie was searching for a new encryption program because nothing Dragon One had was working. Max wondered how many fingers were in this operation by now, because he didn't trust the CIA to keep their mouths shut, but Ellie had assured him the flash drive was *her* station file.

On a pad he made a list of the items in Vaghn's pack. Remembering a pen-light, he added it, then tried the combination of scribbles again. He wasn't ready to believe the scrap of paper was insignificant. It was the same sequence. If it weren't, he'd consider it was doodling, but the repetition said Vaghn was committing it to memory. The contradiction with that theory was Vaghn had photographic recall.

Alone in the air conditioning, he tried different configurations of the same sequence. It read like garbage, and reminded him of a spam email address. Above the fridge, the TV was on CNN and occasionally, he switched it to a local news station till he couldn't stomach the scene. In most instances, they had to use bulldozers to move the buildings off the dead. He wanted to go down there. It wasn't that he couldn't accept Sebastian was dead, it was the lack of proof. But from what Riley described, there wasn't anything left to get even a DNA sample to test. Max sighed, tried another sequence, then rubbed his face. After refilling his mug, he reached for a landline and dialed the morgue.

Sonsoral Islands
South of Palau

The morning sun was sizzling hot by seven A.M.

She'd argued with Travis yesterday about going ashore and when she'd finally caved in, it was too dark to consider it. Exactly what the sneaky sot wanted, of course. One would think she'd be wise to his manipulations because normally his Scots charm didn't work on her. She admitted he was right, but not to his face. He'd be a bother to live with if she did.

Her hand on the throttle, she angled the skiff away from the ship and pointed it toward the shore. She pulled her floppy hat low, her body lacquered in sunscreen. Wearing a tank style wet suit and dive boots, she was protected from any poisonous plant life, and though sweat spilled down her back beneath the neoprene rubber, she came prepared, as Riley had taught her. Circling her waist was a utility belt with her specimen bags, brushes, and a small shovel evenly spread in pouches and loops. She didn't expect to use any of it.

Jim was in the front, watching the land through binoculars. He hadn't said a word since they lowered the rubber boat into the sea. He glanced at her, then back to the island.

"You buggered about going back?"

He frowned for a second. "No. I'm just eager to get something that would explain this." He touched his wound.

"We know there's something alive there, so all we have to do is prove it."

"Capture?"

"Ha! Not on your life. We don't have cages and frankly, nothing on this island is getting on my ship."

He smiled, his body relaxing a bit. Finally, she thought, though he still looked ready to jump overboard. Nearing the shore, she gunned the engine, pushing them onto the sand. They hopped out and dragged the boat further up the beach. She looked back at the ship and waved, and in the distance saw Travis on the bow. He wanted to join her, but she had to have someone completely reliable and trusted to remain on the ship.

For the sake of caution, she tried the radio, then turned her back and looked at the tree line bending in a deep curve on the aqua blue and white shore. Lovely. The south side was rock and she spied the formation Jim mentioned before. Water had eroded a cavity in the stone, hollowed like a yawning mouth. Waves barely made it to the small inlet cave.

She looked at Jim, pleased to see him smile. "You're the guide here, Doctor Clatt." She waved him on.

He chuckled under his breath. "You're the field experience."

"There you go now. I knew you'd see why we make a great team." She marched toward the tree line beside him.

He stopped on the edge and flicked on his flashlight. "In there, you can't see clearly it's so dense."

At the hem of the jungle, she turned to wave to her husband again, then ducked into the darkness. It was bright enough to see, but Jim wasn't taking chances. It made her nervous, a man his age so spooked. Likely well and good that she didn't tell him about the radio making noise. Trav knew; she couldn't hide anything from him, but bone digging wasn't her only goal today. She wanted to find that hand radio. It had definitely come on, but what she heard was up for debate.

"I was digging over here," he said, taking a few steps deeper, then halting in a small clearing. The soil was sandy and the footprints from their last visit were visible. No wonder. The air in the shadowed circle was still and heavy. She felt cocooned, the suffocating enhanced by the climbing temperature.

"Where was the attack?"

Jim pointed, and she moved past him, flicking on her torch light and nudging aside the vegetation to see the ground. She didn't find anything but a couple crab tracks and moved further in, the flashlight necessary now. Piercing sunlight came with the breeze, then went dark. The flicker made it hard for her eyes to adjust. The ground was dense with rotting vegetation, the undergrowth smothering it, and each step tossed the odor of compost. She found an opening in the jungle floor, and with her shovel, she dug but after a few minutes dismissed it and moved left.

Then Jim called to her, and she stood, then hurried back

to the clearing, but didn't see him. He shouted and through the foliage she saw him wave his arms over his head. He was several yards ahead near where he was attacked. She strode to him.

"Don't go off alone. We're stronger in pairs."

"Your brother's words?"

"No, my mum's." She smiled and looked to see what he'd found. It was just a bit of sand about five feet wide but a palm tree had fallen over.

"Take a look at this." He shined the light.

Bridget bent and inhaled a sharp breath. "My word." The gulley in the land had eroded and exposed a small skull. She knelt and drew out her digital camera, snapping pictures. Then she brushed at the skull and lifted it out. "It looks like the skulls found on Flores Island."

Scientists believed it was a tribe of smaller humans and had dubbed the skeletons *Hobbits*. Pinpricks of excitement raced through her blood when she realized this skull could confirm they'd lived and migrated.

"Your prize, sir." She gave him the skull, then photographed him inspecting it. "What's your assessment?"

"Washed up here. The typhoons swallow this island."

"I disagree."

"I concur."

She looked up, her camera poised. Agreeing to disagree? Some men needed to get out of the lab more often, she thought, then said, "How so?"

"That tree was in the ground recently, in the last year or so. I don't think a storm knocked it over. Air barely gets in here."

That proven by the sweat dripping into her dive boots, she thought and studied the toppled palm. It fell left from where it once stood, yet the top was caught in the taller trees, dark green vines woven around it and reaching to the snag. She shined the torch to the tops. It was almost cavelike, only a shimmer of radiance, more sensation than sunlight.

Jim examined the skull. "The remains are old," he said. "Under layers of earth and worn by the sea before they ever landed there."

"It could very well be from inhabitants centuries ago." She thought of the "Hobbit" bones of Flores Island again.

"Perhaps, but . . ." Jim walked to the far side of the tree base and pointed. "This is recent."

She looked down at the thready, dry root system, yet the surrounding earth was wet and held a distinct depression. "A large nut or perhaps just a rock that rolled free?" she said, looking for evidence.

"To make a depression that smooth?" He squatted and gestured to the shape. "I believe it's the heel of a foot."

She looked at him. It was a stretch to surmise that and he knew it. "Just what did you see in here, Jim?"

He met her gaze. "Something small and hairy."

"With claws," she added though she doubted he needed that pointed out.

He stood and watched his steps as he worked his way around the print. "There's a couple more that lead away."

Into the center of the island, she thought, and wasn't ready to venture that deep. All right, she admitted. *I am scared.* She had enough education to know that nothing should survive on this island except plant life, yet here it was. Proof. She took several photos, then waited for Jim to decide.

When he followed the prints, Bridget thought, Mary mother, *now* he's brave?

For extra measure, she drew her dive knife, bloody thankful she could do more with it than cut bait.

Singapore

Barasa nursed his morning coffee as he watched the screen of Vaghn's laptop. Behind the small window waiting for a password, the screen was a vibrant digital language he didn't understand, nor care to. He'd already brought in specialists, all unsuccessful. Its creator still refused to give him the sequence or passwords. Vaghn was well trapped in this bargain, but Barasa admitted he was mildly impressed with the scientist's resistance to interrogation. The vigor and rebellion of youth, he thought, sipping. Or fear of the Professor.

Vaghn would feel regret, he supposed, if he were awake. Keeping him complacent with narcotics simplified Cale's day. He admitted he was far more curious about the outcome than he was concerned with the threats. The Professor and his pretty colleague were a mystery, as was their final purpose. They enjoyed their manipulation. It was a mutual trait. Testing limits was often more satisfying than filling his bank accounts. More sport in it, he thought.

His phone rang, and he responded, still watching the screen. "Yes."

Setting down his coffee, he tried a random sequence for the sake of it. It failed.

"Yes?" He checked the number. Blocked. "Speak."

"Ready your jet, and your cargo."

He frowned at the deep voice he didn't recognize. "For where?"

The caller rattled off coordinates, and Barasa scrambled for paper to jot it down. Annoyed they couldn't simply text it, he knew they were fanatical about trails. "I'm not going anywhere without proof." He tossed the pen on the desk.

"Daedalus."

The call ended without another word, and he closed the phone, studying the coordinates. He was neither a pilot nor a navigator, and the longitudes and latitudes made little sense. It's why he hired people, he thought, and pocketed the slip. Rahjan would know, but it would have to wait until the Ghurka soldier cleaned up a few lingering details.

E Ring
Pentagon

David entered the general's office and thought, *The man hasn't slept.* He didn't know what was going on, but the push to decode the transmission had kept him up half the night. The general waved toward the coffee, and pressed a finger to his lips for silence. David respected it and went to the service, remembering Price making him set this up and keep it hot eighteen hours a day when there was a coffee service in the headquarters. He poured himself a cup and took a seat in the leather chair, sliding his feet to the ottoman. He was okay with this, he thought and took a moment to empty facts from his brain, then pep it up with caffeine. The door opened and Colonel Jansen entered, stopping short when he saw them, feet propped up and quiet. As if on cue, he left his briefcase by a chair, got some coffee, and did the same. It was another ten minutes or so before General Gerardo sat up straighter.

"Stalling isn't going to improve the day," he said. "David?"

He opened the file. "I have not broken the encryption, sir. NSA agent Deets has it and is searching for the primer. However, I've narrowed the send from two east coast companies with the capabilities to send and receive. Pike Silicone. It's a plastics company that trades with China and it's regularly monitored for that reason. The other is Noble Richards Incorporated. One of our military contractors."

Gerardo nodded, and his gaze flicked to Colonel Jansen.

Uh-oh, David thought and continued. "The file needs passwords and I'm tracking it backwards, trying to . . ." he stressed. "It hopped a lot of satellite networks before it landed. The stream maintains a tone for a long time and that helps to track the sounds. This contractor has access and authorization to send data files through government satellites. I couldn't go further. Noble Richards projects are black classified." He shrugged. "Out of my pay grade."

Lately it was the pat answer for not taking an investigation further, a bit of leftover from an administration of secrets and sleight of hand, David thought. McGill had shaken up the CIA and tried to get the agencies to pass information faster, but it was the clearance of each piece that stalled investigations, like now. He closed his file and took a sip of coffee.

"Do you know where it landed?"

"Not yet, sir, but it's definitely Asia. I've traced it as far as Turkey. A network in Istanbul. The hop before that was Zaire."

Colonel Jansen was frowning at the file on his lap, and David spoke his thoughts. "Sirs?" he said. "I can't help you if I don't know the whole story."

"Give it all to him, Hank," Gerardo said, then looked at David. "Your pay grade doesn't go up, but your clearance just did, understand?"

"Yes sir." Like everything else, he thought, a big fat secret.

"The military contractor, NRI, works on Department of Defense Research and Development projects," Jansen said. "They are supervised and required by contract, at the completion of a project to turn everything over to the U.S. government. All computers are cleaned of references by our people."

David eyes rounded. "Forgive me, but what are we talking about here? Ordnance? Communications?"

"Weapons using the latest technology."

David sat back in the chair, laid the file aside, then went for more coffee. "What do you believe it is?"

"Coming from NRI, it could be any number of projects. They'd lost their contract a few years ago for violations, and only recently regained it."

"They shouldn't have. Lobbyists and congress made that mistake," Gerardo growled into his coffee mug before drinking.

David set the carafe aside and faced them. "Then since it's a U.S. company and had restrictions, this communication is an act of treason."

"We feel so, yes," Jansen said.

"How long do we have?"

"Every moment counts. NRI developed an explosive, and we believe it was used in Singapore." His eyes flared. "A canister was stolen. That satellite image I wanted you to look at?"

David nodded. It was in his computer and he'd been running some programs to decipher a single foggy shadow.

"It's from the theft a few days ago."

"I think it's a foot, a very small one. Maybe only four or five inches."

Jansen frowned. "Animal?"

"It's not clear enough even with digitizing it, but if I had to guess, I'd say it's human."

Singapore

Tracking the biomarker on her phone, Safia crossed the water-sheened concrete to the far side to the open doors. Sunlight splashed over piles of buoys and nets tossed against a fence and when she cleared the mess, she bolted. The truck slowed and she pushed harder, zigging around a vendor's truck and the men buying breakfast. When the truck stopped and started backing into a garage Safia walked behind a neat row of forklifts and slipped up to the open doorway. It was a produce delivery from local farmers, she thought, spotting another truck on the other side, men unloading wooden crates of bananas. Behind that was a flower truck. She moved closer when the driver climbed out, then opened the tailgate. From her position, the cab looked vacant. Workers lined up to do the fireman's carry to unload the overstacked flat bed. It was almost empty and no Vaghn. She was about to search the truck herself when her cell vibrated and she backed away to answer.

"I can't reach Riley," Max said. "The biomarker is degrading too fast. It dissolves in seventy-two hours and its got at least forty hours left."

"What's that mean?"

"It's exposed to air. It's not inside Vaghn anymore. We've been juiced."

She looked at the truck, empty now. "Damn." She tried to hail Riley on the comm-link. He'd adjusted it because side by side, the device would reverberate, yet at this distance, it should be clear. She wasn't getting anything. Safia started walking back toward the first pier and put her phone to her ear again. "Max, get Ellie to reach Riley. I think he can hear me, but he's not responding. He had a shooter to deal with."

She heard Max curse, then say, "Don't let another of my buddies die."

Her heart clenched. *Oh man.* "I won't."

Twelve

Riley spotted his shooter. It was easy. He'd made no effort to conceal himself.

The sniper shouldered the rifle and ambled down the scaffolding platform, then paused for a moment to look down at Riley, daring him. No. Challenging him. Then he disappeared into the lift and sent the wire cage down. But Riley was already across the road to the shack, pushing past the workers and running down a dirt hill to the yard below. Behind the equipment, he slowed, his boots crushing shells covering the ground. The lift door was still swinging on its hinges and he used a dozer's bucket for cover.

He'd go for close quarters, he thought, nowhere to hide. Left was the warehouse and though he was near the docks, the land was half a mile back from the shore. Between the heavy equipment and stacks of steel, he glimpsed the bow of the fishing trawler idling in the water, sea gulls circling overhead and diving for scraps. A dorsal fin rode the surf near the hull. They're waiting, he thought, then focused on the neighboring cranes, and the path the guy took down. There were too many levels and places to hide but he had to risk it.

Riley darted toward the warehouse as a shot hit the steel wall. The ring of it brought heads up. *There you are*, he thought, and waved workers back, showing his weapon when they just gawked. He rushed toward the half-constructed building, keeping the machinery on his right, ducking once to search for movement and continue. He glanced around the warehouse, the equipment, then spotted a shadow inside the rear wall. It was the only wall completed alongside rows of unfinished storage buildings, and he hurried closer, sidling alongside the steel frames. He peered. Chains hung from the rafters and pooled on the floor.

"Finn?" Base said gently.

Call signs were necessary he supposed. "Go ahead."

"Drac says the biomarker isn't inside the target anymore. It's gone."

"Copy that." He shouldn't be surprised. He'd shot Vaghn in the leg and he'd needed medical attention. Obviously, it was thorough and the idea of picking the marker out of his butt amused him, though it was better care than Barasa gave his men on the bridge. While Safia thought Barasa was the key, Riley knew Vaghn's brilliance would foresee every angle, and it magnified the feeling they were just breaking the ice on this cocktail. Nobody went to these lengths for a new gun or bomb without big plans for it. They still didn't know what explosive Vaghn had used, but a little went a very long way in damage.

The catwalk hinges scraped and a figure swung down, then dropped to the concrete floor. As the man straightened, Riley recognized the threat before he saw the weapon. Riley fired first, the bullet chipping the sniper's shoulder, and he staggered, losing the gun, but kept coming. Riley braced himself for the attack. Like a Brahma bull, the man bolted with his head down to ram him, and when he was close, Riley leapt aside. The man sailed past, staggered, and Riley threw a roundhouse kick to his kneecaps, clipping him off his feet. The guy hit the ground and bounced.

Riley rushed, grabbed his shirt, relieved him of his curved knife, then dragged him deeper inside the warehouse. He fought.

"Oh no, lad," he said when the sniper tried to gain his footing. "You wanted this."

The man curled himself up and rolled three times fast, breaking Riley's hold, then jumped to his feet. He grinned, then slapped his chest. "Come get me."

Riley smirked and raised his weapon. The man ducked to the side, and Riley followed him with the barrel and fired. It met its mark, lower rib cage, and the guy flung forward. No blood. Kevlar and damned unfair, he thought rushing along the wall. Water reflected movement in the puddles, and he swung his aim high. On a stack of lumber above him, the shooter let go of a bola whip and it snapped around Riley's weapon, the clackers crashing his wrist and jerking the sidearm out of his grip, nearly taking his finger. The captured weapon flew, hit, then spun across the cement as Riley darted behind the ice machines. Leaning back against the metal wall, he flexed his wrist and fingers. The stun still vibrated up his arm.

"Hurting?" a voice said. The sound came from his left, near.

Riley spotted the gun and bola against the loading doors, but there wasn't any cover to get to them and he had to assume the shooter was better armed. He freed the double-edged knives strapped to his calf, and flipped them into fighting position.

Riley rolled his wrists, kicked a soda can and waited for the gunshot.

Safia ran to where she'd left Riley, and as she approached, she heard gunfire. Please don't be him, please, she thought and tried to pinpoint the location. It was distant, the report faint. She bolted past the fishery dock to the unfinished side. Men huddled back, pointed out the direction, and she hurried through the overgrown grasses. Her foot hit something and she stumbled, then turned back. She picked up the sniper's rifle. The firing pin was missing. She slung it, ran to the warehouse and slipped inside. Metal sheeting and lumber were stacked high, making a corridor. She heard movement and moved toward the rear, then spotted the staircase to the catwalk. She mounted slowly, stopping at the top step to search below.

Beyond the piles of supplies, she spotted Riley near the scoops and curtains of chains used to swing buckets closer to the sea. He was armed with knives, and she inched up to search the area. His opponent was moving left and she signaled him, but he didn't see her. Then it didn't matter.

Riley's expression was full of payback and the two circled, then clashed. Riley blocked, his leg swinging high and knocking the man's head. He landed in a crouch, ready to spring again. He never let go of the knives. The shooter wobbled on his feet, shook his head like a dog, and Safia saw the cuts staining his clothes. The attacker threw his fist, and Riley blocked with an upward swipe and opened the other's cheek, a swipe downward cut his stomach. Riley's execution was like a man possessed, but his opponent was skilled, pushing him back by brute force until they were grappling, Riley's long arms keeping his own knife from his face. Safia aimed, and put a shot at their feet.

They bucked apart, and the guy said something she couldn't hear. In the next moment, he was stumbling back from a punch. Riley held his fists up like a prizefighter, each blow snapping the guy's head back. He went down by the third hit. Riley stood over him, breathing hard, then stooped to search him. He pocketed what he found, then rolled him on his back.

Safia climbed down the iron steps and moved around the shorter stacks. She picked up Riley's gun, then approached. The blast of a boat horn drowned out any noise. The man was up and bolting to the gaping doors, but Riley was on him. The sniper grabbed a dangling chain and flung it, hitting Riley in the chest. He caught it and using it like a fulcrum, sailed across twenty feet planting his feet in the guy's chest.

The sniper flew back, hit the cement, and was still only for a second before he rolled to his feet and bolted out the wide doors. The boat horn blast came again.

When she moved around the stacks of lumber, Riley was gone, running after his target. She followed, her direction wider, covering his back. The attacker raced down the half-constructed pier and dove off the edge. Riley was right behind him, gripping his knives as he hit the water in an arching dive. Safia rushed to the edge and sighted through her monocular. He didn't surface. She scanned for the shooter, then saw a dorsal fin.

Riley swam, his eyes stinging as he plowed through the water to catch the sniper. He saw kicking feet and grabbed his ankle, then headed for the surface. He popped out for air, then went back down, forcing the sniper's head down. The man curled his body and Riley caught the silver flicker before the guy swiped a knife, catching his clothing and across his arm. Blood colored the water. The sniper kicked free and swam. Riley crested the surface behind him and reached out. A man on the trawler deck fired into the water, and he dove, the shots streaming past him. When he surfaced, the crew hoisted the nets, the sniper lying inside with tons of fish.

"Well that was a bust," he said, then started for shore. Then he heard rapid gunshots again. Safia stood on the pier, firing into the water. He glanced around as the tall fin neared. He hauled ass to the shore. The shark was faster.

Safia saw the shark lift its nose out of the water behind Riley and emptied her weapon into the big fish. Her breath rushed as she reloaded and aimed again, but the fin was gone, the water red and murky. She kept vigilant as Riley swam, then the shark, riddled with holes bucked the surface. No snack today, she thought, aiming for the brain and fired three rounds. The shark sank under the water and she bolted back up the dock, then worked her way down the scaffolding to the ground. She ran across the shore, the sniper rifle and her bag banging against her hip. Riley was bent over, bleeding, and she called to him. He straightened and opened his arms. She slammed into him, clutching tight.

"Shark infested waters, Donovan." She punched his back and he chuckled, leaning on her, still trying to catch his breath.

"He must like Irish sweet bread," he said, "because the sniper was cut too." He straightened and looked to the sea. The sniper stood on the bow and saluted them.

Safia flipped him off. "So how's the egg on my face?" She looked at him. "Because we were royally suckered."

They'd walked right into it with the marker. "We need to go at this more defensively. Raise the bar," he said, still watching the boat.

"Base, get a mark on the trawler in the water. I want to know when it docks," Safia said into her comm-link, then dug in her hobo bag for a tissue. She blotted the spots of blood and he slung an arm over her shoulder.

"He kicked my butt."

"Not that I saw. You're wicked with those knives, Irish."

He watched his target sail away. "We're left with Red Shoes and hope she uses the phone." She handed him his weapon. Riley checked the sight and load. The clacker hit so hard it dented it. Useless, he thought and tucked it in his holster. "He was familiar," Riley said. "The rescue guy from the river, maybe."

She swung the sniper rifle forward and removed the magazine, then ejected a round still in the chamber. "He's Barasa's, for sure. This is from his shipment to Colombian FARC's that Interpol confiscated." She offered it.

"That's Chinese," he said, examining it. "You won't get prints, he was wearing gloves when he was shooting."

"Leaving it is intentional, then. But he took out the firing pin. That I don't get. Removing it says you care who picked it up." Then she looked past him. "Well it just gets better."

Riley followed her gaze. A small speedboat crossed the

delta to the trawler. The low-slung craft swept alongside the fishing boat, and the soldier stepped to the rail. He jumped from one boat into the other, then waved as it sped north on steep curls of water. She alerted Base.

"Arrogant little puke."

"He was a Ghurka soldier," he said and held out the curved knife. The handle was intricately carved and inlaid with silver. It was standard for Nepalese soldiers.

"I thought the Ghurkas wouldn't stop fighting. To the death kind of guys."

"That's the rumor," he murmured, watching the speedboat shrink in the distance. He recalled a few in Iraq had to be separated because they reacted with such speed that innocent people were wounded by just coming up behind them. "That soldier could have killed me at any time," Riley said, then looked at her. "So why didn't he?"

"A warning," she said firmly. "It's a game to him."

He shrugged, digging in his pockets for the items he took off the soldier. "Apparently the joke is on us."

The cell phone, keys, all of it were realistic looking plastic toys.

Sonsoral Islands

Bridget felt the jungle narrow around her and glanced back. The darkness swallowed, yet fifteen feet ahead, she could see green fronds dappled with sunlight. The fallen trees from past storms tented broad areas on the otherwise insignificant island. The skull inside Jim's bag bounced against his hip as he walked and while she had some specimen bags and a few tools, she was truly only interested in retrieving the radio.

"Jim? Are you still tracking the prints?"

He glanced back. "I'm not sure." He and Derek had gone further toward the center than she'd thought.

Her hand radio clicked, startling her until she heard Travis's voice. "Everything right and proper?"

She unclipped it from her belt. "So far. We've made amazing finds."

"Splendid. Why aren't you heading back?"

She was about to ask the same thing, and realized she was alone. "Jim," she called. "Jim!" He kept going, suddenly driven. Bridget made a rude sound and hurried after him. He stood near a boulder three times his height, vines concealing the jagged rock beneath. He was still and she crept closer.

"You don't follow field orders very well," she said, annoyed when she'd warned him already. Bloody lab rats, knackered in the brain, she thought, then signed off with her husband. Trav wasn't pleased about it. She heard the worry in his voice.

"Sorry. But don't you smell that?"

She sniffed. "A little mold maybe." The air barely moved around them.

"No, over here."

She took a couple steps nearer and still didn't smell anything foreign. Then a breeze kicked up and she got a whiff. She pressed the back of her hand to her nose. "Oh, that's awful."

"Feces."

Feces, however foul, meant living beings. "Saints preserve us, that's brilliant," she said, her gaze darting over the trees, the rock covered in vines. There was something here and a bead of excitement coursed through her, nudging aside her fear. Then Jim knelt and pushed at a cluster of fronds. She bent, blinking with surprise. Under a bush was the radio. It wasn't turned on, but it had been chewed, the hard plastic scarred on the corners.

"I'd say this confirms it's inhabited," she said and still wearing the latex gloves, picked it up, then slipped it into a specimen bag. Inhabited by what, she could only speculate, and she wanted to preserve any DNA on the marks. Yet the fact was, Jim had lost it fifty feet in the other direction.

Jim pushed at the vegetation, exposing the ground, the black earth and sand appearing almost oily. He moved in a squat, circling the boulder, searching for evidence of life. "Few tracks," he said, gesturing, then he sat back on his rear, and waved to her. "More bones."

She crossed to him and he showed her a dainty pile. They were exceptionally small. She photographed it, then scooped up a few and bagged them. "That wouldn't cause the odor, and it's too heavy to be just these rotting trees and coconuts."

Jim moved to the rock, walking left of it, then pushed at the thick vines trapping it. She was on his heels, not about to be left alone with no one to hide behind, she thought. Then she recognized what he was going for and tapped him, offering her knife. He hacked at the vines and the odor grew almost unbearable.

He looked at her. "It's hollow." He shined his flashlight inside and ducked a bit, then made a noise. "Oh yes, this is the source of the odor, definitely."

"What is it?" she said, and on her knees, crawled up beside him. He held back the vines, but they were so thick it was an effort. She peered, then reared back, completely confused. She looked again. A carcass putrefied inside the cavity. She could see grayish hair and pointed teeth still anchored in a decaying jawbone. At this angle, she couldn't pinpoint the species. "A monkey perhaps? Did this attack you?"

He frowned at it, shaking his head and chewing on his lip. "I thought, I mean, it felt . . . bigger."

Her gaze swept her surroundings. Monkey or possibly just a rodent, it still didn't answer how it arrived on such an isolated island. She looked back when Jim asked for a specimen bag and then crawled deeper. Shining his light, he gathered samples. The reek made her move back. She shined her light on the rock, trying to imagine it without the vines, then rushed to the right side of the clump and tried to get her hand under the inch wide vine. She held her shovel sideways, using the edge like an axe. The shape was too uniform on one side, and she chopped harder. The shovel clanged against metal.

Jim backed out, his expression startled. "You have got to be the most amazing archaeologist, Doctor McFadden."

"I've me moments," she said smiling broadly and he crossed to her. "It's almost perfectly straight over here."

They chopped at the vines stopping when the tools hit something solid. Bridget replaced the shovel in her belt, then felt the lines of the boulder that truly wasn't. She pushed at a knot of feeder vines, and her eyes rounded. "Jim," she said. "The knife." She held her hand out like a surgeon, unable to take her gaze off the latch. She sawed at the vines, and he pulled, tearing them back.

"No," she breathed. It was a metal crate of some sort, or part of one. The surface was black with fungus and she scraped at the latch, exposing rivets. "How could this exist in a rust eating climate?

"Galvanized?" Jim said, peering where she'd scraped.

"Has to be. It's had to be here long enough to grow all this." She photographed it, the rush of finding this pushing on her overkill button and the camera didn't stop blinking.

A short pinched noise startled them, and she looked behind herself, her heart in her throat. Jim shined his light. The path was smashed from their footsteps, but nothing moved except the sweat down her spine. Then she felt an unwelcome pull on her skin, a knowledge that they weren't alone in the copse.

Her gaze swept to him. "Let's go."

"I'm right there with you," he said and met her gaze. Bridget swept hers meaningfully to the far right. She glimpsed movement, then suddenly turned and with the shovel, took a swipe at the brush. The spade hit something low to the ground and she stilled, then advanced.

"Bridget, no," he said. "Remember my cuts."

"I have to know." She reached to push at waterlogged palms. A quick rustle of fronds shook the jungle in more than one direction. "Perhaps not," she said and backed up beside him. "Slowly, retrace back to the boat."

He nodded and they walked backwards a wee bit. Bridget cast a glimpse at the formation before Jim handed back her knife and led the way, familiar now. When they reached the edge of the jungle, she stopped, letting the comfort of the sun warm her face. Her heart pounded and she returned the shovel to her belt and replaced her knife in the sheath on her calf. Jim walked on ahead, his step lighter, and his arms full of bone bags. She touched her pouch, suddenly anxious to get in a lab.

That feeling returned and she stepped away from the forest. Her gaze ripped over the darkness beyond, wanting to see something and almost hoping she didn't. Nothing moved and on impulse, she pulled her energy bar from her belt and hurled it into the forest, then turned away, hurrying toward the boat and the man on the shore who couldn't seem to get in it without putting down his precious cargo.

Some people should remain indoors, she thought, and under supervision.

Singapore

The afternoon sun blazed in a cloudless sky. Citizens rushed to grab a meal and head back to work, the hustle stopping for no one. The tall buildings stood close, blocking any breeze and lit to the top with flashing advertising. Riley leaned his shoulder on the wall of a brick building and watched the street traffic. He and Safia had bought clothes downtown, changing in a bar bathroom. In jeans, soggy boots and a sleeveless tee-shirt, he wasn't going to blend well in a crowded city of Asians, but while he was glad to be dry, it was Safia he didn't recognize.

"I like being your backup," Riley said, watching her.

Over the comm-link her voice was soft. "Takes a big man to be second fiddle."

"Not if they had the view I do."

She didn't stop walking, but put more swing in her step. He chuckled and looked ahead of her. She was going after an asset, someone she'd tapped before. Men stopped to watch her and she moved in, teasing them. They had wood before she got close. It was all that cleavage, he thought. She wore a deep blue bustier thing that shaped her like an hourglass, not that she wasn't there already, but her tight jeans were a thing of fantasies. He wanted to peel them off her. She'd applied makeup to give her that Asian look, and pulled her hair tight on the top of her head to slant her eyes a bit. To him, it just looked painful. She was trying to attract the wrong kind of attention and the throwing knife strapped to her thigh wasn't much of a deterrent to the idiots trying to cop a feel of that incredible behind. One tried and got his elbow smacked in the wrong direction.

Gotta love a woman who can kick ass, he thought and followed, his tee-shirt already soaked with sweat. The bandage on his arm wasn't any better. Safia walked by a group of men being useless near a movie theater. Asking after her asset, he heard the response through the personal roll radio and Riley followed as she hurried toward a shabby storefront with blackened windows. A bar, he thought, closing in. She didn't go in but walked past.

"Target acquired," she said.

Before Riley knew what she was about, she disappeared down a side street.

"Dammed impulsive woman," he muttered, but he'd already learned when she was determined, get out of the way. This was the second source she'd tried to question. The first, a cracked out map seller, ran when he saw her, but didn't see the truck coming. Safia was thirty yards away when he flew through the air and landed at her feet. Coincidence? Hardly. Especially when the driver never stopped.

Riley jogged, turning down a side street to head her off. He passed the road and saw her gaining on her source, but the man was the size of a linebacker, and he plowed through the narrow corridor, yanking down clotheslines and tossing trash cans to block her path. Safia wasn't letting up, God love her, and she vaulted the heaps, then disappeared from his sight. He ran south to cut them off and made the next block in time to see her target rush into the cross street.

Safia appeared from the alley, leapfrogging on cans and crates, then jumping. She hit her target's back and they both smacked the ground. She recovered swiftly and pushed her knee in his spine, yanking his hand back and twisting his wrist. With the other hand, she gripped a handful of hair and pulled his head back. Webber cried out, cursing foully.

Riley came to her, glancing around at the spectators, then down at her. "Well that was discrete."

"We don't have time for it." She pulled on Webber's hair and leaned close. "Why you running, Web?"

"Fuck you, bitch."

She knocked his forehead into the ground and Webber howled. "You speak to your mother with that mouth?"

"Mom's dead and you're going to join her. Get the fuck off of me!" He tried to roll over, but Safia put her weight into his spine.

Riley stepped on the back of Webber's knee. "Clean up your act, dirt bag."

Webber spat. "Fuck you too. Who is he? Your bodyguard?"

"Do I look like I need one?" She glanced at Riley, then meaningfully at the spectators and knew the police would nose too close if they weren't careful.

She slipped off, and Riley pulled Webber to his feet. Webber struggled and Riley dug his fingers in his elbow joint. The man howled and folded a little.

He leaned in to say, "I won't be nice if you keep pissing off my girl."

Safia tried not to smile, but Web tipped his head back and snarled, "She's an ice cold bitch, man, and you need to run in the other direction."

"Ahh, laddie, you should have quit while you were ahead." Riley drove three fingers into his carotid artery, and Webber staggered, his eyes rolling. He helped him into the alley. In Malay, Safia shouted at people to get lost, pulling out her knife to push it home.

Webber coughed, rubbed his throat. "What the hell do you think you're going to do to me? I know people."

"So do I," Safia said, nodding to Riley.

"I'm not telling you dick. You know what will happen to me?"

"I'll kill you," she said, suddenly in his face and her knife under his chin. "Don't think I won't. Thousands of people died yesterday and I want the trigger."

"How the hell should I know?" He flipped her a quick angry glance, but his attention remained on Riley standing back, his face impassive. "I'm just trying to make a living."

She stepped back. "I know you've transported for Barasa. Where is he?"

Chris Webber was a black market antiques dealer. He'd been a shovel bum archeologist in his youth, but the money in illegal trade was far more lucrative. It showed in the jade ring he wore. From the third dynasty, she decided. But Webber was closed mouthed, his reputation of never giving up his sources making him rich with black marketers. He was a big man, thirty-five maybe, decently attractive, his goatee perfectly manicured. He might work with the worst, but he didn't dress it, his clothing evenly matched in khaki. It was a contrast to the frayed Chicago Bears ball cap with sunglasses over the brim like an extra pair of eyes.

"Ya know . . . there was a shipment highjacked from a dig in China last month," she said. "They'd unearthed terra cotta warriors. One was outfitted in the armor of the king."

"What of it?"

"That ring was in the first discovery." She whipped out her cell phone and before he could stop her, she photographed him and the ring. "I'm sure Interpol and the China Ministry of Antiquities would love to know where the rest of the relics went? What's the prison term for that?" She glanced at Riley. "Fifty years with fish heads and rice?"

Riley nodded, his gaze never leaving Webber.

"Like you would do a damn thing. You need me."

"Not really," she said with a shrug, then inclined her head to Riley. "But he does and as you've experienced, he's not nearly as nice as I am. Where is Barasa?"

Webber shrugged. "I hope he's dead."

Safia frowned, waiting for the explanation.

"He hired me to get a guy across a few borders, but re- neged on the deal."

"What did you do with this man?"

"I dumped him in the projects." Webber dusted his clothes, swiped at the grit on his forehead and came back with blood. "He wasn't exactly grateful, but I wasn't paid."

Safia glanced at Riley and knew he'd helped Vaghn get from the U.S. to Singapore.

"Answer the lady's question." Riley's tone sent a chill across the back of her neck. He looked ready to tear into the guy.

Webber's face pulled taut. "I snitch and I won't live to see tomorrow."

In three strides, Riley was on him. "Don't, and you won't live to see the sun set." He struck quickly and so lightly, Safia wasn't sure he did, hitting Webber in the solar plexus and a spot near his hip, then cuffing his ears. Webber folded to the ground, gasping for air and clutching his side, but Riley grabbed his shirt and hoisted the two hundred pound man to his feet, then shoved him against the wall. Webber's head lolled on his shoulders as if he was drunk. Riley hovered close, threat- ening. That was just so cool, she thought, and tried not to smile.

Webber groaned, rubbing his stomach and blinking as blood rushed back into his body. "Okay, okay! Christ! Keep him away." He rubbed his throat. "The Philippines."

Safia frowned.

"I got a guy at the airport." Webber blinked, scowling at Riley. "Heard stuff."

"Expand," Riley said, unimpressed.

"They had a prisoner in a wheelchair."

Riley didn't glance at Safia, but both knew he'd shot Vaghn in the leg.

"They loaded him in and took off, without a flight plan."

"Impossible," she said. "They wouldn't get clearance to take off."

"Helps if you grease a few palms. He's got a parliament member on his payroll."

"Tell me something we don't know," Riley said, and Webber flinched, eyed him for a moment before he said, "He's waiting for some go ahead. Like a scavenger hunt, go here, wait, go there."

Riley inched in and Webber threw his hands up in surrender. "Mindanao!"

Safia leaned into Webber's face. "You screw me, and I'll come after you," she warned.

"Yeah, yeah, and you'll bring your muscle." He rubbed his armpit, scowling at Riley.

Safia was too pleased. Webber's cockiness was all show, and she walked away, but when Riley didn't follow, she glanced back.

The antiques dealer let out a long-suffering sigh, and said, "The Crown Hotel." He pulled off his cap, his arm shaking and he switched hands, flexing his fingers.

"The feeling should come back in an hour or so," Riley said, then stuffed a few dollars in his shirt pocket. "You look like you need a drink." He turned away as Webber called out.

"You see Barasa, tell him I'm still waiting for my money."

He waved over his head. "First on my list."

Safia waited at the end of the alley, the neon lights of the bar glowing down on her with the afternoon sun. "I love it when you get all Benihana."

He chuckled. "Speaking of food . . ."

"The airport comes first."

"Let Base watch him," he said and slung his arm around her shoulder, then kissed her temple. It constantly amazed her at how comfortable she felt with him. The car was three blocks away and when the BMW was in sight, Safia hit her key remote to start it and turn on the air conditioner.

A second later, it exploded.

Thirteen

The blast knocked them off their feet and sent the flaming car into the air like a fiery geyser. Riley scrambled to Safia, covering her as the car hit the ground and exploded again, metal debris shattering windows and crashing into nearby walls and people. Car alarms buzzed the air, mixed with screams of pain. He shielded her head as more debris fell, then he rolled, taking her with him as a chunk of engine hit the ground and tumbled along the street.

"Are you hurt?"

"No, I'm okay," she said into his chest. "—all those people. God, there was a mother pushing a stroller right beside the—" She choked, squeezed harder, then she tipped her chin up. Tears welled but never fell, and the fracture in that iron will broke his heart. He swept his hand over her head to her nape and pressed his forehead to hers. She'd spent her adult life fighting and now it was aimed at her, at her doorstep. She sniffled and he eased back, then helped her to her feet. She leaned into him, rubbed her scraped knee.

"Raven, report. Raven!" blasted in their comm-links.

"We're okay. All emergency services to my position. We need ambulances."

She stepped away from Riley, stunned at the damage. The remains of the car were hunks of twisted metal. The people unfortunate enough to be nearby littered the ground like bloody trash, survivors staggering to their feet, clutching wounds. Safia strode to a man staggering from the blast and helped him find a place to sit. Riley pulled a sheet from a drooping laundry line and wrapped it around the stump of his arm.

She went to the next person as Riley moved down the street, checking under debris. He heard a squeak, and when he neared the buildings, the frightened cry grew louder. He rushed to lift a fallen fence and smiled when a little black dog scrambled out and ran to find a new place to hide. He walked toward the explosion. There was little left of the car, the inside hollowed by the blast and fire. He couldn't tell the type of explosive, but knew it was rigged on the car's starter. That meant the rigger had to know how to get around the computer system and Safia's key code. Not good. In the short time they were in this part of town, someone set it. Likely still near, probably watching, the sick bastard.

Riley looked to the rooftops, expecting the sniper, and then down along the length of the street. Bastards will kill anyone, he thought, then turned back. Ambulances arrived, the sirens winding down to a groan. Safia stood near a police cruiser, talking with an officer. She discretely waved Riley on and he kept walking, wondering what story she was giving the officer. With subtle hand signals, Riley told her to 'follow, still watched,' then headed away from the blast area and toward the metro rail station.

People ran past him to view the explosion, and he stopped at a vending machine, shoving in coins and in the dented surface, watched his back. He punched a selection, waiting. The soda dropped, but his shoulders didn't relax till she rounded the corner. He grabbed the can, and she headed straight for him, grasped his hand, pulling.

"It's a turn on, this bossy side of you."

She flicked him an apologetic glance. "We're witnesses, nothing more right now."

Riley opened the soda, offering it to her.

"Thank you," she said with feeling and drank in big gulps, then handed it back.

He finished it off and pitched it in the trash as they hurried away from the chaos. "We need to get out of sight, now." She met his gaze. "They knew what you drove, Safia. That's too close for my comfort. They've been watching since we left the docks and the sniper's gone, so that means a relay team, a new hitter, or they have the ability to triangulate." Riley opened the phone, then popped out the battery. "Maybe it's all three."

She agreed, then hailed Ellie. "Base, sever all communications."

"Repeat last?"

"Cut off all contact, and block any tracking on us."

"Roger that. Executing. Now tell me why I just broke the rules again?"

"We have an Eye. We were lured to the docks, but there's no way anyone could have known where we were today."

"Roger that. Go under until I can check for tracking."

They arranged a time to contact, then Safia shut off the phone and the comm-link, but Riley took them before she dumped them in the garbage. "We don't want anyone else being the target either." Leaving them in the trash was just as dangerous and he opened her phone, removed the batteries, then searched the ground.

"I need something small and sharp." She dug in her bag and handed him a barrette. He used the cleat to pry out a small piece, then crushed it under his boot. "GPS chip. I've had to replace that sucker a couple times." He turned the TDS Recon back on and it worked. "We can't track on it, though. Base can send data to us. It pretty much turns it into a cell phone." He shrugged, still wondering which communications device they'd traced or if it was only visual. "We still need clean gear. Untraceable since they're right on our backs. Max can get anything, I just need to call him."

She walked faster. "Takes too long."

"Ya know, for a spy, your patience is dammed thin."

"See why I didn't stay a NOC for long." She hurried toward a small bus station on the corner of a busy street and pushed through the doors. "Give me a minute."

Riley remained near the entrance, grabbing a newspaper as she crossed to the ticket counter, rising up on her toes to speak to the attendant. Her hand slid under the glass partition separating her from the man, a Singaporean and maybe forty, and he gripped her hands with both of his, smiling so hard his cheeks bulged. Then the man disappeared, and a second later, the employee door flew open and he swallowed Safia in a hug. She laughed and patted his shoulder, then kissed each cheek. Something worked inside Riley to see her smile like that. The attendant let her go, and they talked briefly before she pressed something into his palms. He went back to his cubicle, then slid a black case across the counter. She slung it over her shoulder, waving before she hurried to Riley.

"Prizes," was all she said as they slipped out and walked down the street.

Riley eyed her and reached to unzip the bag for a peek. Inside, it was padded and filled—with weapons, communications, passports, and money. A backup stash, he thought, zipping it. "He keeps this for you?"

"In a locker, I have the only key." She zipped it shut. "Li is a friend." She glanced at him and shrugged. "A couple years ago, his ten-year-old daughter went missing. I saw him on the news pleading for people to look out for her." Her shoulders moved uneasily and Riley understood that Safia wasn't comfortable with her own valor. "I talked with him, learned about her friends. I found her and two others in a slave ring in Thailand and brought them home."

Like the one Sam's wife Viva was caught in. "Bet that was a big story. The news media didn't get you?"

She shook her head. "I worked with the Thai police and a policewoman did the face work."

"A wee bit outside weapons dealers, isn't it?"

She reddened a little. "The Company thought I was on vacation."

"I bet they knew. They always know."

"Not unless you tell them," she said and wiggled her brows. "I can get around that because if the Company had its way, I'd have a handler and video link all the time." She shook her head. "I do a job and live the life enough. I don't need their noses in the only privacy I can grab."

"I want some of that privacy," he said as he raised his arm to hail a cab. She ducked in first and he scanned the area, then climbed in beside her. The driver twisted in the seat, waiting for instructions.

"The Orchard," he said before she could. She eyed their bloody clothing, but Riley waved the driver on, then said in her ear, "Hiding doesn't mean we have to slum it." In Singapore and a few other countries, he went with the best security and that meant pricey. He supposed it was a bit paranoid— till now.

"We still need to get to the airport."

He groaned. "Are you planning on leaping in front of his jet, or just shooting everyone?"

She gave him a sour look. "I opt for shooting. Webber was lying."

"Should have beaten him up some more then."

"Barasa's not going to Mindanao because Webber knows he can't land. If he does, U.S. Forces will take him into custody. He lands only in countries where he can bribe or has government ties. He went to a lot of trouble to keep Vaghn. I'm betting the wheelchair and that he's leaving are true, but Barasa doesn't have connections there, not enough to set down an aircraft. Too many Philipinos want the Americans to come back after the volcano destroyed the bases." She smiled to herself. "Love the Philippines. Best girls' day out."

"Girls' day?" He eyeballed her disguise.

"Don't look at me like that. This takes work," she said, making a sweeping motion down her body.

"Goody for me." He lowered his gaze to the cleavage so wonderfully displayed.

She reddened. "Fly in, get your hair done, nails, pedicure, even have a pair of shoes custom made. My girlfriend Calista is a chef at a resort there and its the royal treatment." She looked as if savoring her favorite taste just then, and then her wistful smile faded as she focused on her bag of tricks.

"I adore that about you," Riley said offhandedly.

Only her gaze shifted. "What?"

"That you can shift gears and be at the top of your game."

Her expression fell. "I'm not, we're not. People are dead and families are destroyed." Her voice fractured a bit. "We need to outsmart them because they're sure doing it to us." Her words snapped, and Riley didn't respond, thinking of Sebastian and was afraid if he let his anger go, he'd do more harm than good.

"Airport," she ordered the driver.

Riley rescinded it, then met her gaze. "Base has a trace." When she opened her mouth to protest, a given, he said, "Slow down a second. I guarantee you Barasa is out of the country by now. And we can't get on his plane. Authorities aren't going to board it without evidence, especially if he's got a parliament official behind him. Let Base learn where it lands."

"We'll lose opportunities."

Riley felt the energy and anger simmering through her. "We're cut off, but Base isn't. For the love of Mike, the car exploded. We still have Vaghn's hard drive to open."

"That won't make a difference right *now.*"

He reared back and scowled. "Really? Thirty thousand were murdered last night along with my best friend. You don't think we need to know how to anticipate it? Know your enemy and his tools," he reminded. "Whatever he's created, we haven't seen the worst of it yet, and unless you're a genius with explosives, we need another expert because ours is dead!"

She flinched at the last word, and he turned his face away,

staring out the window. After a moment, he rubbed his face hard, but still didn't look at her. Sebastian's image floated in his mind. Knowing he'd died horribly hurt more. He didn't deserve this, no one did. Then she laid her head on his shoulder, slid her hand into his palm. He laced his fingers with hers and felt his rising grief slowly recede.

"I'm sorry," she whispered. "I didn't forget. I've just never had to consider any opinion but my own."

"I was warned," he said, then met her gaze. "Compromise with me, Safia. We've seen enough death for one day."

15 minutes earlier
Private Airstrip, Changi

Barasa stood at the hatch as the sedan skid to a stop on the tarmac. Rahjan hopped out and quickened to the jet.

"I'm glad you were successful." The engines were revving and he was just about to give the order to take off.

"Wouldn't be here if I wasn't." Rahjan snickered, mounting the stairs, then stopped at the threshold and looked toward the water.

Barasa followed his gaze and caught the spiral of smoke in the distance. "Excellent."

Rahjan stepped inside, and Barasa noticed the bandaged cuts, the fresh ones on his face. While Barasa was curious, he paid the man to take care of details. His pilot pulled the hatch closed and told them to take a seat.

"The Geek tell you who they were?" Rahjan inclined his head to the rear and the men securing a blissfully comatose Vaghn.

"No, and it doesn't matter, as long as that marker isn't in his ass and the trails are gone."

"It is, but the Feds aren't dead."

He smiled. "Wouldn't be any sport in it if they were."

Dead agents on his hands was considerably different than agents warned off. The technology in the dart shaped marker said the hunters had government funding.

"The Professor won't like the trail."

Barasa frowned. "I don't give a damn what he wants, I'm taking the risks with that *infant.*"

"You're wanted in five countries," Rahjan said, going to the wet bar and pouring himself two fingers of Jack Daniel's. "They'll find you."

Barasa frowned at the alcohol this early when he was still drinking coffee. "You seem pleased at that."

He glanced. "You pay me to head off the unexpected, but I'm not getting caught with you. They're waiting for this." He waved at the jet and their escape. "You land in Mindanao . . ." He shrugged, still holding the untouched glass. "I hope you like *Adobo* and leg irons."

"And what do you suggest?" Barasa freshened his coffee and took a seat.

"Grow some balls and tell this Professor you'll deliver the package in person or nothing at all."

"And you think I haven't?"

Rahjan frowned, thoughtful, then nodded approval.

"I hand over Vaghn and I've got nothing. No weapon, and no leverage. So where he goes, we do. No pass off until we have what we paid for."

"Good. Because you were greedy enough to promise it before you had it, not me." The aircraft taxied. "And I plan on getting paid the last installment."

Barasa raised his cup. "So do I, my friend. Because selling it will make us wealthy enough to retire."

Rahjan didn't respond. He held the glass near his lips and muttered words Barasa couldn't hear, then tossed his drink back in one swallow. Barasa had seen him do the same a couple times before, but he wouldn't explain the ritual. He left the glass on the bar, then dropped into a seat.

"Retire where? Nobody wants you in their country."

Barasa laughed and settled into the sofa as the jet lifted off the ground. "I'm sure I can find a nice island to buy. But till then, tell the pilot to head northwest."

Rahjan lifted a brow. "For how long?"

"One hour. That should give the Professor plenty of time to understand our position."

Rahjan pulled out a web phone and thumbed keys, then met his gaze. "That's Vietnam."

Barasa sipped. "Communist countries love me."

E Ring
Pentagon

The first pots of coffee were brewing by the time the Joint Chiefs were assembled, the scent of after-shave still fresh as Hank walked to the front of the room and dimmed the lights over the large screen.

"We have the perpetrators from the RZ10 theft." A murmur circled the room. "Tests confirmed the acid explosive used on the UK facility match the residue found on the bodies." The picture of the dead taken by Agent Choufani filled the screen. "They are both former U.S. servicemen declared killed in action in Iraq four years go. Dossiers are in front of you. I regret that the trail ends here. They were paid two million, cash, unmarked. It was still in their possession when they were discovered by Interpol. However, the explosion in Singapore has the characteristics of RZ10, but it's not confirmed. The canister was passed off in Turkey by the mercenaries yesterday. Which of course, means the Singapore blast was not RZ10 but something very similar." His glance went around the room and he knew they understood. Not only were they still missing the canister with no trail to follow, someone was capable of creating something worse—and had used it.

He relayed the details and ended with the bad news that the center of the blast was a CIA station. "We know the agent in charge is alive, but haven't had contact. The agent was tailing an arms dealer suspected of international smuggling." He put up the photo of Cale Barasa and from across the conference room noticed Major Beckham's expression change. "Additionally, the information we have at this moment is in front of you." The preliminary reports were thin, but would have to do.

David had narrowed the satellite transmission to NRI and considering it was the company that created the damned explosive, Hank knew they'd found the source. He wouldn't report to the JCS till he had concrete evidence and he had a mountain of information to read and some people to question before he could point fingers. But the burden of securing the RZ10 was his alone, and Hank shouldered the blame for letting it get away. The Intel leak could have come from his end or the UK side and plugging it up had all analysts working overtime.

He crossed the room, stopping in front of Beckham. "You know that arms dealer?"

Beckham met his gaze. "I've seen him before, when I was in Syria a couple months ago."

"He has Hezbollah ties." He'd read the dossier. Barasa was a slick operator, skimming laws and selling weapons to anyone with the cash.

"Then why is he still walking around free?"

"Maybe this is our chance. I still need contact with the station agent."

"Hell, I can get you that." Beckham stepped outside the war room. Jansen followed and away from the door, Beckham placed a call. "The station agent was on his trail then. She'll know his shoe size."

Beckham let the phone ring several times and frowned, ending the call. "No answer. Not like her either."

Hank scowled. This puzzle was not shaping up fast enough. "Get Deep Six on it. Do what you have to. We need to talk to that agent now."

Singapore

Safia took stock in her failures, wondering how she could have done things differently since waking in Riley's arms this morning. Like a ritual, she forced herself to remember the details, imprint them in her mind and put them into her energy to keep going when things felt hopeless right now. From the wide balcony, she stared out into the city, the hot trade wind pulling at her hair. She reached for the rubber bands, loosened, then popped them when she heard the sirens heading to the damage area. The car explosion was on the local newscasts with a rehash of the accidents on the bridge, and the explosion in the station. *We really need to get this out of Singapore.* The people shouldn't have to pay so dearly, she thought and pushed her fingers into her hair, then massaged her scalp. She'd pulled it a little too tight this time, and worked her eyebrows to get some feeling back. She'd already washed off the extra makeup and blood.

She glanced into the hotel room. Riley leaned his rear on the desk, surfing TV reports and looking grim. She lowered her arms, sighing and for a moment, closed her eyes. The wind snapped at her loose cotton slacks, coasted over her bare arms and shoulders, her camisole top making her feel cool and lazy. She was glad Riley talked her into buying it from the hotel gift shop.

He'd been right about other things, and she'd freely admitted it to his face. She liked that he didn't gloat and just kissed her, but after a quick call on a public phone to Ellie, she'd learned Barasa's jet had taken off quite easily from one of the private strips. Vaghn was caught on a surveillance camera being physically carried onto the jet. Sedated, she thought, and they'd seen the shooter board shortly after. She recognized the clothes, but not his face. No question about who ordered it, though the only part of Barasa to show up on the security cameras was his feet. He'd boarded from the far side of the craft, away from view. Yes, I'm watching you, she thought, impatient to get back to her technology. She was grounded from her Intel until Base assured them they weren't pinpointed.

Her comm-links were her only connection to the outside, to the real world, and not the dark and dirty. Without them, she felt incredibly alone and detached. Ellie had all the numbers to the fresh equipment, but Riley made Safia promise not to "battery up" to the point of rigging the devices so she couldn't. A bit over the line, but she conceded when he downloaded the airport surveillance videos. His caution was warranted, she'd give him that. She was rarely the target.

She suspected their hunters had taken the easy route and followed them, maybe a tag team, but getting past the alarm on the car to rig it on the ignition took a specialist. Northern Singapore station agents were fanned out and rousting contacts to learn who could have done it, but Safia didn't waste the mental energy. They had other avenues to search.

She turned back into the hotel room and went to the bag she'd left on a sofa, sitting, then pulling out her equipment. Riley groaned. "Stop," she said. "It's a part of me."

"More like an addiction."

"Yes, true. But it's a lifeline. Other than the criminals and my assets, I rarely talk to anyone sane and good."

"I'm here."

She looked up, and thought, *you are such an ass, Troy. You read people and can't read him?*

He crooked his finger, and she threw her head back and laughed, left the sofa and crossed to him, sliding into his arms. "That would get most men killed, you know. Or at least a couple broken bones."

He ran his hands up and down her back. "I consider it a gift."

She met his gaze.

"From you," he clarified.

"I know I'm a hard case sometimes." His smile widened and she felt her cheeks warm. She blushed a lot around him, she realized. "Fine, all the time." She put up a hand to halt any additions to her flaws, but she wasn't going to whine that her job was solitary. She'd chosen it. "I'm not used to having people I care about around me while I do my job."

His smile softened and something in his eyes scared her a little. "I like you too."

She floated her hands up his arms, clasped them behind his neck. He'd entered her life briefly years ago and disappeared, but at this moment, she felt as if they'd never parted. It had nothing to do with the lives they'd led between then and now, but somewhere else, in a place only her heart seemed to recognize. She could feel it quicken, skipping faster as he lowered his head.

"It's okay, love," he whispered. "I won't hurt you."

"Don't make promises you can't keep."

He paused, his lips a breath from hers. "This one I will."

"Prove it," she said curling her hand behind his neck and pulling him down. She kissed him longingly, a mold of lips and tongue that sent desire pulling through her. It made her eager to be naked, and when his big hands swept her body in a wild ride, she wanted more, and nothing between them. She slid her hands under the hem of his tee-shirt, peeling it up his chest and over his head.

Safia's eyes widened at the slash of scars on his torso. "Riley, Jesus." She stepped back, stunned.

"Not as pretty as I used to be," he said, self-conscious.

"What happened?" He had jagged scars on his ribs, another surgical scar on his shoulder and down both arms.

He sat on the sofa and said, "I was buying conflict diamonds off smugglers and it went sour. Not before the dam broke in Sri Lanka." He shrugged. "I went with it."

Frowning, she remembered skimming an Intel report from Dr. Tom Rhodes on the Kukule Ganga Dam and the acres washed away with hundred of homes and lives. She lowered to the sofa beside him, and rubbed her thumb over a bullet hole near his heart.

"This was point blank." She could tell by the clean shape and from behind, the tear was large.

"Yeah, he's dead though, along with a few of his pals." He leaned back in the cushions, throwing his arm over the back and told her about the dam explosions, and that he'd been in a coma for weeks. It had taken him nearly two years to recover. "I had to learn to walk again." He knocked on his knee. "Lots of new hardware though."

She shifted on the sofa to face him.

"If Logan hadn't been there I'd be dead. Still dead," he corrected, staring at his hands. "He revived me a couple times." He met her gaze. "Kinda puts a lot of things in perspective."

"Like what?"

"I'm too old to be doing this."

She made a disbelieving sound. He was only about three years older than her. "Why, you're fine. You kicked some heavy duty booty today."

"Belfast street fighting," he said. "I don't want to be doing this when I'm fifty."

"What do you want to do then?"

She regretted asking when he said, "Hold my children, love a wife."

Her brows rose, and she stood quickly. "I hope you find that."

"Maybe I have."

She spun around, not at all happy about that suggestive look. "No, not me." He smiled wide. "No! Are you nuts? We don't know each other. God, Riley don't talk like that." She shook her head, rushing out of his reach. "Don't." She turned her back, staring out the window at the waning day. *He doesn't want* me. She was too empty inside for a man like him. A man with a wealth of love and family showing in everything he did. She didn't know if she had it in her to consider more than this mission.

She felt him approach slowly, and moaned softly, awareness ringing through her. She wasn't certain she wanted it. She didn't turn around, rebellion pricking her, and she kept her back to him, but he stayed near, letting her feel the heat of his body, grow accustomed, then, when she could barely stand it another moment, he slid his arms around her waist and pulled her back against him. Safia went soft inside and laid her head back on his shoulder. So nice, she thought, but had to be realistic. She wasn't exactly every mother's dream for her son. God. Even thinking like that scared her.

"Don't believe this is any more than a working relationship. I can't think like that. I can't." She started to push his hands away, but he tightened, leaning his cheek against hers. She released a long sigh and nuzzled his face. How could she fear and want at the same time? "You want what I can't give."

"Have you tried?"

She dropped her head forward. "Oh Riley, why are you digging so deep?"

"I like you. I want to know you. Is that so difficult?"

"In my life, yes it is."

"It can be easy."

She turned on him. "For that I'd have to give it up and I won't."

He reared back, surprised. "Who says you have to?"

"No one. Me." She glared, pushed out of his arms. "Damn you, Donovan." She strode into the other room, flipping at papers and room service menus, then finally stopped and faced him.

"Maybe I was wrong." He walked near, the scars an insult on his lean sculptured body. "Wrong in thinking there was more to you than fighting the good fight."

She tried moving past him. "There isn't."

"Liar," he said, pulling her smoothly into his arms.

Denial was on the edge of her lips, but he covered them with his own. Safia capitulated, her willpower and her excuses disintegrating with every slide of his mouth over hers.

She fought terrorists, the world's most evil, and wasn't afraid of much. But up against Riley Donovan's incredible mouth and tender heart, she felt annihilated, weaponless. And then she didn't care, and kissed him with total surrender.

"There you are," Riley whispered, and felt the change in her, the way her body relaxed into his and let him feel all her luscious curves.

"How many women have you charmed so easily?"

He scoffed, rubbing his mouth down her throat and loving that she tipped her head back. "I just listen," he murmured. "I never got a word in edgewise with my family."

A prick of longing stung her heart, and she tried smothering it, pushing it far down where it didn't affect her work. But it reared and made her want more of this, she thought as his mouth moved over her jaw, then lower. Her hands were busy on his jeans, flipping the button, loving that his muscles contracted as she sent the zipper down. She shed her job with her clothes as he stripped her down to her skin.

"Then let's not talk."

Riley let his gaze roam over her, the scars she'd earned over the years marring her beautiful body. "Not in my plan." He swept his hand down her curves, cupping her breast.

"Smart man, oh yeah," she purred. "That's good." His tongue slid over the thin scar that stretched from hip to navel; then he found another and she pulled him nearer, gliding her hands over his muscled contours. He had them in spades.

"I'm a little out of practice."

"Then you've been doing it with the wrong man," he growled and she inhaled, trapped by his soulful blue eyes. God. She wanted to run, and run to him. He'd slipped under her skin, made her see a life without isolation. Made her want it. She'd never entertained the thought and rarely felt jilted out of a steady love life. Until now. Until she understood and experienced and, God, hungered for it. She'd lived her life telling herself that eliminating fanatics like the group that killed her family was worth giving up that part of herself. But as his hands swept luxuriously over her body, she knew her thinking had changed.

And would keep changing. Riley was stubborn, but hard to resist, especially when he knew exactly what buttons to push. Like now, his hand palming her behind, and doing that slow upward glide that sent shivers of pleasure over her spine. She wiggled deeper into his arms, his mouth plying over her throat, her jaw, then her mouth. Oh man, she liked that the best, she thought, then changed her mind when he lifted her, pulling her legs around his hips, then walked through the suite and tumbled her to the big bed.

"Your reputation precedes you," she murmured as his lips skated over her breast, a warm tongue snaking around her nipple. His lips tugged, and heat spiraled under her skin. He was a charmer, loved women, and she experienced the reality of it in his expert touch. She was just damn glad it was all over her and gasped hard when he slid lower and nudged her thighs apart. His mouth found her center.

She let out a little shriek of his name. He didn't answer, then she couldn't, his lips and tongue doing incredible slidy things and she felt the burn all the way up to her hair. Then she fell off the edge of the world when he pushed her thigh over his shoulder. He devoured her, sliding two fingers inside that made her bow off the bed with a guttural moan.

He rose up, smiling, and in the slickest move, sheathed himself with a condom and slid into her. She inhaled and arched, her body liquid beneath him. She pushed against him, his groan that harsh male sound every woman wanted to hear. He was as helpless as she was, his trembling striking her almost like a blow. She'd never done that to a man, and felt herself sinking when he leaned down slowly, bracing himself. His gaze locked with hers and he tucked his hand under her hips, bringing her to him. With each withdrawal and plunge, he watched her, toyed and stroked until she was hurting for air.

"I adore you," he said deeply, then kissed her, melting away the rebellion instinctively rising in her. In his arms, she reveled in the freedom, smiling when she rolled him to his back and sat up. He pushed deeper and she held his gaze, her hips undulating and taking him with her.

Riley didn't think he'd seen anything so exotic, her dark hair unbound and sweeping her elbows, teasing across her round breasts, and he sat up, pulling her closer, smiling when she laughed, when she asked him to keep rocking her world.

"It'd be me pleasure, love," he said and bucked, grinning when she quaked and lavished in his arm. Her hands dribbled over his body, feeling where they joined. The pulse burst through him, and he pushed her on her back, held her as the sensual eruption clawed up his spine. He pumped harder, a hand on the headboard, the other sliding beneath her hips again and pulling her up to greet him.

He watched her whiskey brown eyes, saw the tears well slowly. Emotions rose with their desire, and Riley wanted her—all of her. Greedy, he withdrew fully, her gasp of pleasure galvanized him, and he plunged again and again.

She cupped his jaw, whispered his name, and he begged, "Give yourself to me, Safia."

Her mouth crushed over his, her body a wildfire beneath him and she held tight, the crush of passion spreading through her and into him. Her little gasps fueled him, her whispers and the slide of their bodies breaking something inside him. He thrust once more, the eruption spilling and she dug her fingers into his hips, grinding as he whispered his truth in Gaelic. They collapsed in a tangle of arms and legs on wrinkled sheets.

He couldn't move, wondering where his finesse went when he was with her, and he struggled to catch his breath when her fingers were sliding up his spine. He leaned back to meet her gaze, swiping her hair from her face. A tear slid into her temple and her brown eyes captured his soul.

"Oh Riley," she said, sweeping her fingers across his mouth. "I hate you and love you for that."

He smiled. "God love ya, lass, you're a difficult woman to please."

She rolled him on his back, laying herself over him and Riley thought he could live a long time just like this.

"You could keep trying," she said.

And he did.

Fourteen

Marina Bay
Singapore

Max frowned when the door buzzed and slid the pan off the burner, then crossed the condominium to answer it. A petite woman smiled up at him.

"Hi. You must be Maxwell."

He recognized her voice. "Ellie?"

She flashed a quick smile. "Yes." She showed him her ID. "I have a key, but I didn't want to barge in, in case you weren't alone." She peered, and sniffed the air. "Cooking?"

"Guy's gotta eat. Join me." Max stepped back to let her pass, then closed the door. "Who would I have here anyway?"

She walked with him to the kitchen. "I never close doorways of thought. Anything is possible."

Well hell. She was just a little thing, and as young as she sounded. Younger now, he thought, yet Safia had said she was a Marine. "How did you make it through boot camp?"

She smiled, and he'd expect to see her dark blond self at a football game or a Dairy Queen, not running intelligence for CIA. He suddenly felt very old.

"Four older brothers. I graduated top rifle score of my series," she said as he pulled the pan back on the burner and stirred. "I was slated for sniper school, but since life expectancy in the field is two minutes and I'm a tech geek, this was safer." On the other side of the counter, she slid onto a stool and said, "I've had to cut all communications with Riley and Safia."

Max frowned. He'd signed off with them when they'd gone to talk to Safia's assets. Then she told him why. "Good God. The car?" Max leaned back against the fridge, thankful Safia used her tech toys to start her car. "Where are they?"

"Underground."

"Good." Though knowing Riley, he was probably enjoying his confinement. "Two attacks in one day is risky, even for a criminal." He rubbed his mouth, tumbling theories over in his head. "The dock attack was a lure with the biomarker." He waved it off. It had the earmarks of a game to the Ghurka soldier. "But her car was stored in the garage here. Anyone could have tampered with it. *If* they knew her identity of the day and where to look." He leapt forward to move the pan off the burner and stir. "Possible, but not probable given the time frame. It's been a day since Vaghn came out of hiding and hell broke loose. However," he said, stopping to search for plates, "she'd driven the car all over town, restarted it. So, it was either planted and detonated by someone on sight, or rigged on the spot to the starter, which isn't that difficult if you know what you're doing. Either way, it was planted while they were talking to the assets."

Ellie gathered utensils and laid them out. "Do you always answer your own questions?"

"Free association. Try it." Max dished up the stir-fry. "Now that we know when it was planted, what do we know that they don't?"

She frowned, sliding onto the stool.

He put up a finger. "We know who they are. They probably don't know us personally, other than we're making trouble for them." Another finger went up. "They're willing to kill anyone, anywhere. We're not. Put that at the top."

"You like lists."

She gestured to his larger than necessary list of items in Vaghn's backpack and Max knew he bordered on obsessive, but he'd brought the damn thing into the station. "Vaghn's backpack. Riley and I looked through it. It was normal guy stuff. Games, music, phone, a pen light, though he had a gun, cheap and pretty dirty. It'd probably misfire if he used it." He took a seat beside her and ate. "Vaghn's smart enough to create any weapon, but he can't do it without that." He flicked at the screen with the duplicate hard drive that wouldn't do anything but exist. "He had a death grip on it from the get-go and the encryption is way out there. They don't know we have a copy, but then, only Vaghn can open it. The little creep holds all the cards. I just want to read his hand."

Ellie laughed softly and Max glanced. "Did you extract anything from the Triad house? They were chatty."

She nodded, moppy curls bouncing. "I confirmed that the incoming caller was the same number that the two phones had in common." She showed him a picture on her web phone. "The only woman. Safia calls her Red Shoes."

Max frowned at the photo, thinking pretty but kind of sharp, as if her elegance was painted in place.

"I did a synthesized wash on the Triad house, removing each, one at a time to single them out. In operation at that moment was a computer, three active cell phones, and four numbers."

"Four?"

"Vaghn's computer is its own communication. Attach a head set with a mic and you're good to go. Satellite capable too." He groaned. "They were all working at the same time, but it was the woman's that was incoming. Red Shoes doesn't match any passport photo so far, and the cell number is dead," Ellie said. "No battery, no signal. It's just parts."

"Smart cookie," he murmured, eating.

"They aren't missing a beat, even with all our interference." Her sad tone made him look up. "Red Shoes would have to be using that particular phone to even start a triangulation. Or at the very least, have the battery back in. I have alerts set up to let me know if she comes online with it." She wiggled the phone, then hooked it on her shorts. "She could just use another one and we've got nothing."

"She's the money and while we *should* follow the cash, we're missing a key piece." She frowned, her pixie nose wrinkling. "If there wasn't a bomb in the pack and right now, let's say no, then what triggered that station explosion?" We have two hitters, Max thought, but he didn't want to voice his thoughts just yet. He needed evidence.

"Forensics is still testing, and I don't monitor the workings of the station, but I do know that there wasn't a gas line and locks were engaged. Anything on site is gone, but all data files are backed up with Langley." She frowned for a second. "The Company would have known because it's automatic, like in a power outage." She reached for her phone. "I've got some friends who might help pick this apart."

Max chewed, swallowed, and shook his head. "Keep this between us. They wouldn't shut down links if they thought it was just Barasa tracking them." Then he gave her a morsel because he needed her help. "We have a new player."

She nodded, quiet for a second and Max didn't think they had the same suspicions till she spoke. "The other stations know she's offline and why, Max. You don't think there's a leak in the Company, do you?"

He scoffed and tried not to burst her bubble. "Wouldn't be the first time. But with the right software, anyone can trace a cell phone. Moms do it on their kids' phones."

"The car bomb was a professional job."

"Oh hell, yes. But the house, another story." He shook his head. "It doesn't add up." When she didn't respond, he glanced up. She toyed with her fork, her brow knitting. "She's fine." He nudged her.

"I know, but—" Ellie met his gaze. "Safia's made enemies. Most are in prison or dead, but some, like Barasa, slipped through."

"She's tried for conviction on him before?"

She shook her head, picked at her meal. "He's produced documentation or paid fines." She tipped a look at him. "Or witnesses disappear. Mostly that. But a case has never made it past international investigation. Never to court. Probably why she breaks a lot of rules."

He could tell that bothered her. "Such as?"

Ellie looked away, pursing her lips, and Max wondered if she was fighting loyalty or her clearance in telling him something that might be classified. He understood that. "You don't have to elaborate."

"Oh, it's not illegal or anything," she rushed to say. "She takes big risks, alone, a lot. She has a few agents who can help her when she needs an extra pair of eyes, but she rarely let's anyone in." She met his gaze. "I was *really* shocked when she asked me to bring Riley online with her communication link to me."

"She did it without authorization."

"*I* did it *for* her. It's a misuse of government equipment, if you want to get technical, but fortunately she's rarely wrong." Her brows knit deeper. "She really doesn't like to be outsmarted. Expect crazy."

"Honey, that's what Dragon One is all about."

"I know. I read your dossiers. Y'all are too old to be so daring."

Max looked up sharply. "Who you calling old, little girl?"

She grinned, taking the last bite of her meal. "My dad is only about eight years senior to you."

Good God. "Well thanks, peanut, that just made my day."

NSA
Near Washington, D.C.

When Nolan Deets admitted he couldn't break the encryption on the satellite transmission, his frustration settled somewhere between his shoulderblades. He'd created a program for David's stream and each effort bounced off its firewall. A transmission this deeply encrypted was never good news. Without the program to run it, he'd tried duplicating it, unsuccessfully. The encryption was for this particular data strand. Nothing else like it, he thought, and glanced between the two computers and the rapid attempts to decode. But a piece of the stream wasn't doing any of them much good, and David Lorimer was trying to gather segments. So far, it had bounced to eleven different server locations across the globe.

He turned to the third computer and opened a window, then dialed the phone. The video screen came up with David's image.

"Any luck?" the analyst said.

"If I had more time to understand the creator maybe, but no. Breaking it is impossible, at least for me."

"Oh hell."

"Yeah. It's kicking at all my brain cells. I think there might be a certain sequence of steps before you enter the primer to unlock it. If you don't, it automatically alters the firewall and locks me out."

David frowned. "I've never heard of a program that does that."

"Got to admire the genius behind it, eh? The encryption was made for this stream, and its black secure. I can't go at it much more. The firewall is like fabric weaving tighter. Eventually it won't allow me to bump its wall."

"Jeez, I need to take lessons from this guy."

"Do we know who created it?"

"Not yet, but it was sent from NRI to Asia."

Nolan's featured pulled tight. "Then we're running out of time."

David frowned.

"It doesn't matter were it landed right now, but who has the codes to open it," Nolan said. "Someone went through a lot of trouble to hide this—in every direction. From the Sat

Send to all this coding. It makes it that much harder to re-trieve the transmission. I wouldn't want to advise you on your job . . ." David looked eager for the advice. "But in your trace, look for a server that's on, but inactive. If they're hiding it with encryption, you can bet the final resting place of this thing isn't in friendly hands," Nolan said. "And they have access to it."

"Yeah, and we don't."

Singapore

Safia groped for the ringing phone and rolled on her side, then switched on the light. She checked the number, frowning, then answered. "Beckham, do you have any idea what time it is here?" Thirteen hours difference, she thought.

"You weren't asleep."

"But I was very busy." As she spoke, Riley nibbled a path over her bare hip, then up the curve of her spine. She shivered and tried to listen to Beckham when she wanted the entire OP to just go away for a little longer.

"This line is not secure," he warned.

"Then why are you calling me on it?" How did he get this number anyway? Then she realized Ellie gave it up.

"We need to know what you do," he said cryptically. "Nang Qi Road is significant."

"I'll say." She glanced at Riley and knew he'd heard. That was the station address and she felt a familiar rush chase up her spine. They knew what caused that destruction and if the Joint Chiefs were calling, it meant military grade explosives.

"Call back on secure lines through my Base."

Beckham confirmed the time, but before he hung up he asked, "Why didn't anyone alert HQ that you were unharmed?"

She frowned, glanced at Riley. "Ask them. Base followed SOP before the cut off."

"Someone dropped the ball then."

"It was a little crazy," she said and ended the call, then contacted Ellie. "The reason you let Beckham have contact was what?" Riley touched her shoulder, but Safia pulled away, angry with Ellie for breaking her orders.

"The DDO ordered it."

"No excuse. He's not in the field. His car didn't explode and kill a dozen people!" She shouldn't have to say a word. Ellie knew her job, and it made Safia wonder who was pushing her buttons from the other end. Besides Beckham. "Someone knew our moves. We were tracked!"

"Negative. No trace on you or anyone in the area then."

That brought her up short. Then they were tailed, she thought and the bomb placed while they were close.

"And I scrambled Beckham's signal, or I wouldn't have allowed the call."

"I want to believe I can trust you to have my back, Ell."

"You can!"

Safia ignored the sting in her tone. Ellie was good at her job, but a little intimidated by authority. "Then keep them away till I give the order. I want isolated lines before any further contact and that includes the JCS or the Company."

"They can cut me off," she warned.

"They aren't that stupid," she said, then ended the call and looked at Riley. "Why would the Thailand office not confirm to the Company?"

"You work alone, Safia. How often do you hand over information?"

"Good point," she said. "I don't. Base does. I rarely speak with Washington or Langley." She let out a breath, shaking off her annoyance. "They get in the middle of it and muck it up, like they're doing now. They have a bird's view, not the rats'. I know what I'm doing. I've been chasing weapons for ten years."

He frowned softly. "Killian's wife did too."

She smiled slightly. "We started with drug smuggling rings. Alexa used her assets, I use mine." She shrugged. "She had more patience to get under deep cover." Alexa was a beauty and she used it to distract, to slip into the very homes and lives of arms dealers. A pair of tits and ass for the good ol' U.S.A. she used to say. Safia masqueraded to get close to follow the dealers to the transporters. But Alexa had built a cover reputation on moving weapons through her antique business and took them out of circulation. They would have made a great team if not for Lania Price and her compulsion to manipulate everyone.

"She's pregnant. Due anytime."

Safia stilled, then laughed to herself. "*That* I want to see. Kids terrified her."

"Not you?"

She eyed him, and knew where this was leading. "Not at all. Children are always the innocent. They do as they're taught and shown." She'd been showered in love as a child, her mother her best friend even when she was a teen and rebellious. Then she looked down at her hands. An old ache, one she hadn't visited in years, churned to life. "No, kids don't scare me." She met his gaze, and swallowed. "And since we're being so honest, I can't have any either." She flipped back the sheet and marked the scar from hip to navel. "Terrorists made sure of it."

His features tightened with sympathy, yet when he started to speak, she pressed her fingers to his lips. "Don't. Please. I've heard it all."

He caught her fingers and said, "I'm sure you have. I'm a guy, I can't judge and don't want to, but thanks for telling me."

She lifted a brow. She didn't know what to make of that, but with Riley, she had to think differently. Visiting old pains was useless, especially when nothing would change.

"Are you always this prickly when you wake?"

"Yes. Intolerably moody." She didn't think that would discourage any ideas of continuing this interlude, but couldn't entertain any either. She swung her legs over the side of the bed. "Get that tight behind moving, Donovan. The JCS will want to have a chat with you and Dragon One."

He grabbed her back, wrestling her to the bed, and then hovered over her, naked and strong. "Let them wait a wee bit longer."

She was all for that, but . . . "They *are* the boss of me, you know."

He held her gaze as he nudged her thighs apart, settling between, and Safia arched, tingling heat skating up her body. "Bad guys wait for no one." Yet she slid her hand down his chest, fingers wrapping him, guiding him.

"I have my priorities for the moment." He filled her in one smooth push. "Tactical assault on a sour mood."

She smiled. He'd already succeeded, but of course, she didn't tell him that and let him keep trying—delicious mood achieved.

Jason stirred, feeling as if he were climbing out of a dark, narrow tunnel. He didn't want to come out. His skin felt on fire and he stopped moving, his breathing too fast. The last thing he remembered was that Rahjan guy injecting him with some drug. Everything else was a blank. He couldn't name the day but he listened to his surroundings. On a jet, he thought. Yet the murmur of a news reporter drifted and he smelled the aroma of food. His stomach recoiled and cramped. He kept his eyes closed, the seat vibrating beneath him. He licked his lips, his tongue swollen and fuzzy. He felt a presence lingering near, but his lids were heavy and he didn't give a damn about talking to anyone. He wanted to stay right where he was until the pasty taste in his mouth went away.

"Wake up," a deep voice said. He recognized Rahjan and he mentally flinched, expecting the sting of his curved knife again.

Rahjan nudged him hard and he forced his eyes open, suddenly shivering uncontrollably. Was this detox? "What the hell did you give me?" God, it hurt to talk.

"Morphine, a little cocaine." He shrugged big shoulders

and Jason noticed the fresh cuts on his face. Good. "Any-thing to shut your ass up. You scream like a woman." He handed him a bottle of water and Jason broke it open and drank. He snatched it back. "Slowly, asshole," he said. "I don't want to clean up your puke."

Jason grabbed for it and the guy held it out of his reach, smiling, then tossed it to him.

"Prick," he muttered, yet felt his stomach churn, his mouth watering. Christ. It took several minutes before he could move without his stomach coiling, and he leaned out to look down the aisle between the seats. There were about a dozen regular airplane seats in the rear behind him, but the front looked like a living room with sofas and tables. Barasa was stretched out on a section, watching a flat screen TV. The news reports on the explosion were on every channel. The number of dead changed with each broadcast, but Jason didn't want to see it and turned away. They were unearthing bodies now.

The remnants of the drugs lingered, his mind still foggy, and he inspected his wounds, surprised to find them covered in fresh bandages and a soft stretchy covering. He could feel the tug of stitches in his thigh and thought of Donovan. He'd made his life miserable and he hoped the bastard was blown to smithereens. Though he never cared for the saying, it satis-fied. This deal was planned to the minute until Donovan.

He grabbed the blanket someone had tossed on him and pulled it over his head, then reached from beneath enough to close the shield on the window. He drifted back to sleep, wondering how he was going to get out of this with his life—and his money.

Marina Bay, Singapore

Safia was impressed. Even short team members, Max and Riley were formidable. They'd had several hours until the satellite link up and Max had gone to the team jet, *Dragon 6*, and retrieved gear. It filled her condo. She stood back as Riley connected wires under the dining table, now in the living room as a command post, of sorts. He rigged her obscenely large-screen TV for the satellite connection to Deep Six. More equipment, scanners, listening devices and ammunition lined the coffee table along with some Thai take out. Max, she'd learned, was a bottomless pit. The guy loved his food.

She glanced at the clock and the countdown to link with Deep Six. Ellie had followed orders and blocked against any breeching. After the car bomb, Safia wasn't trusting her own network.

Riley backed out from under the table, and stood. "That should do it." He turned it all on and he said, "We have tone." Safia watched the flat screen and smiled when the feed blinked to life.

"Wicked cool," she murmured.

Riley smiled. "And for your enjoyment . . ." He tapped keys and she watched the flat screen divide, satellite feed on the left, already searching for Red Shoes' phone, the right waiting for video connection from Deep Six and the brass. Holding its place was a white screen with a red and gold dragon curled around D-1. The team covered all the bases and her coffee table was spread with a few gadgets she didn't recognize. Max promised her a lesson, and she smiled when he showed her a hand control for the computers. He smiled for the first time since returning from the jet. He'd stopped near the station blast sight, she thought. Uncovering the dead was a slow, gory process and she thought of the 9-11 victims. No loss is easy to take, but Max couldn't accept that Sebastian didn't exist anymore. He hadn't witnessed it and without a body to bury, it was tough on him.

"We're all set," Max said.

Safia glanced around. The stools from the kitchen counter were at the dining table, a line of computers and screens. She hoped Max could control it all because she wasn't planning on hanging around here. Barasa's plane was in the air. Despite all this technology, they hadn't advanced the Op enough to stop thousands of deaths.

Impatient for progress, she picked up a lidless box, frowning at the tiny button-like devices secured in foam, then frowned at Riley, holding it up.

"GPS markers," he said, gathering electrical lines and binding them. "Max builds them into just about anything. He's logistics and very protective of the equipment. D-1 doesn't have endless government funds."

"I can get us what we need."

"I knew you had pull."

She smiled. "Not really, but I can throw a good tantrum when necessary."

"I want to see that."

"You've seen enough," she flipped back in a low tone and he chuckled to himself. She turned, reading through the recent reports from the field while Riley tried for the umpteenth time to open the hard drive.

Less than eighteen hours alone with Safia just wasn't enough. But Riley knew better. She was afraid of him now. Scared of what she was feeling, he supposed, but he didn't try to ease it either. She was tied so tightly to her job, she dismissed any relationship out of hand. Too quickly. But if she thought what was going on between them was a one-time thing, he was ready to change her mind. He'd never had a woman touch his soul like the pretty Egyptian. But then, she did that years ago in Serbia too.

When she'd come out of her bedroom, the one room he'd yet to see, she was back to being cast-iron CIA. Putting a chink in her armor was second to opening the hard drive. Ellie, separated the cell phone streams just before the explosion and learned that one line wasn't used at that particular time. But Barasa, Red Shoes, and Vaghn's were all active.

Right now, the computer firewall was just pissing him off. He rubbed his face, then pushed his fingers into his hair. "The sequence is useless. Ellie's run a program that would try any combination. It failed a half hour ago." Logan wasn't having any success, but he was also preparing to join Tessa with a National Geographic expedition.

Riley rested his rear on the edge of the tall stool, smiling his thanks when Safia handed him a fresh cup of coffee. She was guzzling back a pot and still yawning. The reasons made him smile, and she blushed and turned away, but he caught her sexy glance. The last time he saw it they were tumbling across the sheets and falling on the floor.

Focus. He stood as if it would clear his head, then crossed to the empty dining room, grabbing the bag of trash from Vaghn's hideout. He started to toss it, then decided to have one more look. He dumped it on fresh newspaper and examined it again.

"We've gone through that. It's rubbish," Safia said, leaning against the counter. "And it's starting to stink."

He agreed. Finding nothing new he shoved it back in the bag, then hesitated, staring at the paperback novel, then flipped through it. "Vaghn didn't read this book. There's something in it." He looked up. "He didn't read fiction, said he never learned anything new and that he made fiction real with his weapons." Riley ran his finger down the spine of the book, then looked at Max. "When have you known Sebastian to not abuse a paperback?"

Sitting in front of a computer, Max spun on the stool. "Never."

"Look at this. The spine isn't even cracked." He tossed the book to Max and Safia stepped closer.

"Sebastian got his money's worth and never exchanged books," Max told Safia. "If he didn't—hadn't—owned the Craw Daddy, he'd have a bookstore." Max turned the book over in his hands, then gave it back to Riley. "Other than the stains, it looks new."

"Then why throw it away?" Safia asked.

"Exactly."

Riley flipped through it again, spotting a graphic, then read the paragraph before it, realizing there was some sort of code in a grid of symbols.

But the hard drive files were locked up, the only access they could get was Vaghn's email and a War Craft gaming program. It was like bashing his head against a wall, anything he tried got bumped back and it was harder the next time. He picked up a slip of paper Max found, and at the computer, he compared the scrambled doodling sequence to the novel. "Two symbols make a close match. The trash sequence he doodled is similar to the graph."

"*Clever* boy," Safia said and grabbed a pad and pen, then sat beside him.

Riley punched in a search. He'd done it once before but didn't try it with only the symbols. He found an email that nearly matched and opened it.

"Max was right. It was a spam address and sent to millions, but it's just garbled trash. The average person would delete it. Vaghn deleted the email, but he replied. It was empty."

"How many replies?" Safia said. "If he sent that out, we're so screwed."

Max nudged her. "Don't ask for trouble, but good conspiracy. What I don't get is what that does." He flicked at the screen that was a multitude of swirling colors.

Riley used the hand held scanner and uploaded the novel's symbols, then Safia took the paperback with her to the table and copied the grid containing it.

"Only one symbol matches," she said, "And there isn't anything like it on a keyboard."

"Ellie says it's not a keystroke, it's a graphic," Max said, the comm-link itching in his ear. He highlighted it, dropped it into a new file, then opened the graphic. "It's wider than the other numbers and letters. Different font too." He enlarged it. "It's the letter I."

"More to it," Safia said from his right and Riley stood to look. "See the curls on the edge?" Max enlarged it again and she pointed to the scrolly ends of the letter. "The lines don't match up."

"It's got something under it," Riley said. "Another layer."

"I think it's three dimensional," Safia said. "We don't have its program, so it'll view differently. Try reversing it."

Max did and the image on the screen flipped. "Ooh-rahh," he said, leaning in closer. "Greek letter, Iota. The back of the graphic is different from the front. Looks like glyphs or cave drawings."

"Man, this guy is just scary smart," Safia said, peering.

"I don't get the purpose," Max said, pushing back from the computer, frustrated. "Because it doesn't unlock Vaghn's hard drive programs."

Riley frowned. "Then we're still missing a piece."

"Or three. Maybe they have some of it," Safia said, inclined her head to the flat screen suddenly flickering to life.

Riley crossed to the living room and faced the screen as the image cleared. "Lorimer," he said when he saw the analyst.

"Hey Riley, how are the new knee caps holding up?"

"Enough to keep me standing," he said, smiling. He was still on crutches last time he'd seen David.

Safia sent him an arched look. "Is there anyone you *don't* know?"

Riley leaned in, pulling off his headset to say, "You, lass, and not nearly well enough." She sputtered, blushing. "Though I must say, we covered a lot of territory last night."

She didn't have a response. A first, he was certain.

Riley was about to put the headset back on when his attention focused on a familiar face in the background behind David. Safia nudged him, nodding to the screen, and wanting an explanation. "Colonel Henry Jansen," he said lowly, the mic still off. "He was my company commander when we met. A captain. Going after Sam was disobeying his orders."

And they were asking for his help now? "He busted you?"

"It was hard to get a conviction when we were a success *and* right. But no one would give up who put the crunch on the rescue. It should have been the NATO commander, but Jansen's the one who told me to drop it and never look back." Riley left the Corps, more disillusioned, a little under pressure, but it was Sam who convinced him to give up the Fundraiser hunt. He'd moved on, but he wanted the truth to put it to rest. When he stepped out of camera range, she glanced at him, confused.

"They're calling you, Agent Troy, not me."

Off camera, she gripped his hand, and murmured, "We're going to find out the truth of that. It will just have to wait a little longer."

Then she took a step in front of the video camera and folded her arms, her hip cocked. It made him smile. She was just cruising for a fight and he sat back to watch the show.

fifteen

Situation Room
Pentagon

General Al Gerardo rolled a quarter over his knuckles as they waited for the satellite link to operatives in the field. Almost anyone who worked with him knew of the tell, Hank thought. He was concentrating, and since it usually spawned brilliance, people backed off. Gerardo had just been informed that Dragon One was involved, but the agent in charge had put a lock on communications after her vehicle had been bombed. Shut down so tight, they had to learn that from another station. Beckham charmed her Intel officer into giving up a contact number, but only for a limited time and she jammed everything else around the number to keep her agent underground.

No one in the room needed an update on Dragon One. General Joe McGill had made a personal call and Gerardo already debriefed the brass sitting round the oak table on D-1's recovery of Silent Fire and the schematics, along with nearly a dozen arms dealers in toe tags. No one was going to bark at the help where RZ10 was concerned. The consensus was locate and destroy it. A-sap, priority one.

The connection made, he kept the volume down, listening to the bit of conversation between Singapore and Deep Six.

Hank pulled his mic away and leaned to Gerardo and said, "McGill's sacred six, capturing Price, and a higher clearance than most of the people in this building? How come they're not on the Company payroll?"

"They'd have to take a pay cut," Gerardo said. "And they don't follow anyone's orders but their own. Look at their Service Record Books. Donovan disobeyed direct orders and went into Serbia alone to get a pilot left for dead."

Hank's features tightened, and he looked at the screen. "I know Donovan." He recognized the agent's name now. "The pilot was Captain Sam Wyatt. Donovan was court-martialed for disobeying orders, but not convicted. I was with NATO forces then. They wouldn't allow the *Nimitz* to launch a search because of the heavy fighting near civilians, but Donovan didn't listen. Agent Troy helped them back to the border. Donovan insisted command stalled a rescue to get the NATO countries and congress behind the conflict."

"Did we?" Gerardo asked.

"Our hands were tied then, sir. U.N. was in peace negotiations, NATO pretty much in control."

Gerardo arched a brow. "Who was the Intel liaison?"

Hank's brows knit for a second, then smoothed. "Lania Price."

"There's your answer and she's in Leavenworth." He looked at the screen. "I have no problem with Dragon One. They can get places we can't and I've never seen a more ingenious group of guys."

"Confucius say, don't ignore stolen food when you're hungry?"

"Roger that," Gerardo said, then caught the quarter and faced the screen. Under his breath he added, "You want to tell Donovan it was Price or shall I?"

"Do me the favor, sir. He probably wouldn't believe me. I wouldn't. I was a boot officer and followed orders." It wasn't one of his shining moments, Hank thought. Gerardo nodded, stepped back and they looked at the screen.

The woman at the other end of the link was lovely, but showed very little of her surroundings. "Agent Troy."

"Colonel. Tell me what you have that concerns my Op?"

"A shipment of RZ10, a thermobaric explosive was stolen from the UK facility," Hank began. "The explosion in Singapore has the characteristics of the chemical."

He debriefed her on the power of the chemical, its movement, the bodies found in Turkey. "The canister's trail ended with the mercs, but Interpol traced them through several training camps in the Middle East. They had help. Secondly, Marianna Island intercepted a stream in your area. A very large one. We believe it was sent from Noble Richards Incorporated. It made several hits before it landed. As of this moment, we don't know where. We have only a fragment of the stream, but it is deeply encrypted."

She folded her arms, waiting for more and giving nothing up. How did we earn this kind of distrust, he wondered, then continued.

"NRI created the RZ10. Specifically Dr. Kenneth Black."

"What's Black say?"

"I'll find that out in a few hours, but we understand Dragon One is hunting fugitive Jason Vaghn."

"Actually, he was in their custody until I interfered. We're here because Intel didn't pass, and sir, while I'm bitching, the sensors on the station did not pick up the explosive."

"It's not released and it's classified."

"Not from me," she said with all candor. "I hunt weapons, sir, and if there's a new one out there, I need to know about it. I can't find them if I'm going in blind."

"Understood, Agent Troy," Hank said, feeling chastised. "Be advised, I'm not the last word."

"But the two-star behind you is and he's listening."

Hank glanced and caught Gerardo's shoulder shaking with a quiet laugh. "I see why she gets the job done," Gerardo said too low for the others to hear.

"The only items we brought into the station were Barasa's

discarded phone and Vaghn's pack." She gave them a list of the fugitive's items. "We don't know if the weapon was in one of them or not. But from the reports, he's capable of concealing it."

Donovan stepped into camera range. "We need forensic proof but Vaghn created the weapon that detonated here, no doubt about it." The lens pulled back to include them both. "The timing of calls to the explosion is just too neat and Vaghn was Black's chief R&D designer till he was convicted."

"He designed the containers," Jansen said, referring to his notes. "He understands its capability and the formula, obviously."

Donovan raked his fingers through his hair, looking frustrated. "You have to stop underestimating this kid, sir. He's been in prison planning this payback for a long time." Donovan sighted instances that should have sent up red flags, but none of it mattered now. "Black is part of it. In the middle of the trial, Vaghn shouldered all the blame, and trust me, this kid has no guilt. All charges on his boss were dropped and Black is back to business as usual. You think Vaghn rots in prison for five years doing nothing?" Donovan shook his head. "Any weapon he creates is worth more on the market, and the buyer is playing Vaghn and Barasa like a cello. A few thousand have died to protect this guy and kill us."

"What a prick," he heard and Hank glanced off screen. The generals, admirals, and the president's national security advisor looked as discouraged as he felt.

"We downloaded his hard drive, but it needs a password. We can't open the files or programs. We can do minimal searches, but with the exception of mail program, it's all encrypted."

"As was the stream that was sent from NRI."

"The weapon's schematics," Donovan said firmly.

Hank agreed. "According to cryptologists, every time they try to open it, the stream locks tighter."

"I'm not sure how this fits, sir, but we have a sequence

that we've tried and it hasn't worked on the hard drive, however, we matched a graphic to a novel."

Hank frowned. "Repeat last?"

"The novel was delivered to Vaghn." Donovan explained the discovery of the novel in Vaghn's flat with its postage wrappings, the scribbling, and Hank suddenly realized the advantage of Donovan's connection to Vaghn. No one would have thought to look deeper.

The station agent turned to a laptop and Hank's screen filled with a graphic. "We found this in a sequence that was in an email Vaghn had received, along with a few million other recipients disguised in one big spam send. This "I" character was in the body of the email within a sequence of random letters and numbers. Just junk," she said. "However, it was the only character in the random set with a different font, and a shadow. When singled out and enlarged, we learned it's a graphic. Then we compared it to the one in the novel."

A second window opened and showed the novel's square grid made to look like a carving or a tombstone. Vertically, the middle of the sequence matched. He shook his head, admiring their skill.

"You have the stream," Troy said. "I think we have the program that runs it. The Iota graphic must be some sort of key. The sequence from Vaghn's note pad, and the sequence in the novel contain a match to the Iota, but they are not identical."

"Excellent work, Agent Troy, Excellent."

"Thank you sir, but Dragon One was the talent there. My Intel is sending what we have to Deep Six."

"NSA is working on the encryption." Hank hesitated for a moment, then asked, "Donovan, what do you think is going on?" The man's features hardened and Hank was certain he remembered him.

"Vaghn's made a deal with someone a lot more powerful than Cale Barasa. Barasa's part was to deliver Vaghn, get a weapon as payment. That means Vaghn will be making more, with financing. He has expensive tastes, the price tag will be high. Don't be surprised if it turns up elsewhere too." He took a step closer. "Sir, the security in the UK survived because killing those men would send more agencies after their ass. Eliminating the RZ10 carriers effectively obliterated any connection to follow. They're cleaning up any trace as they go along."

Hank wondered why he didn't mention the car explosion, then glanced as a new picture digitized on his smaller screen. It was taken at a distance, yet clear enough to recognize the woman wasn't ugly.

"She's the money," Troy stepped up to say. "Barasa has met with her once in two months, a little over forty-eight hours ago." She told him the events since then and Hank was surprised the two were still alive and mentally listed a dozen more questions that needed answers. the laptop hard drive, once cracked, could give them a location.

"My Intel says one call was incoming just before the explosions, one call after. From Vahgn's computer but we aren't positive. That first number we believe belongs to this woman, and right now that is all we have to go on."

Hank glanced again at the photo of a woman taken at a distance. "We'll run it."

"Quickly please. They are ahead of us and we've already lost a member of Dragon One."

Hank's face shaped with sympathy, and he rubbed his mouth. "What do you need?"

She took a deep breath and said, "Forensics on the station, flight plans for her jet, a positive ID on her, the Ghurka soldier, *and* a global trace on that phone number twenty-four seven."

"Global?" Big area, lady, he thought.

"Until we can identify and track her, yes. They know how to vanish, sir. When it comes on, we chase."

"That's pretty thin."

"If you have a better solution, speak up. Barasa has the laptop and the inventor. He doesn't need a diagram. He has all he needs to be a mobile bomb squad and sell them out of his trunk."

Over the Philippine Sea

From his seat inside the aircraft, Jason peered at the island below, a fat emerald plopped in the deep blue water. Lagoons shaped the southeast, and white sand outlined the four-mile stretch like a torn hem. He spotted clusters of buildings surrounded by dense jungle before the Lear jet touched down. The jet trembled as it powered down and taxied, and he kept watching out the window till the aircraft stopped just outside the hangar. Then that prick Rahjan stood near his seat.

"Get the fuck away from me or I'm not getting off."

Rahjan grabbed his arm and yanked him out of the seat, nearly hurling him toward the door. Jason stumbled, caught the back of a seat, his leg on fire again. Rahjan pushed and he went to the hatch, ignoring the man waiting as if to catch him. Squinting against the bright sunlight, he descended slowly. The air was fast and steamy, perspiration already gathering under his arms. Didn't matter, he reeked like an old gym bag anyway.

The hangar was surrounded by lush trees and blooming flowers, looking more like a resort, and he admitted, it felt like it. A few yards away beneath a shade awning, a woman sat in a folding chair and as he neared, she stood. The voice on the phone. Beautiful, he thought, and she reminded him a bit of his older sister, polished and perfect—almost icy. He limped toward her and the uniformed men standing just beyond the awning. This was getting more interesting by the moment, he thought and she waved, just a little trickle of her fingers. Immediately, a man brought a wheelchair forward and though he hated that he needed it, he was grateful.

The driver pushed him to her and she waited till he was near to say, "We've spoken. I am Odette. Welcome."

He shook her hand, a weird comfort coming with the presence of a woman. "When will I meet him?"

She smiled with gentle patience. "Soon. He's anxious and considers the change in plans for the best."

Yeah, sure, more control, Jason thought and felt his embarrassment when she frowned down at his clothing. Her gaze snapped somewhere beyond him and didn't leave. Jason hooked his arm over the back of the chair and looked at Barasa, surprised to see men searching, then stripping them of weapons. It amused the shit out of him, and he glanced at Odette. Utterly expressionless, he thought, entertained. Getting between rivals, he didn't need, but Barasa had underestimated this woman, badly.

When a white van pulled to a stop, his wheelchair driver followed Odette to the side. Jason was about to climb in when the man scooped him up and gently sat him in the rear seat. Jason felt his face heat. Man. A little overkill.

"You will find the Professor more accommodating, Doctor Vaghn."

"Jason please," he said. His colleagues had refused to address him by his degrees, jealous probably, but he'd grown used to not hearing it.

"We will give you time to clean up and dine before the meeting, neh?"

He nodded and relaxed for the ride. Before they were out of site, he looked back to see Odette striding toward Barasa.

"Explain this." He gestured to the armed men and their collected weapons.

"You have no need of them. This island is completely secure and the property of the Professor. He makes the rules."

"I'm not staying."

She arched a tapered brow. "Your jet has been disabled, so yes, you are."

Anger burned through him and he wanted to smack that superior look off her pretty face. "You have him, without a trail!" Barasa said, stopping so close she was forced to look up.

"And your actions required us to ignite the prototype," Odette said calmly. "Now he has to create it again, so I suggest you enjoy the Professor's hospitality. As of this moment, Dr. Jason Vaghn is no longer your concern. Touch him again—" her gaze flicked to Rahjan— "And you will feel the consequences."

Barasa didn't respond. He knew when to back off. She was surrounded by guards in her territory, and keeping her mollified would gain him the weapon he needed. Beyond that, he didn't care. Then she asked for his phone and frowning, he offered it. She opened the back and removed the battery. He took a threatening step and her gaze jerked to his.

"How do you think they tracked you?"

He'd assumed so after finding the marker on his car, but any number of people could have put it there. "Your own phone?" A slimmer version was clipped to her waistband.

"No one knows who I am, Cale." She waved to the right at the limousine with the doors open and a chauffeur standing near. "They will take you to your accommodations." She turned away as a roofless Land Rover pulled to a stop. She slid into the rear, closed the door and never once looked back. His gaze followed the vehicle till it rounded a curve and vanished behind the jungle. He looked at Rahjan and smiled.

"You're hot for her?" the Ghurka said, surprised.

"Powerful women often do that." Barasa would reserve further judgment till he met the Professor. But there was no doubt in his mind that Odette would be trouble. She took every action against her grand plan as a personal affront to her beloved Professor. He was anxious to meet the man who had control over so many. Especially her.

He crossed to the car, and didn't wait for the porters. If she was so efficient, she'd see to it.

Sonsoral Islands
Philippine Sea

The marine archaeology research ship *The Traveler* cut through the seas with ease despite the storm pounding the decks. They'd sailed around the worst of it, yet the season brought afternoon squalls almost like clockwork. Bridget sipped hot tea and watched the rain pebble the windows. It soothed her. She'd loved storms since she was a child in Ireland, though she preferred to remain a spectator. She got wet enough with her job.

At a desk in the corner, Travis charted the weather patterns and would compare them to ocean currents. Silt dunes and shifting sand, especially under the power of a tsunami, had already revealed several shipwrecks. The Asia seas were filled with them, pirates, East India Company, Dutch traders. Her wreck diving passion was getting a workout on this expedition. Lightning cracked, brightening the sky and striking the water. She smiled. Jim flinched. In the window's reflection, she could see him sitting at the waist high desk behind her. The table's surface was a scratch resistant white Plexiglas, about two inches thick, and beneath it glowed with soft lights. It enabled scientists to see the finds clearly and separate dirt from fossil. Jim was bent over, micro glasses giving him a bug eyed look when he had basset hound eyes to start. He sorted the bones, trying to make a skeleton. They hadn't had the time or the facilities to construct a formal land dig site, and neither of them wanted to go back without more answers. They'd discussed the excursion and evidence with the team. Travis wasn't enthusiastic about the return trip, but agreed to send the photographs to some colleagues. He agreed with her that Jim had not found monkey footprints. Even meerkats would explain the footed claws, but she was accustomed to dealing with facts. Even archaeological speculation had to have evidence to back it up.

Jim made a familiar sound, a sort of closed mouth aww, and she smiled, went to the table. Bones weren't the usual finds for a Marine archaeologist but she had knowledge of skeletons. Jim had assembled pieces of a spine, pelvis, and two ribs, none of them complete. At the top was the small skull they'd found first by the tree. Testing would determine the species family and related bones, but this reconstruction was simply a place to start.

Bridget reviewed the outing in her mind and other than Jim and his penchant for running off, the metal crate made the least sense. She turned back to the window and the counter, switching on the lamp and spreading out the photos. A crate not a cage. Whatever was in it was long gone, and while they couldn't take the time to tear down the vines and see how much was there, she believed the crate was never opened. The latch she'd photographed had been sealed. Again, she could speculate that the growth of vegetation could have done it, but it wasn't a concern. The bones would tell them more. She glanced past the spread photos to the work yet to complete for the expedition, but she was still within her deadline. If anything, the National Geographic Society was accommodating. It showed in the equipment surrounding them, some of it unnecessary for her expedition and brought up from storage when they'd found the bones. She lowered the light and drew her magnifying glass, studying the photo. After fifteen minutes, she straightened and stretched. Her theory was the same; solid metal surface, galvanized and riveted. She wished now that she had a sample of the metal, yet still felt it was smashed to the boulder so hard it flattened it, and that brought up Derek's idea that it was dropped from an aircraft.

She'd made a reverse mold of the radio, then digitally

scanned and uploaded it to make it three-dimensional. There were specialists from NGS looking at it right now via satellite transmission. She turned back to the table, noticing that Jim had formed a wrist and one finger.

"You're certain?" she said peering and noting the angle of the joints.

"I'm going by a primate but yes." He glanced up. "This is my field. Putting the pieces back together."

Did he think she didn't notice after all this time on a ship? The waterproof cases stacked behind him, filed and cross-referenced was proof of his obsession. He'd matched bone fragments smaller than a pea.

"Analysis?"

"Feline."

Her eyes flew wide. "Cats are hunters and there isn't anything to eat on that island."

"Except each other."

"Cannibalized? Few animals eat their dead."

He pointed to a bone. "Those cuts are teeth marks." She drew the magnifier over the fragment, then measured the width and gouge. "It looks like the marks in the radio," she said. "But the jaw with the teeth from the boulder doesn't match it. The tooth length isn't long enough."

He gestured with his tweezers, poking the air. "Long scrapes mean long teeth, and they lose their strength." She brought the mold from the counter and he showed her. "Not curved either, but almost buckteeth."

She frowned, and he added, "Like a saber tooth, though not that long since these aren't large." He nodded to the table of bones, then picked up her radio mold, lifting his micro glasses to look. "I'd say three maybe four teeth tightly grouped." That meant the animal gnawed like a dog on a bone, rather then chomping as if biting into an apple.

"A cat with buckteeth?" Was it bred that way or adapting? The more they learned, the more her curiosity grew. They had no conclusion and they'd accept it. It was part of their trade. She was about to turn in for the night when Derek entered, looking a bit green. He went to the small icebox for a bottle of water. He'd drunk half of it before he waved, a paper caught between two fingers. "This is so rad," he said. "Bones P-three through P-eight are male, human."

"Oh God."

"Not hobbits, either. A child," he added. "And the best part, they have animal DNA."

"What?" That brought Travis from his charts. "Animal mixed with human?"

"And yes, Andrew checked the calibration of the machine," he said when she opened her mouth to ask. "He'd trained on it and when he saw that spectrograph he about wet his pants."

"Don't be getting so knackered about this," Bridget said. "It wasn't a proper dig. The finds are contaminated and inconclusive." She was curious, but not willing to stake her career on it. Especially with the strange test results. Improperly grading a site went against her education, and ethics. She'd agreed for Jim's sake, but didn't debate taking it further academically. She simply couldn't turn back now.

"Repeat the tests."

"Andrew is, but says it's in the marrow, matured like that."

The evidence was stacking, she thought and tried not to get too excited and re-read the printout, then picked up the small skull missing its mandible. "This is not feline," she said, turning it. "So we have human and animal bones, with animal DNA." She shook her head. "Impossible. Human and animal can't mix. Even if it could, it would take a couple generations of breeding for it to masticize in marrow." A shiver passed up the back of her neck, the thought and the images that followed were revolting. It was simply not possible. "I want to carbon date it all," she said. "Let's prepare samples for the NGS labs." She grabbed her notebook, and with Derek went below deck to join the lab rats.

Manassas, Virginia

In the rear of the staff car, Hank Jansen watched the scenery pass without much notice. Noble Richards Incorporated stretched across twelve acres and four separate buildings with testing hangars, and a security system that rivaled the Pentagon. Even his Joint Chiefs of Staff credentials kept them held at the north gate for longer than it should have. The Department of Defense paid most of the bills, dammit.

The concept that NRI had sent the transmission when they'd lost their contract for failing to control the R&D and maintaining the DOD testing standards did not bode well for the home team. The trial that followed had been lengthy and closed, resulting in the chief designer's imprisonment. However, then the weapon had been a laser rifle, not the thermobaric explosive RZ10. Nor were an estimated thirty thousand lives already lost because of it. Hank was still receiving information, but little came from the Singapore government beyond a possible gas leak. The experts told him otherwise.

His driver slowed the vehicle and braked to a stop outside the entrance. Hank left the staff car, not waiting for the JAG attorney or Major Beckham as he walked through the wide glass doors and into the foyer of Noble Richards. He stood on the mosaic of the company logo and saw NRI's president walking toward him. Bruce Cannel was one of those guys who wanted everyone to know he was really an aging hippy by keeping his red hair long and in a ponytail, but coupled with Cannel's barrel chest and jowly cheeks, he looked like a man who refused to grow up.

"Welcome, Colonel. I was surprised when security apprised me of your arrival."

Not enough to delay them for a half hour, he thought. "It's urgent. Can we speak in private?"

"Certainly." Cannel's expression remained impassive, and

he kept his silence as he escorted them up two floors and into his office. The JAG attorney and Major Beckham behind him, Hank entered. Cannel moved behind his impressive desk, gesturing to the chairs positioned in front. Hank remained standing, aware of the intimidation tactic. The chairs were lower than the desk, therefore behind it was a superior position of negotiation. Hank had no intention of bargaining. He wasn't leaving without Black and the encryption primer to the file.

"What can I do for you?"

"We need to have any and all information on the research and development of RZ10."

Now Cannel looked confused. "I don't understand. You already have it, as per the court orders and the contract. Your people took the hard drive, the files. All of it."

Hank set his brief case on the man's teakwood desk and opened it, then handed Cannel photographs taken of the explosion site at dawn this morning. "This says otherwise."

Bruce gave it a cursory glance, then handed it back. "It's impossible. We didn't manufacture it. DOD did." Cannel's gaze flicked to Beckham standing at parade rest behind him. Hank didn't have to turn around to know the man was dishing out his finest "I will eat you alive" look. He'd seen it make grown men piss themselves.

"A satellite transmission, encrypted, was sent from this company," Jansen said. "With Doctor Kenneth Black's authorization. Black was the director of the thermobaric project."

Cannel frowned slightly. "We have other contracts besides those with the government, Colonel. Dr. Black isn't involved in anything with the Department of Defense that I know of."

That I know of. Covering his back and already giving the "I have no recollection of that, Senator," answer he'd unfortunately heard before. "He sent a transmission and he is the creator of RZ10. A blast occurred that has its characteristics." The man did not need to know it was stolen. But Cannel's watchdogs had failed to monitor his own people. We should have destroyed the damn chemical.

"Those combined tell me Dr. Kenneth Black was still in contact with co-creator Jason Vaghn."

He shook his head. "No reason and Jason is in prison."

"He's been out for nearly a year, and he escaped the country a month ago," Beckham said.

Cannel didn't look happy about that. "Regardless, you have no solid evidence that RZ10 did this," Cannel said, gesturing to the photos. "Transmissions are sent from here all day long, and giving that information to you breaks contracts with other clients."

"I understand, of course. But we are certain of the origins." Hank paused, his gaze direct. "If someone misused it or falsified authorization, then that's your concern. But I need to speak with Dr. Black for clarification." When Cannel hesitated, Hank said, "Now please."

Cannel eyed him, then let his gaze slide past him to Beckham. Finally, he turned to his phone, grasped the receiver.

"We'd rather you didn't alert anyone."

Cannel practically tossed the phone onto the cradle, then walked around the desk to the door. Hank glanced at Beckham. The major smirked and mumbled, "Ass bag," under his breath as Hank followed Cannel.

Without a word, the company president led them through the floor to the east side. Sunlight flooded through the long stretch of plate glass windows, but there was no one there to enjoy it, the space taken up with a receptionist's desks and hallways. Both were empty. They passed through a room filled with cubicles and Hank caught the graphic design of hiking gear or spelunking as he followed.

Cannel slowed, turning slightly to say, "His office is in the corner." He stopped before it and knocked.

The reply was a gunshot.

Hank pulled Cannel from the door as Beckham approached from the side, his weapon drawn.

"Clear the floor, sir," he said softly. Hank ordered Cannel and everyone out.

The JAG attorney dropped his briefcase and moved behind the major. Both were armed. Beckham grasped the doorknob and opened it, pushing it as he inched inside, aiming to the corners, then moving further inside and out of sight. He returned a moment later, and said, "It's clear."

Hank walked briskly inside and stopped short. Doctor Kenneth Black was in his chair, his head thrown back, half his skull and brains sliding down the window. "Christ almighty."

"That puts a damper on things."

He glanced at Beckham. "Where did you hide a sidearm?" The man's uniform fit like a glove.

"Sock," he said, throwing the safety. "I'll secure the floor and make the calls."

Hank stopped him. "We need analysts in here, and NCIS. We have to keep a lid on it."

Beckham arched a brow at the suicide.

"Before the news media. Lieutenant," he said to the attorney making copious notes and the young man looked up. "I want JAG to seize his papers now. Get any court order you need." Hank glanced around the office that belonged in a Bogart movie. "He had the answers to that transmission and where it went." Time wasn't their friend and he felt the clock ticking away till the next explosion.

Beckham nodded and left. The JAG followed, needing crates to get started. He'd find a reason not to be here too, he thought. He looked back at the body and sighed. His suspicion of treason was true. Kenneth Black had sent the transmission, but the reason was still locked inside its contents. Hank moved to the desk, looking at the blotter and the weapon Black still held. From his position, he could see the serial numbers were sanded off.

So he buys a gun off the street and offs himself just before he has to talk, Hank thought, inspecting his left hand for a note, then checking the floor. He ignored the framed photo of

Black's family, his kids about the same age as Hank's own as he leaned over the desk. A green file lay a few inches from Black's gun. Hank used his pen to open it. It was empty except for a fresh piece of paper printed with three words.

Icarus is rising

Sixteen

Jason felt better than he had in years, prison included, after a few hours on the island. Bathed, his wound properly dressed, he wore fresh clothes that made him feel like he was on vacation. He wasn't and the pain in his leg reminded him of it as he left the master suite. He investigated the bungalow, finding a stocked kitchen and a spa pool in the shaded backyard. He was alone in the suite, the bedroom larger than his last apartment, and decorated in blue and white that soothed him, reminded him of home. The island breezes kicked at sheer white drapes, and he crossed the living room to French doors thrown wide. On the deck, a linen-draped table was shaded by a giant umbrella.

"For your dining pleasure," he murmured. The table was set for lunch with his favorite; a turkey club sandwich with extra bacon. He didn't wonder how she knew, it just felt good that she cared to learn it. Taking a seat, he picked up half a sandwich and ate. A hundred yards away lay the jungle, and beyond that, the China blue seas. He didn't know where he was, and he'd bet Barasa had his doubts too. He'd heard him give the coordinates to the pilot. Let them power struggle. Odette had made good her promises and that was aces to him. He propped his sore leg on the padded footstool and sipped a light Riesling from a chilled goblet. Irish crystal, he decided, holding it to the light. He thought briefly of Donovan, then dismissed it. The man was a constant reminder of all Jason had lost.

Since the trial, Jason hadn't relished pleasures like this. His family had disowned him, his inheritance held in courts. Convicted felons didn't hang around Nantucket and certainly not with his family. Yet he'd grown up with everything and he missed it, longed for the moments when he didn't have to worry about his next meal. It sucked.

He set the crystal glass aside, picked up the last half of his sandwich, and bit into it. He'd enjoy it while he could, and not for the first time, he mulled over the identity of his benefactor—a man far more educated than him. Jason had his skills, but they paled to the ingenuity of this plan. It would come to a head soon, he thought, eager to finish and disappear with his millions.

Cryptology Division
NSA

Nolan brought up the graphic sent from Dragon One. Damn clever to find it, he thought, then studied the stream again. D-1 had the program on the download from Vaghn's laptop. Nolan had the stream. He loaded the captured hard drive into his dummy computer, no link to the outside to keep any nasty bugs or snoops from getting in. Prior to D1's sequence, he'd tried his own decode program, but the system rebelled. He'd tried so many sequences of the scrambled numbers and letters, he felt he was on his last couple of tries. Another complicated fail-safe Vaghn had created. A couple more and it wouldn't let him back in. Permanently.

Last time, he thought and wondered if he'd be fired for this.

He worked backwards, dropping the graphic into the password window, then entered the sequence. It failed and he could almost feel the system tightening its guard. He tried it again, leaving out the Greek Iota.

He blinked as the graphic expanded to three dimensional and on the screen, it turned, rolled on its side, then came upright. The program opened. Data streamed and configured.

His eyes widened and he grabbed the phone, dialing General Gerardo. The chairman of the Joint Chiefs answered on the first ring. "Agent Deets."

"I have it open and it's as suspected, sir, weapon schematics."

"What is it? Sidearm, rifle?"

"Sir, I'm too old to be facetious, but you really need to see this one for yourself."

Gerardo ordered him to the Pentagon and Nolan hung up, staring at the screen.

"We're in big trouble." And it was already in the hands of a weapons dealer with Hezbollah ties.

Jason knew he'd nodded off when a soft whisper stirred through his brain. He blinked and sat up.

Odette stood beside him, her hand on his shoulder. "Is everything to your satisfaction?"

"Yes, extremely." He rubbed his face, then sipped water. She took a seat across from him and crossed her legs. She'd changed, her clothing more casual in black cropped slacks and a white top, her bare arms tanned and sculpted. "What do you do for the Professor?"

"I'm his voice when he needs it," she said succinctly. "When you're ready?"

"Now is good." He wiped his mouth with the linen napkin.

She stood, then a uniformed maid stepped through the wide doors and handed him a cane. Christ, the servant couldn't be more than thirteen and wouldn't look either of them in the eye. A moment later, the girl was gone, backing into the shadows of the house. He held the cane to the sunlight. The leopard carved into the handle was remarkable. "Thank you," he said, then stood, testing it.

"Join me, Jason. He's eager to know you."

He followed her out of the house and kept the pace as they strolled down the gravel road to a cobbled path stretching across the manicured lawn. He glanced behind. Near his bungalow were more like it and he wondered if Barasa was in one. Did she offer him the same comforts? The bastard needed to die, preferably with Rahjan.

"He is still here," she said, and he glanced, flushing that she could read him so easily. "But neither will bother you again." He hoped so.

Ahead he saw another house in the distance, then beyond, nearer to the jungle, were several more buildings. Except for their size, they were identical, terra cotta roofs with covered porches. The setup reminded him of a village.

He frowned at the children, following three as they ran across the lawn laughing.

"He's adopted them," Odette said softly. "When they are of age, he sends them all to boarding schools in England and France." She shrugged as if it bothered her. "He provides well in all ways. We are fortunate."

"Me especially," he said. Man, this was some big money. How did they get electricity? Generators must be buried or he'd hear them. Then there was food, supplies, and fuel. "You must be self-sufficient here. No quick run to the store for milk and eggs, huh?"

"Mostly imports. There are the gardens and fresh water through osmosis." She gestured to a large fountain spilling water from the mouth of a giant cat. "Piping to all units."

"Running water is a luxury I don't take for granted," he confessed. Soaking in a tub full had barely made up for living in the slums.

She touched his shoulder. "You will not lack here, Jason."

As they approached the largest house, a man sitting on the

porch stood and descended the wide veranda stairs. Jason stopped and looked at Odette.

"You recognize him?" she said, smiling.

"Anyone in the scientific community would." Now he understood the secrecy and destroying all trails. If even a suggestion of his involvement in the explosion in Singapore emerged, the law enforcement of every nation would descend on them.

Jason walked forward, smiling. "Doctor Thibaut, an honor and a pleasure."

Haeger Thibaut was a philanthropist, a biochemist and a physician. And those were the degrees Jason could recall off the top of his head. Aside from specializing in genome research, he'd been nominated for the Nobel Prize years ago until moralists and critics compared him to Frankenstein for his groundbreaking cloning research with livestock that was commonly used today.

Jason shook his hand and felt like a groupie to a rock star. Thibaut's millions were in patents and wise investments, a portion in a Swiss bank account with Jason's name on it, yet he didn't wonder why Thibaut had secluded himself on the island. If he owned one, he wouldn't leave either, but the admonishment from the scientific community sent him here. Jason knew how it felt to be ridiculed by your colleagues. He hadn't seen the man in the news except when he held some benefit for an orphanage. Only the tabloids and media pried into the reasons behind his isolation because he'd donated millions and had adopted several children himself. Jason wondered if one was the maid in his suite.

"Come my friend, get out of the heat."

He didn't mean the porch and as they walked, a young boy trailed behind them with an umbrella on a long pole. The whole thing had a 40's Caribbean vibe going, and Jason felt himself relax. They chatted about the advances in science and Jason knew he was slobbering.

"So tell me, Dr. Vaghn, who tried to take you from Barasa's men?"

Jason glanced, and didn't see any point in not answering. Donovan was dead and probably his entire team was, too. "That was my fault," he admitted to a man he considered one of the greatest minds of the twenty-first century. "I knew they were watching. I didn't know it would be that close or that it was Dragon One." When Jason was finished giving the details, he waited for Thibaut's reaction.

He only nodded, looking thoughtful as his long thin fingers stroked his goatee into place. Then he looked up, tugged at his shirt collar and said, "Would you like to see your laboratory?"

"Yes, definitely. A lab?"

"I think you'll be pleased."

They walked toward a building, and Jason thought if this is a lab, he was going to like it here. A copy in appearance to the other buildings, it had an orange tile roof and pale yellow walls with white trim, the porch shaded the wood door and dark wicker furniture. A plantation rocker like his mother's rested near the door. Palms and coconut trees bent over the stone pathway, shading them from the heat. The boy with the umbrella waited at the end of the walk. Old world attitude for a modern man, he thought. They crossed the threshold and that's where the similarities ended.

Jason looked at Thibaut and smiled. Thibaut waved him in. "Should you need assistants, don't hesitate to request them, but I know you prefer to work alone."

He glanced at the man. "What else do you know about me?"

"Everything, Dr. Vaghn. I wouldn't have solicited your assistance had I not known you were brilliant and worthy of the challenge."

Jason felt his shoulders pull back without will. His own father had never spoken to him like that. All he'd done was try to browbeat him into the family business of politics, he thought bitterly, and walked the corridors between steel tables and computer stations. At the farthest end, he stopped at a case with a glass front, then swung a look at Thibaut.

"Where did you get that? *How* did you get it?"

Thibaut smiled, the lines in his long face deepening. "Nothing is impossible with the right plan, Jason."

His gaze returned to the gunmetal-gray canister suspended inside the case. It was shaped like an hourglass, a titanium fortification between the two components. He should know. He designed the container. RZ10.

It was dark classified. How did Thibaut even know it *existed*?

Marina Bay
Singapore

Riley glanced up when a buzzer sounded, his gaze searching the condo for the source.

"Here," Safia said, walking to the intercom controls near the foyer. "I'm surprised it works." She tapped *talk*. "Yes?"

"Someone need a jet jockey?"

Riley grinned. "Sam Wyatt." Safia's expression brightened and she rushed to the door with him. "Should I be jealous you're so excited?"

"He was half dead when I saw him last." She shrugged. Smiling, he threw open the door, but Safia slipped around him. For a second, she just stared.

"Hi Sam. I'm Safia Troy."

Sam frowned, confused, then glanced at Riley. "Serbia Safia?"

She looked over her shoulder at him, arching a brow and he smiled. "Unforgettable. Told you."

She yelped when Sam suddenly scooped her in his arms, hugged her tightly and planted a smacky kiss on the cheek. "Thank you, darlin'." He set her down. "My wife'll probably talk your ear off about it. Fair warned."

Riley waved them inside, but Safia held back to greet Logan.

"It's a pleasure to finally meet you," he said, his smile somber. "Thanks for helping find Sebastian's killer."

She gave his arm a squeeze. "I want him too."

Sam and Logan unloaded their luggage, waving at Max, who was on the phone with Colonel Jansen last Riley checked.

"Dragon Six is on the Changi airstrip, gassed to go," Sam said, working his shoulders and looking around at the setup. "Chopper is on the roof."

"We're waiting," Riley said. "NMCC, Deep Six, Interpol, Scotland Yard, are all on alert and Deep Six has satellites tracking one phone number. The cryptologists have what we have." Riley felt the helplessness and thought, with all this technology, they couldn't find a stronger link than the woman in Red Shoes? "I bloody hate waiting for something else to happen."

"I can tap into the aviation network," Logan said, crossing to the computers. "The language barrier might be a problem, but didn't you say Barasa landed in Vietnam?"

"On the ground for a few hours," Riley said. "He didn't leave the jet, but dinner was delivered."

Sam tipped his cowboy hat back, and said, "Some people just *know* how to spend their money."

"Like Viva?" Max said, winking at Safia and she looked at Sam.

"She buys helicopters like women buy new wardrobes."

"Your fault for teaching her how to fly one," Max said from across the room.

"You try saying no to her, see where it gets you," Sam said, his smile telling them he didn't have a voice in the matter and didn't care.

"Helps that she's *loaded*," Riley said, passing Safia on his way to the kitchen. "Why isn't she with you, anyway?" Riley came back with a six pack, handing them out.

"In New Orleans with Sebastian's sister," Sam said, pinching off his cowboy hat and tossing it on a chair. "Jasmine and Sebastian have lots of relatives, but they were their only real family," he told Safia. "Killian had to return home. Alexa can't fly. She's too far along." Sam accepted the beer, smiling. "He's so pathetic. Calls her every fifteen minutes, it's a wonder she gets any rest."

"You know Alexa and I were trained at this together."

He nudged the air with his chin. "Riley mentioned it."

"When she delivers, I'd like to know."

Her lips curved in a smile Riley had seen before, the kind women exchanged that warned men not to even try to understand what was behind it.

"I think you'll be around." Sam sipped his beer, hiding a smile as he walked to the printer, grabbed a sheaf, then dropped onto the sofa, catching up. Logan was at the computers, his fingers flying over the keyboard. Riley gauged Safia. She wasn't accustomed to input and opinions.

But Safia stepped back, her gaze moving over her condo and the men filling it. No one except Ellie had ever been inside. She preferred it that way, private, hers only, but realized she liked seeing people here, despite the reasons. There's another first. Dragon One certainly cornered the market on tall and good looking, and while they couldn't pass for brothers, the friendships were close, in each other's lives enough to know how Viva Wyatt spent her money. A chopper wardrobe. She loved it.

Riley moved up beside her, and she gravitated to him.

"You have that 'I need to do something right now' look," he said.

She tipped her head, met his gaze. "That hasn't been the wisest course of action so far, I'm not rushing in."

His brows knit for a second. "It's not your fault. None of this is."

She shook her head. "Vaghn would be in U.S. custody and no one would have his weapons."

"They'd just find another one to sell. We're assuming we brought it inside the station in the backpack."

"I thought of that. Motion sensors would have gone off if someone crossed the courtyard. The sensors inside would have detected it before we passed the key lock."

"I think that one had help," Riley said. "Any enemies we should know about?"

She scoffed. "Plenty, if they knew I was chasing them. I can't be one hundred percent, but my cover is in tact." She shrugged. "I'm inconsequential, Riley. I don't get that close, just watch, listen, track, report. Maybe cause them some trouble, but Interpol makes the arrests." She waved at the set-up. "Dragon One is more involved than I've ever been."

Riley thought she underplayed her role, but dismissed it for the moment. "What were you doing before trailing Barasa this time?"

"Tracking LAW rockets to Syria." His eyes flared. She just shrugged. "Barasa was transporting them. They ended in a Hezbollah training camp." At his look she said, "Yes, it was risky since females are worth less than a camel to those guys. I was disguised as a water boy, but I couldn't get close enough before Barasa handed off the weapons." She gestured to the screen waiting for the Deep Six connection. "Major Mitch Beckham destroyed the arsenal. I followed Barasa here."

Riley's brows knit as he tried to find a piece he knew they were missing. "There are a handful of explosives that could have blown that wide a berth; It would take a lot, but they all need something to ignite it. A detonator, a match. The bigger that is, the wider the radius."

Safia hurried to a free computer and pulled up the satellite image of the station house. "About a five block radius."

"Yeah, but look how even that explosion is," Max said.

Almost a perfect circle, she thought. "Jansen said the RZ10 creates a vacuum and collapses on itself. But we saw a lot of debris moving outward. The blast pattern proves that.

The RZ canister was stolen twenty-four hours before the station blast. It *could* have been used then, but Vaghn was still in hiding." She looked at him suddenly. "You think there's another player?"

Max twisted on the stool. "I do." Safia frowned. "It doesn't add up. The map seller was killed by a hit and run. Then Webber runs from you *and* lies. Why run if you're going to lie?"

"Riley scared him." They stared and her shoulders suddenly fell. "Okay, fine. You're implying I was the target and we have a new suspect. But I haven't a clue who it could be. If it was RZ used at the station, then the chemicals have to show up on tests. Forensics went in for it that morning. It should be done already." She slipped on her ear mic and hailed Ellie. "We have confirmation on the substances?"

"Negative. Homeland is stalling."

Safia frowned, glancing at the ceiling as if she could see above. "Go to Dr. Wylie, Forensics."

"I'm not sure—"

"We've been down this road. It's an order, Base." She signed off and looked at Riley. "We don't have time to mess around."

"Man, I thought Viva was impatient," Sam said.

Riley shook his head, pinching the air, a measure she thought was a little skimpy. Safia gave him a shove.

"Found the plane," Logan called out, twisting on the stool. "It landed on a little island in the South Pacific. It's still there, but all communication to the island is down."

"Down?"

"Like the dark ages. No in, no out. The piece of land is listed as unoccupied."

"So is this apartment," she said and crossed to him. "Bring up the map, please."

Logan did, then transferred it to the flat screen. She stood back a few feet. "Micronesia? The Truk islands?" she said and looked to Logan.

"Close. Palau. The outer rim. A scatter island. Five miles off any coast, international waters, untouchable. As for commerce, it's useless. Half the size of Guam."

"Bridget took a side trip south of there, Sonsoral Islands," Riley said. "Monkeys and sea shells." He told them about the scare, the scratch marks on the archaeologist and they were well into a discussion when he noticed the incoming call warning was blinking.

Logan turned away, worked the computer, then pointed the remote at the flat screen. "The Brass is calling. We're live again, people."

With the team, she faced the screen. "Colonel Jansen." She nodded and noticed the latest director beside him now. "Director." Dr. Roger Shiplet was new at the job and while he'd run the gauntlet of senate hearings, she didn't know too much about him. But when the director of the CIA got this close, it meant they were scared. She'd seen the damage, the lives taken. RZ10 was on the loose and she knew it would just get worse if they didn't bag them all.

"Dr. Black is dead, a suicide," Jansen began and relayed a few details. "Baring the investigation, we have his computer and Deep Six is working to learn where the stream ended. In the meantime, cryptologists have unlocked the hard drive and the stream."

Their bleak expressions said nothing good was coming.

Cale admired the ingenuity of the island. A sanitarium for the peculiar. There was little he could do but enjoy the comforts availed to him, and he couldn't recall when he'd breathed unpolluted air. The scents surrounding him were incredible, a fruity fragrance lingered. This far in the ocean, the winds were stronger, keeping the muggy heat back where they left it in Singapore.

Odette spared nothing, providing them with accommodations, clothing, and food. Servants catered and vanished. Cale felt like the wealthy socialites he'd seen on the Riviera where he was never welcome. Clearly, the Professor had amassed a wealth Barasa could only imagine possessing. He stepped off the porch and strolled toward the cobblestone paths, obeying the signs, a declarative prisoner now. He studied the buildings in the distance, tall palms and twisted pasir trees shadowing the roofs. He supposed Vaghn was somewhere over there happily creating weapons of mass destruction. He was eager to see this device that went undetected by Vaghn's captors. The level of secrecy was annoying, and he'd done too much to be so uniformed, yet the money soothed that; half of his nearly spent.

He'd not learned anything about the men who'd interfered, yet knew they'd keep hunting. Just not here. Odette assured him of complete encapsulation once here, yet he'd spotted the occasional guard and it elevated his suspicions. Why post guards on an isolated island?

A servant dressed in white rushed near, offering him a bottle of water so cold it sweat with condensation. "Sir?"

He took it, frowning when the teenager wouldn't look him in the eye, then watched as he ran away as fast as he'd approached. He followed, the aroma of spices floating on the air, and saw the teen dart into a building. House staff, he thought. He'd not seen many. Things just appeared. He'd never heard them when they'd delivered a meal after his arrival.

Rahjan tried investigating, but already complained of being forced back. The guards were undisguised, though he hadn't seen any weapons since his arrival. When he crossed another sign directing him elsewhere, he considered they were there for him. He didn't see anyone on the island that didn't have a job. He turned back toward his bungalow, and he glimpsed a figure in the distance. Awareness pulled through him.

Odette. She walked between buildings with a determined step, two people hot on her heels and trying to catch up. The woman loved giving orders, he thought and stepped off the path and under a tree to watch her. She stopped near a fountain in the landscaping, gesturing to the tall stone back and the giant lion head spilling water from its mouth. He frowned when she marched left and disappeared down a path under the trees. From the air, he'd seen dense jungle nearly to the white shore, the buildings barely visible for the trees, yet while his bearings were a little off, the sun wasn't. He was in the middle of the island and though it warranted a search, he'd wait till nightfall. He pushed away from the tree and headed back to the bungalow, anxious to meet the Professor.

Then he saw him, a trail of children behind him like the pied piper.

It wasn't until he neared that recognition dawned and he understood the secrecy and money influencing this deal. He glanced around, wary that this was an elaborate setup, then looked back at the man. He'd brokered a weapons deal with one of the world's leading scientists. Someone easily recognizable and with enough international influence that he'd never be a suspect. Yet when he smiled and extended his hand, Barasa knew *he* was the only suspect, and if he wasn't careful, Hager Thibaut would feed him to the wolves.

Nolan strode down the halls of the Pentagon. He'd been here exactly three times in the last year, and didn't care to hang around. Too many opinions to spoil the intelligence. He preferred the isolation of his office, the bank of computers and a list of work. Field duty was interesting, and addictive, but he had a family to consider. He waited for the security to pass him through and stopped outside the war room, waiting again for his clearance inspection. The guard started to take his laptop and he held it out of his reach, shaking his head.

"Make a call," he said and when the Sergeant hung up, he nodded Nolan through. He stepped into the war room, and crossed to the front. They were expecting him and the group of men didn't look all that happy to be gathered. National security never took a break. A mantra that annoyed the hell out of his wife. He greeted Gerardo and Jansen, then opened the silver laptop, linking it with the screen monitors. From Deep Six, David brought Dragon One on line.

He addressed the brass around the table. "D-1 had the program off Vaghn's computer. We had the schematics. Neither opened without the password. The graphic had the codes imbedded in the lines and swirls." He worked the keyboard and demonstrated the steps necessary to open the files. "Vaghn assured no one could get inside unless you had all the pieces and knew how to put them together. It gives him complete control and likely why they mowed people down to protect him."

The brass scowled and Nolan explained.

"You needed all the pieces," he said. "The graphic is deciphered with the sequence, yet minus the symbol in the password." He gestured toward the larger screen and brought up the letter, Iota, then demonstrated opening the program and the schematics. "The pieces have always been there in the spam mail. The order of it was in the novel, and the Greek 3-D letter, well, you had to know to remove it from the sequence." Nolan tapped keys. "This is what they were so desperate to conceal."

The weapon materialized in three dimensions on the large screen.

He got the reaction he'd expected, the same one he had.

The weapon was housed inside the latest web phone.

Ironically called the Icarus.

Marina Bay
Singapore

"Oh no he *didn't*," Safia said.

Riley sat back in the sofa. "*Jaasus.*"

Safia wouldn't be still and peered closer, then swung a

look at Riley. "It's the latest gadget, everyone has one or wants one. It's a hand-held *computer* capable of sending and receiving in five different methods. And worse, it's cheap here. How can we track that?"

"There's more," Nolan said and Safia looked at the screen, just learning the NSA agent was a college roommate of Logan's. "With the programming he's created, it can be ignited from any phone containing its number."

"What's the bad news?" Logan said.

Safia snapped a look at him. "If that's not bad enough for you, you need to seek therapy."

He just shrugged. "There is always more, Safia."

"The schematics in the stream are CAD capable. Computer Assisted Design," Nolan explained. "CAD programs in various forms create anything from a footstool to a guided missile. Complete with a shopping list and the construction steps. Vaghn's program is designed to recreate it." Nolan pointed out the capsule to hold the explosives. "The only chemical strong enough in that small amount is the RZ10 or maybe nitro and a little C4."

Safia spoke up. "What you're saying is these plans can take an ordinary web phone or a Blackberry and convert it into one of these things?"

"Yes, unfortunately, I am."

"Then we are up a creek because Jason Vaghn sent out a mass email, containing the sequence and the graphic. Thousands could have exactly what we do right now."

"They'd have to be very smart to figure it out," Jansen said, moving up beside Deets.

Safia folded her arms. "They don't have to. Bad guys are paying Vaghn for that information. Push button terrorism. Undetectable. Vaghn made this for mass murder, sir. No other reason for it exists. The schematics are his insurance, a secondary deal should the one with Barasa fail."

"Agreed. Where do you want to go from here, Agent Troy?"

"ID on the woman?" *Did these people not take notes?*

"She has a passport, but no driver's license, no education or hospital records, or fingerprints on file. Not even a birth record."

That sounded like a NOC to her. "A ghost?" Safia said. "Passport name?"

"She goes by Odette Thibaut."

General Gerardo moved up behind them, startling Jansen. "The name didn't jog, but she's his voice." He leaned over the computer and played it like a master. A photo filled the screen. "Dr. Haeger Thibaut, biochemist, medical doctor. He's as overdegreed as it gets. He has several patents and he's worth millions and spreads it around too. That makes him well loved." Gerardo looked at the camera, directly at her. "If we have anything connecting him, we'd better be dead certain and in triplicate. He's well connected."

Safia frowned, then tapped keys to pull up a CIA dossier. The first was photos of Thibaut with Mandela, the German Chancellor, a Saudi Prince, and three American Presidents. Splendid. Influence as well as millions to back it up. "He owns the island where Barasa landed. They're all there."

"We have no confirmation the RZ10 canister is with them. We'd have to be within twenty feet for sensors to pick it up."

"Then we need to get on that island for a look."

Gerardo shook his head. "That would take an executive order for an assault on a private citizen who has a clean record and no evidence to connect him to the theft."

"Sir—?" She glanced at Riley. "Then you're tying our hands and frankly, I've gone after perps with less evidence. He's harboring a fugitive and an arms dealer, what more do you want?" Gerardo shook his head, but Safia spoke up. "You people lost this stuff and now that we're close you're locking us down because he's well connected?" Her sour expression told him what she thought of that. "I can get around this."

His brows shot up. "Are you threatening me, Agent Troy?"

Behind her, the team groaned, but she stepped closer. "Time to fish or cut bait, sir. If the RZ10 is your top priority, then get us authorization to go get it."

"Safia," Riley said softly. "You're biting the hand that feeds."

She met his gaze. "You say I was the target, but Sebastian and a few thousand are dead. What would you do?" She didn't give him a chance to answer and looked at Gerardo, her hands on her hips. "Well sir?"

Gerardo surprised her by smiling. "Agent Troy's opinion not withstanding, I'm not one to let political friendships and big money make a difference," he said. "So who wants to start chipping at this guy?"

Off to the side, Beckham smiled. "I'd be happy to learn his lingerie size." The general scowled at him, but Safia just smiled. Beckham liked stirring up controversy. "Oh yeah, and that's really his daughter." He scoffed and went somewhere off screen.

Gerardo looked at Safia and frowned. "You're not satisfied?"

"No. That takes time we don't have. They have all the components they need," she reminded. "I request this Op go Delta classified, sir." It would sever all communication outside the operation.

He scowled blackly. "You don't have a lot of faith in us, do you, Agent Troy?"

Images and painful memories flashed through her mind. "Experience has taught me otherwise, sir."

"Then I'll see what I can do to restore it."

She nodded, signed off, then faced the team. They stared at her, sort of dumbfounded. "What?"

"You don't play well with others, do you?" Sam added and Riley winced.

Safia lifted her top and showed Sam the thin whip scars

that curled her spine. "Not when my own people did this to test *my* trust."

His eyes widened and he glanced at Riley. "I don't need anymore, do you?"

Riley met her gaze and Safia felt his compassion from across the room. "I never did."

Deep Six

David felt like a mole in a dark corner as he worked the computer of a dead man. It gave him the creeps, but he'd already learned why the man put a gun in his mouth. *He's committed treason for Vaghn.* The fragment Marianna Island post picked up had the same encryption as the hard drive. Now they were learning the steps to open it, but Agent Deets was on top of that. David's assignment was to learn where the transmissions landed and in whose hands. Black's NRI records were in Department of Defense possession now and while the NRI president, Cannel, tried protesting, a call from the National Security Advisor shut him up. Threatening to broadcast a charge of treason had that effect on some people.

He'd deciphered Black's authorization, and NRI's list of transmissions in the Marianna time zone. Black received several emails with attachments from one address. A quick IP search confirmed it was Vaghn's computer. The hard drive programs were encrypted, the computer itself was not. David's curiousity made him work faster. A debrief was already scheduled and the JCS waited for no one.

He filtered the transmission but didn't need to know what was in it to do his job. The final send came from another computer, a laptop probably to avoid detection. The collected data was delivered in one single feed transmission through the NRI satellite network that rivaled the CIA's.

He leaned back in the chair and watched the coordinates of the transmission hop to the places he'd tracked so far. The satellite screen to his left digitized with his previous tracking and linked with the pattern from Black's send for Vaghn. When it hit Zaire, his pulse quickened. Zaire, Johannesburg, Sri Lanka—"Bingo."

David pushed off from the counter and spun his chair to face Beckham. "Transmission landed in Kolkata, India."

"Excellent."

David turned back and tapped keys, trying to access the server. "One problem."

Beckham made that hand rolling motion.

"Even if we had the transmission open, we can't erase it from here. Vaghn insured it with a back bomb virus. If we try to erase it, it will launch." Crazy smart, Donovan had said.

"Then we have to physically destroy it," Beckham said with a glance at Colonel Jansen. "Now, I'm happy to volunteer, but D-1 is already in the area."

Jansen agreed and Beckham contacted Dragon One. Max Renfield came on the line and Jansen explained.

"I'm on it," Max said. "David, set up a focus trace for that server, and be my navigator once I land. Colonel? Dragon Six is too obvious and frankly, you aren't paying for the fuel, sir. I need a jet and a pilot." Jansen turned to do just that.

"With all the cautions they've implemented," David said quickly before the connection ended. "There's a good chance it's rigged to blow."

"I don't like the sound of that."

"When you find it, contact me. I've got your back."

Max bent and smiled into the video camera. "Now there's a change."

Jason soldered a wire, then sat back and removed his goggles. He'd gone right to work assembling the first device. Odette had brought him dinner, to check on his progress he supposed. Barasa was still waiting for his payment because he was still on the island. Thibaut wouldn't allow him to leave. Bet that pissed his ass off. Odette had made it clear Thibaut's plans came first, and though he had not revealed them, it wasn't part of the bargain to know. No questions for ten million. How Thibaut knew about and stole the explosive fuel still baffled him.

Yet simply handling the RZ10 made him jumpy. It was too volatile, and he'd reproduced only a 4 gram solution for the prototype. It didn't have the capability of RZ10, but it was close. However, keeping the mix separated was delicate work and the containers inside the device he created were fragile enough to be easily breakable on ignition. He'd almost blown himself and half the island up, he shook so bad.

Grabbing his cane, he stood, stretched, then went to the small fridge for a soda. He strolled around the facility, working the stiffness out of his leg. Untouched sleeping quarters were adjacent to a small kitchen. He didn't concern himself with it. Thibaut had people waiting on him like a king. Yet oddly, not one servant had spoken a word, only nods and hand gestures to communicate. Deaf, dumb, he didn't know, but Thibaut had adopted the unadoptable, he'd read once, insisting every child needed a home.

He stepped onto the veranda shielding him from the hot sun, the breeze pushing at his loose clothes. He walked down the porch, humming a Jimmy Buffet tune as he strolled toward the other buildings. He was nearly at the door of one when he heard his name. Dr. Thibaut crossed the yard to him, smiling.

"Jason. I didn't know you were taking a break. I'd have given you a tour."

"I'm sorry, I was just curious. How many houses do you have here?"

"Several, and that's a dormitory for the staff and the children." He pointed at the pair of two-story buildings with a tree shaded courtyard between. They walked and to the right of the dorms, he saw a colorful playground, children swarming like bugs on a burger. Money wasn't a problem, he thought, noticing the large pool before they stepped inside the coolness of the dorms.

There were individual rooms each child had decorated themselves, the colors bright, cheery. A bell rang, the halls filling with children, and Jason's throat burned with envy when the kids surrounded Thibaut. He called each by name and asked about their day, their homework, yet they answered in a language that sounded like Malay. Thibaut brushed his knuckles across a smooth cheek, bent to kiss the top of a downy head. The children completely ignored Jason, and he stepped back. Finally, Thibaut untangled himself from the group when an older girl called out and the children quickly dispersed into the rooms. A little dark haired girl paused at a doorway, waved at Thibaut, then disappeared into the room. Jason glanced. Thibaut's face was lit up like Christmas. He ignored the prick of jealousy and followed him out, then crossed the yard to a laundry where several workers were pulling white sheets from lines and snapping them with crisp folds.

"How many people are here?"

"Under a hundred, but that still generates a lot of care." He pointed out a dining hall near the dorms, and his own private labs tucked under trees near the fence. "Feel free to investigate, Jason. But please obey any signs you see. And I suggest you not enter the jungle for any reason. It's not safe."

He looked at the forest beyond tall fencing he suspected was wired with electricity. "Safe from what?"

"Pirates have landed here a few times, and the wildlife is dangerous."

Jason strained to see anything. The island was isolated, and he wondered what Thibaut was really keeping out of his compound. There should be nothing on it except maybe birds and monkeys. He was surprised people survived this far out in the ocean.

As if reading his thoughts, Thibaut added, "For the sake of your life, don't test it."

Thibaut pushed back his sleeve to show old scars, three claw marks that nearly wrapped his entire arm. While he wondered what did that, Thibaut didn't offer. Jason had a good thing going. He wasn't about to blow it by being nosey. He respected Thibaut too much to press it. Thibaut would tell him if it was necessary, he assured himself. Yet with the RZ10 here, Jason knew U.S. authorities wouldn't stop until they found it, and him. He was trapped and way out of his league, yet questions lingered. Why would a man of Thibaut's caliber want any bomb and what was the target? He couldn't think of a single reason for the rage behind it, but then, all he knew about Thibaut came from the media. Thibaut walked with him back to the lab, escorting him to the door. The simple act felt restrictive, shrinking the tropical island around him.

"When will you have the first one complete?"

"Three hours, maybe. You've given me everything I need to be productive."

Thibaut's smile was slow, a greater knowledge behind it, and a little guilt over what he was doing surfaced. A heartbeat later, Jason brushed it aside. *This is how you make the real money.* He stepped into the lab and went back to earning his keep, quickly.

Seventeen

Under a cloudless sky, Odette waited on the porch as Jason crossed the lawn. The sun fading, the lamp posts illuminated his path, flickered with his swinging arms. He appeared more teenager than an accomplished scientist. "Don't be nervous," she said and he blinked as he mounted the wide steps.

"It's that obvious?"

"We're unveiling a tremendous device, Jason. We're all nervous."

She escorted him inside Haeger's home and smiled at his reaction to Haeger's wealth and power in the beautiful furnishings, the priceless art covering the walls. A Matisse hung over the mantel of a rarely used fireplace. Beneath her heeled shoes was a richly dyed carpet, a gift from a Saudi prince she'd never met. Haeger wouldn't allow it, the disrespect too archaic for his tastes. But that didn't mean he couldn't take their money. Odette gestured to the far corner, then cleared her throat softly.

In a high backed leather chair, Haeger spun about, smiling. "Ahh, Jason a moment of truth, ey?"

"Yes sir." Jason shifted from foot to foot.

"Be still, Vaghn. You act like a schoolgirl."

Jason turned, scowled. "What is he doing here?"

Barasa stepped from the dark near Haeger's desk, a short crystal glass cupped in his palm. "Viewing the prize everyone wants so badly."

"It's a matter of prudence, Jason. Mister Barasa has fulfilled his end of the bargain and I imagine wants to leave, neh?"

Barasa only nodded, remaining back and while she didn't want to be near the arms dealer, Thibaut insisted he be informed or he would pry into dangerous areas. Haeger crossed to the living room, briefly gripping her hand. Fulfilling his ambition was so close.

"I need the laptop," Jason said.

Odette went to a delicate Queen Anne table and flipped the computer over, replacing the wi-fi card and the battery, then powering it up. Jason frowned. "A caution. Nothing more. We can be traced with it."

"Only the number. The encryption will firewall any trace. I created it from your program," he said to Haeger.

"You continue to confirm my faith in you, Jason," Haeger said. "How very ingenious."

"Clever clever," Barasa said, folding ungraciously into an oxblood club chair.

"An added precaution," Jason said with an anxious shrug. "Dragon One might have copied it, but their only opportunity was between the boat pickup and the chopper on the bridge so I doubt it."

Odette looked pointedly at Barasa, blame for the failure his alone.

"It's of no consequence to us." Thibaut waved that off. "The American agents could have sent it elsewhere before they were killed, but deciphering it needs a master."

"Like you," Jason said with a cheeky grin.

Jason typed in the sequence and over his shoulder, Odette observed each keystroke. The screen blossomed with color, the shape confining to a letter. Interesting. Haeger stepped forward and added a familiar tune to the detonation, and when they'd completed the task, she went to a desktop, then accessed Jason's Swiss account.

"You have another portion of your money," she said and Jason frowned.

"A little incentive," Haeger said. "We are so close."

"I won't fail you," Jason said, looking almost offended. "I haven't."

"Yes, I know. You've done everything I've asked, Jason. Thank you." Haeger held out his hand, and Jason rushed to shake it, beaming. He was so eager to please, just as Haeger had predicted and used it to his advantage. "Consider remaining with us, will you?"

Jason's features tightened and he glanced between the two. "Really?"

"I can almost guarantee you'll have challenges no one can match."

He was cryptic for a reason, she thought. None could be trusted with the final outcome, and while Odette understood every aspect, the specific targets were unknown to her. So he thought. Haeger loved his secrecy and she was happy to keep it for him.

Barasa moved in closer, his after-shave too strong. "I'll retire for the night," he said, then glanced down at the device. "Good job, Vaghn. You've become useful again."

Odette lifted her gaze. He bid Haeger, then Jason good night, smiling beautifully and showing white teeth. Then he glanced her way, held her gaze for a moment before he let it slide down her to her shoes. It was insolent, vulgar, and it pricked her spine. She didn't let it show. *Let him believe he's safe.*

She looked down at the simple device, smiling. Haeger's glory. The Icarus.

And she'd have the honor of setting it all in motion.

Kolkata, India

The four-hour flight didn't mean squat to the temperature and Max felt every degree as he swiped at the sweat in his eyes, then discretely glanced at his TDS Recon. He kept his heading, yet doubled back once to see if he had a tail. So far, no watchers, he thought, and following the GPS, he turned a corner, the street wider, but the foot traffic was a maze of dark heads and colorful clothing. He longed for Singapore, and at least a breeze. He pulled the bandana from his neck and tied it around his forehead. Rambo dorky, he knew, but it wasn't as if he didn't stand out anyway. He'd never considered himself fair-skinned till he landed an hour ago. The beacon triangulated and he tucked himself out of the stream of people moving past and waited for the satellite to narrow on his positions. There weren't enough towers to make it any faster. He bought a bottle of water from a vendor and leaned back against the stucco wall in the shade. It wasn't much of a relief. A couple yards away, a shopkeeper pushed up a striped awning, then threw back the sliding windows to show off bins of neatly stacked fruit and vegetables. The lanky owner splashed water onto the walk, sweeping away the night's debris, the tidy shopfront a sharp contrast to the filth littering the streets.

He checked the TDS Recon, then looked up the street. He drank, trying to wrap his brain around the knowledge the server was inside a church. A Catholic church. St. Thomas of something he couldn't translate was across the street and down a block. Taller than any building around it, the stained glass and tall spires felt out of place, though he knew there were more Catholics in India than in Rome. He pushed away from the wall, pocketing the Recon as he crossed the street and stopped on the avenue between the church and another row of shops. He tried following the lines gathered on top of rough-cut telephone poles. The tangle of wires led off in every direction, some linking to buildings, some directly into windows like a clothesline. Birds flocked and nested in the tops.

"Welcome to Dell tech support," he muttered and searched for the electrical box. He needed to find the power source, then he'd find the server. It wasn't blowing hot on thermal and that meant it probably had its own cooling system. Following the broadest lines, he realized they branched off to a modest house behind the church. The rectory, he realized and knocked. The door opened and a round apple-cheeked woman smiled, telling him the priest was at the local hospital tending the sick. Once he showed his ID and asked if he could search, she was more than kind. Inside, he tried to follow the antique wiring and while they had a computer, the operating system was too old to handle the server, not without the hundred gig it likely needed. The housekeeper followed him from room to room, wringing her apron. Finding nothing, he thanked her and went to the door. She quickly wrapped a hunk of herbed bread in a cloth, then pushed it into his hands.

Cool. Never one to turn down food, he thanked her, and bit into it as he went back to the church. He found a junction box that couldn't handle three more bulbs, let alone a blade server. His gaze slid around. Typical church, it had a center aisle, with a portico flanking the pews. Beneath the portico was lined with heavy wood doors, arched and carved. Inside one, he found stacks of hymnals, buckets, and mops, the next sparsely filled with altar linens. He walked along the outer wall under the portico. An old woman sat in a pew, her head down and covered in a blue scarf. Max stopped to the left of the altar, but didn't need to search it. It was barren of vestments and the elements of mass. He glanced at his watch. Service would start in a couple hours. The only item large enough to house a server was the holy water font, and that would be too difficult to get to without notice. Max lifted the broad steel bowl and looked beneath anyway.

Frustrated, he took a seat in a pew while the Recon triangulated. The sensor picked up within ten feet, but in close quarters that was a lot of ground to cover. He let his gaze wander over the cathedral. Paintings of the Stations of the Cross lined the walls beneath the portico, niches carved into the stone and holding candle stubs. Ahead the crucifix loomed, and his gaze slid to the vestibule, the antechambers. He spotted the confessional and the tiny green light over the narrow door.

"My mother would love this," he said under his breath and crossed to the wood cubes. The side-by-side doors were identical, the Indian craftsmen leaving their mark in the intricately carved latticework doors of scented sandalwood. The light over the left side said the priest waited to hear a multitude of sins. He opened the door and stepped in, his upbringing pushing him to cross himself and kneel to say the proper words.

"Bless me, Father, for I have sinned."

The priest chuckled when he told him the last time he was in this position.

"Do you pray and repent?"

"No Padre, sorry. I just try to be one of the good guys," he said, then stooped to lift the cushion and the wood plank beneath. More cushions. "Father, can you lift your seat? The cushion, I mean."

The partition slid open. "Who are you?"

"Diplomatic Security. I'm looking for a box about eighteen inches wide and a little taller."

"A . . . bomb?"

"No, but it would be a good idea to clear the church, just in case."

The priest in rough brown robes left the confessional, and Max stepped around the door to the clergy's side. He pulled off the cushion, tossing it out, then tried to pry up the wood. It wouldn't budge and he flipped out his knife and slid the blade under the rim, then pried it up. It was glued. Wood cracked.

"My son, son," the priest protested.

"Sorry Father, it's important." Beneath the wood was silver insulation. He pulled it back and Velcro ripped. The blade server was a slim black box. Max opened the commlink to David Lorimer at Deep Six.

"Is it hot?" Max really didn't want to disarm explosives today.

"No indication, but that's it."

"I thought it would be bigger. Now how to destroy it?"

It had its own cooling system and now that it was exposed, Max could hear it operating. He backed out of the confessional and suddenly felt a sharp poke in his back. Instantly, he recognized a gun barrel—which said a lot about his life—and he raised his hands, turning slowly.

"Oh now that's just sacrilegious."

The priest aimed the weapon as he pulled off the rough cassock, then tossed it aside. Big trouble, Max thought. He's got a silencer and probably help close by.

The man searched him. "Put your hands down." He dug the weapon into Max's side and his chin nicked the air. "That way."

They crossed in front of the confessionals and the well of souls lit with candles. Max's steps slowed when he spotted a pair of legs draped in priest's robes on the floor inside the antechamber. Aw, man. He was damn tired of the innocent dying because of a freaking genius hell-bent on mass destruction. He faced his captor.

"Ya know, this isn't working for me."

The man raised his weapon. "I will shoot."

Before he could fire, Max grabbed the barrel, shoved it down, and threw his elbow into the man's face. Cartilage gave, and the man reflexively pulled the trigger, the round chipping the marble floor. Max hit again, tearing the weapon from him, then flipping it to grip the stock. But his opponent was skilled, a spin kick knocking the gun from his hand. It skated across the slick polished floor as his opponent executed a side kick. Max saw it coming and grabbed the man's boot mid-air. He couldn't balance, couldn't move.

"Not so slick now, are you?" Max said, and violently twisted the boot, the force driving the man to the ground. Max heard the guy's knees crack as he hit the marble, but his attacker rolled, then struggled to his feet, obviously in pain. The old woman roused from her prayers, rushing toward the door. The fake priest grabbed her arm and used her as a shield.

"Oh you big chicken shit," Max said and threw himself at him, breaking his hold on the old woman and taking him to the floor. "Run lady!" Max immediately locked his legs around his chest, and his arm around the guy's throat, bending his neck and squeezing. His opponent fought, fists hammering till Max thought his skin would split, but he kept pressure, pushing harder when he glimpsed the dead priest again. He heard the soft crack, then applied pressure. The hard snap rang in the hollow church, and the man went slack. Max pushed off, and the dead man rolled over, smacking his head on the marble steps and splitting it like melon.

He glanced away, then up at the crucifix. "Sorry." He pointed to the dead man. "Bad guy." He relieved the body of weapons, taking back his own, then searched him. No labels, no ID. More mercenaries.

He retuned to the blade server to search for the leads to the power source. Buried under it, he supposed, then gripped the server and yanked it from the confessional seat. Sparks snapped, but the cables refused to give it up.

"Not on my watch," he snarled and tore it free, then marched out the door, dragging it behind by the torn wires. He crossed the street and waited a few moments for traffic to congest, then like skipping rocks, he hurled it into the street. Cars crushed it, and Max waited till parts fractured under tires, then called David.

"It's done, destroyed."

"Any problems?"

He glanced back at the church. "Nothing I couldn't handle, but pass onto the big Kahoona. Agent Troy was right. Terrorists have knowledge of the Icarus. They were waiting and willing to kill to protect it."

Like everything else in this mission, he thought, ending the call. He was so ready to get them on their own territory, and take them down to hell where they belonged.

Barasa sipped iced pineapple juice, the remains of the morning meal shared with Thibaut cleared by servants in silence. Till Thibaut gave the order, his life was at his whim. He snickered a laugh to himself and set the goblet down before he dropped it. The drink was laced with something. Why, he wasn't certain. Thibaut had already effectively disarmed him and his jet. And where was Rahjan? He'd sent him to search for his flight crew. He hadn't seen them since they were escorted to a lounge in the hangar. An unnecessary tactic. He wasn't leaving without his weapon. But there was one more piece he needed.

"The perfect delivery system? You've yet to produce it."

Thibaut insisted he had it, yet as per the agreement, he had given no explanation. Barasa licked his dry lips, his words slurred, but he straightened, hoping it cleared his head.

"Have you noticed the others on my island?" he said with a wave.

Barasa frowned, glancing around. "The kids?"

Haeger nodded.

Cale blinked, rubbing his face when a girl about eight years old walked up to Thibaut. Haeger smiled at the child, brushed the back of his bony hand across her cheek. The girl turned her face into it and kissed his palm, mewing yet never speaking. Thibaut dragged on the thin cigar, then took the child's hand. He whispered something to the girl Barasa couldn't hear and the child nodded. Thibaut ground the glowing cigar into her palm. Barasa winced, yet the child didn't flinch, and only tipped her head curiously. After a moment, she drew back, shaking her hand. He puffed the smoke again, then opened his arms. The girl launched at him, clutching, smearing blood and burned skin on his clothes. God, how was she not screaming in pain? Not hating him for wounding her?

Odette walked near and pulled the child back, directing her to another with shushed words in a language he suspected the Professor developed. As far as he could tell, no one could communicate with the children except Thibaut and Odette. Part of a larger plan, he thought and when Odette returned, he lifted his gaze to hers. How could one so beautiful be so vicious?

"Interesting," he said, trying not to show his revulsion.

It sobered him quickly. Children. He'd bred children to deliver weapons of mass destruction. A little army from what he'd seen. Thibaut had clearly established his own community on the island, yet none of the children he'd seen were over twelve or thirteen. Where did they go when they were older? His gaze flicked to the two guards at the far edge of the lawn, but knew they were hired. Too many faces had a familiar past.

Yet the children were all different nationalities. Some Indian, Malaysian, Thai, Norwegian perhaps, then he remembered Thibaut had orphanages in those countries. Barasa frowned for a second. Thibaut had taken them from the streets, feral children with the instinct to survive. A registered orphan risked being missed and he was all about secrecy. Cale thought suicide bombers were twisted. He gave them weapons, but didn't allow their causes to touch his life. Suddenly, he met the older man's gaze. "Your goal?"

Thibaut sat forward, his palms propped on the top of his cane. "Absolute proof I was, and still am, correct. DNA and gene manipulation is possible. They are as obedient as animals."

Thibaut's thin glance slid to him, and Cale experienced a moment of fear he'd never known. There was no way to predict this man, or the woman standing behind him. His gaze lowered to her hand on Thibaut's shoulder, gently caressing.

Thibaut covered it, patting, then turned her hand to kiss the center. His gaze never left Barasa's.

It was a telling moment in the relationship between the twisted pair; devout to the point of madness.

He looked away, ashamed to be part of this. He'd no delusions about himself. He was a criminal, with many graves beneath his feet, as Rahjan would say. For the risks he took, he was rich, and the men who joined his organization well paid. Some forced, certainly, but he'd given the families the money. That whisper on the streets offered up men when he needed them. Yet he followed a personal set of rules that included avoiding any involvement with the underaged. Countries hunted child killers harder than political assassins. His gaze slid past Thibaut to the children playing happily about a hundred yards away. Barasa never experienced that kind of freedom and safety. He envied it. A child of the streets himself once, he'd foraged for food and a place to feel safe for the night. He would have given his life for a little affection, for someone to show they cared if he'd existed. Instead, he'd been bought and sold till he was skilled enough to fight back. He could have been one of these children.

He lowered his gaze and suddenly understood the mechanism Thibaut had used. Love was a weapon in this man's hands, and the degree he'd taken it became clear when the burned child returned and Cale saw her sweet cherub face. More importantly, her eyes. The irises were a bright, icy blue, but her pupils were elongated—feline.

Jason stepped back slowly, careful not to disturb the fronds disguising his position. The group clustered on the lawn near the end of the large porch sat under the shade of a massive round tent, the afternoon sun haloing the children dressed in blistering white clothes. Realization struck like a fist to his stomach, pushing the air from his lungs. He moved back, feeling his way before he turned and hurried toward the lab. He worked his way beyond the sunlight, the jungle dense enough to conceal his shadow.

He tried to block the last few moments, but his mind refused. Like a video stream it repeated the look on the child's face as Thibaut burned her. Obedient, almost lovingly suffering for him. He'd heard enough, the long porch echoing their voices.

He didn't have a problem with Thibaut exacting revenge on those who'd marked his work as Frankenstein. They just couldn't wrap their brains around the fact that no matter what he did or had done, it advanced science and discovery. Jason understood. He'd wanted to be a leader in his industry too. Thibaut was the forerunner in DNA sequence interlacing, and while hundreds of universities and institutions were using the methods scholars once deemed unethical, not one voice had credited Thibaut for its roots. That kind of insult was tough to swallow. It festered in the patient planning of his revenge.

Jason understood that too. His device was the result of five years of designing in his head because anything he wrote in prison was immediately confiscated. Odette had contacted him only a few days after the trial with the proposition. He'd had five years to design, but it took him less than a day to turn it into schematics. Thibaut paid to have the first few devices, but after that, it was his to sell for every dollar he could get. He'd no intention of being penniless ever again.

He slowed near the dorms, skirting the playground, pool and yard. His lab was about fifty yards beyond, slightly isolated, yet as he hurried, he noticed the same child in the same swing he'd seen before. He stopped, studying the child, trying to pinpoint what bugged him about it. Well, more than the robotic kids. It occurred to him that the lights were still on from last night. Now that he thought about it, he hadn't seen the dorm lights go off after he'd delivered the device. He realized they never went off. No one on this island slept. And not one child was over the age of twelve, thirteen max. Odette said the rest were in boarding schools but Jason wasn't convinced.

His gaze shifted to the jungle beyond his lab. The buildings a hundred yards behind it were off limits. Thibaut's own labs were there, and while Jason was curious and tempted, he didn't want to get that close to Thibaut's work. Just sell him his. He was almost finished and reconsidered remaining with Thibaut when he understood that Thibaut had taken his greatest accomplishment and planned to use it for revenge. The children would deliver the bombs—and the puzzle of his targets suddenly fell into place.

Changi Airport
Singapore

Max had to give Colonel Jansen credit. The man knew people, he thought as he walked away from the Lear jet used for diplomats. A cush ride at supersonic speeds was the only way to go, he decided, turning his phone back on.

A second later, it rang in his hand. He glanced at the number before answering it. "Jasmine? What's up, honey?" Viva should be with her because Killian had to fly back for Alexa.

"It's mean, Maxwell. Someone's bein' just mean."

"Take a breath and tell me who it is so I can kick his ass."

She laughed over her tears. "If my big brother is dead, then why am I getting text messages from his phone?"

"Excuse me? Say again."

He hadn't heard wrong. "Send it to me as an email. Can you do that?" He'd personally kill the person doing this to her.

"I'm southern, not stupid, Maxwell. But tell me true," she sniffled "Is there hope?"

Her voice sounded so broken and empty. "There's always hope, honey. Sit tight. I'm on it." He ended the call and at the edge of the flight line, a sedan pulled to a stop. The driver got out and addressed him, but Max put up a finger, pacing as he waited for the text message to arrive from the other side of the world.

When the chime sounded, he opened it.

A-L-I-V

Max blinked. *Ohgod.* He immediately called Ellie. "Base, track the GPS in this number." He rattled it off.

"That's your friend's phone. It's not on, Max. We tried this before."

His grip tightened. "But not on text messages sent after the explosion."

Over forty-eight hours after, he thought.

"I'm on it, listing as search and rescue assistance."

The proper paperwork, he thought and knew she didn't like breaking the rules, yet while she kept a steady flow of information, it was at Safia's request, not the CIA's. She'd probably lose her job for this, or possibly, her clearance. "Thank you Ellie. At least we can say we tried everything."

Max looked at the message again, then sent it to the rest of the team and slid into the staff car. Max rubbed his palms on his jeans, looked out the window at nothing, trying to keep a handle on his imagination and mentally listing what they'd need to help find Sebastian. Spotlights first, he thought, glancing at the predawn sky.

Ellie called again. *"I have an address and you're right, it came from his phone."*

A little burst of hope spurred through him and Max rubbed his mouth. "Give me the location and tell the rest of the team to meet me there."

Sonsoral Islands

The Traveler rendezvoused with the Palau police craft on the Philippine Seas, and Bridget stepped onto the police boat, greeted the officers, then walked to the bow. The vessel was underway in moments, and she waved to Travis on the deck of her ship. She didn't have her radio. It would interfere with the police bands they'd said, but she'd tucked her cell phone in her bra, yet left it off. She'd done it for Travis. He was against notifying the police because there wasn't anything they could do about the finds, but she felt too strongly about this. She had the clinical proof. They'd completed several tests three times to confirm their findings. She dipped her hand in her pocket and rolled the tooth in her palm. Removing the tooth from the jawbone had been difficult, and it was the first sign the bones were newer than she first thought. She studied the tooth, but knew the curves of the enamel by memory now. Narrow and pointed, it showed no signs of filing. She'd been wrong. It was human. The jawbone of a child with feline DNA.

The boat neared the island, two men lowering a rubber craft over the side. Bridget went to the rail and flipped the rope ladder down. An officer offered help, but she stayed him with a wave and went over the side. Two officers joined her, and since she'd been here twice already, she started the engine and steered them in. The tide was perfect to get them over the reef. The two men watched the land approach, and though they hadn't said a word, the larger of the two jumped out and helped beach the craft.

She was here to show them were they'd found the bones and mark it for further investigation. The island belonged to Palau, but so did the entire chain that stretched for a few hundred miles. The Palau government didn't have the money or the interest to dig. But Bridget wasn't letting it go just yet. Maternal instinct reared when she thought of the bones, the child gnawed by cats. She couldn't ignore it. Though most of the bones were old, she dated several as recent as five years. There was no way to match DNA without something to compare it to, and searching missing persons records was a task for the police.

Bridget slung her wet sack on her shoulder, then led the two men into the jungle. She held her light down, searching for prints as she meandered toward the boulder. She wanted the chance to look at the case again, but it proved impossible. The vines were too heavy and her earlier cuts had made little difference. She glanced at the officers. One was photographing it. She showed them the dugout in the rock, and the remains.

"Animal," one man said.

"I thought so too, but no." She drew specimen bags and gloves, pulling on the latter, then knelt to take more samples while the other man snapped photos.

She ducked in, holding her breath against the stench, then swept up the remains. Too new to smell this bad, she thought again, then backed out and stood. She dusted off her knees and saw the sole of a boot. Frowning, she took a step. The younger officer was flat on his back, his throat cut. She immediately took off in a run, heading back toward the shore and *The Traveler*. The other man thrashed behind her in the woods, warning he'd shoot her if she didn't stop. She managed a couple more yards before his body impacted with her back. She fell hard, her chin scraping the sand. She barely caught her breath before he yanked her off the ground, then pushed a pistol barrel into her throat.

"I have no problem killing you," he said. With the other hand, he pulled the camera strap from around his neck and tossed it down.

"Why?"

He shrugged. "Not my job to know."

She felt numb, her heart beating hard in her chest when she realized he didn't need her alive. He'd already killed a man to get her. He searched her, and she slapped at his hand when he cupped her crotch and slid his hand between. He felt her breasts, and she fought, but he did it anyway, pushing his pistol into her side when she elbowed him. He pocketed her cell phone, then took her knife always strapped to her calf.

"Walk." He gestured with the pistol. "That way."

She obeyed, her sense of direction twisted, but he used a

compass on his watch and Bridget recognized the clues she'd missed; the bulges in his short vest, the scars on his face and throat that looked like knife slashes. But it was the lack of emotion in his eyes that terrified her. He pushed her none-to-gently ahead, directing her and the jungle thinned, the trade wind breeze pushing the trees. Several more yards and she stopped.

"Maary mother," she said under her breath. They were on the other side of the island—and there were more of them. Fear pulled at her skin when she saw the four men with rifles on the beach. "You bloody bastards."

"Aren't we all," he muttered and nudged her ahead. She walked, escape further out of her reach, and she thought of Travis and her sons. *They'll go mad.* Several yards in the water, a speedboat rocked on the waves. Long with a small cabin and some extremely large engines, it was a racing boat and not built to take them into open seas. So what were their plans for her? Transport her again? Hostage for ransom? Who did they think would pay besides her husband on a professor's salary?

Then one man left the group and came to her, taking her firmly by the arm, then walked her into the water to the speedboat. The rest didn't follow and walked back up the shore and into the woods. "Where are they going!?"

But she knew. To leave no witnesses. *Oh Travis.* For a breath, she considered going over the side of the boat and if she had to, die with her husband. But the leader pushed her down to the floor, then secured her feet to her hands with plastic slip ties. She looked up at him as he tossed a white tarp over her. A moment later, she felt the jolt as the craft moved, the engine vibrating beneath her. The betrayal and murder thumped at her temper. Bridget didn't know anyone this powerful, this clever, but she knew—her brother did.

Eighteen

Odette wrapped her jacket tighter, then leaned to turn up the heat inside the luxury car. The day was warm for the region, but she preferred her home in the tropics. She wouldn't be here for long regardless.

Against her judgment, she glanced at the child seated on the opposite end of the leather bench seat. The girl lightly gripped a small school bag that matched her clothing, a blue blazer, and plaid skirt copied from a nearby girl's school. The child didn't speak and stared ahead, humming to herself. Occasionally something bright caught her attention and she watched the scenery pass.

Odette had chosen the fairest, the least suspicious. She ran her hand lightly down the waterfall of gold hair, then drew back and turned away.

She thought of Haeger, all he'd done for her, given her, and she did not want to fail him. She had taken great pains to enter the country unnoticed, the papers to deliver the child to her new parents passing through scrutiny when they learned of Thibaut's beneficiary. His name still carried a golden touch she was happy to use. The driver continued for another four miles before she ordered him to pull out of traffic. She left the car and walked around the rear, then opened the door. The child stepped out and continued walking without a backward glance. Odette smiled proudly and watched her cross the street, beyond the security that wasn't completely in place yet. A chubby girl in the same uniform waved, then frowned when her girl ignored it and kept moving between the crowds outside the building. The white stone double colonnade front was barricaded from street traffic and when her girl walked between the barriers, a young guard stopped her. She behaved exactly as planned. The man smiled and let her pass.

Odette slipped back into the car and ordered the driver to leave. She placed a call. "Number two is in place. Enjoy your glory."

She closed the phone and relaxed as the car headed for the airport and her jet, already cleared for takeoff.

Singapore

Max called Sebastian's number and kept calling so Base could get a triangulation on the signal. Ellie had to jump a satellite to stay in range as Dragon One converged on the collapsed buildings. The signal came from the edge of the blast zone. While Riley wondered how he got out of the CIA station before the explosion, he was grateful.

Riley glanced at his friends. "Max, see if David can help narrow the signal." He looked at Safia. She had her phone to her ear and she tipped it away to say, "I've got emergency services coming. But they're busy nearer the blast sight. I'm trying to round up some help."

Max already had a million candle watt power shining down around the rubble. Riley walked onto the rubble, Max beside him, his expression grim.

"The battery's signal is dying. It's not on anymore." Max checked for it on his spiffy new flip phone, and Riley glanced at the yellow dot tracer. "He's been under there for nearly three days."

"He didn't survive this to end it now, buddy. We work

faster," Riley said, giving Max's shoulder a squeeze before he turned away.

In the blast, the roof and upper floor slid off like books off a stack and crushed half the lower level. Riley realized the signal came from between two buildings, an alleyway, and he prayed there were air pockets in there somewhere. The pile was damn high.

He grabbed a cinder block and tossed it, his teammates moving mountains of wood, furniture, and concrete like a well-oiled machine, yet it was a slow process. They had to shore up the weight of the upper floor as they went along. Beyond the destruction, people loitered to watch.

The team worked without talking, sweating in the heat to clear a path, and Riley glanced over his shoulder, frowning when he heard the roar of a diesel engine.

"That's a humvee," Max said without doubt. They hurried to the street as the green humvee rode over the rough terrain and stopped, half tilted. The doors opened and five men in camouflage uniforms left the truck, walking briskly to the center.

"Agent Troy?" The Marine sergeant looked at Riley. Riley shook his head, stepping aside.

Safia advanced. "I'm Troy. Thank you for helping." She shook hands. "A fellow Marine is under there somewhere. Alive. We need to dig him out." The men went immediately to assess the damage and she looked at Riley, smiled, shrugged. "U.S. Embassy detachment."

Max led the men to the spot, but paused to kiss her cheek. "Thanks Safia."

She blushed. The squad spread out, and in a fireman's line started the long process of removing rubble. Max and Riley were in the front, working stone by stone. They were forced to stop to check the stability of the structure and brace it before continuing. Safia was between them, stripped down to shorts and a tank top, and moving as fast as the Marines.

Riley suspected she had a little guilt going and looked back at the crumbled building. Nothing compared to his own. He should have let someone else go after Vaghn. It was a favor he could have done without.

"He saved my life, you know?" Max said. "He did more than that. I was seventeen, lied about my age to enlist." He inclined his head to the youngest Marine helping them dig. "I was deployed to the Gulf and scared shitless. Sebastian noticed, never mentioned it, but he kept a watch on me. Made me double check my weapons, that sort of thing. He didn't cut me any slack either. I dug a lot of bunkers. A real hard-ass, but it wasn't tough to take orders from him. They always made more sense than the officers'."

Riley sensed Max needed to talk and while he knew the story, Safia listened.

"My fire team was in a skirmish on the Kuwait border. Iraqis coming in ten directions and they didn't know what the hell they were doing. Like a bunch of eight year olds playing Army in the backyard. Ran right into the open." He let out a breath, his shoulders sagging with the weight of old memories. He grabbed another hunk. "I was in charge of the fire team, no hunkering down and waiting. We went looking for it. Shoot everything, drive some more, shoot everything again. The humvee got hit. The mortar tossed that puppy in the air."

He made an exploding sound and Safia smiled as she gathered and tossed. "Didn't blow it up though. I broke my shin and my guys were pretty banged up too. Iraqis pinned us down. We ghosted a few, but they had reinforcements bringing bigger ordnance. Saddam was tossing kids at U.S. forces like cannon fodder." Riley glanced and noticed the Marines listening intently. "We had to get out of there." He shrugged. "I shot pain killers in my leg, then we threw six grenades at once and ran like hell. We didn't get far, the enemy pinned us down." He smiled to himself. "Then a banged up humvee comes flying across the sand, a gunner manning a fifty cal, shooting his way to us. He rides over the dunes, crashes into the enemy fortification. Gunner lays down some cover fire, Sebastian is out of the humvee, firing at anything." Max's smile widened. "Crazy bastard. He gets back in the humvee, rolls out and races to us, slams on the brakes—the Vee slides sideways and nearly tips over. They're heavy things, an iron brick with a motor. It sits down so hard the door opens. He shouts, 'Need a lift, devil dogs?'" Max looked past her to Riley, smiling.

"Devil dog express," Riley said.

"So, crazy really is what D-1 is all about?" Safia said.

"That and the hokey pokey."

She laughed, gripped more concrete and behind her a couple Marines snickered.

Max and Riley tried to lift a chunk of the cement wall, then dropped it, the weight too much. "We need a hoist," Max said, glancing around. He was about to call the Marines over to help when Riley heard, "Make a hole!"

Men parted for Safia wielding a sledgehammer, and she slammed it down on the block. It cracked, but she wasn't done, slinging it back and bring it down with a growl. It fractured, and they hurried to move chunks aside and get another layer closer to Sebastian. Marines watched her for a second as she took her anger out on the cement till she couldn't swing anymore.

The young sergeant glanced. "Wouldn't want to be on her bad side," he murmured and continued lifting chunks.

Yes, but her good side is so intriguing, Riley thought, noticing more locals coming to help. Something tightened in his chest when a boy, skinny as a switch with his head wrapped in a blood-stained bandage bent to help.

"David got a triangulation on the last location?" Riley asked Max.

"Cell towers fell, coverage isn't good, but this is it." Max moved slowly inside the lean-to pile, the weight above threatening to collapse further. Riley sent the Marines off to find more wood to shore it up and two trotted off. Logan knelt and held the Sonar Shield, a flexible cone-shaped listening device that worked on sound waves. A thank you gift from R&D after the Thailand mission.

Riley ordered everyone back for a moment. It picked up breathing, and Logan aimed the device.

"Mine's not that small," Safia said in a whisper.

"The inventor made it."

Logan glanced to level them a "gimme a break" look, and they stepped further back. Logan had to stop to wait for men to brace broken walls, then crawled deeper. He called out for Sebastian. One time, two, three . . . still nothing. Then Logan said, "Coonass," and Riley thought the call sign had less syllables, more force than his name.

Logan ducked back out. "Nothing."

"We keep digging," Riley said, and went back to work. Logan went to the other side of the fallen structure to find another way in. "Give me the Sonar." Safia handed it over, and Riley held his breath and aimed. "Coonass," he said, not too loud. The feedback in the headphones buzzed his head. He grabbed a chunk of cement and hit a pipe once, let it ring, then did it again. His heartbeat slowed as he waited, forced his breathing shallow and quiet.

He waited. Tap . . . tap.

"We have tone!" Riley stuck his head out. "He responded."

Max, Sam, and Logan smiled, giving each other a shoulder shake, then Max was there, instructing them how to move the pieces. Safia worked the hammer, breaking chunks the Marine quickly carried away. The largest piece shifted, and Max kept vigil on the structure growing precarious the more debris they removed. Furniture and a fridge blocked one portion, an unstable slab hanging over them as Riley dug.

"Where is he?" Riley sat back, swiping his sweaty forehead with the back of his hand.

"Riley! We have another way in," Logan called and Riley left the tunnel and rushed around to the street side.

The entire upper floor was shoved off, but the staircase was intact. Logan swung an ax to chop it away. Riley pulled the pieces aside, then heard the whine of a power tool. Safia strode over the debris, a small chainsaw screaming in her hand. Men grinned. It looked brand new.

"Yes, I nipped it." She lowered the engine. "Tell me where."

He directed her and she cut away at the staircase, the guys moving the remains. When she grew tired, Max took over, but there wasn't room in the small space. Riley stepped back beside Safia.

"I have a medical chopper standing by, and a room at the hospital," she said, swiping at the sweat under her chin.

He slipped his arm around her waist, and she tipped her head on his shoulder. "I've never prayed before. Not till now." She met his gaze. "Sebastian, this city. They didn't deserve this and need some hope."

She still blamed herself, Riley thought and didn't try to convince her otherwise. He knew from his own experience, guilt didn't leave till you let it.

Max cut away at the staircase, his goal the wall beyond that covered the top floor. Riley stepped into it, the chain of Marines removing debris faster than he could hand it over. Spectators gathered, the police trying to keep locals back from the danger. Nothing was stable at the end of the blast zone. They pried dry wall and Logan shined a light, then lurched back and smiled. Sam and Riley moved in with him, and Max splashed light into the small gap. Riley looked in.

Sebastian. He wasn't moving.

The leanest of them all, Riley stretched over the concrete and touched his throat. "He's alive."

Sebastian's cell phone lay in his lax palm, slats of wood pinned the left side of his body, only his hand exposed, another tumble of trash covered his waist and chest. One leg was free. No telling what injuries he'd suffered and like moving toothpicks, they went slowly. Another hour passed before Logan could get close enough to him to inspect his wounds.

Sebastian still hadn't moved. Logan handed Riley the phone, then checked Sebastian's vital signs and probed for wounds. He looked up. "I need a backboard, neck brace, and air casts. His ribs and wrists are broken." Riley could see the bone pushing through the skin, but took hope that it was the only place he spotted blood.

Max couldn't stop smiling even as they eased Sebastian onto the backboard. Logan went to work. Max knelt near and said, "Coonass, wake up, you spatula wielding redneck."

He didn't move, and Safia grabbed Riley's hand as Logan injected him.

"You still owe me twenty bucks on that Saints game," Max said.

Still he didn't move. Max glanced at Logan, then said, "Another week and it doubles."

Sebastian shifted minutely. Riley let out a hard laugh, grabbing Safia to his side and squeezing. He felt his eyes burn. Thank God.

Sebastian's lids fluttered and before he opened his eyes, he swallowed, then asked, "How's my little sister?"

"With Viva," Sam assured. "Jasmine will be happy it wasn't a ghost or voodoo."

Sebastian smiled, then winced. He couldn't move. Logan had him strapped down and his wrist in an air cast. With the embassy Marines, Dragon One lifted the backboard and slowly carried Sebastian to the waiting ambulance.

"Why call Jasmine?" Riley had to ask, walking alongside.

"Only number I could remember," Sebastian murmured, his mouth bloody and swollen. "Sometimes speed dial sucks."

Riley grinned and realized that trapped, Sebastian couldn't see the keypad and could only dial with his thumb. They settled the board on a gurney and pushed it into the truck.

"Don't you think you should call Jasmine?" Riley said,

nudging Max. He scrambled for his phone and dialed, his grin so tight Riley thought his face would split. Riley couldn't stop smiling himself and glanced as Safia moved up beside him. "This is a good day." He bent, kissed her softly.

Logan climbed into the ambulance with Sebastian, promising to call. Max joined them, and put the phone to Sebastian's ear the instant he was inside. As the ambulance pulled away, Riley, Safia and Sam stood on the debris with the embassy detachment, hot, sweaty and happy for the first time since landing in Singapore. Riley let out a loud ooh-rah, the Marines joined and a cheer rose. Locals brought water and food, and for a moment, he enjoyed the relief—and a new understanding of his family's pain.

An hour or so later, the Marines climbed into the humvee, and Riley thought he was never that young, but only youth and stupidity would have sent him into Serbia with just a sidearm and a radio. Then again, he'd done dumber things and age had little to do with it.

The chime of phones had everyone patting pockets, and Riley answered his just as Safia put her own to her ear. He listened, meeting her gaze.

"You need to get in the air, Odette has already landed once," Beckham said. "In Norway."

That was a long flight from the South Pacific not to be noticed. "You didn't track her moves?"

"They flew under radar over Chinese air space. She doesn't have the phone with that number and she was on the ground less than an hour."

Safia frowned at Riley. "Long enough to set a bomb."

"That's why there's a jet on the airstrip," Beckham said.

Riley was already behind the wheel of the rental truck, turning over the engine.

Safia climbed in. "What do they expect us to do? Shoot it down?"

Sam hopped in the back. "Sounds like a plan to me."

Offices of Major General Gerardo
Pentagon

"Do you want the short version?" Beckham said, dropping a stack of files and books on the conference table. He crossed to the coffee service, bypassing a teacup for a mug and poured.

Hank's gaze flipped between him and the stack, then settled in for a debriefing. "Fire away."

Major Beckham returned to the table. "Haeger Thibaut is older than he looks, that much I'll say. His bio says he's the son of a NASA physicist who was among the Nazi-held scientists we smuggled out of Germany during the war. Ring any bells?" He prodded.

"Operation Paperclip. We captured, then smuggled Hitler's V-2 rocket scientists with the help of the resistance. Then we employed them with the Joint Intelligence Committee for missile defense." JIC was an arm of the Joint Chiefs of Staff then. Now the government had ten agencies doing the research and development.

"A smart move to have the brain power in our control and away from the Russians then," Gerardo said, then shook his head, his look doubtful. "It was a moral stretch to hire the same people who'd killed our troops, and expect them to protect our people later. Even Eisenhower's final address mentioned that bringing them into the country was a mistake."

Hank supposed it was the Hitler ideology they feared and not the scientists themselves. "We kept tight control."

"Not enough because Thibaut wasn't a child then. He was near twenty, a prized prodigy under the tutelage of scientists at Dachau. Like Sigmund Rascher."

"Oh good God." A sick feeling worked into his blood stream. The concentration camps were infamous for human experimentation, freezing, poisons, even twisted attempts of sewing twins together to force them to conjoin. "Wait, he'd be eighty, at least."

From a file, Beckham slipped out a black and white photograph and slid it across the table. It showed a young man grouped with several older. In the background, he recognized the dated gear on the soldiers. End of conflict, WWII. The line-up of scientists numbered over a hundred, yet his attention went to one young man, tall and underfed. Something about the way he folded his arms, almost defiant and turned away from the others made him want to slap him. Another photo slid easily across the table. In color, Thibaut stood with Mandela.

"Does that look like an eighty year old man?" Beckham said. "That was taken six years ago."

Hank's brows shot up. Thibaut looked forty-five, fifty at the most. "Where did you find this?" Hank pulled the files close, splitting them with Gerardo.

"Amazing at what people have published on the internet. These photos are from the *grandson* of a German Jew who was freed from an encampment in the mountains. On My Space." He chuckled. "Isaac Hieberg, the kid, found them in an old trunk in his grandfather's home in Morocco. He was on some 'I need to know my roots' quest and tried to put the pieces together. When it came to before the war, he had nothing except what was in the trunk. He was kind enough to ship it to me with the promise to return it. He's an American born and raised." Beckham searched his pile of books and files, selected a thick leather binder, opening it on the table. Inside was a journal with yellowed papers inked in German. "Eye witness accounts. The translation was as close as we could get. Dialects make it tough." He shrugged. "Mostly it's the story of Grandpa's run to freedom, eating rats, losing a finger to frostbite. However, he goes into detail about the scientists and their journey. He was turned over to the American forces and lived in the U.S. for several years before ending up in Morocco. He writes about meeting this scientist and being terrified of him." He tapped the photo of Thibaut. "He mentions three times that he'd seen him at the Dachau prison camps. Grandpa Hieberg was a survivor."

That sick feeling magnified and Hank felt his palms sweat. Donovan tried to warn us, Hank thought.

"I had our analysts do a bone structure match to Haeger Thibaut, born Henrick Knapp. In most recent photos, he's rarely without that straw hat, but analysts feel its good enough to stand up in court. Fingerprints of Knapp taken before entering the U.S. in the 40's match the thumb print for Thibaut's last passport."

Hank sat back. "Plastic surgery can reverse the clock, but why wasn't this guy vetted by the Secret Service? He was in the White House."

"Who would refute him? Without documented corroboration, no one could deny his identity as the elder Knapp, because he's really the son." Beckham shivered dramatically. "God, that's just creepy. No record of any surgery, at least not under either name. No personal documentation like birth certificates, so legal names couldn't be proven. They were running for their lives in the middle of a war zone then. We made allowances. The father doesn't show in paperwork or records and I can't find out what happened to his mother."

"Don't bother. If he's eighty, she's dead." Hank still couldn't wrap his brain around this.

"Knapp or Thibaut did return to Austria to get her, but after that there are no banking accounts nor even a home loan. Last time he used his jet was a month ago, a brief trip to Turkey, although his funding shows up as recent as three months ago to international adoptions or something."

"He was in Turkey or Odette?"

"Don't have confirmation yet. Her most likely. Air traffic control recognize flight numbers, not the owner's registration."

"Bring in more help," Hank said. "Get a psychiatrist in here, a profiler. He's assumed his father's identity." When Beckham protested, Hank put up a hand. "It doesn't matter right now. This is the man turning all the keys." He tapped the color photo. "If he's got the fountain of youth, fine, not a concern now. And get a body language expert." He flicked a hand at the war photos. "He's got attitude for a kid who just left the laboratories that committed the biggest atrocities of this century."

Gerardo leaned forward. Hank glanced and saw the quarter rolling again. He waited. "He's been planning for a long time. Odette did the dirty work and she's still doing it," he said with a glance at his reports. "He was on the inside and knows how we work. Procedure might have changed with technology, but he's informed and worse, knows our handicaps and circumvents every roadblock." Gerardo was quiet for a few seconds, the quarter rolling evenly across his knuckles. "It's in the targets."

"I'm betting on Dragon One's theory that he's exacting revenge on all who spurned his greatness," Beckham said and Hank agreed. "A man who deals in facts, he was ruined for experimenting on DNA splicing and his work on genome with stem cells. Where did he get the stem cells? The DNA to torture into submission?"

"What did you learn about this Odette?"

"Nothing. Not one thing that isn't connected to Thibaut. There is no birth record for that name and her fingerprint is a manufacture." Hank and Al looked up at once. "Her passport is a fake."

Gerardo read the report and said, "She had diplomatic papers for an adoption. To a cabinet member. They let her pass and no search. She could have a purse full of those things to plant."

There was a long silence before Hank spoke up. "Wasn't the Nobel Prize award a couple years ago for DNA, stem cell research?"

"For the principles of introducing specific gene modifications in mice by the use of embryonic stem cells," Gerardo read off a report. "Oddly, it's his human experimental research with Rascher at Dachau that's the basis of it."

"This guy's fucking Mengella," Beckham said and didn't apologize for his language. "We need to take him *out*."

Hank frowned. Beckham looked like he wanted the job. "Crazy never takes a vacation, sir."

Dragon Six was too large to outmaneuver a Lear jet, not that Riley planned on a dogfight. Jansen came though with an aircraft regulated to generals at Central Command. Inside, it ran a close second to Air Force One. Flyboys knew their technology and it was filled. Logan would be in heaven, Riley thought, but he wouldn't leave Sebastian's side till Jasmine and Viva arrived. Riley sympathized with the Cajun. When it hit how long it would take to be one hundred percent again, he hoped that laid-back Louisiana patience helped. Riley had set himself back a couple times trying to rush his legs to heal.

Safia sat behind the cockpit, watching the trace of the jet. Intel said Odette had landed, drove to the center of Oslo, then did a one-eighty back to the plane. It was as if she'd lost her way, though there was definitely a method to her madness.

"Secrecy is one part," Riley said. "But why these countries, why right now?"

"Didn't they fuel the plane?" Sam asked.

Safia frowned. "Yes, of course."

"Can you get me the fuel invoice?"

Safia turned back to the console, adjusted her headset and gave orders for Base to hunt. Within four minutes, Safia held her hand out to the printer, then handed the sheet to Sam. He bent over a counter lining one wall, and scribbled in the corner, calculating fuel ratio.

Then Sam straightened. "She's got under a two thousand mile radius. Not enough to get back to the island. She has to make another stop."

Riley walked to the cockpit, spoke to the pilots, then looked back. "We can get behind her on a return trip over Northern England. MI 6 is on alert if she lands."

"Force her to the ground," Sam said. "The jet's got the maneuverability."

Riley knew that was pushing it, but that was the fighter

pilot talking. "She might ignite it over land. Interpol has her stats so she'll be tracked when she lands again." They didn't have proof, just pieces. Catching her in possession of the explosive device was a close second to taking her out of the equation. If it wouldn't cause an international incident, he'd press for elimination as soon as the jet was over water. But Odette was a cog. Riley wanted the creator of this death march.

The signal from Deep Six pinged in rapid succession, and Safia twisted on the stool toward the screen. "We can't trace the jet. It's flying over Russian airspace. One tiny breach and we'll be shot down." She looked at him. "The Russians won't help us. We're wasting fuel chasing her."

"We need her flight plan," Sam said.

"Well." Safia shooed him. "Get busy, Wyatt."

Sam glanced at Riley, amused about something, then Riley said, "What's in Oslo, Norway?"

Sam rattled off all things familiar; tulips, wooden shoes, hashish market, legal prostitution. Safia rolled her eyes, smiling, then her expression fell. "Nobel Peace Center," she said. "Beckham said his work was dismissed, ridiculed till it ruined him. His name was first stricken from the list of Nobel Prize contenders ten years ago. Oh this is rich . . . two scientists on this year's list were his students." The imagery and data filled the screen. "She stopped within two blocks of the Center. Beckham has local law all over it."

On the computer, Sam brought up the path the jet had taken. "She's got no prejudice. Refueled in north China. Bet that was pricey. Next stop, she left the aircraft, then went by car, same routine. She's never on the ground more than an hour or two, then off again. Last check, she was two blocks from the Genome Research Institute, Germany."

"She's planting in institutes that ridiculed him," Riley said. "Fuel range was?"

Sam looked at Riley. "As far as Greece I'd say."

"Which institutes denied recognition to Thibaut?"

Sam's features pulled tight and faced the screen, tapping

the keyboard like a mad man. "Nobel Peace Center Oslo, Oxford, Kuzusa DNA Research Institute, Japan. GRI, in Germany, Genome research, Sorbonne. Take your pick."

"She hit two of those so far. Where can she get without refueling?" Safia asked.

"The Sorbonne."

Riley turned to the cockpit, giving orders to the pilot. Safia got on the line to Deep Six to send a blanket communiqué to National Gendarmerie in Paris. It would take every officer they had, but they needed to clear the streets and the Sorbonne.

"We have a big problem," Riley said, backing away from the computer screen.

"Is there any other kind lately?" Sam said.

"The Sorbonne is awarding chemistry doctorates or something there. A ceremony." Riley looked at Safia. "It will be packed with people by nine A.M."

"Three hours?" Sam left his chair and went to the cockpit. "We need to get this bird on the ground now, boys." The discussion was short and when the pilot stepped out, Riley leaned in to see Sam slide into the pilot's vacated seat.

"Deviating from flight patterns will get us an Interpol F-16 escort, with shoot to kill orders," the Air Force pilot said.

"Wouldn't be the first time." Riley sat and strapped in, then looked across at Safia. "We're about to break a lot of rules."

She dropped into the chair and quickly buckled herself in. The jet's speed increased and Safia's eyes widened as it banked sharply toward France.

Singapore

Max stood near the hospital bed, Logan on the other side. The monitors beeped with the tempo of a strong heartbeat. Sebastian was tucked neatly under the covers, a petite nurse popping in frequently to check on him. Sebastian came away from the explosion with a broken wrist, ribs, a fractured scapula and right arm. He was lucky. His internal bleeding was minimal, the swelling contusions purple and iced down. The surgeons spent several hours removing shrapnel and glass from his body and according to Logan, Sebastian had enough pins in him now to set off sensors as bad as Riley. Logan checked his breathing and his IV, deciding his drip was sufficient to keep the pain at bay.

He looked at Max, frowning. "He'll recover," he said.

"I know. You do good work. But I'm curious as to how he got out before the blast. The sensors in the station house didn't pick up the explosives. They were all in the house long enough to detect it."

"JCS said it was classified and not out for distribution, but I don't think it was the Icarus device that did this kind of damage."

"Riley has the same theory. RZ implodes and this stuff didn't. Not completely."

"I read the data. It will outward blast if it's not completely enclosed," Logan said, then gestured to Sebastian. "He was at the edge of the blast radius. He was heading elsewhere before it went off."

"Then it wasn't meant for us, but for Safia," Max said. At least it wouldn't be a surprise to her. "Either her cover is completely blown or it's from the inside."

"It's both."

Max looked up, startled. "Hey old man, don't talk."

Logan offered Sebastian water.

"I saw a car on the perimeter cameras," Sebastian said, breathing a little hard. "Went to look."

Logan and Max exchanged a glance.

"Motion sensors went off. I saw the driver hop the court-yard wall, go into the garage area. Then he's back out twenty seconds later." Sebastian's eyes closed and Max thought, he's going back under. Yet when they eased back from the bed, Sebastian said, "He went right, I went left. 'Cept I was on foot." With his unbandaged hand, he reached for the cup, eyeing Logan back when he tried to help. He sipped, then said, "He planted, for certain, but not meant to cook more than the station house."

"The blast radius was massive. You were four city blocks away from the center," Max said. Nearly a half a mile.

Sebastian frowned and Max knew he was thinking of materials that could accomplish that. "It's possible RZ10 was in the station house. Ever heard of it?"

Sebastian's eyes flared and he struggled to keep them open. "Shoulda never been made," he slurred, then gave up, sliding into sleep.

Max looked at Logan. "Just once, I want to be ahead of these assholes."

Outside the Sorbonne, Paris

Sam put the jet down flanked by an Interpol escort. Safia still felt the stomach-rolling ride and was glad Gerardo was pushing his stars around. They didn't have time for questions or explanations. Clear the streets, fast and no one will die, she thought as Riley stopped the car. She kissed him once, then hopped out and walked toward the building while Riley continued driving to the far side of the grounds, pausing halfway to let an Interpol agent out. Sam was with the French police.

She neared the barriers, the triangulation of the phone between towers narrowing. Paris traffic rushed by. Gendarmes blocked the roads in and rushed to clear the area. The Sorbonne was emptied a half hour ago, thank God.

She glanced at her web phone tracking the signal. Odette was near and using her own phone. Safia stopped, searching the terrain. "It's in the same block."

"I'm coming toward you." Riley's voice came through her ear mic.

Then she saw her. "Finn, target acquired."

Odette Thibaut was under a block away, poised gracefully between the open door and the limo. Ready to jump in and run, Safia thought as she stepped into a phone cube to shield herself, then focused the monocular. Even without the red shoes, she'd remember the woman. But it was Odette's gentle expression that puzzled her and she followed her line of vision, then rushed briskly closer when she spotted a young girl, maybe nine, weaving behind the barriers. She wore a French school uniform, a green plaid skirt and dark blue jacket with some insignia on the pocket. Safia lost sight of the target and moved to see the girl approach the doors. A gendarme stopped her, turned her away. The blond girl clutched her book bag and danced like she had to pee. The guard smiled and directed her somewhere inside. He let her pass. Safia's focus went back to Red Shoes.

"Triangulation is blocking the signal," Deep Six said. Safia knew it.

Odette paced and as if it would work, spanked her phone.

"We have it locked."

"Excellent. Team one, keep clearing the buildings, two, the park. Double time."

"Roger that," she heard Sam say, amused to hear French with a Texas accent. French police were on the same frequency.

Streets had been blocked for a parade honoring the recipients, population was sparse, but the families and friends of the recipients were early and allowed access. French secret police, Interpol and CIA agents converged, moving efficiently to not cause a panic or alert Odette. The signals crossing were a problem and isolating hers was difficult, even for Deep Six.

In seconds, she saw police and French citizens hurrying away from the Sorbonne. "A kid went in to use the bathroom, female, 10, long hair, blue book bag." No one responded.

"Deep Six?" She glanced and realized no one was getting a signal through. Her comm-link blinked in and out.

"Raven . . . run." Riley's voice sounded panicked.

She stopped short and immediately started in the opposite direction. She didn't question him, and pushed her legs to take her further from the buildings.

". . . going to blow."

Oh, no it's *not*, she thought, running faster. "Deep Six! Jam the signal!"

"It's coming in from another phone!"

"Take it all out, all of it." She glanced back, searching for Odette. The limo was gone. Safia alerted French police to the vehicle, but couldn't get a confirmation. The jamming blocked everything except the PRRs.

"Safia, run!" Riley said. *"Steal a car. Get out of there!"*

Her arms pumped and she pushed between people, warning them. "Bomb," she said in two languages. People stopped, stared as she ran past. Then she shouted, "Police!" and waved. They got the message, the stampede of people following her, mothers grabbing up children and bolting.

"Raven, I'm a block west, keep going, don't stop!"

"Finn, come back?" she said, breathless.

"Your right, go to your right!" she heard, obeyed, and the car appeared. Riley slammed to a stop long enough for her to dive in through the window before he hit the gas. "Get down! Down!"

She shifted in the seat. "Why isn't the jam working?"

"It is, on the cell towers. They went satellite with a new phone. 'Icarus is rising.' That's the code to set it off. A text message, for God's sake."

"Go! Go! Oh God, those people." She looked back and didn't see the schoolgirl come out.

Then the blast hit. The Sorbonne courtyard imploded. The explosion didn't go up, it went out, flattening everything. The percussion shattered windows a block away, tumbled buildings, cars, and people flew like matchsticks swept off a table.

Despite their speed, it kept coming, a rolling force that crushed everything in its path.

"Riley." She grabbed his shoulder. "We aren't going to make it."

Spinning debris knocked two floors off a building with a giant shove, hurling the rubble toward them. Riley pushed her to the floor seconds before it impacted. It kicked up the rear of the Land Rover, the ground rushing toward his face. The force tossed them ass up and over—inside three tons of machine filled with gasoline.

The vehicle landed on the roof, but the crunch of steel didn't end, debris shooting over the car. Riley reached for Safia but the after-blast kept coming, knocking the Rover so hard it pushed it several feet. Thunks of rubble stabbed the car for a full minute before it stopped. The city froze as the shock vibrated. Alarms sounded, the cry of police cars nearing.

"Safia." She didn't answer and Riley struggled under the crushed metal to reach her. He couldn't. "Safia?"

Riley flipped out his knife and cut his seat belt straps, smacking his new knees, then maneuvered out the broken window, his jeans catching on the crushed metal. Above him, the tires were still spinning as he kicked out the remaining glass and the nose of the Rover threatened to tip and crush him. She dangled limply from the seat belt, and he knew no other way to get her out except to cut her free. When he did she dropped only inches and didn't move.

Please no, he thought, noticing the blood staining her face and shirt.

He stretched his arms and caught her shirt, then her shoulders. Around him, people scattered, staggered with wounds. Riley inched in as close as he could, grasped her under the arms, and carefully eased her from the wreckage. Glass sprinkled. She wasn't moving.

He sat on the street, holding her, using his sleeve to blot the blood. Her head lolled listlessly back over his arm and his heart fractured. He touched her throat for a pulse and sighed, relieved he found it. He clutched her, then stood and carried her from the wreckage.

"Deep Six!" he hailed through his mic. "I need shelter, now. Safia's wounded."

"*How bad?*"

"She's unconscious and bleeding."

With David directing him from ten thousand miles away, Riley hustled, Safia cradled in his arms as he bolted through the streets of Paris.

Nineteen

Paris

Inside the hotel room, Riley could hear the sirens and knew if he stood at the balcony, he'd see the smoke. He'd get reports later and shifted on the bed, watching Safia sleep. She'd woken once, then lapsed into unconsciousness, but the doctor Ellie had sent assured him she didn't have a concussion. Four stitches later, he was gone.

He let his head drop back onto the pillow and didn't really want to examine why she was so deep under his skin. Usually, he went for the casual relationships, and he admitted he'd never had much trouble with women, and attributed it to being the youngest with four older sisters, each with an opinion she insisted on sharing with him. They taught him early that pleasing most women was simple, if he'd just listen. Safia wasn't so easy to read. Whenever he expected a reaction, he didn't get it. He felt almost raw around her, and it was damn hard to focus when her smile took his breath away. He experienced emotions so caveman primitive it scared him, and reminded him of his youth in Belfast—the urge to shelter, protect her as he had when IRA fighting came too close to his family. His sisters showed him strong women were resilient, often a damn sight more than men. Every buddy he'd ever shared a drink with said they couldn't handle battle. He'd like to introduce him to the Donovan women, and Safia Troy, orphan, loner, and a woman who cared deeply about the people caught between terror and their innocent lives. Like hers, he thought, his brows lifting. He smiled, laughed to himself, and smoothed his hand over her shoulder, his thumb circling the little triangle birthmark on the back of her arm.

Carefully, he pushed her hair off her temple and watched the dark strands sift through his fingers. He was scared for her, he'd admitted, and had to get a handle on this need to protect and take her away from the dangers. She wouldn't allow it for a second and he wanted to stay on her good side. For a long time.

She inhaled and breathed deeply, and he smiled. She shifted. "Ow," she said dryly.

"Don't move so fast."

"Not a problem," she said, being still. She finally opened her eyes and smiled slightly.

"Don't scare me like that again."

"Sure."

He chuckled lowly, then bent to kiss her forehead. She sat up in increments, and touched near her hairline. She felt the stitches. "You do that?"

He inclined his head to the door a few feet away. "CIA physician just left. Gerardo pulled out all the stops." And Ellie, he thought. A doctor had been waiting for them and now they had fresh clothes, phones, and food. The agent was amazing and he couldn't wait to meet her.

"He's a good general." She didn't try to stand just yet and shifted in the corner of the bed. "What's the damage?"

Riley met her gaze and said, "First reports are seventy-four injured, twelve dead."

Safia let out a long breath and sank back into the mattress. "It could have been thousands," she said.

"David delayed long enough to get more people out of there. Odette is wise. She used another number and phone through a satellite hop."

She met his gaze. "I saw a child go in the Sorbonne a few minutes before the detonation. I think he's using children to deliver the bombs." Riley scowled. "I didn't see it, but I think she'd arrived with Odette." She shrugged, then rubbed her shoulder. "Since she had diplomatic papers, no one inspected the aircrafts. She's changing methods."

"She knows she's tailed then."

"Panicked bad guys will screw up."

"I doubt it." He nodded to the end table and the printout waiting for her. "You need to read that. Beckham has Thibaut's history."

She shifted, grabbed the report and read. Riley heard her sharp intake of air, then watched her finger slide over the page as she re-read sections. "He's disgusting." She looked up. "Adopted or whatever, that girl walked robotically into that building. This says we're dealing with a sociopath with no remorse."

"Hell, I knew that," Riley said. "But he should be dead from old age, and he's not."

"Some people would kill for whatever he's taking to stop the clock." She accidentally elbowed him and when he flinched, she immediately pulled up his shirt. His ribs were purple.

"Not broken." Her gaze flicked up. "I swear." She touched it a little harder to be certain and Riley chuckled to himself. "And they say the Irish are stubborn."

"The Egyptians took forty years to build the pyramids," she reminded. "A useless marker in the middle of the desert. That's persistence." She grinned. "I hate the desert, by the way."

"I'll remember that."

"What do we have?"

"She's going to his island. She knows she's tailed now. The bomb went off."

"She's just following orders," Safia said. "We'll never get on that island with approval, Gerardo said so. Thibaut's too well-connected. He was at the president's birthday celebration, for God sake."

"And you thought the president would say no when he learned Thibaut was a Nazi we harbored, probably still experimenting on children?" He flicked at the report that made him want to wash.

"God, I can't even think that demented to understand what he'd do next." She stood, her balance waving for a moment. "And Odette helped him every step of the way. I want to shoot that Jimmy Choo knockoff-wearing bitch between the eyes!"

"I didn't think otherwise."

Her temper deflated a bit and she said, "Sorry. Sam okay?"

He nodded. "He's at the plane on the flight line. French military."

She crossed to the phone. "Their equipment is not up to date. I'm not handing control to those pansies."

He chuckled to himself. "Actually, it's in our hands."

She looked up, about to dial. "Ours?"

"Yours and Dragon One."

"God. How did you do that?" Giving over to civilians was not the norm.

"Called in a big favor or two."

"Make it three. Ellie is the best shot in the Company and she can do it free falling a thousand feet per second. Besides, I want her in on this. I trust *her*."

"Satellite picked up Barasa's jet still on the island too."

She smiled widened. "Where are we staging?"

"Guam."

"Wish it was the Philippines," she murmured, turning to the stack of clothes. "I could use a vacation."

"When it's over, I'll take you to Ireland."

She turned sharply. "You have family there."

"A lot, yes." She shook her head, and he left the bed, prying a pair of jeans from her hands. "What frightens you so?"

She tipped her head and met his gaze. "I don't know. Family, people asking questions I can't answer. Being near them threatens their lives." She shrugged.

"Or is it just me?" Riley waited, almost breathless.

Safia tipped her head, her gaze sweeping his features. His dark hair held a little Irish red and she wanted to sink her fingers into it right now, take him into the next room and—"No," she said. "You're the only one who doesn't scare me."

"But you keep running." He jerked his hold on her. "Let me in, Safia."

"I have, more than you realize." She stared at a spot on his chest, and felt something inside her melt away. A little smile coasted over her lips. "I've thought about you often over the years." She lifted her gaze to his. "You don't know how impressed I was that you went after Sam, alone. That was the worst fighting I'd seen yet, but there you were, so determined to save your friend."

"Reckless and dim-witted is more like it."

She waved that off. "It wasn't the bravery, but what made you brave, Riley. A friend. Your boss, for that matter. If I'd died out there, I'd be a star on the wall and nothing more." She tipped her head, folded her arms over her middle. "I was envious. Sam's alive because you're friends. For a long time I wished I'd jumped on that chopper with you."

"Dragon One is a team at its very roots."

She scoffed softly. "I know. Each one of you has an ax to grind with the D-oh-D, but here you are, doing the job you were meant to do all along."

"I can say the same about you."

"Oh I won't deny that. I still have some axes of my own, but I give a damn and that's what keeps me doing it. One life isn't meaningless, but I've learned to move on, get the terrorist, then hunt the next. It's not such a big cost to me, but I've seen too many lives destroyed by a death. Saving one father so he can love his child is always good enough reason." She frowned, swiped at her cheek and was a little shocked to see tears. She laughed shortly to herself. "After my family was killed I cried for weeks," she said suddenly. "I was numb and I don't remember most of it till I left for college, but I was tired of crying and swore I wouldn't do it again." She shook her head, sanding her fingers until the tears dried.

"Too much time alone, I'm thinking."

"It's easy to be detached that way." She looked up. "But you, your friends, this, it gave me the up close and personal reasons why every agent keeps fighting. Don't look so sad," she said, nudging him, then regretting it when he winced. "I chose the life. I knew what I'd get in return."

He smiled gently, a little amused. "I doubt it."

"I didn't have some wild epiphany or anything, but—" her brow knit for a second, then smoothed—"Just a reminder of who I am, I think." She patted the skin over her heart. "Here." She searched his handsome face. "Thank you."

He brushed his mouth over hers, and said, "We've no debts between us, you and I. Only what's right here." He laid his palm over her heart, then pulled her deeper into his arms. He held her, rubbing her back in slow circles and for a second she wondered if it was for him, or for her.

"You know," he said. "I've liked a lot of women." She smiled and he pushed her hair back, watching his moves. "But never once said I loved them."

She started to turn away from him, but he cupped her jaw and made her stay put. "I love you Safia Troy." Her eyes teared. "I think I have since the moment I saw you and—" he shrugged a little—"I was just waiting for you to come back so I'd remember."

She swallowed. Her heart pounded in her throat as she fought the instinct to run because she wanted this, wanted him.

"I *can* love you. Like you've never been loved before—if you'll just let me."

Tears fell and her lower lip trembled. Riley groaned softly.

No one spoke to her like he did, so honest and simple. And Safia hoped. For this moment, she hoped for a future she couldn't imagine, and the truth slid easily from her lips. "I love you too."

It was his turn to tremble. No cheeky smiles, no sexy innuendos, but a softening in his handsome features, the way he looked when he made love to her, and he lowered his head. His mouth was a breath from hers when he said, "Ahh, that's my girl."

Then he kissed her. It was instantly different, slower, patient in commitment, and Safia felt the floor tilt and slipped her arms around his waist, then stepped into the warmth of his embrace. His hands rode down her arms before they wrapped her tightly, his mouth making a slow smooth ride over hers. Desire pulled at her, and pushed her hands under his shirt.

She drew back enough to ask, "How long before we fly to Guam?"

"Long enough."

The jet touched down, the jolt drawing her back to the moment. The instant the pilot let down the hatch, Odette left the aircraft, and strode across the darkened flight line to the man standing near the car. When she approached, his smile fell.

"I'm sorry. I failed you." She got into the car and waited impatiently for him to join her.

"You're upset." He sat back, sliding off his hat and laying it on the seat between them.

"Of course I am. Months of planning. We were so careful. I barely got out of France." The French Secret Service caught her just before takeoff, but a call from someone, she didn't know who, and the guards pulled back.

"They knew it was you, then."

She snapped a look at him. "No, they knew it was Barasa. That's how they found any link to us. I told you he wasn't the proper choice."

"Then it's my fault."

She scoffed and knew Haeger didn't take blame for anything. Did he realize how close she came to being apprehended today? She never wanted to be that close to those men with guns again. She inhaled and let it out slowly, turning her face to the window. The headlights splashed across the vegetation, and she glimpsed movement in the jungle. She frowned, leaned closer.

"The messengers were to place the devices without suspicion," he said.

"They still don't know about them," she said glumly. "But they are following us now, you know that." She gestured to the ceiling, to the sky above.

"And for that reason, I can set them off from here."

Her gaze snapped to his. "What about the Sorbonne? It went off too early. The text was sent, but the signal stopped. The girl wasn't to respond for several hours."

"Perhaps she panicked." He flicked a long boned hand. "Dismiss it and go on, my dear. It's the only way to learn new discoveries. Leave the old ones behind."

"When then?"

He tilted his head, looking thoughtful. "I know you're as anxious as I, but we have the evening to decide and dinner is waiting for us. Your favorite, fresh scallops."

Odette smiled weakly. "Thank you. Will Barasa be joining us?"

He shook his head. "Let him leave at first light and take his men with him. They have too much interest in the children."

She inhaled sharply. "They touched them? Who?"

"Not yet, but you know behavior, it won't be long before they do."

Odette's gaze narrowed. The children didn't go near any males. Thibaut kept them separated for just that reason. So why were they even near the guards? She looked at the black jungle again. The guards understood the retribution for touching one of his subjects. Death.

"Don't worry, my dear," he said patting her hand, then squeezing, unaware of her thoughts. "We still have Jason and his wonderful laptop to do it for us."

"He's another man that needs to leave our island."

His smile was sly and Odette wondered what he had planned for the scientist.

Somewhere over Malaysia

The flight from Paris to the South Pacific wasn't so daunting in the Gulfstream jet when you had the comforts of a four-star general at your fingertips. Riley'd caught some shut-eye on the first leg, but it was time to get busy on condensing reams of information. Riley studied the topography of the islands, the intelligence handled through Marianna Island post, and while Owen was good, he sort of missed Ellie's voice. She was on her way to Guam, in charge of intelligence for the Op.

In the first row of seats in the rear, Safia snacked on whatever she could find, and right now, it looked like microwave Chicken Marcella and bags of pretzels. In the rear, Sam snoozed, stretched out on four seats, his boots hanging over the edge, his hat covering his face. Logan was on Guam with Max, Viva and Jasmine at the Singapore hospital with Sebastian. Spec Ops was on their way to lend a hand.

Safia's web phone vibrated across the tray, and she didn't stop eating or reading to answer it. "Send it to the jet," she said after a moment, then closed the phone and left the chair. "There's a message coming in. Base says it's for you."

Riley frowned, withdrew his web phone, but it wasn't signaling. She went to the computer and tapped the keys swiftly, then stepped back. "On your private number." She glanced. "I didn't know you had one."

"It's for my family," he said and experienced a quick, hard chill. "After months in the hospital, a direct line was the only way to keep them off my back. But no one's used it in a year." Riley turned on the stool, facing a larger screen. He expected a text message or voicemail, and blinked when a video popped up. Its clarity hit him in the chest. "Oh bugger me."

"Who's that?"

"My oldest sister. Bridget."

She laid a hand on his shoulder. "Oh Riley."

On the screen a man stood behind her, his head and neck covered in black cloth. Bridget was exposed, her clothing dirty, yet she appeared unharmed. The man grabbed a handful of deep red hair and pulled her head back. Bridget spat in his face. Riley smiled slightly. She was giving him hell. He didn't wonder how the captor knew of her, but the threat was clear. Keep coming and he'd kill her.

Sam moved up behind them. "Oh Christ, Riley. What can I do?"

"Try to reach Travis on the ship. He wouldn't let her go without a fight." He must be going crazy, Riley thought. "Tell him to sail to Guam."

Sam turned away as Safia leaned in. "Rewind, please," she said and Riley complied. She focused on the mask. "The fabric is moving. He's talking. Turn up the volume."

He did and the voice was loud and clear through the speakers. "*Continue your pursuit, and she dies. It's that simple.*"

Bridget twisted against her captor. "*Come blow his bleedin' arse out of the ocean!*" she shouted. Her captor struck her, knocking her head to the side so hard Riley heard her teeth click. Bridget worked her jaw, then said, "*Oh your mum must be so proud of you, beating women like you do.*"

"I love her," Safia said, then at the computer linking to Deep Six, she requested a trace. Ellie, Safia thought, would have done it without asking.

On the video, the man made the mistake of moving a fraction closer and Bridget drove her elbow into his groin. But he anticipated and jerked back.

His laugh made Safia's heart skip a beat. "*You almost killed me with that one.*"

Her phone slipped from her hand and she scrambled to

catch it, then turned away. She paced, and when Riley started for her, she waved him back and stepped to the rear. Tucked against the bulkhead, she stared at the toes of her shoes and told herself it was her imagination. She was keyed up and grasping for information. *Be sure.* She went back to the computer and rewound the feed and then sat, not really watching, but listening to the audio. She turned it up, and knew the second the hairs on her arm moved with a chill.

"We have to get her back now."

"No question about that."

She met his gaze. "No, now. Remember my initiation, the prison?"

He nodded, a tightness climbing over his skin.

"I'd recognize that voice anywhere." She pointed to the screen. "That's my torturer."

Riley's features pulled so tight he felt it. He looked at the hooded figure standing behind his sister. "Then he's a CIA asset."

They'd been betrayed.

No one slept. There was constant movement, people. Jason tried to investigate the island but each time, he was deterred by the adolescent population. He felt watched, and in such an isolated place, he wondered why. It wasn't like he could fly a jet off the hunk of rock or swim, for crissake. A couple times the children crowded him and forced him in a new direction. Obedient little minions for Thibaut, he thought, walking slowly, questions rising constantly. What *didn't* they want him to find? How did he control them; drugs, brainwashing? What was Thibaut hiding that he needed armed guards? There were only a few men, and while he noticed the guards didn't even look at the children, how many visitors did Thibaut have here anyway? It was the lack of older children that bothered him. Odette mentioned the boarding school, but as a fan of the man, it was news to him, and considering the guy made certain any grand charitable gesture he made was in the papers,

Jason went looking for proof. A quick search and a hack into some education networks, and Jason knew it was a lie.

He walked toward the big house as he thought of Thibaut's home on the northern tip of the island and as he approached the walkway, Odette stepped out, looking lovely and refreshed.

"I didn't know you'd returned," Jason said.

Her smile was oddly Cheshire. "You wanted to speak to Dr. Thibaut?"

"You actually." He inclined his head, and she descended the steps and strolled with him down the cobblestone walk. Overhead the sky darkened, the breeze quickening. It fit his mood. "There are no children of Thibaut's at boarding schools, Odette. I looked."

"I'm offended that you did, Jason."

"Why?"

"I thought you trusted us, but I understand your curiosity. Please know that his name sometimes carries a stigma from his past, neh? And letting it join the children in their new life wouldn't be fair."

"I suppose so." Names changed to protect the innocent, he thought.

"You've a very curious nature, is there anything else you'd like to question?"

He let out a breath. "The guards."

"Ahh, yes. They're protection. Children are curious, they wander. The jungle isn't the place to play."

Bullshit. If Thibaut had control over their pain factor, then he could control their barriers. He let it go, unconvinced. But he wanted off the island. He'd completed the weapons, and Thibaut had taken them away with the canister. He didn't want to be near that shit again. "I'm ready to leave."

She pouted but it just didn't fit with her face and demeanor. "We so hoped you'd join us and perhaps continue his work."

That would be years away. Thibaut was fit and healthy, not one foot in the grave. "I'm not that smart."

"But you and I would be."

He blinked.

"I have been his student since I was a child and have earned three doctorates—medicine, behavior science, and biochemistry."

He whistled softly. "Congratulations." He forced a smile, maintaining easy conversation, yet inside he was screaming, she wasn't his assistant, as he first thought, but his partner. Odette, he surmised, did not like her authority questioned or her mind demeaned.

Without realizing it, she'd steered him back to his private bungalow. Four more cottages were grouped a half acre apart, Barasa's the furthest, nearer the airstrip. At the door, she reached inside to switch on the porch light and he noticed little things—the perfect almond shape of her eyes, their odd blue gray color, her ink black hair always twisted up and showing her long neck. The graceful way she walked, like a ballerina. His gaze lowered to her cleavage, then swept away.

"It's alright to look, Jason."

He met her gaze. "You are a very beautiful woman."

The corners of her mouth tilted, a secretive Mona Lisa smile. "Thank you." She tilted her head. "If you've a need, I can arrange it."

When her implication dawned, he said, "No, thank you." He knew there were only kids here, so where would she find—oh gross. He wasn't a pedophile.

"Fine. Enjoy your evening." She turned away.

"About ending this, leaving. I can't spend my money here." U.S. agents were hunting the RZ10 and him. It was a matter of time before they found it. Jason wanted to be as far away as he could before that happened, but it was all up to Thibaut. And apparently, Odette.

She looked back over her shoulder, her expression sublime. "Barasa will leave soon. Tomorrow, I believe."

"I hate that bastard."

Again the secretive smile appeared as she said, "Then I will take you where you desire myself. Two days? I suffer jet lag, neh?"

He nodded, and as she walked away, he tried to understand how she'd just hoodwinked him into complacency. At least he'd be away from here. The entire island was a mystery he wanted to investigate, but couldn't. Jason harbored the suspicion there was a lot more going on here than kids and some mind control.

Anderson Air Force Base
Guam

Riley stood on the flight line, waiting for the SUV to bring his brother-in-law from the docks. Behind him about sixty yards, the hangar was buzzing. Sound echoed from inside as technicians worked to set up the ops center. Without will, his mind crowded with images of Bridget and while he knew she was a tough bird, she was in the hands of a man who'd tortured Safia at the sanction of her supervisors. That alone twisted his gut till he had a hard time breathing.

The car shot across the tarmac and screeched to a halt. Travis was the first man out, striding toward him. They embraced, then Travis introduced the crew. None of them looked as if they'd had any sleep in days. He could at least make them comfortable. They walked toward the hangar.

"How did this kidnapper know about her, Riley?"

"He's rich, powerful and pays to be informed. The man I was chasing is with him and we have a history." He reminded Travis about the trial, yet didn't reveal what Safia called her first real lesson in intelligence. Travis didn't need to worry more. A killer had his wife.

They stepped into the hangar, and Travis stopped short, his gaze skimming over the men and equipment. "I didn't know Dragon One was this big."

"It's not, Trav, but it helps to have your country backing you up when you need it."

Travis glanced. "We could use that on the British."

A Belfast boy, Riley had deep feelings about England's possession of Northern Ireland. One country, he thought, then dismissed it. "People owe us." He gripped Trav's shoulder. "I will get her back safely, I swear it. Trust me."

"I do, lad. I really do."

Riley would die before he'd let his sister suffer.

Safia walked near, introducing herself. "She's alive and unharmed. Let me show you what we have." She escorted Travis and his crew to a group of tables with computers and screens showing the satellite imagery.

Travis took one look at the weather screen and said, "When are you scheduled to leave?"

"Forty minutes."

"You're going to get hit with that storm."

Safia frowned at the screen, then Riley said, "The family weather man." He inclined his head to Trav. "Climatologist and an oceanographer. He's never wrong." Riley turned to the teams. "Listen up! Change of plans. We have to beat a storm." The crews moved faster.

Thibaut's satellite dish was their first target while authorities in four nations worked to locate the Icarus devices Odette had hidden. That she had touched down with the security alerts blanketing each city said that Thibaut had paved the way for this long before it started. Let the diplomats sort that out, he thought, then asked Travis, "You said you found bones on the island?"

Jim Clatt quickened to catch up. "Bridget was showing the police. Some of the bones were new." Jim started explaining, but Riley stopped him and called the teams in for a debrief.

"I told her to forget about it," Travis said.

Riley stopped, frowned. "Forget what?"

"We went back for a second look and found something."

The teams gathered and Jim Clatt started in. "We found animal and human DNA. Marrow actually. Dr. McFadden found cases, like metal cages, but solid. She said they hadn't been there that long."

Riley frowned harder, and couldn't image the connection to the bones. He didn't *want* to imagine.

"We found the creator," Safia said and Clatt's expression fell. "Genetically engineered children."

"I thought as much," Travis said. "Nothing could sustain life on that island. They were dropped there. Left to die or survive."

Jim touched the marks on his throat. "And they did."

Cale woke with a jolt, his naked body trapped to the bed, his mouth sealed in duct tape. Breathing was a labor. His gaze flicked around the dark room, his eyesight blurry from the drugs. With the drapes drawn, only the hint of light stirred at the edges. Nothing moved. Then the light on the beside table switched on, and he turned his head. A small figure sat in the chair just beyond the glow. A woman, he decided. Odette. He wasn't amused.

Then she rose, her shape defined in icy white, her moves soundless. She pressed one knee on the bed, then swung her leg over and straddled his hips. Her skirt slid up her thighs, and that she was naked beneath was an instant turn on. He grew hard quickly as she laid over him, rubbing. Her accented voice was throaty in his ear.

"I know you sold a weapon you did not have."

Barasa tensed.

"It was forbidden. You knew this. After his glory, you may have your payment."

She leaned back, his groin mashing to hers and he felt her wetness coat him. He wanted her, a woman so bold to slip into his room. Her body was a willowy silhouette, her skin flawless in the lamplight. Around her neck was a silver chain, the pendant between her breasts and hidden by the neckline of her simple blouse. She didn't strip and he wanted to see her tits, their round shape perfectly artificial. His gaze rose to her face, beautifully uplifted, her hair twisted high, a couple jeweled sticks securing the thick dark mass.

He met her gaze, his look questioning the gag. Was she afraid of what he would say? God, he wanted to fuck her. Isn't that what she'd come for? His gaze lowered, watching her hand stroke him smoothly, then she laid over him, a blanket of flesh and woman. "You think I screw Thibaut?"

His gaze slid to meet hers.

"Don't you?"

She smiled and rocked her hips, rubbing on his cock. He wanted inside her, for her to ride him, but she was in control, and he couldn't do a damn thing. She leaned back, pulling her skirt higher. He watched as she guided him inside, then slid down. She let out a deep-throated sigh, and he groaned, her body incredibly wet and tight. Then she moved with a smooth undulation, her tempo increasing by the second. He wanted more, harder, and he bucked, needing to grab her hips and jam her down on him. He pumped and opened his eyes, his climax shaking through his hips and up through his bloodstream. She never took her gaze off his face, and when he groaned behind the gag, climaxing hard, she slid the stick from her hair and flicked it sharply. A tube slid off, the light glinting on a thin blade. His arms were restrained, but one was secured to the table, his knuckles resting on the cool wood.

"There is always a price for disobedience," she said, then lashed her arm down. He blinked, wondering what she was up to a moment before the pain swept up from his wrist. He looked to the side. His little finger lay on the table an inch from his hand. He howled behind the gag. The bitch! The fucking bitch! He fought against his bonds, screaming that he'd kill her.

As if she understood, she leaned down in his face, her dark hair sweeping his bare chest. "You ruined the perfect plan. Timing is essential and your greed," she stressed, "has cost us."

She met his gaze, and Barasa swore he saw a silver sheen in her eyes.

"Neh? I can still take another." She let the blade slide over the back of his hand, leaving a blood trail.

He shouted behind the sticky gag.

"Good. Now the Professor considers the bargain still solid. Leave quietly and disappear. Do not disappoint him again, Cale. I will kill you."

She dismounted, then pushed a cloth into his palm to stem the bleeding. With another scrap, she plucked the finger off the table and as if selecting a candy, she dropped into a bag. The blood seeped instantly, but it didn't stop her from stuffing it down between her breasts. She stepped back out of the light, and Barasa heard nothing more. Not a footstep or a door.

He howled, trapped, and knew Rahjan wouldn't hear him on the other side of the house. He jerked at the bonds, and the lamp crashed to the floor. He rocked the bed, struggling, but the fiber-filled tape refused to release him. If anything, it felt tighter.

Then the door opened a fraction, a pistol barrel coming around the edge before Rahjan stepped into the room. No matter how much he wailed, the man wouldn't come near till he'd inspected every corner. He walked to the side of the bed, and his expression warned before he yanked the tape off his mouth.

Barasa spit. "Cut me loose."

Rahjan's knife appeared and he obeyed. "Who did this?"

Barasa sat up. "Who do you think!"

Rahjan smiled a fraction, but his amusement fled when he saw Barasa's hand. "She's a vicious little thing, isn't she?"

"I'm going to kill her! She has to know that." He shoved

Rahjan with one hand, clutching the other as he went to the bathroom and grabbed a hand towel.

Rahjan tried to examine Barasa's hand, but he didn't want help. Mortified to be caught so, the humiliating evidence would never leave him. He grabbed a small first aid kit from under the sink and when he tried to doctor the wound, Rahjan pushed his hand aside and bandaged him.

"It's a clean cut. What'd she use?"

Cale shook his head, confused. "A hair decoration."

Rahjan snickered and even Barasa's glare didn't shut him up. "Tied and sliced up by a woman who did what first?" His glance swept meaningfully to Barasa's naked body roughly wrapped in sheets.

"She's a good fuck." Barasa tried to be amused. He wasn't. He had, in a base sense, just been raped and mutilated.

Odette would pay for this, as would her Professor. Yet trapped, weaponless and outnumbered, he didn't know how.

Outside the bungalow, Odette leaned against the exterior wall for a moment, reveling in her revenge and the sex that satisfied a need she hadn't intended to exact. But the man was horny for her, and it was too easy to manipulate him. She was certain her message was clear. There were no second chances.

When she heard a crash from somewhere inside the house, she pushed off and strode across the lawn. She cornered the cobbled path and movement startled her. Immediately she slipped into a defensive stance, then relaxed as Haeger stepped into the lamplight.

His gaze locked with hers. "Pleased with yourself, my dear?"

She glanced away, embarrassed to be caught. His presence spoke of distrust yet he knew she'd needed to punish Barasa for his failure. Why did he involve himself? "Yes. Quite. You insisted on revealing all to him." They had disagreed on this matter from the start. "He will disappear quietly now. He's aware we can reach him even after he leaves here."

Haeger nodded, his gaze lingering over her wrinkled skirt, her feet bare and dirty from her hike though the jungle. She tugged at her hem, the lingering sensation of Barasa's body filling hers still intense and the memory brought a rush of heat between her thighs.

It vanished when Haeger stepped near. "Did he satisfy you?"

She blinked, her face warming. "Haeger."

"We have shared everything, my sweet." He brushed the back of his knuckles across her cheek. "Your revenge is a beautiful, deadly thing." His thin lips curved, deepening the lines in his face. "Perhaps Jason would have been a better choice to relieve your needs."

She scoffed. "One had nothing to do with the other. This is *my* reprisal."

His dark gaze narrowed. "Everything you do is my business."

She tipped her chin up. "Not this." Barasa offended her, not Thibaut.

He didn't argue further, yet eyed her with a disdain that stung. "Fine then. You reek of him. Rid yourself of it."

Odette stiffened, a retort on her lips, yet she kept silent, and she rushed past him to obey, her trophy still tucked between her breasts.

Twenty

Anderson Air Force Base
Guam

Inside the hangar-turned-command-post, Safia stared at the screens. Just outside, a jet was prepared for the incursion. Beside her, Riley waited for the links to complete and get the go ahead to launch. "I need a favor."

He simply waited.

"You take it," she said. "Take the lead."

He frowned. "They won't agree, not with Bridget at risk."

She was already shaking her head. "My worst nightmare is on that island, Riley. I want him, but not at the expense of the mission. We need to take out the dish and tag the canister. I'm not exactly in my element here." She waved at the Op center set up a few yards away. "There is no other logical choice."

His brows knit for a second, and then he nodded. She sighed with relief and hugged him. "Thank you." She tipped her head back, then noticed they had an audience, but she didn't give a damn. She kissed him until Max called out. Twice.

"The good fight calls," she said, then hustled around gear and men.

The staging for the high altitude jump was chaotic. Special Forces were on hand from Okinawa, but Dragon One had the lead. Safia didn't want to be the official authority, but with the bastard holding Bridget, she had less at risk than Riley.

As she approached, Max had his face in a screen, working to digitize the feeds. "Street cameras?"

"Ellie got me the video cameras from around the station. I've got vid from three hotels on the same street and the mall diagonally across the street."

"This is what you've been working on all this time?" He'd had his face in the screens since they'd arrived. "This have to do with the phone numbers Ellie was separating from the Triad house?"

Max nodded. "Sort of. We focused on the one phone that wasn't active. It was a disposable phone, used maybe four times and in the trash somewhere in Singapore."

"A dead end," she said, and her expression told him to get to the point.

"Not quite, but what's interesting is forensics said while there were traces of the RZ formula in the blast zone, there was also Centex in the house blast and your car." He glanced at her. "The Icarus has the capability but with the RZ10 everything collapses."

"It did, Max, we saw it. You did."

"So did Sebastian."

Her eyes flared.

"The motion sensors woke him. He saw someone, put it together and split fast. That's why we found him so far away from the station. But it's been bugging me how the blast sight was so round. RZ10 from what I learned," he tapped the thick report on the desk beside him, "ignites in isolation. It's the reason we don't use it. We can't control the blasts outside a closed area. But look at this vid." He brought up three videos simultaneously. "Three locations, a block up the street, diagonally and then here, two stories up on the shopping center across the street on the corner."

Safia nodded, her gaze flicking between the views.

"This is the clearest." He played it and Safia saw a figure leave a car and rush over the courtyard walls, then under the house. There were no basements in this part of the world, the water table too low, so most private homes were on cinder block stilts this close to the water.

"Male, at least six feet, fit," she said.

The figure returned to the car, sliding in and driving away in under a minute. Max tapped keys, another view came up, and she watched it play from a different angle. She nudged him. "What do you really want me to see, Max?"

He sighed, and showed the last stream. It was a police camera positioned at a street post. The local police kept a handle on crime, or at least tried with little shacks for the cops all over the city. She'd seen them abandoned more than occupied, but she'd forgotten about the cameras.

"This is from the mall camera." Max slowed the video down and when the same man hurdled the stone wall, he dropped to the other side and straightened. Then he swept his hair back with his right hand and the street lamp gave off enough light for her to recognize the contours of his face. Max froze it and digitized it for clarification. But she didn't need it.

Recognition was instant and she stepped back suddenly. After a moment, she looked at him, a little pale. "Keep this between us. He's mine."

He frowned.

"Search his personal phone records for that disposable's number. Can you get in a back door?"

"Logan can."

"Go under the wire and give him some rope. If I'm right, he's made calls to Bridget's captor."

Max's features pulled tight as he understood. The CIA asset held Bridget captive, and if the Mole panicked, he could give orders to kill her in the clean up. Barring that, they needed proof for a trial.

"This Op is blacked out so he won't have any way around

it. It takes several officials to sign off and then they'd want to know why. He's out of the loop, at least."

"You've every right to be pissed off, ya know that."

She patted his shoulder. "Oh you haven't seen angry yet, Max, but I'm going to *love* bringing him in."

Deep Six and the JCS were calling. Safia stood on the X for the video feed. Around her, Dragon One and the Marines moved in. She glanced back at the men in Black Ops gear, their faces painted, most rechecking their weapons. Sam winked at her, then slipped another weapon in his leg pocket. Riley, on the other hand, was stashing knives everywhere.

She faced the screen. Several thousand miles away, General Gerardo and Colonel Jansen were clear as a TV show.

"Agent Troy," Gerardo said. "Status to launch?"

"We're on tap, sir. Thank you for the teams." She gestured to the Marines with Max and Sam now bent over a table going over the assault again. They'd split into two teams, Safia, Riley and two marines, Sam, Max and two more. Launching with a full squad would take two aircrafts and frankly, they didn't have the time. A storm was rolling in.

"If I didn't send them," Gerardo said, "I figured you go in alone."

"Not quite, sir." She smiled, then gestured to Riley beside her. "However, in the best interest of this Op, I'm turning over command to Agent Donovan," she said and the colonel frowned. "He and the teams are more experienced in this type of operation." She flashed a smile. "I'm the watch and snoop type." And the last time she jumped out of a plane was in training. She was not looking forward to it.

"Donovan," the general asked.

"We're good to go, sir."

"I realize this puts an emotional strain on you, Donovan, but the priority is the canister and the dish."

"Understood, sir. But I won't be leaving without her." This was their one chance, Riley thought. The weather and the moon would play a role when they dropped from thirty-five-thousand feet onto the island. Intel reports showed the island was wired, including the airstrip. Electrified fencing and armed guards. It didn't make a wit of sense. He expected trouble.

"Thermals are off the map and from what we've seen,"—he gestured to include Safia, "there are more on the island. We believe they are children."

Gerardo frowned. "They are his, all legally adopted."

"Over fifty, sir?"

His brows shot up. "Good grief. An orphanage?"

"An army of detonators, sir. No one would suspect a child, and they could get in anywhere. Agent Troy witnessed a child entering the Sorbonne when guards were turning everyone else back. She never came out."

"Do what you can for them. I don't suggest confronting Thibaut. He's a sociopath."

"Yes sir, off the map. But he's also brilliant. He has a contingency plan. He *will* detonate. Given the profiler report and the guy's history, he's been fixated on this for decades. Despite all we've done, he's exactly where he intended to be, in complete control."

Gerardo nodded and Riley's gaze dropped to the quarter he flipped over his knuckles. "It's never an easy decision," he said, a little philosophically. He looked up. "I've spoken with the president. If you cannot recover the canister, we'll level the island."

Riley didn't question it and nodded. Tagging the canister for detonation was a lot more comforting than trying to transport it. They needed to be far away before the jets dropped their loads. He signed off and the image softened to a blur.

Max and Sam were on another link speaking with Beckham. At Deep Six, he would monitor the incursion and feed Intel. Riley did a time hack with Beckham and the teams, then he glanced at Safia. She stood off to the side, staring at the floor, her arms folded over her middle. The stance was familiar now and he knew she was battling something. The man who'd tortured her held Riley's sister and his worry was right up there with hers. Bridget was not equipped to handle it and he prayed she was bound and gagged somewhere and left alone.

He crossed the hangar as a door screeched open. Around the jet, crewmen rushed to remove chocks and blocks, preparing to roll out. "Hey," he said and she looked up. "You okay with this?"

"Oh God yes," she said, grasping his bicep. "I don't speak commando." She waved at the men just finished loading parachutes and gear into the aircraft. She leaned in. "Last time I jumped was in field training. I'd hoped it was the last. Guess not."

He smiled. "Five years for me, Amianan Islands, ballistic missiles pointed at South Korea and a NATO delegation."

Her eyes widened, and she patted his shoulder. "I made a good choice then. Clearly, you're the one wearing those smart trousers today, Irish." He chuckled lowly and Safia felt something give inside her, fade the tension locking her spine a little bit. "We both have a lot of payback in this, huh?"

"I'll ghost him for you."

She laughed shortly. "Ah my knight, the masked man is not a priority."

"It is if it will wipe that look off your face."

She frowned softly.

"He scares you."

Her expression fell and she turned away. Riley drew her into privacy, but the noise around them made him lean in.

"*I* scare me more," she said. "I think of those days and I want to torture him back so much it fills me with nothing but this *ugly* rage."

"You're stronger than that and him. You survived."

"Sometimes I wonder. It changed me. I should have walked away from the Company right then."

"But it taught you not to trust Price."

"Yes well, Price didn't hire the asset to do that to me, Riley. Adam Kincade did."

His features pulled tight. "Why didn't you say anything? I don't know him, but the team does."

"He'd arranged my incarceration. It was his asset. Still is. That's why I was getting all the tips. For every arms dealer I brought in, another got away. The asset was committing the crimes we were fighting."

"The station is one thing, but the car?"

"I thought so too. But not passing information that D-1 was in the area? That I survived the station explosion? Putting a block on forensics with Ellie?" She shook her head. "I'm betting he rigged the car."

"That took talent."

"Oh yes. I checked his record. Adam was a specialist. Like Sebastian."

"I recall something Sam said, in Thailand. Adam wouldn't go in to rescue a diamond cutter's kids held hostage until we did. He wanted to ghost the captors, we gassed them."

"His asset was probably in the middle of that. Ya know, there are so few people I could trust," she said sadly. "With Lania, Kincade was the lesser of two evils." Safia held his gaze, then moved closer, loving that his arms opened and trapped her in warmth. He rubbed her spine and she softened, laid her head on his shoulder. "They give us all a bad name, ya know?"

His short laugh vibrated against her cheek. "But you give the CIA a good one." She looked up and he smiled, kissed her.

"Time to fly," Logan called, tapping his watch.

Riley grabbed his helmet off the rack, Safia behind him, their jumpsuits swishing with the stiff fabric. At the doors, he spared a glance at his brother-in-law sitting at the weather desk. Travis nodded, offering a half-hearted smile, then turned back to the screen. But Riley caught his sad expression. He felt the same, a guilty chill tight over his skin. He pushed it down as best he could. Once the storm was on them, it would get a little dicey. They had to do this fast before the weather grounded the jets.

He jogged across the flight line to the jet, the engines screaming. He cast a glance at the darkening skies, then stepped onto the lift. The storm would provide cover, but it'd be hell getting off the island. As the hydraulic lift rose and closed, Riley hoped Jansen had some tricks up his sleeves.

Over the Sonsoral Islands

Thirty-five thousand feet in the sky, the unpadded walls magnified the noise. The temperature dropped rapidly at this altitude, and she could see frost forming on the crew chief's window near the hatch. Safia tested her oxygen, then eyed Riley back when he reached to help hoist the chute higher on her back. The only woman, they were being chivalrous, and she understood that, especially with these guys, but this ritual steeled her nerves. She wasn't crazy about jumping from a perfectly good aircraft. Not from nearly seven miles up.

Safia cinched the nylon harness, then gripped her helmet and wedged it on. "I hope I remember how to do this," she mumbled, the sound going through the PRR mic sets they all wore.

Riley pointed to himself. "Five years," he said. She took little comfort in that and backed up against the bulkhead as Max shifted past, holding his load bearing vest so they wouldn't catch. He wore a ring of Centex. She didn't want to be anywhere near him, though she supposed jumping onto an island that had enough RZ10 to level Texas wasn't any smarter.

Riley met her gaze and she saw the worry in his expression. "We'll do it and get her. Ellie's got thermal on isolated locations." She patted her pocket, her Recon inside.

They were out of time. While law enforcement searched

for the bombs already planted, Thibaut and Odette could fly out on his jet at any moment or set bombs off from their easy chairs before the teams could get close enough to take out the satellite dish. The islands were in the U.S. strand. Interpol would have no recourse except to shoot the jet down before they could ignite an Icarus. Satellite Intel could only jam so many signals in so many parts of the world at once. Safia knew Ellie and Deep Six would go right to the source, and block the island. That included the team's communications.

She'd memorized the island geography, but none knew what to expect. Bridget's exploration team confirmed that the bones collected were human, with animal DNA—and all children. Safia glanced at the photo encased in plastic and neoprene. Riley's sister. She'd memorized her face, listened to a recent recording of her voice. This wasn't the way she wanted to meet his family. Riley snapped his static line, and she looked up. He tugged at her gear, double-checking and duplicating the others doing the same. She'd hate to have the parachute pop off before she had to pull the rip. This was their one shot, the last moonless night and to be a success, they had to breach the island security without setting it off. Why Thibaut needed it this far out in the ocean gave her the willies.

Thibaut had the entire island wired with defense systems she was sure they couldn't break. The man was as dangerous as Vaghn, and they'd learned to circumvent intelligence and be extremely methodical. She expected as much complication on the island as she did anywhere else.

The buzzer screamed inside the aircraft, the green light blinking brightly. Jumpers lined up and she tightened her chin strap, then clipped her jump line to the static line. An Air Force crewman opened the hatch. The icy wind screeched inside, beating the lines. Riley was ahead, lead man out, and he glanced back once, wiggling his eyebrows, his smile cartoonish before he bit down on his oxygen regulator, then vaulted into the darkness.

At the hatch, Safia stepped up and held onto the frame, the wind threatening her grip. Endless black lay below, and she thought, *I am* such *a dumb ass.*

Then she jumped.

Wind streaked past as she fell to earth. Like Icarus, she thought, feeling her skin and muscles flap like paper with her speed. This is so not fun, she thought and focused on the marker topping Riley's helmet. When it kept flashing, she realized he was spinning in the air, then flattening out, tucking and rolling. *Oh for pity sake, he's playing.*

She had her hand on the rip, watching the altitude meter on her wrist because she couldn't see the ground. A good thing, she thought, her stomach rolling. The altimeter ripped off feet-per-second too fast to see. She watched it anyway, thinking this is a long time to drop into hell. Then it stopped and blinked. She pulled, the chute yanking her back up and filling. She let out a long breath, controlling the lead lines and guiding herself past the shore. But not in the jungle, she thought, jerking on the line. Night vision showed her the target.

Her boots hit the ground and she tucked, rolled, then on her knees, she drew the chute in fast and tight, then raced to Riley. He was several feet from the jungle, already out of his jumpsuit and burying his gear. She released her harness, then removed the oxygen and her helmet. Riley cracked a chem-lite. Safia peeled off the jumpsuit, then replaced her load-bearing vest and weapons. Riley eyed her dull black skinsuit and vest doubtfully, but didn't have time to reassure him she was well-armed.

Intel said the security fence was deeper inside, and just short of landing in the center of Thibaut's little town and risking exposure, this was their choice. There were sensors in the water. Mirroring her, Riley had cyborg-looking night vision goggles on his forehead, his weapon forward, ready to fire. The NVG's would record the Op, yet their only communication were the PRRs, Personal Roll Radios that were always on, voice activated. If Thibaut had detectors, they wouldn't catch the PRRs. They had to memorize the island. Any device with a satellite connection could be tracked by Thibaut's dish. The idea was use the PRRs till he found out they'd stopped in for a visit.

Safia kept a vigil on the jungle as they waited for the rest of the team to draw close. Sam and Max were on the other side of the island beyond the runway.

The Marines hustled near, kneeling, facing the opposite direction, watching their six. The fence was further in the jungle, bordering a section of the village of the damned rather than the island itself. Outside the barrier was dense and inhabitable. There was no path from the sea to the land. No docks. The only people welcome were flown in. Crossing the security fence and doing it silently would take timing. There was no record of the construction, and reception was blocked. A scramble tower, they assumed. Intel couldn't give them more than that.

Riley signaled and they moved forward, two more teams on the east side of the island and mirroring them. They had under two hours to take out the satellite, find and tag the canister—and Bridget—then get off the island. It had taken them forty minutes to get to the ground. Safia felt Bridget was the priority. Get her out and bomb the place. Only Dragon One was in agreement. The JCS, not so much.

Riley advanced, Safia moved to his right, parallel, exchanging places once, then overlapped. The Marines mirrored them, constant new eyes with each step. They checked their bearings with the other teams. Max's team would target the airport and Sat dish. Riley's team would search buildings to find the canister. Slow and dangerous when they didn't have much time. Riley signaled her and she moved to his side, and they progressed in short increments.

"*We've got movement,*" Sam said, his deep voice gone to a rumble through the mics.

Safia adjusted her night vision lens. Riley took position beside her. She searched for the movement, but couldn't see beyond. She shook her head.

"Guards?" Riley said.

"Yeah, decked out for the rodeo," Sam said. *"No pattern. Close quarters."*

"Even the odds, D-3," Riley said. "Draw back, take it down by the water. Buzz me when you're at the fence. We're heading in."

Timing was crucial with the advancing storm. The winds were pushing it faster. On the northwest side of the island, they advanced. There were three buildings ahead, she recalled, then two more several yards further in. They were about fifty feet from the fence when the air suddenly changed, grew heavier. Another step and a putrid odor rose from the ground.

Riley glanced at her, frowning. She nodded. He signaled his team, but didn't have to ask if they smelled it. Two more steps, and she frowned as the ground shifted beneath her feet, cushiony. Her boot soles slipped on something slick and soft. She gained her balance, then cracked a chem-light. She held it low, sweeping it, then staggered back.

"Look at your feet."

Riley bent, slipping a chem-light from his pocket, and swept its green glow slowly over the ground—exposing a severed arm.

"Oh God." Safia moved her light around. "There's more, oh Jesus." She stepped back, Riley beside her. The foulness of decay rose up in heavy waves with each step, and she pressed the back of her hand to her nose. He tossed the chem light and Safia tried not to vomit. There were more, many more.

"It's a mass grave," Riley said, scowling. "I saw one in Serbia with Sam. Tanks were coming and troops didn't hang around to bury the dead."

"But it should smell far worse. It's covered in lime, intentional."

The Marines drew near. "God, that's rank."

She shined the chem-light. "Look how small." She lifted her gaze. "They're children."

Riley coughed against the stench, knelt. "They've been gnawed on."

"Don't say that," she whispered. "Eaten?"

He cracked a second chem-lite and tossed it in the pile. Safia reared back, aimed her weapon, her gaze scanning. Limbs and skulls protruded, the layers of lime bright in the night vision.

"Oh I'm going to enjoy seeing this guy bite it," she said and frowned when Riley cracked another chem-lite, and bent to look. Safia turned her face away, but the tiny decayed hand stayed in her mind. She watched the terrain instead.

"Disgusting, but Bridget was right." He tapped her, then with the chem-lite, he pointed to the ground. She really didn't want to look closer, but did, squatting. She'd grown accustomed to the odor. The hand was small, maybe a two year old, but the nails were exceptionally long. With a gloved hand, she turned it over to see the back.

She looked at him sharply. "That's the strangest thing I've seen." The back was covered with fine dark hair. "Your brother-in-law said they found animals with human remains." She waved at it, then wished she hadn't. "Is this the source?"

"Can't deal with that now, but it looks like it." He inclined his head and she came to him, leaving the horror behind. Nearly fifty yards in, they found the fence.

"Satellite picked up enough to get that it runs through the jungle but only on this side." Thibaut kept them contained, she thought, glancing back.

Riley was at the fence, searching, then finding whatever he needed. He pulled out some electrical gadget and attached wires and clips at the top and bottom. Safia scanned her surroundings, the night vision picking up movement. She aimed right, lowering to one knee. Then a feeling she never ignored passed over her spine. "We're not alone."

"They've been following since the graves. They're in the trees."

Safia kept her head straight but behind the goggles, her gaze swept up. The night vision outlined a small figure in the tree, crouched. Dark, a lot of hair or mud, she thought, but could see little else.

"Dragon Three, you see anything unusual?"

"Yeah, kiddy campsites."

Max brushed at the ashes, and glanced around the tent. Of sorts. It was constructed from dead leaves and branches, strips of a bangi tree used for rope. Sam knelt near, watching his back. Max pushed up his NVG'S and cracked the chemlite, sweeping it slowly.

Sam leaned in to see. "It's like a fort. A kid's fort."

"Not wild animals, or they wouldn't have beds and utensils," a Marine said, pointing. The lean-to was filled with scraps that probably washed up on shore, but the Marine was correct, Max made out a spoon shape and a few daggers. Then he realized they were made from bones. Jesus.

"Thermal says there are people housed all over here, most in the two story buildings at the northeastern end."

"Commune life."

"Yeah, but what kind of commune?" a Marine said.

"Sick and depraved so far," Max said. "Move out. Let's get this done."

The teams advanced. They had planes to disable, and guards to subdue. The fence perimeter surrounded the island except for the northern corner, the largest building on the tip. Thibaut's house probably, but the weird kids were here. South. The nutty professor didn't know his projects had escaped, Max thought as the team halted near the fence line, throwing rope into the trees, and climbing. When Riley warned them of the break in the electrical fence, he put up a fist. Although they could hear it as well, he counted off his fingers, and heard Riley say, "Take the hill."

Dragon Two and Three went over the fence, and dropped to the ground like apples from trees. He glanced back in time to see the static course through the metal.

"Divide and conquer," Max said, and they advanced rapidly to the jet hangar and guards' post beyond.

Barasa glared at the door when he heard a knock but didn't get up from the stuffed chair. "Does no one sleep on this island?" He wanted to be alone, but the caller entered, and Barasa kept his glare on Thibaut as he crossed the living room.

He tisked at Barasa's wound. "A woman scorned," he murmured. "Dangerous, wouldn't you say?"

"I want my weapon." The soft click of a bullet chambering echoed between them. Thibaut didn't react a fraction.

"I've come to deliver it." He reached inside his jacket. Barasa lifted the gun.

"Careful. Professor."

He withdrew the shiny black web phone, already turned on. "You have only to call this number." He tapped the screen and brought up the string of digits. "The detonation message is ready."

Barasa frowned and gestured with the gun for him to leave it on the coffee table. When he did, Barasa pushed out of the chair and stood on shaky legs. Liquor and painkillers did little to ease the throbbing in his hand. He still felt the finger though it was no more than a stump now. His anger swelled and he pointed the barrel at Thibaut's forehead.

"Release my crew and jet. I'm leaving."

Thibaut nodded, an odd smile on his thin lips. "It will be done within the hour, and I suggest you be quick." He looked meaningfully at his bloody hand. "Before she decides to cut off something vital."

Thibaut glanced around as if looking for something, then turned away and left. Cale sank into the chair and laid the gun on his thigh, then reached for the bottle of painkillers.

He gave up, his arm pulsing now. He needed better drugs and shouted for Rahjan.

No one answered.

Riley went over the fence, instantly looking at Safia as she vaulted and dropped a few yards away. She didn't move for a second or two, and the fence rearmed. She straightened and rushed to his side.

"No going back," she said softly.

He gripped her hand once, then signaled. The team advanced.

Ahead, a single building stood apart. Several yards to its left a pair of two story structures glowed with light, and satellite said there was a pool and a playground. The dorms housing his freaks, Riley thought as they spread out and moved. He felt rather than saw Safia beside him and mentally slapped himself to keep focused as she rushed ahead, taking position for the next advance.

"There's no one out there," she said. "No movement at all. But lights are glowing."

"Surveillance says they never go off," a Marine said before they rushed to the single building, sliding along the side to look into the windows.

Then the sky opened up and rain fell in heavy gray sheets. "Well this spoils the party," Safia said, drops peppering her face. Lightning flickered overhead, the storm boiling.

Riley stopped at the entrance, Marines spread out, covering another. No lights, no movement. Riley pointed to his eyes, the window. *What do you see?* The Marine made a cutting motion across his throat. *Negative, nothing.* They entered the building, methodically clearing the hall, each room. The Recon on his wrist showed negative thermals except for a small fridge. The building was half home, half lab, he realized, glancing at a single bed, recently slept in. There were glass tabletops, lit from below. Only one was on, the counter barren. At the end, he spotted a glass cabinet. Empty.

"It was here," he said when she moved up beside him. His hand-held sensor was off the charts with detecting the RZ components.

"This is where that little brat built them." She pointed her weapon down and flipped on the laser light. It illuminated empty web phone boxes stacked under a worktable. "Oh hell, there's at least a dozen empty cases."

Riley mentally counted the stops Odette had made and the ones that had already gone off. "That means about six are out there. Step it up." They cleared the next room meant for storage, then moved out the rear and into the dark. The team spread out to the next location, but Safia tapped Riley, and they knelt behind thick bushes and pushed up the goggles.

"This is where we part for a bit."

"Oh hell no."

"Ellie has three isolated thermals. That way." She pointed back over her shoulder, then showed him on the Recon's screen. "There's a stream that cuts the island in half on the windward side."

Riley remembered the brook from the topography. "And what do you think you're going to do alone?" But he knew.

"Find Bridget."

He shook his head. "Not without me."

"Riley, why do you think I'm pared down?"

Her gear was minimal, and aside from that skin suit, she had no armor protection. "You planned this."

She nodded. "I can move faster alone, you know that. You have to get the canister. When hell breaks loose, Bridget will be a target."

She was right, but he was in command, responsible for accomplishing the mission, and that included his sister. Safia laid her hands on his chest and held his gaze.

"I'll find her. We have thermals to follow. The only other hot spot near there is the dish and D-3 has that covered." When he simply stared, she said, "Tell me I'm wrong." He didn't speak. "It has to be this way. She can't die because of this man."

Riley sighed hard, cupped the back of her head, pressed his forehead to hers. "Thank you. You're the only person I trust to do this."

She gripped his arm. "The thermal is isolated and still. Another is moving, but they are not far from each other. It must be her." Though from the look of the topography, Bridget was buried under rock, but Safia didn't mention that.

Riley nodded. "I know my sister. Tell her Travis and her crew are unharmed first. She'll be bonkers." He withdrew a knife, flipped it handle out. "In case you want some payback." It was the Ghurka soldier's, her torturer. This time, she knew his face. She'd studied the photo she'd taken from the docks. She stored the knife in her boot, then moved away, her weapon forward. She glanced back, then suddenly rushed close to kiss him. "I love you madly," she said with feeling, and heard his quick inhale. "Do *not* get shot."

"You either." He leaned in and she felt his breath on her cheek. "We're due a future, you and me."

She wanted that, badly, yet threatened it as she turned away from him—and any chance of backup.

Twenty-one

Deep Six

When the Marine's video feed showed the graves, the bodies, there was a collective gasp inside the Op Center. Hank was equally disgusted. None of it was getting off that island, he thought, then from behind the long console, he said, "Get as much footage as they can."

Beckham nodded, then spoke into the headset like a defensive football coach, moving between techs and analysts to stay on the ball with the Ops center in Guam. The video play started once the teams had hit the ground. One Marine on each team had the feed. When Troy split off, Jansen cursed.

Beckham twisted a glance. "You knew she'd go after the sister, right?"

"I expected Donovan to break from mission protocol." His shoulders lifted, fell. "He's a maverick, and it's his sister."

"I knew Troy wouldn't wait."

Jansen arched a brow. "You're that familiar?"

"No, sir, I'm not," Beckham said and Hank detected a blush in the big man. "She shot me down *many* times." He snorted a laugh, watching the feed, the satellite showing the movement on the ground. "People mean more to her than the Intel."

In his experience, it wasn't the norm with the CIA. "How did she last this long?"

Beckham covered the padded mic curved in front of his mouth. "For just that reason, I guess."

"Let's hope she's right this time."

Hank watched the screen and the link to Dragon One, and Chambliss in Guam. "Keep Intel flowing, our people are still on the ground." He glanced at the clock, then the weather map. The window was closing, and his final orders depended on their quick execution and departure. Gerardo was overseeing their retrieval, but with the storm stirring up, it might be a rescue.

Safia hurried through the jungle, the ground more stable. The image of the bodies and their abuse blossomed and it pushed her faster. If they could do that to children, then what would they do to Bridget? She sprinted through the forest, slowing and tipping her head when she heard the sound of rushing water. The stream. The island was small hills and craggy valleys on this side, a natural volcano, Bridget's husband had said. She pushed at the fronds, her pace slower and heightening her awareness. She paused on the edge of a clearing, freezing in her tracks. Familiarity magnified through her and with it, an insurmountable rage.

Oh, no it isn't, she thought and moved quickly to the right, and saw the small waterfall. Recognition dawned. Indonesia, my ass, she thought, but when Kincade and Price had air lifted her out of the jungle, it was in a jet with blackened windows. Her gaze flicked, night vision goggles defining in iridescent green, and she spotted an opening east of her position. She glanced at her Recon. Thermal reading showed three bodies nearby, none of them together. She had to assume they were combatants and not anything electrical. There wasn't any power running in this direction. Most of it was centralized near the buildings. Gas generators, she thought and moved in a crouch a few feet, then stopped to check her surroundings and continue.

She was at the south end of the small island, the area blocked by jungle and cloistered with decaying trees and vegetation. The geography showed a cliff on this side. Each step brought up the moldy smell and she followed it, spotting a shape that had too many straight lines to be natural. She headed toward it.

Jason paced his bungalow, watching his bare feet kick out almost in time to the thunder pushing closer. He wanted off, now. The manipulation around him was tough to fight, and his options were few and at the mercy of Thibaut, Odette and Barasa. He'd no reason not to believe Odette would keep her promise. She was the only one who had, really. He considered offering money to Barasa's pilot and crew, out-paying the arm's dealer. Loyalty wasn't a commodity Barasa had in spades.

Thunder crashed loudly. Seconds later the flash of lightning lit the rooms and silhouetted four figures and the weapons pointed at him. Laser sights dotted red targets on his chest and head.

Shit. Slowly, he lifted his hands. From behind, someone grabbed his shirt, pushed him to the floor face down. A knee in the back, his hands yanked behind, then slip ties locked on his wrists. The commando searched him, then yanked him to his knees and pressed a gun barrel to the back of his neck while the others moved methodically through the rooms. Lightning blinked like camera flashes. The tallest came forward and Jason looked up. He recognized the gear and fear shot up his spine. The U.S. had found him.

The man stared back through night vision goggles, then suddenly pulled them off. "Where is the canister, Vaghn?"

Jason blinked. "Oh holy shit! Donovan?"

Riley dragged him to his feet. "*Where is the RZ10?*"

Jason recognized the murderous look. "He took it back. Thibaut took it back. I swear!"

He released him in the direction of a Marine. "Gag him."

Jason swallowed, shock rippling through him as Donovan hand-searched the cottage. Alive? How? His shoulders sank and he didn't fight the Marine when he gagged him. Not that he could. Running wasn't an option with high-powered machine guns trained on him. It was over. He was looking at a firing squad if Donovan had his way.

A Marine led him to the rear of the building, a solid grip on his arm as he pushed him ahead. Donovan gave orders he couldn't hear, but after several yards, the Marine forced him to the ground near a fat tree and secured him. Then they took off, leaving him in the rain. Wind bent branches, trees swayed, and he let his head fall forward. Well, he'd at least have the money for lawyers. He resigned himself that Donovan was in control, but money would move mountains, and he'd get off the island. They were obligated to take him along. He stared at the darkness. Twigs and leaves stirred in gray sheets of rain. All the lights were out. Under the tree, he was a little dryer at least. A flash of something slick near the fence made him strain to see more. The sky boiled and lighting struck, rippling through the metal fence and across the ground. Jason watched helplessly as the charge divided and climbed up tree roots, splitting trunks. He tried to move away. With his back to the tree, it was impossible, and when the blue charge reached him, he watched it channel into his wet feet, then up his legs, exploding his organs under his skin.

Bridget worked the ropes with her teeth, then stopped, pretending to sleep when she heard a noise. Two days in this filth was enough. She'd been drugged and hooded since the speedboat and she knew her husband was going barking mad. If they hadn't killed him, she thought, her throat tightening. She focused on the ropes again, any reason not to worry over her fate, then suddenly realized her hands should be tied behind her back. She'd seen American TV shows. He wanted her to escape. Well, why? she thought sitting back. She'd already tried it once and got tossed in this place. Her eyesight was accustomed to the dark enough to make out the shape of a doorway and bars. Somewhere beyond was a green glow but tied up, she couldn't see the source. She felt the wet rope give and struggled harder, her heart pounding as the knots slipped free. She stood, wrapping the ends around each fist and wanted to kiss her brother for teaching her this.

Riley will come. She didn't doubt it for a moment. She moved to the cell door, her boots slopping in water, and pushed. It gave a fraction, making a squishy noise. The scents were Malaysian, maybe west Truk Islands. She'd no notion why they took her and killed that poor police officer. The finds on the islands had yet to be researched and though the bones were young people, they'd been on the island for quite some time. She patted her pockets, but they'd taken everything and really, given the sort, she was lucky to be dressed. Her sunscreen tube dangled from her belt loop. She pulled it off, and removed the tube from the hook. She strained to bend the hard metal. She could pick the lock. Not that she knew how, but this was such a special time. Straightening the hook as best she could, she knelt on the wet stone and worked to open the lock and not make any noise. The tumblers clicked, and she covered her mouth before her surprise went verbal. She pushed the door and it swung without a sound. She scowled at the hinge, noticing it was the only spot not covered in mold. Atrocious place, she thought, then heard a noise. She backed into a corner, listening and couldn't tell the direction. She tipped her head and waited for it again.

Instead a broad figure stepped from the darkness and Bridget thought, oh bloody hell. "I don't suppose there's a quick way out of here," she said. "Directions?"

Bridget turned and sprinted in the other direction. His footsteps pounded behind her and suddenly she turned, gripping the rope between her fists. As he reached, she caught his hand in the rope and twisted and yanked as Riley taught her. The man stumbled but didn't go down. She let go of the rope and took off. The floor disappeared under her feet and she fell on her arse, slid down an incline and hit a wall. He was there and grabbed her by the hair, pulling her up.

"Oh alright. Bloody freaking hell. Stop!"

"Yes, stop," a voice said calmly.

The man spun toward the sound, pulled Bridget back against his chest and pushed a gun in her throat. Then a green light stick tumbled through the air, hit the ground and rolled.

"We have a visitor," he said, sounding delighted.

Safia forced herself to remain calm when the man of her nightmares held Bridget against his chest, a gun in her throat. "I have a job to finish, remember?" She kept her body hidden beyond the wall, her aim steady.

He visibly stiffened. "You are better than I thought."

Safia hated the sound of his voice, the way it made her cringe and focused on the face that looked nothing like the bruised mess she'd glimpsed before. "I know who you are now, and who holds your leash."

"You think you'll stop him?" He scoffed, inching closer. "He is most helpful. How do you think they possessed the canister? Or bypassed surveillance, the satellites?"

A chill swept over Safia and she realized Adam had done more than use this man as an interrogator. What did this guy pass along to other enemy combatants? He took another step. "Careful, I'm really trigger-happy today. How about you release her and we can end this, hum?" A useless request, she knew.

"But I'm not done with her." He dug the gun in Bridget's artery, forcing her head to the side.

"I am, in case anyone is interested," Bridget croaked.

"Bridget." He held her as a shield, moving constantly and it was too dark to get a good shot.

"Yes," she gasped, and Safia heard the terror in her voice.

"No sudden moves, alright?" She nodded, but Safia knew Bridget was insignificant to this man, and she searched for a way to disarm him, or at least get Bridget out of his grasp enough to shoot. But he wasn't letting go of his only insurance.

Carefully, she drew the Ghurka knife and pinched the blade. She inhaled and threw. It missed her mark but hit his thigh, sinking deep enough to make him flinch.

Safia didn't hesitate and fired. The bullet impacted his shoulder. Blood splattered Bridget's face. He grunted, firing repeatedly, but Bridget hit his arm, going wild. He wrestled her for a second, but before Safia could put one in his forehead, he pulled Bridget in front of him and emptied his weapon.

Safia felt two bullets impact her chest.

The woman flew back a few feet, struck the ground and didn't move. *Oh sweet lord, no.* Bridget yelled, calling him names as she struggled in his grasp, jamming her elbow into his gullet over and over. It had no effect and he twisted her, cupping her face, his fingers digging into her jaw. She felt the heat of the weapon still in his hand.

"Now who will save you?" he said and her anger magnified.

His bloody shoulder glistened and she slammed her fist on the wound and kept pounding. He groaned, grabbed her by the throat and shoved her away. Then he backhanded her. She hit the wall, the breath knocked from her lungs and she slid to the wet floor. He clamped his wound, glancing at the body and muttering in a language she didn't understand. Then he faced her, raising his weapon.

"You are no use to us now."

Bridget stared down the barrel of the gun. Oh God save me, she prayed, trembling, thinking of her husband, her family, and what this would do to them. She inched to her feet, the gun barrel following. If she were to die today, she wasn't doing it on the ground.

Out of the corner of her eye, she saw movement. The woman shifted a fraction, then a wee more. How? Her captor spun, dragged her with him and took aim. But the woman was faster, rolling to her back, something clenched in her teeth. Bridget heard a *thip* sound, but didn't see anything, yet her captor stiffened, his hold going lax. Bridget twisted, but he held on, staggered a couple feet, banging into the stone wall and taking her with him.

The woman stood, rushed near, her weapon drawn, and Bridget saw the small blowpipe as she spit it aside.

"You're going to die slowly," Safia said, peeling his hands off Bridget, then motioning her back. "It's not a full dose." Her captor tried to speak, his lips working without a sound. His back hit the wall and he tried to remain upright, but his legs buckled. Safia looked down at him and when he tried to reach his gun, she kicked it aside. The Ghurka was twitching on the ground.

Safia knelt, her braid swinging over her shoulder. She flipped it back as she said, "You'll convulse for a while, then your skin will burn, as if its peeling off, I'm told." She tilted her head. "The rest you'll discover soon enough." The man spat at her, tried to talk, but couldn't. He choked, blood bubbling from his lips. The shoulder hit nicked his lungs. She leaned in close, wrapping her fingers around the knife still buried in his thigh. "I told you I'd find you." She gave the knife a hard twist and he howled without a sound. She stood and grasped Bridget's hand, pulling her away. Bridget glanced back and inhaled.

"Don't look," Safia said, moving further away and leaving a chunk of her past with him. "Are you hurt?"

"No, not enough to bother. Who *are* you?"

"Safia Troy. CIA. I'm a friend of your brother's."

"Riley's here? Well, of course he is."

Safia stopped, met her gaze. "He's a little busy right now and said to tell you Travis and your crew are unharmed. Not a scratch, and they are in Guam, safe."

Bridget sank a little, her eyes tearing. She covered her mouth, gripped Safia's arm. "Thank you. I thought they killed them like the policeman." Bridget patted her chest, trying not to cry out her joy, then with a few deep breaths, quickly pulled herself together.

Safia led her further down the corridor and felt her demons fade with each step. She glanced back once. The asset quivered on the ground and she felt no remorse. She had scars no one could see because of that bastard.

"What did you use?"

Safia urged her ahead. "Thai poison, highly effective. *Ya Pit* plants, a little fire cobra venom. I've handled it enough that I'm immune." Or she wouldn't have held the blowpipe in her mouth so long. Safia stopped at the edge of the stone corridor, then withdrew her spare pistol. "Take this."

"I can't, I can't." Bridget shook her head violently, and Safia could see the shock of the last moments working to a head. It was just too much to handle. Witnessing the very bad was tough for the good people. They just couldn't assimilate that some were inherently evil.

"Listen to me." Safia smoothed her hand over Bridget's hair and saw Riley in her pretty features. "Take a breath, let it out slow. Focus on me." She pointed two fingers to her eyes. She had little time to make Bridget understand just how much danger they were in right now. The gunshots would bring the guards. "My plan was to find you and get you to shore first. But we've seen what's out there, its not an option. This isn't just a kidnapping, it's bigger. They've manufactured state of the art bombs and two have already killed thousands." Bridget's scalp pulled tight and Safia was damn impressed when her shoulders went back.

"I'm alright. I am."

"There are children here. Don't trust them. They're brainwashed to deliver the weapons." *And God knew what else.*

Bridget's green eyes widened. "Maary mother take the bastards."

"You need to protect yourself in case we get separated."

"I won't be plannin' on that, I tell you."

Safia's lips quirked. "Have you ever fired a gun?" Bridget shook her head. Safia put her fingers around the weapon. "Use two hands. It kicks back a little, so tip your face out of the way. Aim for the center of the target. Not the head, or heart, just get a couple shots into them. That will stop them."

"It didn't stop you."

She patted her stomach. "Liquid body armor. Great for holding in those unsightly bulges *and* to get the target to drop his guard." She flashed a smile though she could still feel the impact and knew she'd be bruised. "Keep shooting till they don't move, Bridget. You won't get a second chance."

Bridget looked down at the gun, then flipped the safety as she'd instructed. Safia showed her how to tuck it away for the fastest retrieval. "Ready?"

"I keep thinking of that poor police officer and yes, I'm ready."

Safia lead the way, water rivering around their feet. She searched for a new way out, a fresh chem-lite glowing in her palm. They moved carefully, weapons drawn and she took a corner, then spotted a break in the rock. Water flowed toward it and they rushed past cells. Then a timid voice said, "Take me with you."

She froze and backtracked. Inside a cell was a child about six or seven huddled in the corner. Bridget moved up to look. "Oh my God. She's just a baby."

Safia grabbed her hand and led her away, but Bridget yanked free. "We can't take her with us," Safia said sternly. "She's safer here. We will come back for her."

"Release her to head to shore."

Safia shook her head, and recalled the mass grave and the animals. "It's not safe there either."

Bridget's brows knit, but she didn't question. She turned back to the girl and said, "We will get you out."

The child simply stared, then suddenly lurched from the

floor and swiped wildly at Bridget, claws catching her clothing. Safia rushed to break the hold, then pulled Bridget down the wet corridor.

"Oh my lord. She's wild, completely feral."

More than that, Safia thought, and they climbed to the surface.

"I will not disobey again." Bridget looked back at the hole in the prison. "What is going on here?"

"The evidence you found on the island is the same that's here, I think. But newer."

Bridget's skin paled. "So it's real, the DNA genome mix?"

"Not my field, but from what I saw, yes."

"*The Island of Doctor Moreau,*" she whispered and Safia agreed. This was the strangest operation she'd ever worked. Safia climbed down off the rocks, using her knife to scrape the moss and give Bridget a better foothold. She shouldn't have bothered. Accustomed to climbing the side of a ship, Bridget was agile and sure-footed. They neared the first building. Half of it covered by the jungle, it was the only one this close. Safia suspected they released the experiments from there.

They crossed the grounds, from cover to cover. Bridget tapped her and Safia looked where she pointed. She shined her laser light. "Cages?" They inched nearer. Tall and narrow, no more than a dog walk, the cages were under the trees. She examined the frame, the ground.

"Those are paw prints," Bridget said softly. "A very big cat, I'd say."

"But no locks." She spied the laser over the cage. The latch was electronic. "Geez, the fence is down. Let's go."

She approached the building, and ordered Bridget to remain outside and concealed. She was surprised to find it unlocked and entered, clearing the first few yards inside, then motioned Bridget to follow.

"We're looking for a container." She showed her the RZ10 canister on the TDS Recon. "If you see it, don't touch it." Bridget nodded and Safia was three steps ahead of her, clearing the first two rooms. One step into the next and she knew today would not improve.

"Is that a birthing room?" Bridge murmured behind her.

Safia entered slowly, her gaze flicking over the surgical table, the storage cabinets filled with instruments as she checked the corners of the room. The laser sight on her weapon touched on the lab equipment stretching the length of the wall. But it was the table with stirrups like an ObGyn that made her muscles clench.

"Not so unusual."

"On an island of children?" Safia said. "There is only one grown woman here." The only one mature enough to develop babies, she thought and moved around the surgical table. How bad did your life have to be to submit to this, she thought, moving into the next room. Inside she stopped, her gaze darting over the glass cubes that lined the wall, each filled with clear liquid and holding the remains of an infant in stages of uterine growth. Some of them had eyes shaped like felines, the iris long and narrow. On another Safia recognized the clawed hands and feet, the dusting of hair covering the entire body. One had a tail.

Bridget moved beside her and the scientist was calmer, more clinical than she expected. "There was one on the Sonsoral Islands, a survivor that attacked Jim," she said and looked at Safia. "Why would he do this? I've never seen anything so horrid."

"Neither have I." Safia suddenly looked away, struggling to slow her breathing and not vomit. The twisted shape of the babies, the incision that said he dissected them was painful to see. "This guy needs to be six feet under," she said.

"The children?"

She shook her head and turned back into the birthing room. "He's used them to breed creatures." Safia took a breath, managed to push the images aside as Bridget moved up beside her, peering. Safia handed her a monocular. "It's got a digital camera. Will you photograph it?" Bridget nodded and took several. Safia blotted the sweat on her throat and forced herself to look at it all again and grow accustomed. A dozen years at her job, she knew she never would. Not with this. She searched cabinets for the canister.

"It's alright to have a soul, Safia," Bridget said softly, photographing. "And one that hurts when others are abused." She tilted her head. "I suspect that's why you're a CIA agent, hum?"

She smiled weakly. "Riley does not realize how knowledgeable you really are."

"Let us keep it that way, hum? Wouldn't want himself to get a big head over it." Bridget stooped to look more closely at the specimens. "I found the discards." She told her about the cases, then flicked a hand at glass cubes. "This is more proof."

Safia went to a storage locker, opening it, finding lab coats and surgical scrubs. "He's left some beyond the fence too. Some survived."

"The scientist in me wants to know. But the mother—" she shook her head. "This is the making of nightmares." She handed back the monocular, then picked up a file, flipping through it.

"Do you really want to know?" Safia said.

Bridget closed it, shaking her head. "I've read enough."

Safia checked the last possible spot, then led them out and to the next building. She hurried toward the entrance on the east side, making Bridget wait as she cleared each section for occupants. They searched, but it was empty and she stopped at a window. The moonless night kept shadows down to a minimum and she scanned for the teams, then looked down at the Recon.

Bridget tapped her and gestured to the computers. She shook her head. Thibaut's work needed to be destroyed, all of it, she thought. "F35 Raptors are going to flatten this place in a very short time." She turned her wrist so Bridget could see the counter. Safia put the PRR in her ear. "Raven to Finn, come back."

"*Roger that.*"

"I have the red haired package."

She heard his shuddering sigh. "*Thank God. I owe you.*"

"And I'm collecting, don't think I won't." He chuckled, and Safia pulled out her ear mic and held it for Bridget.

"Ri-Finn, the package is fine."

"*I love you,*" Riley said and Bridget smiled. "*And I'm sorry.*"

"Ahh, every life needs a wee bit of adventure," she said, then handed it back to Safia and she slipped it back in her ear.

"We're two kilometers southeast of you. The asset is terminated."

"*Feel better?*"

"Yeah, he tried to kill your sister. I'm good with taking him out."

"*That's my girl.*"

Safia smiled and glanced at Bridget. Riley's sister gripped her hand and squeezed. "We found cages, empty. Be on guard for some big cats. Finn, I searched a lab, the experiments are worse than we thought, but no canister."

Riley didn't respond and her worry peaked when she heard him grunt. She shelved it, and moved back from the door, then went left, overtaking another corridor to a door at the end. Bridget was her shadow. Safia paused at the doorway, slipping down night vision and studied movement. She could barely make out the satellite dish and checked her thermals. The teams were moving fast, D-3 was at the dish.

Suddenly, she worked off the night vision and the pack that shaped to her spine to pull out a spare PRR. She was glad she had the chance to use it and explained the personal roll radio. "It's voice activated. You're going to hear things you won't understand or don't want to, but be careful, talking will give up our position. Tap the pad at your throat to turn it off."

Bridget nodded, waved to the weapons and darkness. "It's not my element, you know."

Safia heard the trickle of fear in her voice and understood. It wasn't exactly hers either. "I'll get you back to Travis, I swear it. Stick close to me and follow my orders." She reminded her not to trust the children.

Bridget nodded and Safia pulled down the night vision and stepped out the door.

"Be advised," she heard Max say. *"Guards are subdued, and ten minutes till charges set on the dish. When it blows, so will our cover."*

She glanced at Bridget. "Dragon Three, we're coming to you." Safia headed out, weapon trained as she gave Riley's big sister a lesson in search and destroy.

Riley bolted, tucking behind a cottage. He didn't see the porches or the décor inside, but locations for the canister. Their chemical sensors were useless in the rain, but the chemical wasn't. Unblended RZ10 was no worse than Centex. Combined, it was catastrophic—and it did not dilute.

With him, the team drew in and surrounded the cottage. He signaled and they pushed through the doors, laser lights from rifles marking the room. They cleared each, quick, methodic, then moved to the next. Inside he found bloody rags, a jumbled bed, and assumed Barasa was running scared right now.

"Airport secure. Jet disabled," Max said, sounding breathless. *"Found Barasa's pilot and crew imprisoned, negative threat. No canister."*

"Copy that. Barasa's out there somewhere." He picked up a shirt he recognized then tossed it. The arms dealer was last on his to-do list. "Dragon Two headed northwest, the two story."

"Roger that. At the dish. Get ready for fireworks, sports fans."

Riley motioned and the team rushed across the manicured lawns, the cobblestone path slick with rain. The storm tide was already flooding some areas, then Ellie's voice came through the comm-link in his left ear. *"Base to Dragon Two. Be advised, fence is not armed. Possible thermals. Your Six."*

Riley kept running, rain slickening their gear and making them too visible. At the dorms, he tucked to the wall and looked back, signaling for the team when he spotted figures moving in the trees. The lightning strike, he thought, but couldn't investigate and moved to the windows of the dorm. First look, it was empty.

"Dragon Two, thermal and movement, your three o'clock. Confirm?"

Riley edged around the far side of the building, night vision visor up because of the lightning. He did not want to go blind out here, but risked a three-second look before the next flash of lightning. It showed him the thermal readings. A line of children marching toward the large house on the point. Like eye sockets in a skull, the house windows glared light in the storm and he wondered why the lightning strike hadn't shorted out the generator. It was a party over there.

"Roger that. Children." Despite the storm tearing up the lawn, they moved in tempo and maintained the line. Robots, he thought as a tall man stepped onto the porch and ushered them inside. What the hell was this loon doing? Riley gave orders to check the dorm for occupants and in less than three minutes, the Marines reported.

"Negative, no IP's." Indigenous personnel. *"Looks like a kindergarten school. Creepy."* Considering the children were mostly between six and nine, he agreed.

"Dragon Two, my six. Let's check out the party." Riley signaled, and his team worked around the playground, but he didn't mistake the shapes in the shadows. Feral children on the loose. The team ran in bursts, using the trees and plantings for cover. He crossed in front of a waterfall spilling from the mouth of a stone cat.

"I see a theme going on here," a Marine said as Riley advanced alongside the building and looked inside. The Marines spread, two watching their backs. "A celebration, sir?"

"Apparently." The music was calypso, and the children

were dancing, but it was his first close look at Thibaut. All Riley thought was *pedophile*. He was tall, lanky, yet it was his long bony hands and the way he touched the children that turned his stomach. He saw no way for this to end well, and when the children moved out of his way like the parting of the seas, Thibaut went to a large desk with a computer.

Riley saw the table lined with Icarus phones. He narrowed the focus on his goggles and shifted for a better look. Vaghn's laptop was open, and the screen showed the locations in blinking dots. *Icarus is rising* was printed across the screen. Oh, crap. Now he knew why Thibaut was celebrating. He was going to ignite them from here.

"Drac, what's your twenty?"

"Behind the dish. Charges are hot."

"Target has phones like a party line. Raven, report, Raven!"

"We're opposite D-3's position," Safia said. *"Package is with me. Vaghn is dead."*

Riley ordered the teams toward the front of the house, beyond the glow of light.

Deep Six

Jansen watched the screen. The storm was on them, sea conditions rising to level three typhoon status. The window was shortening by the seconds.

Beckham turned in his chair. "Raptors are in the air."

"What? By whose order?"

"Gerardo."

Jansen turned to the phones, connecting with this boss. "Abort sir, they're still on the island."

"The window is gone. It's now or never. Get them off, Jansen, now."

Beckham turned to the console, contacting the teams. "Raptors locked and loaded. ETA four minutes. Bug out."

Hank watched the jet path. At Mach 3, the bombers would drop the load and be back in ten minutes. Whether Donovan and the teams were off the island or not.

Twenty-two

Max quickly packed the charges around the waist of the satellite dish, the rain hindering, but once he had them rigged, he pushed in the detonators and set the timer charge. He pocketed the deadman trigger, slung his rifle forward and signaled the team to move north. They were in the center of the island, the big house yards ahead. His senses went on alert and he suddenly spun, bringing his weapon to his shoulder.

A moment later, he heard, *"Raven to Drac, did you see that?"*

"Give it a wide berth, ladies, really wide."

Black and slim, the big cat strolled, not noticing them when the jungle was full of sounds and some god-awful smells. Max signaled the team to move away from the dish.

"Thermal said it was people."

"Definitely not." He followed the cat with the gun barrel, sighting for a kill. Beyond the cat, Safia and Bridget ran to the north near the house. The panther's gate looked all wrong.

Sam appeared at his right, the Marines in tight formation and flanking. "It's an experiment, too docile."

"Look at its skin. It's been cut up," one Marine said. The hind end was missing squares of flesh, the healing process half done.

"Let it pass," Sam said. "It's got a target."

The house. He warned D-2 and went to join the party.

* * *

On one knee, Riley kept in the shadows, watching and waiting until Safia and Bridget rushed near. He broke form long enough to nearly crush his sister and kiss Safia before Max, Sam and the Marines moved in close. He looked at D-3, at Sam. "Bug out. Get my sister off this island, please."

"It'd be my honor, partner." Sam urged Bridget. "Come on, darlin', no time for square dancing." Bridget grasped Riley's hand briefly, then drew her gun and followed Sam into the jungle toward the shore. The Marines trailed.

Riley looked at Safia. "You gave her a weapon?"

She shrugged it off. "Lots of crazies out tonight." She watched the house, swiping rainwater from her face and smearing camouflage paint. Thunder rumbled loud, but the PRR picked up a whisper. "No sign of the canister?"

Riley nodded ahead. "I'm betting it's in there, with him."

"But we're not invited to that party." She flashed a cheeky smile.

"Then let's crash it," a Marine said from behind. "And blow this psych ward."

Riley signaled to widen the area. "Let's see who comes out, huh?" He nodded.

Max hit the detonator. The explosion was instant, fire wreathing the dish and shooting into the sky. The rain did nothing for the boil of smoke and flames, the rip of metal. The dish tilted, then hit the ground. They could feel the vibration from here.

Safia glanced at Riley. "Knock knock."

Odette whirled in the chair. "Was that the storm?"

Thibaut frowned at the windows and walked to the front door, then threw it open. Wind shot through the house, stirring papers and flowers, and making the children go still. A word and they followed him as he stepped out onto the porch. "We have company."

"Barasa wouldn't dare." Odette rushed to his side. Flames licked at the satellite dish in the distance. "Haeger, it's all ruined."

"Not entirely," he said, his casual air confusing her.

"Get the canister, dear." She scowled at him and he glared. "It's why they're here." In a moment, she returned with it. When figures moved from the darkness into the glow of the house, something changed in him. Odette didn't like it.

He smiled, taking a step down, disregarding the rain and the weapons.

Safia inched forward, Riley on her left.

"Hello, Safia."

Every muscle in her body locked and she frowned, glancing at Riley. How did he know her name?

"We were neighbors once."

"I don't have neighbors."

"Cairo, after the bombing. You lived with me actually."

Safia paled, her weapon dropping a fraction. Riley barked at her and she brought her aim to her shoulder. "You're a liar and an abomination." She back stepped, using the shadows.

"You have my mark on you."

Her skin crawled and she searched her memory, her childhood, after her family was killed. The neighbor wasn't there, leaving her alone to mourn mostly. She'd gone back to the States a few weeks later, living on campus until classes started. She shook her head. He grabbed Odette's arm and she protested with a little squeak, but Thibaut ignored it to twist her arm and show the mark on the back. It was far darker than hers, but clear. A circle with a short line in the center. Theta. "Have the Delta still?"

Her gaze flicked to Riley's and he knew as she did. The triangle.

Safia kept aiming, a thing of nightmares standing in front of her.

"The canister is ours." He waved to Odette and she walked down the first two steps. Riley recognized the RZ10. Safia trained her weapon on Odette.

"But the bombs are not."

Punctuating his words, the explosion ripped again, bright flames blossomed over the island. Riley arched a brow. "Now you can't set them off."

"But I can, with your satellite." He lifted the web phone. "Jump hardware. My personal favorite. It too is yours."

Riley immediately tapped his link to Deep Six. "Block the Hawkeye! Block the Hawkeye! Now! Now!" He aimed at Thibaut's head, children in the path. "Don't do it pal."

Deep Six

"What's he talking about?" Beckham said, the entire complex hopping with Intel. "Why is he still on the island? Christ."

David tapped keys. "Oh God. Icarus is rising. He sent it directly through the satellite, not the phone."

"Impossible. The dish is down."

"He used ours! He's jumping off the Hawkeye."

"Stop it!"

"Trying, sir. I can't retask it with a keystroke." He rerouted the controls, and grabbed the joystick, watching the screen and pushing the ten-ton satellite out of range.

"David," Beckham warned.

"I can't get up there and push it myself, sir."

Come on, you billion-dollar piece of hardware, move your butt.

Riley aimed, but children crowded Thibaut, his face obstructed. Odette was at his side, smiling prettily and Riley thought she was the essence of ugliness, obedient as a dog, and just as guilty.

"You can't pull the trigger, can you?" The children draped him, the phone in his hand.

"Coward."

"See how effective?" Thibaut went on without missing a beat. "They're my products."

Riley stepped up. "Enough of this *shite*." He drew his knife from behind his neck and threw, putting the blade in the only place he could. Thibaut's throat. "Bug out, now!"

Odette screamed for her mentor, then dropped the canister, lunging at Riley. But Safia got in the way, throwing her weight at the woman. Odette hit the ground, and rolled several feet, then jumped to a crouch. Riley went for the canister, but Thibaut broke it, letting the mix spread and melt. He lay on the steps, clutching the canister to his chest as his children crowded him like monkeys. One looked up, tears in her feline eyes, but when she opened her mouth, she had no tongue.

Then Logan's voice came over the wire. *"Finn, get your ass off that island now. Raptors are on their way in. ETA two minutes to drop. Two minutes! Get in the water! They'll level the island with you on it!"*

Riley ordered everyone to the water.

Odette looked down at Thibaut, then to the teams. For a moment her features softened, young and innocent, as confused as a child. Then everything about her sharpened, and she launched at Safia. Riley fired, the bullet hitting Odette in the side. She tumbled backwards, then twisted and landed on her hands and knees. Safia blinked. For a second Odette was motionless, her silver gaze shooting to Thibaut, the children, then she turned and ran—on all fours.

"Safia!" She rushed to Riley just as a bone-chilling cry howled above the storm.

The team turned and aimed as the darkness erupted with mud soaked children. Naked and emaciated figures rushed across the manicured lawn in packs, wild creatures vaulting past them to Thibaut.

The old man's eyes widened as the largest landed on his

chest, howled and ripped the canister from his grip and tossed it aside. The feral children struck, shredding clothing and flesh, dragging their rivals into the jungle as Riley and Safia bolted to the water, Thibaut's terrified screams barely resonating over the wrath of the storm.

Behind Bridget Sam yelled. "Keep going! In the water, in the water. We're out of time. Base, where's the ride?"

"You should see it on the horizon."

They ran down the shore, but Bridget saw only boiling black seas. The Marines were already in the water, dropping gear and fighting the storm current.

"We got to get wet," he said and taking her arm, pulled her into the water. "Swim! The jets are two minutes away!"

"But Riley—?"

"He'll get off, come on!"

She dove and swam, the water white capping and she fought the waves battering them back. The water churned white and her eyes widened as a submarine broke the surface like a black whale.

"Ohh-rah," Sam shouted over the crack and bash of thunder. "Sometimes I love the Navy." The sub surfaced, leveled, and she saw lights on the bridge, figures moving in the dark. "Stay with me Bridget," he said and she swam, but it felt like a rip tide, drawing her back to shore and draining her strength.

Sam grabbed her shirt, pulling her with him as men in dive gear crawled over the side of the sub's bridge like rats escaping a flood. Four men tossed a bulk into the water and it instantly inflated. Men dropped into the rubber boat, the motor churning, and heading toward them. She looked back at the island and didn't see Riley or Safia, then swam, praying with each stroke. Waves covered her head and she choked, then felt hands grab her shirt, pull her above the surface. Sam pushed her butt, then rolled into the boat as the waves rose and fell, nearly capsizing them. The rest of the team climbed in, the SEALs shouting questions at her, then the boat turned on a swell and headed to the sub. Bridget held onto the boat ropes, but couldn't take her gaze off the shore, waiting for Safia and her brother to appear.

Barasa remained hidden but when the satellite dish exploded, he knew he couldn't wait any longer. He hurried to the aircraft, hailing Rahjan but getting no response. He rushed to the jet, waving at the pilot. He was bruised and filthy, but wanted to get out of there as much as the rest of them. He approached the aircraft and slowed when he saw a little girl standing near the steps.

"Go away." He waved her off, giving her a little push. She didn't move, tipping her head in the odd curious way he'd seen before.

"I am yours."

"No you're not. Get out of here." He mounted the steps.

The child followed and Barasa rushed to push her back.

"No, go! I don't want you. Go." The girl was on the verge of tears. Gunshots peppered the night, the crush of rain wilting the child's clothes and hair. He saw a figure closing in on his position. The jet engine didn't start and he shouted at his crew.

Barasa looked at the child waiting patiently, unaware of her surroundings except for the only duty Thibaut had assigned her. "You sad pitiful thing."

Harvested from the streets or cloned, they were experiments. Bad ones. Deny, and the animal instinct takes over. Not to survive, but to do as instructed like Pavlov's dog to please the master. She had no mind of her own, no life to look forward to living. He mounted the steps, and when the child rushed after him, he lifted his weapon.

He was doing her a favor, he told himself and pulled the trigger. The bullet impacted with her forehead, and the child fell, that fawning expression still on her face. He took the steps, shouting for the pilot to get them off the airstrip. He heard a sound, a growl, and glanced around, still mounting the steps. The storm raged, wind snapping at trees, rain stinging his face. Then he saw a human shape on the aircraft rudder, crouched on the fuselage. The noise came again. The figure prowled closer and suddenly leaped. Cale barely recognized Odette as she impacted with him, taking him down the stairs to the ground. The force knocked him breathless, his shoulder cracking, and she was on him, her nails scratching his face, tearing his skin, and he felt claws, saw the silver sheen in her eyes. My God, what did Thibaut do to this woman? He battered her back easily, but she was agile, leaping from spot to spot, making him twist and turn. She bolted, jumping over his head and landing like the mixed breed experiment she was. Then she ran, hit his back, knocking him to the ground. His head hit, pain rigging his brains. She straddled him, her knee on his throat. His eyesight blurred, his breathing labored, then she howled, a long tearing cry before she swiped her claws across his face. Pain seared. She struck again and again, tearing his flesh. Then she raised her hand, fingers arched.

"You destroyed the perfect world. Mine."

She struck him in the throat, the claws slicing into his skin. Barasa choked for air, felt his blood spill warm and wet as she ripped her hand away and held up her prize. His Adam's apple.

She uncoiled, tossed it aside, then went to the child. She knelt, brushing bloody hair off her face, straightening the child's clothes. Then she scooped her in her arms, tears falling as she looked to the black sky. Jets streaked overhead. His last vision was Odette slipping into the jungle, her dead cargo cradled in her arms—and the bombs quickly falling to earth.

Riley swam, coming up for air, then diving again as the jet shot overhead. The maverick dropped on target, the center of the island. The sky lit up like Christmas, the RZ10 pushing out. The percussion splashed across the surface, the suction of the vacuum pulling the water up like a wall, then shoving in a giant wave.

Not again, Riley thought and let himself flow with it, knowing he couldn't fight the tsunami. He gulped air, and looked for Safia, felt her beside him. He could see the dark shape of the rigid inflatable boat and headed for it. The effort drained his strength and he rose to the surface, swiping his face, looking for Safia and his team. Heads bobbed. The wave of the blast pushed them further out to sea with the speed of a roller coaster ride. White water coiled and tossed, the sea ink black and pushing them further apart. He shouted, turning in the water. Where was she? He saw the teams locked in a ring, floating tethered, but no Safia.

Don't do this to me, Lord, not now. The wave crested and he spun in the water, rain pelting his face. He saw a hand and dove for it. He swam toward the darkened shadow twisting in the water. He grasped her shoulder, working to her arm and swam to the surface. She choked and struggled to keep her head above water.

"Body armor!" She sank below.

Riley dove down, Safia falling fast and struggling to peel the skin-suit off her shoulders. He reached, drawing his knife and hooking it in the neck, but the Kevlar wouldn't cut. Panicked, she fought the suit, the pressure telling him they were falling too deep, too fast. Lightning flashed above and Riley realized she wasn't fighting it anymore. Frantically, he yanked at the suit, and once her arms were free, its weight slid it off. He held her and swam to the surface, the last few feet without air. He broke, sucking in a lungful as the jets screamed overhead.

Safia was limp, and Riley swam one armed toward the RIB, the lights flashing on the water. A rope slapped the water and he grasped it, wrapping his fist and men drew him in. The sea rocked violently, the jets closing in. Someone grasped his shoulders to pull him in.

"No, her first, CPR CPR!"

The SEALS hauled her over the side, one going to work as Riley pulled himself into the rubber boat. He scrambled, pushed the SEAL away, doing it himself, breathing for her, forcing her heart to beat again.

"Come on baby, don't leave me now," he said, counting presses, then breaths.

The boat brushed the sub. "Sir! We have to get onboard, now sir."

"Not without her."

"Sir, we have to dive—"

He grabbed the Seal by the throat. "Not without her!" The man nodded, pried his hand from his neck, then helped him carry her body to the ladder, men working hand over hand in a storm. Riley felt himself dying inside, mentally ticking off a full minute since she'd moved last. *She's not dead*, he chanted. She's not.

Hand over hand, crewmen and his teammates helped them down the forecastle into the bridge hatch, water spilling and draining through the grate floor. The hatch sealed, the deep dive warning ringing inside the submarine, but Riley bent over Safia, performing CPR again. Max and Sam stood with the teams, passing towels over their faces. Footsteps shook the metal floor as a doctor and medics rushed the narrow passageway. Riley kept up the routine.

"Riley," Max said. "She's gone."

"No, she is not. She's cast iron. She's tougher than we are, for God's sake."

Bridget put her hand on his shoulder. He shrugged it off, never taking his gaze off Safia as the doctor charged fibrillator paddles. He warned him, then hit her, the charge arching her torso off the deck.

Riley checked for a pulse. "Nothing, again."

"Sir, she's gone."

Riley grabbed the paddles, hit the switch, and held his breath till the charge light blinked. He shot her again. She bent to the charge, and he felt her throat, waited a breath, the longest heartbeat of his life. "Pulse!"

She made a sound. It grew louder and he choked with her, pushed her on her side. Water spilled and he heard her hard intake of air. Then another. The doctor was there, hovering, calling to her to open her eyes. Her head lolled and Riley gathered her, propping her up as she coughed and struggled for fresh air. The doctor injected her. Riley caught her face.

"Safia? Look at me, baby." She didn't, breathing. "Safia?"

"Ow." She opened her eyes, let out a long, slow breath. "Well, that was wild, huh?"

Riley laughed, holding her tight and over her head, looked at his friends. Bridget swiped her tears, hugged Max and Sam. Riley looked at Safia, and she touched his face, smoothed her fingertips over his lips. She swallowed and the tears came, and she let them flow, choking, laughing, then dragged her arms around his neck.

"No more," she said in his ear. "I don't want to do this *any*more." He didn't ask what changed her mind, he sort of knew. Three hundred feet above them, fighter jets obliterated the island. And with it, went her past.

He leaned back, caught a towel and wiped her tears. "You promised not to scare me like that."

"Then talk to R&D about that body armor. It doesn't float."

The teams laughed, shaking a shoulder, a pat on the back and over her head, he met his sister's gaze. Bridget sobbed to herself, patting her chest the way she did, and Riley knew in his arms was his reason for living.

"Make a hole!" The teams parted and General Gerardo pushed between, smiling down at them. "Well done, Agent Troy, Donovan." He acknowledged the teams, shaking hands. "Well done."

"Thanks for the lift, sir."

"Jansen thought it might make up for not giving you one in Serbia."

Riley looked down at Safia, her amused smile making him grin. "All squared away, sir, believe me. No chit to call in."

"I'll be certain to let him know."

4 days later
CIA station, Thailand

Safia pushed through the doors of the graphics company, a front for the station. This one worked more area than hers, at least a dozen officers in the field from this shop alone. A few were sitting behind desks working satellite transmission like Ellie.

A young man came around his desk to block her path.

Safia flipped out her ID badge and looked the man over, then inclined her head behind her. Armed security entered and the look on the young man's face was priceless. Paler and oh my God scared. He stepped aside and she continued.

She'd waited for this moment for a long time. Long before the mission, she thought. She remembered with clarity, the pain, the desperation. Yet the instant she'd seen Adam's face she knew for certain, no one had her back. It held sway over her, pressed into the way she worked, and how she related to people, she thought with a glance at Riley. She slipped her hand into his and laced fingers till they reached the door. He pushed it open. She strode past the next layer of assistants and analysts to the room in the far corner with two glass walls.

Adam was already on his feet, putting a file into a brief-case. Riley remained outside the door, looking very Secret Service. Safia stopped in front of the desk. He'd been in Lania Price's back pocket from the start. She'd trained him to re-lease information to lure the bad and ugly. She'd traced the thermobaric fuel back to him. This guy didn't know squat about fighting fire with fire. There were rules, and then there were *rules*.

"Happy?" he practically snarled.

"Deliriously."

"You killed a good contact. How do you think we captured half these fanatics? Inside Intel tips we could never get."

"Yes we could. You took the easy route with a hired gun, a killer."

"What do you call yourself then?"

She inhaled, her shoulders throwing back. "An American. You, on the other hand, are a traitor." She glanced at Riley, and said, "My love, would you be so kind?" She looked at Adam. "I want to watch."

Riley chuckled to himself as he walked behind Adam Kincade, gathered his wrists, and closed the handcuffs.

"This isn't necessary." Adam made a face at her. "I deserve the respect of my position. I've been doing this longer than you, Troy."

"Well then." She folded her arms and cocked her hip. "Now we know you've been doing it *all wrong*." The last she gritted through clenched teeth.

Riley led him around the desk, and Kincade stopped, met her gaze. "It wasn't all bad."

She scoffed, itching to slap him stupid. "You set a bomb for *me*. I have video." She loved the gray color of his skin just then. "Why did you do it? Money, a chess game, why?" He was trusted, and even Alexa Gavlin swore by his loyalty.

His expression hardened. "I take orders too, Safia."

Her eyes flared. "Then you won't be alone in your prison cell."

"It's bigger than you think," he muttered and she frowned.

Riley led him around to the expressionless and rather large Department of Justice authorities waiting to question him on U.S. soil. They even had a jet gassed to take him home. She hoped it was a stripped down Flying Tiger with jump seats.

When Kincade was out of her sight, she inhaled and let it out, a smile breaking across her face. "This is a good day."

Riley moved near. "Are we done yet?"

She smiled. He sounded like a kid after a long trip. "I hope not. You have some promises to keep."

"Then let's go home."

South Belfast, Ireland

Riley took a sip of Guinness and watched Safia with his sisters. They crowded around her, asking about her travels and never once about her job. She'd saved Bridget's life and they were all especially grateful. Riley liked being the one to show it and planned on long hours for the next few decades.

Only Sebastian was missing, in New Orleans with Jasmine, proving to the rest of his family he wasn't dead. On the slope of the lawn, Sam and Viva were stretched out on a blanket. Sam smoothed a hand over her barely rounded tummy. It was the calmest Riley had seen him since he got the news. Viva waved at him, rolling her eyes at Sam, then grinned. He waved, but his gaze automatically slid back to Safia. She looked great in yellow.

"For a man who's *never* wanted for female attention, I don't believe I've ever seen such a sappy grin, Donovan."

Riley looked at Killian, then down at the sleeping infant tucked to his chest. "Look who's talking, lad. Sappy's your middle name. She's beautiful. Alexa's looks, thank God."

Killian didn't take insult and watched his child wrap her tiny fingers around his index finger, then looked to his wife flipping a Frisbee with Max and Riley's nephews. If he could, he grinned wider.

"She's a remarkable woman," Killian said softly and Riley knew he meant Safia. "I'm really glad Alexa has someone who relates to her past. She won't join Dragon One now, and frankly never got the itch to go back." He shook his head. "I'm glad. Maybe we'll both sleep better."

"I don't think you'll be getting any shut eye for a while,"

Riley said, glancing at the infant wrapped in fuzzy pink blankets. When she fussed and Killian reached for a diaper bag, Riley could barely contain himself. "I wish your troops could see you now."

With a black look, Killian shooed him. "You'll get yours."

He wiggled his brows. "I already have it."

His attention went to Safia, her face upturned as she listened to his mother. Something tightened hard in his chest. He loved her beyond any feeling he could have imagined, and knew he didn't want to live without her. The women in his past paled to who Safia was inside, in her soul. *She* was the good fight, the woman worth knowing. True to herself, she'd joined Dragon One and agreed to become operation commander, a seat Killian once held. He was taking a break to be a father.

When his sisters grew animated, he decided it was time to rescue her from the stories of his misspent youth. She was getting it in detail by now. The one thing he wanted to spare the woman he loved was a *complete* list of his faults.

Safia tried to listen but as he neared, her attention strayed. She supposed it would be rude to run off somewhere private with him. But that's all she wanted. No work, just time to love him. The easiest thing in the world, she thought as he neared and gave her that crooked smile, one just for her. It made her heartbeat skip, her blood move faster.

He winked at her as he leaned and kissed his mother's cheek, then said, "You'll have years to lambaste my exploits."

"Ah! We're getting to know Safia better so we can have fun at your expense," his sister Colleen said, her four-year-old son wiggling on her lap.

"Sorry Colleen, that won't be happening," Safia said as she stood.

Riley grinned, pulled her close. "Finally, someone in my corner."

His sisters made a racket over that, but Safia said, "I've got your back on this one."

"Ahh my very own champion. Just what I always wanted," he said, steering her away, and over his shoulder made a goofy face at his sisters.

She nudged him. "Stop. You're such a tease." She walked with him down the slope of the yard.

"Overwhelmed?" He slid his arm around her waist, and she leaned into him, loving the comfort and the way she fit so nicely in the crook of his shoulder. "They're spectacular. And I know why you turned out so terrific."

"Yes, hen-pecked and coddled since I was born."

"Oh for pity sake." She laughed softly, and suddenly Riley darted to the side, behind a Guelder rosebush pulling her close. She clamped her arms around him. "I love you, Riley Donovan."

"God, I can't breathe when you say that."

He swept his hand over her jaw, sank his fingers into her hair and Safia purred, closing her eyes. She just wanted to soak this up, replenish this wonderful feeling he gave her. Every minute with him was a minute she never had with anyone else. Yeah, she thought, Riley was in her soul. "Can I claim jet lag?" She opened her eyes. "I love *this* island, by the way."

"If you think you're getting off it any time soon . . ."

"Trap me." She held her wrist out. "Please."

"Ahh, you'll miss it soon enough."

"Ha. The last month was more action than I've seen in years. Snoop and listen girl." She pointed to herself. "Besides, I get to be the boss of you now."

His smile was slow. "Maary Mother."

"Be sure to wear your smart trousers."

He laughed, a rich warm sound and Safia knew beyond her heart and in her soul, this was where she belonged, surrounded by new friends and family—and ending each day where she felt truly loved. Right here, in Riley's arms.

Yup, she thought. Shoulda jumped on that chopper.

And be sure to catch Lucy Monroe's new book,
WATCH OVER ME,
coming next month from Brava . . .

"Dr. Ericson."

Lana adjusted the angle on the microscope. Yes. Right there. Perfect. "Amazing."

"Lana."

She reached out blindly for the stylus to her handheld. *Got it.* She started taking notes on the screen without looking away from the microscope.

"Dr. Ericson!!!"

Lana jumped, bumping her cheekbone on the microscope's eyepiece before falling backward, hitting a wall that hadn't been there when she'd come into work that morning.

Strong hands set her firmly on her feet as she realized the wall was warm and made of flesh and muscle. Lots and lots of muscle.

Stumbling back a step, she looked up and then up some more. The dark-haired hottie in front of her was as tall as her colleague, Beau Ruston. Or close to it anyway. She fumbled with her glasses, sliding them on her nose. They didn't help. Reading glasses for the computer, they only served to make her feel more disoriented.

She squinted, then remembered and pulled the glasses off again, letting them dangle by their chain around her neck. "Um, hello? Did I know you were visiting my lab?"

She was fairly certain she hadn't. She forgot appointments

sometimes. Okay, often, but she always remembered eventually. And this man hadn't made an appointment with her. She was sure of it. He didn't look like a scientist either.

Not that all scientists were as unremarkable as she was in the looks department, but this man was another species entirely.

He looked dangerous and sexy. Enough so that he would definitely replace chemical formulas in her dreams at night. His black hair was a little too long and looked like he'd run his fingers through it, not a comb. That was just so bad boy. She had a secret weakness for bad boys.

Even bigger than the secret weakness she'd harbored for Beau Ruston before he'd met Elle.

She had posters of James Dean and Matt Dillon on the wall of her bedroom and had seen *Rebel Without a Cause* a whopping thirty-six times.

Unlike James Dean, this yummy bad boy even had pierced ears. Only instead of sedate studs or small hoops, he had tiny black plugs. Only a bit bigger than a pairs of studs, the plugs were recessed in his lobes. They had the Chinese Kanji for strength etched on them in silver. Or pewter maybe. It wasn't shiny.

The earrings were hot. Just like him.

He looked like the kind of man who had a tattoo. Nothing colorful. Something black and meaningful. She wanted to see it. Too bad she couldn't just ask.

Interpersonal interaction had so many taboos. It wasn't like science where you dug for answers without apology.

"Lana?"

The stranger had a strong jaw too, squared and accented by a close-cropped beard that went under, not across his chin. No mustache. His lips were set in a straight line, but they still looked like they'd be heaven to kiss.

Not that she'd kissed a lot of lips, but she was twenty-nine. Even a geeky scientist didn't make it to the shy side of thirty without a few kisses along the way. And other stuff.

Not that the other stuff was all that spectacular. She'd always wondered if that was her fault or the men she'd chosen to partner.

It didn't take a shrink to identify the fact that Lana had trust issues. With her background, who wouldn't?

Still, people had been known to betray family, love and country for sex. She wouldn't cross a busy street to get some. Or maybe she would, if this stranger was waiting on the other side.

The fact that she could measure the time since she'd last had sex in years rather than months, weeks or *days*—which would be a true miracle—wasn't something she enjoyed dwelling on. She blamed it on her work.

However, every feminine instinct that was usually sublimated by her passion for her job was on red alert now.

If you liked this book, try Alison Kent's
NO LIMITS,
out this month from Brava . . .

By the time his guest returned, freshly showered and shampooed and dressed in his things, Simon had thrown together a breakfast of scrambled eggs, bacon, coffee, and toast. He didn't immediately turn around and greet her but focused on piling the food on paper plates, digging into his box of grub for sugar and powdered cream.

Concentrating on what was simple kept him from facing the complications that came attached like baggage to Michelina Ferrer. It was a different sort of baggage than what he'd been dealing with the last few weeks, but her being here was still going to weigh heavy on his mind.

Dealing with Bear and Lorna and the property would be enough to try any saint. Add King to the mix, and, well, Simon's patience wouldn't pass the first test. And now he had a mystery on his hands, a crime that needed more explanation before it would begin to make sense.

That was the only reason he finally turned around, the only reason he lifted his gaze from the food he carried to the woman standing in the frame of the kitchen doorway toweling dry her dark hair.

Her face was the same one he'd seen on *Page Six,* on magazine covers, on TV. The same one from his billboard. The same one . . . but not.

Her skin was scrubbed clean. She wore nothing glossy on

her lips, nothing colored and glittery on her eyes, nothing to smooth out her cool ivory skin. She had freckles on her nose, two small red zits on her chin.

And her eyes were sad and scared, not sassy or sultry or seductive. A big problem, her eyes. An equally big one, her unbound breasts beneath his gray T-shirt, the curve of her hips and thighs in his long-legged briefs.

He set the food on the table, cleared his throat, went back for the Styrofoam cups filled with coffee and for plasticware. He didn't turn back toward her until he heard her sit, the chair legs scraping across the worn linoleum, the creak of the wood beneath her weight.

The table hid most of her body. He could still make out the shape of her breasts, the fullness, the upper slope that made him wonder about the weight he'd feel beneath. But there wasn't a damn thing he could do to avoid her face, so bare and exposed, or her eyes.

He had to look at her to get her story. He had to watch her expression, see the truth, her fear, find out how much she knew or had guessed or thought about what had happened. This is what he did—gathered information, ferreted out intel, zoned in on the pertinent details, used it all to come up with a plan of action.

He needed one. Desperately. One that had nothing to do with her body being naked under his clothes, one that addressed the fact that she was Michelina Ferrer. And she was miserable, frightened, and lost.

He couldn't help it. He feared that juxtaposition—what he knew about the celebrity versus what he sensed about this woman with her armor washed away and fearing for her life—was going to make it hard to keep this job from turning personal.

Kathy Love's done it again with her sexy paranormal,
DEMON CAN'T HELP IT,
available now from Brava . . .

Jo breathed in slowly through her nose. What had she just agreed to? Seeing this man every day? She pulled in another slow, even breath, telling herself to shake off her reaction to this man's proximity.

Sure, he was attractive. And he had—a presence. But she wasn't some teenage girl who would fall to pieces under a cute boy's attention. Not that cute was a strong enough word for what Maksim was. He was—unnerving. To say the least.

But she wasn't interested in him. She decided that quite definitely over the past two days. Of course that decision was made when he wasn't in her presence.

But either way, she should have more control than this. Apparently should and could were two very different things. And she couldn't seem to stop her reaction to him. Her heart raced and her body tingled, both hot and cold in all the most inappropriate places.

"So every morning?" he said, his voice rumbling right next to her, firing up the heat inside her. "Does that work for you?"

She cleared her throat, struggling to calm her body.

"Yes—that's great," she managed to say, surprising even herself with the airiness of her tone. "I'll schedule you from 8 a.m. to—" she glanced at the clock on the lower right-hand of the computer screen, "noon?"

That was a good amount of time, getting Cherise through the rowdy mornings and lunch, and giving him the go ahead to leave now. She needed him out of her space.

If her body wasn't going to go along with her mind, then avoidance was clearly her best strategy. And she had done well with that tactic—although she'd told herself that wasn't what she was doing.

"Noon is fine," he said, still not moving. Not even straightening away from the computer. And her.

"Good," she poised her fingers over the keys and began typing in his hours. "Then I think we are all settled. You can take off now if you like."

When he didn't move, she added, "You can go get some lunch. You must be hungry." She flashed him a quick smile without really looking at him.

This time he did stand, but he didn't move away. Instead he leaned against her desk, the old piece of furniture creaking at his tall, muscular weight.

"You must be hungry too. Would you like to join me?"

She blinked, for a moment not comprehending his words, her mind too focused on the muscles of his thighs so near her. The flex of more muscles in his shoulders and arms as he crossed them over his chest.

She forced herself to look back at the computer screen.

"I—I don't think so," she said. "I have a lot to do here."

"But surely you allow yourself even a half an hour for lunch break."

She continued typing, fairly certain whatever she was writing was gibberish. "I brought a lunch with me, actually." Which was true. Not that she was hungry at the moment. She was too—edgy.

"Come on," he said in a low voice that was enticing, coaxing. "Come celebrate your first regular volunteer."

She couldn't help looking at him. He was smiling, the curl of his lips, his white, even teeth, the sexily pleading glimmer in his pale green eyes.

God, he was so beautiful.

And dangerous.

Jo shook her head. "I really can't."

He studied her for a moment. "Can't or won't. What's a matter, Josephine? Do I make you nervous?"

Jo's breath left her for a moment at the accented rhythm of her full name crossing his lips. But the breath-stealing moment left as quickly as it came, followed by irritation. At him and at herself.

She wasn't attracted to this man—not beyond a basic physical attraction. And that could be controlled. It could.

"You don't make me nervous," she said firmly.

"Then why not join me for lunch?"

"Because," she said slowly, "I have a lot of work to do."

Maksim crossed his arms tighter, and lifted one of his eloquent eyebrows, which informed her that he didn't believe her for a moment.

"I don't think that's why you won't come. I think you are uncomfortable with me. Maybe because you are attracted to me." Again the eyebrow lifted—this time in questioning challenge.